Where
WILDFLOWERS
Bloom

Books by Ann Shorey

AT HOME IN BELDON GROVE

The Edge of Light
The Promise of Morning
The Dawn of a Dream

SISTERS AT HEART

Where Wildflowers Bloom

❧ Sisters at Heart ❧

Where
WILDFLOWERS
Bloom

A NOVEL

Ann Shorey

R
Revell
a division of Baker Publishing Group
Grand Rapids, Michigan

Published by Revell
a division of Baker Publishing Group
P.O. Box 6287, Grand Rapids, MI 49516-6287
www.revellbooks.com

Printed in the United States of America

Library of Congress Cataloging-in-Publication Data
Shorey, Ann Kirk, 1941-
    Where wildflowers bloom : a novel / Ann Shorey.
        p.   cm. — (Sisters at heart ; bk. 1)
    ISBN 978-0-8007-2074-2 (pbk.)
    I. Title.
  PS3619.H666W48 2012
  813'.6—dc23   2011036154

Scripture used in this book, whether quoted or paraphrased by the characters, is taken from the King James Version of the Bible.

This book is a work of fiction. Names, characters, places, and incidents are the product of the author's imagination or are used fictitiously. Any resemblance to actual events, locales, or persons, living or dead, is coincidental.

Published in association with Tamela Hancock Murray of the Hartline Literary Agency, LLC, Pittsburgh, PA.

The internet addresses, email addresses, and phone numbers in this book are accurate at the time of publication. They are provided as a resource. Baker Publishing Group does not endorse them or vouch for their content or permanence.

12   13   14   15   16   17   18   7   6   5   4   3   2   1

To Sharron,
my sister at heart

*Y*ou can do this," Faith Lindberg told herself as she gazed into the hall mirror and straightened her bonnet. "After all, it's only for a short time." Once she gathered the courage to talk to Grandpa about her plans, she knew they'd be leaving Noble Springs.

She slipped her well-worn copy of Randolph Marcy's *The Prairie Traveler* into her carryall. Her grandfather said he wanted her to take over managing the store. He hadn't said she couldn't spend time reading when there were no customers.

The onyx mantel clock in their parlor chimed the half hour. Grandpa had been very specific—meet him at eight o'clock and he'd show her what to do before Lindberg's Mercantile opened for the day's business.

Faith hurried out the door, grateful that the morning sun promised a pleasant day after a week of rain. Maybe she wouldn't have to bother with lighting the store's cranky wood-burning stove. Its warmth drew elderly gossipers the way a freshly iced cake drew bees.

Her boots rapped a rhythm on the wooden boardwalk. After several minutes, she passed the livery and tossed a wave at the man working out front. Noble Springs's courthouse rose tall and proud off to her right. She turned, skirting the square. The mercantile stood across the street, next to a drugstore and the newspaper office.

Once under the sloping porch roof, Faith noticed the closed padlock securing the store's entrance. Odd. Grandpa left home half an hour ago. If she'd known he wouldn't be on time, she wouldn't have rushed.

She looked up and down the street, but at this hour most everything was closed. She shook her head. They always walked the same streets from their home to the store. She could not have missed him.

Faith settled on one of the benches in the shade and took her book from the carryall, but after a couple of pages she snapped the slender volume closed. He'd been forgetful lately. Maybe he stopped to visit a neighbor and lost track of time. She would retrace her route, and then if no one had seen him, double back across town.

Past Courthouse Square, she knocked at the first house on West High Street. A woman holding a squalling baby opened the door. "Miss Lindberg? Isn't it a little early to come calling?"

"I apologize, Mrs. Bennett. I'm looking for my grandfather. Did you see him pass by this morning?"

"No." Mrs. Bennett frowned. "Why? Is he missing?"

"He was supposed to meet me at the store. He wasn't there." Her anxiety rising, Faith backed away from the door. "So sorry to trouble you."

Stops at the rest of the houses yielded similar results.

In front of the livery, the stableman bent over a wheel on a black phaeton, polishing each spoke with a grimy rag. She stopped short.

"I beg your pardon. Have you seen an elderly gentleman this morning? He would have passed here about an hour ago."

He straightened. "Using a cane? About my height?"

"Not quite as tall as you are, but yes, he walks with a cane and favors his right leg." Her voice rose. "You've seen him?"

"I did. Earlier on. Besides the cane, he was carrying a chair."

"Carrying a chair?" Faith's mouth fell open. "Whatever do you mean?"

He dropped the rag over the dashboard of the buggy and walked toward her. Up close, he looked to be nearly six feet tall, with a tanned face and deep brown eyes. A partially healed scar ran along one side of his neck, tracing a thick red line from his jaw to a point behind his left ear. Another veteran, starting over.

"I mean just that, miss. He came by here at first light, stepping right along, with a bentwood chair hooked under one arm."

Faith rubbed her forehead, dislodging her bonnet. This had to be the strangest thing she'd heard in a long time. She took a deep breath and let it out with a puff. "Which way was he heading?"

"Sorry. I didn't pay attention. We exchanged nods, and he went on his way." He shoved a hand in his hip pocket. "Guess you're looking for him?"

Obviously, she thought, but didn't say so. "He's my grandfather. He was supposed to meet me at our store—Lindberg's Mercantile—at eight, but he never arrived."

The stableman's brown eyes filled with concern. "Your granddad is Judge Lindberg, then? And you must be Miss Faith."

She nodded.

"I'm Curt Saxon. If you'd like my help, we can search for him together. I'm a pretty good tracker."

"I don't know what kind of tracking you can do on town boardwalks—"

"There's more than one way to track. Sometimes you need to think like the quarry."

"I don't think of my grandfather as quarry, Mr. Saxon."

A muscle twitched in his jaw. "You said he was planning to meet you at the mercantile. I'll walk back that way and see what I can see. You can come with me or wait here."

"I'll go with you. He's my grandfather."

"Let's go then." Mr. Saxon set off along High Street. With his long legs, he was soon half a block ahead.

Sighing, Faith decided to try a different route and crossed the street, following picket fences and peering into yards. By the time she reached Courthouse Square, Mr. Saxon had vanished. Splendid. Now they were both missing. Suppressing a flare of temper, she stalked up the steps in front of the mercantile and flopped on a bench, arms folded across her middle.

She turned at the sound of footsteps on the porch. Mr. Saxon walked toward her, grinning. "Found him."

Faith jumped to her feet. "Where is he? Is he all right?"

He held up his hand with a calming gesture. "He's fine. C'mon. I'll take you to him."

She glanced at the neighboring businesses. No one in sight.

Apparently sensing her reluctance, he scowled. "Rather not be seen with me? Then go around to the alley. Your grand-dad's in the shed." His boots pounded on the boardwalk as he descended to the muddy roadway. "I need to get back to the livery."

She flushed at his brusque tone. "Thank you for your help."

"Don't mention it." Crossing the street, he strode away.

Faith left her carryall on the bench, dashed behind the store, and peered into the storage shed. Grandpa sat at a makeshift table comprised of short boards resting across two sawhorses. An oil lamp flickered next to a stack of loose papers.

"What are you doing out here?"

He leaned back in one of the bentwood chairs from their kitchen. "This is a busy place this morning. First that new fellow from the livery stable, now you. Can't a man have some peace and quiet?"

Faith jammed her hands on her hips. "Grandpa! You told me to meet you at the store at eight this morning. It must be going on nine by now."

"No need to take that tone with me, young lady." He removed his watch from his pants pocket and flicked open the lid. "By George, it *is* after nine. Must have lost track of time."

He stood, bewilderment clouding his eyes. "Why were you supposed to meet me?"

aith stared at her grandfather, fear prickling through
her. They'd had a long discussion the previous evening about her need to learn the business. She put her hand on
his arm, his flannel shirt soft under her fingers. "You wanted
to show me the ledgers, who should get credit and who had
to pay up front. That kind of thing."

"Why would I want you to operate the store?"

She felt like she'd been punched in the stomach. "Papa
and Maxwell were killed two years ago at Westport." She
spoke in a gentle voice, as though she were breaking the news
to him for the first time. "You thought I could manage the
mercantile for you now that I've turned twenty."

He placed a hand over hers. Comprehension flooded his
face. "You're right. You should take over. I've decided to write
my memoirs." Grandpa gestured at the papers. "I've seen a
great deal in my seventy years. When you get married, your
children can read them."

If she ever got married. There was only one man she
wanted, and like so many, he hadn't yet returned from the war.

Grandpa blew out the lamp, jingling a ring of keys in his
right hand. "Come with me. I'll show you what to do."

Her mind reeling at the swift changes in his behavior, she trailed him to the door of the mercantile and watched while he selected the correct key and clicked the padlock open. They'd no more than stepped over the threshold when a woman wearing a fashionably gathered dress pushed into the store.

"Your sign says you open at nine every morning but Sunday." She made a show of lifting the watch she wore on a chain around her neck and pointing at the dial. "It's nearly half past and your shades are still drawn."

Grandpa patted Faith on the shoulder. "Please uncover the windows while I assist this lady." Leaning close to her ear, he whispered, "She needs to pay up front. No credit." With a bland smile, he turned back to their customer. "What can I show you this morning, Mrs. Wylie?"

Her skirt swished as she walked to a shelf displaying samples of china. "Mr. Wylie said we should have better dishes now that he's opened the wagon factory. We will have to entertain buyers, you know."

Faith half-listened to their conversation while she rolled up the shades between the window displays and the interior of the store. Mrs. Wylie seemed interested in the newest tableware that had arrived from back east. Thankful that Grandpa had recovered his wits and could help the woman, Faith located a feather duster in the back room and proceeded to flick dust from the new cookstoves on display. From there she moved to the hoes, rakes, and shovels, straightening handles in the racks.

Studying the merchandise, she decided that the first thing she'd do would be to enlarge the dry goods area by transferring the farm implements to a far corner. The farmers knew what they wanted, but ladies liked to browse. Even though they'd be selling the business as soon as Grandpa agreed, it wouldn't hurt to make the store more inviting in the meantime.

Her mind spinning with ideas, she continued her circuit of the room until she reached the placard Grandpa had allowed her to mount on the wall behind the case holding oil lamps.

She'd copied a list from *The Prairie Traveler*, titling it "Necessities for the Overland Trip to Oregon." The catalog of supplies represented the first step. Now she waited for an opportune moment to broach the subject of leaving Missouri to journey west. Both she and Grandpa would be happier away from reminders of the war and the losses it represented.

The voices in the background faded while she read through the items they'd need. Wrought iron kettle, coffeepot and heavy tin cups, iron frying pans, tin buckets . . .

"Faith, would you come over here, please?" Grandpa gestured from a counter across the room. Plates, bowls, and a cream-and-sugar set were arranged next to a ledger. "Here is the price for each piece. Tally the numbers and write the amount at the bottom. Mrs. Wylie will pay you while I pack her china for delivery." He took a small silver key from the ring. "This'll open the cash drawer." While she unlocked the drawer, he tucked gold-rimmed plates into a barrel filled with wood shavings.

Mrs. Wylie leaned toward Faith and spoke in a confidential whisper. "Truthfully, my dear, I'll have to wait to settle with you until Mr. Wylie obtains a few more orders for wagons. Could you see your way clear to put my purchase on your books for a month or two?"

Faith's heartbeat increased. How was she supposed to refuse without offending their customer? She looked toward her grandfather for help, but he continued stacking china in the barrel, paying no attention to their conversation.

Harold Grisbee and Jesse Slocum, two of her grandfather's cronies, entered the store and sought chairs next to the cold stove. Instead of talking to one another, they focused their attention on Faith and Mrs. Wylie. Faith tried to remember her grandfather's dealings with customers on the Saturday mornings she'd helped by dusting shelves and sweeping the floors with oiled sawdust.

Mrs. Wylie drummed her fingers on the countertop. "Just give me a statement of what we owe you so I can be on my way."

Faith met the woman's impatient glare with a steady gaze. "I'm sorry. We require cash. If you can't pay today, we'll be glad to put the dishes aside until you have the funds." Her heart boomed in her chest.

Mrs. Wylie's face turned a mottled red. "Well! I've never been so insulted." She dug in her reticule and dropped a gold piece on the counter. "Make sure you give me the correct change, young woman." She swung around to face Grandpa, who watched with a grin lifting one corner of his moustache. "I'll expect these to be delivered right away. And don't hold your breath waiting for me to trade here again." She swept from the store, banging the door closed.

Over the chuckles of the men next to the stove, Faith turned to her grandfather. "I'm so sorry. I didn't know what else to say. You told me not to give her credit."

Grandpa threw his head back and guffawed. "She'll be back before the week is out. You watch and see. She knows better than to ask me to carry her on the books, but she thought she could put one over on you."

Faith slumped against the counter. "Do you deal with customers like her every day? I wanted to tell her to go home— without her dishes."

"You'll find most of the folks who shop here to be agreeable. Not too many bad apples in Noble Springs."

The entertainment over, the men near the stove busied themselves placing red and black pieces on a checkerboard and debating whose turn it was to begin. She stopped Grandpa on his way to settle the dispute. "Before any more customers

15

come in, please show me where to find the list of people who shouldn't receive credit."

He scratched the top of his nearly bald head. "Now where'd it go?"

While Faith watched, he riffled through the pages of the ledger, then bent over and brought a group of similar volumes from the shelf below the cash drawer. A musty smell rose from the pages of the dustiest books as he searched. "Put it somewhere safe, I reckon." He chuckled. "It must be safe if I can't find it."

Grandpa lifted an invoice that had fallen from one of the ledgers and turned it over. "I'll make you a new list. Keep it in the cash drawer." He licked the tip of a pencil and scribbled a half-dozen names.

She peeked over his shoulder. "That's all? I can remember that many easily."

"There's more, but right now I can't call the names to mind. They'll come to me." Frustration shadowed his words.

Faith frowned. The man who could recite most of Longfellow's poems, including the newest ones, couldn't remember names of people he saw almost every day. She brushed her lips across his smooth-shaven cheek. "You're tired. I heard you up pacing last night. Why don't you see who's winning the checker game? I'll put these books away."

"You sound like a mother hen. I've got a barrel of chinaware to deliver, remember?"

"Wait until this afternoon. The druggist's boy can help you when school's out."

"I'm perfectly capable. I'll go borrow Simpkins's horse and hitch the wagon."

The stubborn set of his mouth told her that argument would be useless. The thump of his cane against the floor punctuated his departure.

"Never been a woman could tell Nate Lindberg what to

do, Miss Faith. Not Miz Clara, rest her soul, and not your mama, neither. Might as well get used to it," one of the checker players said.

She nodded, ready to reply, when the bell over the door tinkled and a young woman she didn't recognize entered. Dressed in dove-gray watered silk with a high white collar and matching silk bonnet, she formed a picture of modesty. Her eyes didn't meet Faith's as she walked to the fabric display at the rear of the room. Faith glanced at the list of names and hoped she wouldn't have to handle another request for credit.

The bell tinkled again and soon several customers demanded her attention. One by one, she helped them with their purchases, always keeping an eye on the woman in gray.

During the flurry of activity, Grandpa returned. Tipping the barrel of china at an angle, he rolled it toward the door. Faith shot a glance at him and waved over the head of her current customer toward the checker players. When they looked in her direction, she pointed at Grandpa's back and mouthed, "Help him."

Chairs scraped. The men stepped to either side of the barrel.

"You're in my way," Grandpa said, his voice gruff, but he allowed them to support the weight while he hefted the delivery into the wagon.

"It's hard for some people to acknowledge their age," a sympathetic voice said.

Faith started. She'd been so focused on Grandpa she hadn't noticed that the woman had returned from the rear of the room, carrying a bolt of moss green fabric in a paisley print. Her hazel eyes were filled with compassion.

Drawn to the caring in the depths of those eyes, Faith blurted. "He's my grandfather—all the family I have left. I worry about him."

"Many of us have little family left these days. I believe the Lord put us here to comfort each other. To be sisters and brothers to those who have none." She spoke as one stating a fact, not an opinion.

"I . . . I never thought of things that way."

" 'Woe to him that is alone when he falleth; for he hath not another to help him up.' That's from the Bible."

Faith's heart warmed toward this woman with the kindly eyes and soft voice. "Are you new to Noble Springs? I don't recall seeing you before."

"Fairly new. My job ended, so I came to stay with my brother." An impish smile lit her face. "He was alone." She removed her glove and extended her hand. "My name's Rosemary."

"I'm Faith." The woman's palms were callused. Whatever job she'd had, she'd been doing manual work.

After she completed her purchase, Faith watched her leave. When Rosemary opened the door, she whistled two soft notes. A sable and white collie appeared from under the steps and trotted along the boardwalk at her side.

Faith sighed and turned away. How nice it would be to have a friend like Rosemary.

Two of Faith's former classmates, Marguerite Holland and Nelda Raines, breezed through the open door in a cloud of flower-scented cologne. "Did you see her? Bold as brass. Like she's as good as the rest of us."

Curiosity piqued, Faith asked, "Who are you talking about?"

"Why, that vulgar girl who just left." Nelda lowered her voice. "She was a *nurse* during the war. Can you imagine? Touching men's bodies, and having the gall to walk around like she had nothing to be ashamed of."

3

aith bristled at the two women. "I hope someone with her compassion was with my father and brother when they died. I think caring for wounded soldiers was a courageous thing to do. Godly, you might say."

"Well, you might say that. I certainly wouldn't." Nelda glanced around the store. "Where's Judge Lindberg? I need to talk to him about my mother's account."

Sensing another unpleasant encounter, Faith's stomach muscles tightened. "You can talk to me. My grandfather left me in charge."

"No, thank you. I'll come back another time."

"That would be splendid." She decided not to mention that she'd be in charge the next time they returned as well.

When they left, she closed the door, then dropped into one of the chairs next to the stove. She felt like she'd been thrown into Pioneer Lake and expected to swim.

Faith tapped a finger on the wooden arm of the chair. A glance at the clock told her the newspaper editor should be in his office at the *Noble Springs Observer*, although one never knew with Aaron Simpkins. He loved to act like a big city reporter. He could be off chasing rumors of bank robberies or someone's barn going up in flames. Noble Springs hadn't escaped the unrest that seethed through the Ozarks in the wake of Lee's surrender.

Faith popped out onto the covered boardwalk and hurried next door, fingers crossed that Grandpa wouldn't return in her absence and find the mercantile unattended. When she entered the office, her nose prickled at the smell of ink and hot lead.

Mr. Simpkins smiled at her from his desk, his gold-rimmed spectacles glinting in the light. "No new reports. The telegraph's been silent this morning." His smile faded to a look of sympathy. "Miss Faith, it's been a year. I hate to say it, but you need to accept that Royal Baxter is dead, even if we don't have confirmation. I'm told some men were so—" He cleared his throat. "What I mean is, we may never know all the names."

She pressed her lips together. She'd accept no such thing. "Thank you, Mr. Simpkins. I'll stop by again."

He shook his head. "Feel free to drop in any time. But the answer will be the same."

"I hope so. If he's not on a casualty list, then he's alive. Somewhere. Good day."

She trotted toward the mercantile only to stop abruptly at the sight of the delivery wagon tied out front. Grandpa opened the door, his brown eyes snapping with anger. "You went off and left the cash drawer unlocked. Anyone could have walked in and robbed us blind."

Her breath caught. Although managing the store would be temporary, she intended to do her best. Faith stared at the toes of her boots through tear-blurred eyes. "I'm so sorry. I just forgot." She felt his thumb lift her chin so she could look into his face.

Grandpa patted her shoulder. "We all make mistakes."

He handed her the small silver key, then stepped inside and propped the "Closed for dinner" sign in the window. "It's nearly noon. Let's go home."

Curt Saxon leaned against the doorway of the livery stable and watched while a yellow wagon rolled by. He didn't need to read the black letters spelling "Lindberg's Mercantile" on the side to recognize the girl on the seat next to her grandfather. The owner of the livery had told Curt her name when he asked soon after hiring on as stableman. But until today she hadn't noticed him.

He traced his index finger along the scar on his neck. Did he look that frightening? Miss Faith's expression when he'd asked her to follow him said he did. He'd have to change that impression.

The wagon stopped in front of a two-story brick home farther down the street. Once the judge and his granddaughter entered, Curt stepped into the dim interior of the stable.

"Mr. Ripley. With your permission, I'll take dinner break now."

"Told you, call me Rip." The owner of the livery stepped from the tack room. A gnome-like man with a curly black beard, he clutched a half-eaten sandwich in one hand. "You don't need my permission. We got no one wanting a horse now anyway. Go on with you."

Curt thanked him and left the stable. Instead of turning toward West & Riley's, the restaurant across town, he walked toward Judge Lindberg's house. He'd find something to eat later.

When he reached the front door, he grabbed the knocker and rapped before he lost his courage. The door opened almost immediately.

The judge peered out, frowning. "Yes?"

Sunlight poured onto the polished entry hall floor, washing up against the hem of Faith's blue dress. Her arms were folded across her trim waistline. She appeared as irritated as the old man sounded. From the looks of things, he'd interrupted a family dispute.

He removed his hat, mentally berating himself for his poor timing. "Wondered if you'd met up with your grandfather." Curt directed his comment at Faith. "I see you have." He turned to Judge Lindberg. "Miss Faith was worried when she couldn't find you this morning."

"Not really worried," she said.

"I wasn't lost," the judge added.

Feeling foolish, Curt took a step backward and replaced his hat. His impulses seldom went as hoped, and today was no exception. "I've come at a bad moment. Please excuse me."

"Now, now. Come on in, young man. We were going to take dinner. You're welcome to join us."

Faith's eyes widened. "About those dishes for Mrs. Wylie . . ." She nudged her grandfather. "We need to deliver them first."

He moved away from her, his expression obstinate. "Not necessarily."

Curt remained on the stoop. The rich fragrance of baked ham swirled toward him from the entry hall, urging him to accept the invitation. On the other hand, Faith still wore her bonnet and an inhospitable expression.

She turned toward him. "I apologize. I just learned of a late delivery to a customer, and we really must attend to it first."

"It's a barrel full of china," the judge said, his tone cross. "There's no 'we' to it. You can't wrestle anything that heavy from the wagon."

"The two of us could do it, sir," Curt heard himself say.

Faith gave him the same look he'd seen when he asked her to follow him that morning.

He tugged at the neck of his shirt, trying to cover the angry slash. No doubt there were scars in the Lindbergs' lives, as well. Some showed, some were hidden. Everyone had them these days.

Before Curt could form words to reassure her, the judge spoke. "You know where Cletus Wylie lives?"

"The wagon maker? Yes."

"Good, because I can't remember."

Faith stood at the open door until the wagon traveled out of sight. She prayed Grandpa would be safe. The stableman seemed trustworthy. But with all of the men displaced by war, it was hard to know who was honest and who was out for what he could steal.

Her gaze wandered to the maple tree bristling with red flowers next to the boardwalk, then to the weeds coming up in their muddy yard. Her thoughts went to the delayed delivery for Mrs. Wylie. Grandpa said he'd searched for the woman's house for over an hour this morning. A customer he'd delivered to many times in the past, and today he couldn't find his way. The sooner she could convince him to leave for the west, the better.

Back inside, she removed the ham from the warming oven and cut several thin pieces, then split leftover breakfast biscuits and placed a slice between each one. She dropped chunks of pickled watermelon rind on the meat before covering the filling with a biscuit top. By the time Grandpa returned it would be too late to sit down for dinner, so she wrapped their food in linen napkins. They could eat at the store after reopening for the afternoon.

After a moment's thought, she prepared two biscuits for the stableman, bundling them in a clean towel. The least she could do was feed him after he helped with the delivery.

Minutes ticked on, and the two men didn't return. Faith busied herself tidying the kitchen. Every few minutes she checked the case clock. If they didn't hurry, they'd be late opening the mercantile for the second time in one day. With ten minutes to spare, she wrote a note telling Grandpa she had gone to the store, dropped their food into a basket, and left the house.

Her worries about the stableman mounted with each step through the warm afternoon. Buggies and riders on horseback passed by, but no yellow wagon. At around a thousand souls, Noble Springs wasn't so big that they couldn't have gone to the Wylie's house and returned before now.

Trusting the stableman with her grandfather had been a mistake. She'd stop on her way past the courthouse and report him to the sheriff.

What was his name again? Curt Saxon. Scar on neck. He ought to be easy to spot. As she turned south on Court Street, Faith heard wagon wheels squawk behind her. A horse blew and rattled its harness.

"Miss Faith!"

She swung around.

The stableman stood in the wagon, reins taut in one hand. "Your grandfather's hurt. I'm bringing him home." He held out his hand. "I need your help."

Faith fought a grip of nausea. Her grandpa was the only part of her life that had survived the war. She ran to the wagon and allowed herself to be hoisted up.

"Where is he?"

"In back."

She pushed the curtain aside. Grandpa lay pale and silent on a wide plank turned lengthwise on the wagon bed. Faith hiked her skirt, scrambled over the seat, and knelt beside him. One temple was swollen and oozing blood. She jerked her bonnet off and rested her head against his chest, grateful to feel his heart thumping against her ear.

The wagon swayed as they covered the remaining distance to the house. Faith rested on her heels and called forward. "For mercy's sake, what happened? I thought you were going to help him."

"Wasn't my fault, miss." A defensive note crept into his voice. "His game leg gave out and he fell. Hit his head against the endgate."

"How long has he been . . . like this?"

"Can't be more'n ten minutes. Cletus Wylie helped get him loaded." He stopped the wagon. "Be right back. Going to get Mr. Ripley to help me."

The two men, one tall, one short, eased the makeshift litter out of the vehicle. Faith ran ahead and opened the door, then hurried through the house and motioned them to follow her. She pointed at a cot next to the wall in a small room behind the kitchen. "Please, put him there."

Grandpa moaned when they moved him, but didn't open his eyes. Faith's heartbeat threatened to choke her.

She turned to Mr. Saxon. "I know we've been enough trouble to you already, but could you ask Dr. Greeley to come?" She rubbed her throat, willing herself to be calm.

"Already did, miss. Stopped on the way. He's with a patient. Said to tell you he'd be here directly."

She drew a chair beside the cot and sank onto it, clasping one of Grandpa's hands between her own. "Thank you." She addressed both men in a quavering voice.

"Glad to help." The owner of the livery stable tugged at his curly beard and shuffled his feet. "Reckon I best be going. I ain't no doc."

Mr. Saxon moved to one side to allow his employer to leave. "You don't mind, miss, I'll wait out front until Doc Greeley gets here."

"Thank you," she repeated. "I'm grateful for your help."

After he left, she stared around the small room. Intended as sleeping quarters for a house servant, the space had been unused for years. Dust tickled Faith's nose. Not a good place for Grandpa, but as it was the only bedroom on the first floor, it would have to do.

Faith heard voices in the entry hall and then Dr. August Greeley appeared in the doorway. His white hair flowed around his shoulders, framing the precise white goatee on his chin. "The young fellow out there said your grandfather took a fall." He patted Faith's shoulder. "Don't you worry. I'm sure he'll be right as rain in no time."

The doctor dropped his medical bag on the floor and bent over the cot. She watched while he raised one of Grandpa's eyelids. "Hmm." After placing an open pocket watch in one hand, he closed his fingers over the unconscious man's wrist. Lips moving, he counted to himself.

"Pulse is steady. Can you fetch me some water so I can clean off this blood?"

Faith jumped to her feet, glad to have something to do. In moments she returned with a basin filled with warm water from the reservoir on the stove.

Once Dr. Greeley had swabbed and bandaged Grandpa's temple, he sat in the chair Faith vacated and wiped his hands on a towel. "He should come around any minute. After he wakes up, he'll need to be watched for a few days. Blow to the head's a serious matter, 'specially on old fellas like me and Nate here."

Faith looked past the doctor at her grandfather. She could barely discern the rising and falling of his chest as he drew breath. She squeezed a question past the iron bands of fear that circled her throat.

"What if he doesn't wake up?"

$\mathcal{F}$aith sensed a presence behind her.

Mr. Saxon stood in the doorway. "I saw this happen when I was soldiering. Most always, they came around." From his expression, she knew he meant to be comforting.

"Most always?" She knit her fingers together and rested her chin on her clasped hands. "What happened when they didn't? Did they—?"

Dr. Greeley interrupted. "Nate's lips are moving." He shot a stern glance at Mr. Saxon. "No need for worrisome comments."

"Sorry. I didn't mean to offend." His face turned stony. "I'll be going now."

Faith glanced between him and the doctor. "Just one moment. I made up a meal for you since you missed your dinner." She returned to the kitchen and handed him the towel-wrapped food. "You've been more than helpful. I can't thank you enough."

"No trouble." Without his ready smile, his face relaxed into weary lines.

After he left, she noticed her bonnet on a table in the entry hall. It had been brushed clean of debris from the wagon.

Grandpa's cane hung from the edge of the table. Another kindness for which she owed thanks to Mr. Saxon.

"Miss Faith? Your grandfather's asking for you." Dr. Greeley motioned to her from the bedroom doorway.

"Praise God. He's awake." She stepped around the doctor and bent over the cot. "How do you feel?"

"My head hurts. What happened?"

"Mr. Saxon said your bad leg gave way and you fell. Your head hit the wagon."

"Where were we?"

"At the Wylies', delivering china. Don't you remember?"

He started to shake his head, then winced. "Nope. Last thing I recall is young Saxon directing me to the Wylies' house." Grandpa shifted on the cot and looked at the doctor. "August, what happened?"

Faith's eyes widened. "I just told you—"

Dr. Greeley held up a hand to stop her. "You fell and hit your head," he told Grandpa. His voice was matter-of-fact. "You'll need to stay home and rest for a few days. Mind yourself when you walk about."

"Well, I can do that all right. Faith here is running the store now."

She smiled, relieved that he remembered.

Grandpa took her hand. "Why am I in the servant's room? What happened?"

A pulse throbbed in her throat. She stared at the doctor, sending him a frantic question with her eyes.

He warned her to silence with a slight shake of his head. "You fell and took a bad blow to your temple. Rest now. Faith will bring you a cool cloth for your forehead in a moment." The doctor lifted his medical bag and clasped Grandpa's shoulder. "I'll stop by tomorrow to see how you're doing."

Faith followed him from the room. As soon as they were

out of earshot, she asked, "What's the matter with him? He keeps asking the same question."

"I've seen brief amnesia with head injuries before. It's nothing to worry about—unless he's still asking tomorrow." He tilted his head, an avuncular expression on his face. "Just be patient with him for now. Most of all, don't let him move around too much. If you need firewood split, or other such, best call on a neighbor."

"I can do firewood. Have been ever since . . ." She blinked away quick tears. "Since Papa and Maxwell left. They showed me how." She opened the front door and stood to one side. A chilly breeze slipped past her, ruffling her skirt. "How long do you think it will be before we can go back to the store?" Faith hated herself for asking, but the only time Grandpa had closed the mercantile was when they received the news from Westport.

" 'We'?"

She nodded. "Grandpa has asked me to take over for him. Now . . ." She waved a hand toward the rear of the house. "I can't be in two places at once."

"Nor should you be. I thought your grandfather was rambling when he said you were running things. I don't know what possessed him—a young lady such as yourself involved in commerce. It's not proper."

His tone riled Faith. "I can manage the mercantile, and I plan to. What's proper has changed since the war."

"Things haven't changed that much, missy." He wagged his finger at her. "I've known you since you were born. I'll thank you to show some respect."

"I could hardly refuse my grandfather's wishes, could I?" She stifled her irritation. "Can you suggest a person who might be able to stay with him so I can tend the store?"

"Absolutely not. Your place is right here."

The following morning, Faith jolted awake at the sound of her grandfather's cane tapping across the downstairs floor. She flung the covers aside and dashed halfway down the stairs to the landing in time to see him fully dressed, walking out the front door. Gray daylight outlined his form as he moved out of sight.

"Mercy sakes! Grandpa!"

If he heard her, he didn't stop.

No time to don a robe. She flew down the stairs after him and caught up just as he crossed at the end of their block. The mud in the street squished between her bare toes and wicked along the hem of her nightgown.

Grandpa stared at her with astonishment. "What are you doing out here? You're not even dressed."

"Grandpa, what are *you* doing out here? You might fall again. Come with me, and let's have some breakfast." She slipped her arm under his.

"Eggs and potatoes. Not that oatmeal pap."

"Eggs it is."

As the sun crested the horizon, roosters crowed insults at one another from behind nearby homes. Out of the corner of her eye, she noticed a curtain drawn back in their neighbor's window. She turned her head and waved, grinning. Might as well give folks something new to discuss.

After eating, Grandpa paced back and forth in the entry hall. "You sure August said I have to rest at home?" He addressed the question on one of his trips past the kitchen door.

Faith turned from the basin where she was washing the breakfast dishes. "The doctor was very clear on the subject. 'Rest for a few days,' he said. He'll be here later to check on you."

Grandpa settled onto one of the kitchen chairs, a glum expression on his face. "I can't be still for that long. He'll have to tie me down."

Her heart stirred. Maybe there was a solution for both of them. "Would you like me to bring you your papers? You can work here."

"Would you do that?" He brightened for a moment, then his moustache drooped. "What about the mercantile? We can't leave it closed. People depend on us."

Faith crossed the room and dropped a kiss on his bald spot. "I have an idea."

Dr. Greeley arrived a few minutes after ten. "How's your grandfather this morning?"

"He's stopped asking about his accident. But he's restless. He's not used to being idle." Faith hung the doctor's hat on the hall tree. "I told him I'd bring him some papers from the store, so he'd have something to do."

"Good. No reason he can't be up and around, but he needs to refrain from strenuous activity for a bit."

"That you, August?" Grandpa stepped out of the parlor.

"None other." He studied his patient. "Except for that bandaged head, you look like you've recovered."

"Nothing wrong with me. A sore head's all. You got time for a game of checkers?"

Faith recognized opportunity. Before the doctor could answer, she said, "While you two are busy with your game, I'll dash to the store and get your papers, Grandpa."

Surprise, followed by irritation, crossed the doctor's face. "I wasn't planning—"

"I shouldn't be too long." She favored him with a winsome

smile. "Thank you. It's very kind of you to stay." She whisked upstairs and grabbed her shawl and bonnet.

When Faith reached the town square, she bypassed the mercantile and entered the office of the *Noble Springs Observer*. Mr. Simpkins eyed her with surprise.

"How about if I come tell you if I hear of more casualties? Save you the trouble of dropping in so often." He sounded a touch sarcastic.

She folded her arms across her chest. "Fine. I won't bother you again. But that's not why I'm here. I have a question and figured if anyone would have the answer, it would be you. No one knows more about Noble Springs."

He straightened in his chair, chest puffed. "Ask away."

"Yesterday morning, a woman named Rosemary was in the mercantile. Two of the ladies who saw her told me she had been a nurse. Do you know where I might find her?"

"Only one person like that around here. What would a decent gal like you want with her?"

Faith blinked at the open prejudice in his voice. Why was it permissible for a woman to care for a child who was ill, but not to help injured soldiers? "I have something to ask her. Where does she live?"

He walked to the window and pointed east. "Follow King's Highway about three blocks. Saxons live on the left, gray house, white fence around the yard."

"Saxons?" Faith swallowed. "Does she have a brother who works at Ripley's Livery?" As soon as she asked, she remembered Rosemary saying that she'd come to Noble Springs to live with her brother.

"Yep. He showed up around six months ago, but she hasn't

been here that long. People are stirred up since the war ended. Some folks leaving, some coming. Be glad when things settle down."

Faith thought of her own plans to travel to Oregon. "I can understand not wanting to remain around sad memories."

"Wherever you go, you take yourself with you. Memories and all." He combed his fingers through his rumpled blond hair. "Might as well stay put."

She moved toward the doorway. "Thank you for your help."

"Welcome. Say, I noticed your grandpappy didn't open the mercantile this morning. Been some customers pass by."

"We'll be open this afternoon. You can tell anyone who asks."

Once out on the boardwalk she turned east, but her steps slowed as she neared the gray house. Knowing that Rosemary must be Mr. Saxon's sister altered her intentions. She hated to impose on the family again, after all that had happened yesterday, but the woman was her best hope.

Behind the picket fence, a neatly maintained yard with raised flower beds framed the front walk. Rows of seedlings lifted their leaves toward the sun. Faith couldn't help but contrast the tidy garden with the tumble of weeds in front of her house. Some people had a knack for coaxing flowers out of the soil. She wasn't one of them.

She reached for the latch on the gate just as Rosemary appeared on the gravel pathway leading from the rear of the building. She wore a faded blue chambray dress and carried a trowel. Her fingers were covered with dirt. The sable and white collie trotted at her heels.

Rosemary's eyes widened. "You're Faith, from the mercantile." She wiped her hands on her apron. "This is a surprise. Please, come in." She led the way to the porch steps, removing her sunbonnet as she walked. Glossy black hair tumbled loose from its pins. "Fiddle." Rosemary shook her head, freeing the curls. "Gardening isn't the tidiest task."

Faith smiled, enjoying the woman's casual response to her unscheduled visit. Some people she knew would fly into a dither at unexpected guests. "I can't stay but a minute. I know it's presumptuous of me, but I'm afraid I came to ask a favor."

"Please, sit." Rosemary gestured toward two wicker chairs on the covered porch. "How can I assist you?"

"I need help, and you're the first person I thought of." Heat rose up her neck. Now that she was here, she knew how forward her request would sound. "My grandfather fell yesterday."

"That was your grandfather? My brother told me he'd taken an old gentleman home." Her eyes twinkled. "He also said he met a pretty girl with eyes the color of lake water."

"Oh, goodness." Faith didn't think of herself as a pretty girl, not with her straw-brown hair and sturdy figure. She couldn't compare with the ladies pictured in *Godey's*.

"And the favor?" Rosemary asked.

Faith talked fast, before she could lose her courage. "Grandpa's not to do anything strenuous for a few days, so he can't go to the mercantile. I can't leave him alone at home. I need a nurse to look after him so I can open the store. Would you come?"

Rosemary paled. She stood, shaking her head. "No. That part of my life is over."

Faith recoiled at the vehemence of Rosemary's response. "I . . . I'm sorry. I didn't intend to insult you." She rose and moved toward the steps. "I'll be on my way. Forgive the intrusion."

"Wait." Rosemary held out a soil-stained hand. "Please understand. I came to Noble Springs to start fresh. You called today because you heard the gossip about me, didn't you?"

Embarrassed, Faith nodded.

"We lived in St. Louis when the war started. Within a year, Jefferson Barracks was transformed into a hospital complex for the wounded. I felt the Lord calling me into nursing, and offered my services to Major Surgeon Randolph." Rosemary closed her eyes for a moment. When she opened them, they glistened with tears. "So many wounded men—hundreds— and not enough hands to care for them. In spite of his hesitation at using a female, Major Randolph agreed. I had quarters on the post with the other ladies who eventually arrived, so it wasn't until I left a few months ago that I fully realized how much I'd be condemned for my service."

Faith looked at the floor, wishing she could escape. She knew she'd been guilty of similar self-righteous thoughts.

"Judge not, that ye be not judged" ran through her mind. The pain on Rosemary's face illustrated how deeply she'd been hurt by finger-pointing and whispers.

Faith met the other woman's eyes. "You can't imagine how small I feel right now. I'd give anything not to have intruded."

Rosemary's expression softened. "It's I who must apologize, burdening you with my story." Her lips curved in a half-smile. "A simple 'no, thank you' would have been sufficient. Truly, I'm happy you stopped by, whatever your reason. I'm lonely here. As you can imagine, I haven't been flooded with invitations to join the ladies' sewing circle or literary discussion group."

Faith snickered. "They're boring anyway."

"Yes, I expect they are." Rosemary chuckled, then turned serious. "If you can overlook my refusal, I'd be pleased if you'd come by again one day for tea and a real visit."

Faith covered the distance between the Saxons' home and the mercantile at a rapid pace. Too much time had elapsed since she left Dr. Greeley with her grandfather. The doctor would be furious.

Her thoughts tumbled over one another like the darkening clouds massing overhead. Without help, she had no choice but to remain at home with Grandpa. What would happen to the business? They still had a ways to go to recover from the deprivations of the war.

The wind changed, thick with the scent of rain. A few more minutes and she'd be home, but first she needed to collect Grandpa's papers from the shed behind the mercantile.

The floor creaked when she stepped inside. Everything was as he'd left it yesterday morning. Faith placed filled sheets on top of the blank pages and glanced at the words in her grandfather's spiky handwriting.

I am now seventy years old and have had a most eventful career, a history I propose to write for the benefit and satisfaction of my descendants . . .

Feeling like a spy, she rolled the papers into a tube and closed the door of the shed. When Grandpa wanted her to read his recollections, he'd offer them to her.

Fat raindrops splattered on the boardwalk. Faith tucked the manuscript pages inside her shawl, protecting them with her arms, and strode toward home. When she passed the livery, she darted a quick glance at the doorway, disappointed when she didn't see Mr. Saxon. His kindness yesterday deserved greater thanks than she'd displayed. Perhaps she would drop by with a plate of spice cookies tomorrow. That should bring a smile to his face.

In the distance, three men rode in her direction along High Street. The one in the center was mounted on a tall black stallion. He sat straight in the saddle, his hat pulled low against the rain. All three men wore canvas overcoats. As they approached, Faith ducked her head so she wouldn't be caught staring. Her hands clutched the papers under her shawl. She dared another quick glance.

The rider on the stallion looked like Royal Baxter.

On Friday, Faith stood at the kitchen table rolling spice cookie dough into balls and dipping them into a bowl of sugar. The fragrance of molasses and cinnamon swirled from the oven. Cooling cookies rested on brown paper spread over a shelf under the window. Once the final batch left the oven, she'd take a plateful to the livery.

She hummed while she worked, grateful that she and Grandpa had Dr. Greeley's blessing to return to the mercantile on Monday. Faith prayed that their enforced absence during the week hadn't affected trade.

Her mind returned to the riders she'd seen on Tuesday. They were adequately dressed and well mounted, so they didn't look like displaced stragglers. Could the tall man on the black stallion really have been Royal Baxter? She'd had only a glimpse through the falling rain. Besides, she hadn't seen him since she was sixteen. Time and war changed a man. No telling what he might look like today.

The smell of smoke stung her nose. Faith jerked the oven door open and removed a pan of scorched cookies. Grandpa poked his head into the kitchen. "You making charcoal in here?"

She giggled. "Just one pan full. Want some?"

He entered the room and squeezed her shoulder. "Believe I'll try one of these instead." He lifted one of the sugared treats from the cooling shelf. Around a mouthful, he asked, "Are we still going to have sweets when you're busy at the Mercantile?"

"Of course. Wouldn't be supper without dessert, would it?"

Faith approached Ripley's Livery with her gift of cookies tucked into a basket. Neither Mr. Saxon nor Mr. Ripley were visible, so she entered the shaded stable. The smell of horseflesh and manure assailed her the moment she stepped inside. Thick underbrush swayed beyond the open rear doors, propelled by wind that gusted around the enclosure.

Mr. Ripley peered at her over the top of a stall door.

"Afternoon, Miss Faith. What brings you here? Granddad ailing again?"

"Thankfully, no." She took a quick glance around, hoping to see Mr. Saxon.

"You looking for Curt?"

"I brought a token of appreciation for him—for both of you—for helping us the other day. It was a trying time."

He closed the stall door and walked to the center of the building. Tipping his head back, he bellowed, "Saxon! Lady to see you."

A flush burned Faith's cheeks. "I just came to deliver a thank-you." She held out the basket. "If you'll take this, I'll be on my way."

"What's your hurry?" He pointed at a ladder leading to the hayloft. "Here he comes now."

She bit her lip. The last thing she wanted was to seem to be pursuing the stableman. Minutes seemed to pass as she watched him approach. A smile creased his face.

"Miss Faith. What a fine surprise."

"These are for you and Mr. Ripley." She thrust the basket at him, her tone formal. "You helped us so much on Monday. I wanted to thank you properly."

Mr. Ripley stepped close and lifted the napkin. "Well, looky here, a heap of cookies." He reached inside and removed a handful. "Mighty nice of you, Miss Faith. Anytime you want my help, just holler."

"Thank you," she said, taken aback. This wasn't going the way she'd planned. Mr. Saxon was the one who'd done the most on her grandfather's behalf. Faith lifted her head and caught a glint of amusement in his eyes.

"Looks like you brought plenty." Mr. Saxon cocked an eyebrow at his employer. "Good thing too. Rip's fast on the draw when it comes to food."

"Thought I'd take my share and go sit in my office so's you two can visit." Crumbs danced on Mr. Ripley's beard while he spoke. He winked.

The afternoon was going from bad to worse. She should have waited until tomorrow and left the cookies when she and Grandpa walked to the mercantile. Faith looked at Mr. Saxon, the flush on her cheeks hotter than ever. "I mustn't keep you from your work."

"Can't think of a more pleasant interruption. Matter of fact, I was planning to call on you and Judge Lindberg tomorrow." He shifted the basket from one hand to the other. "Can I offer you a ride to church on Sunday?" The scar on his neck flared. "It's a long walk clean across town. Might tire your granddad, being so far and all."

Faith drew a deep breath and exhaled slowly. She'd already wondered if they should miss church until Grandpa was steadier on his feet. Mr. Saxon's suggestion would be a solution, as long as he realized she agreed only for her grandfather's sake.

"I'll tell Grandpa of your kind offer. I'm sure it will be most welcome." She extended her hand as though confirming a business arrangement. "Until Sunday, then."

After Faith left, Curt could still feel the daintiness of her fingers against his palm. Such small hands were better suited to cooking than commerce. Her blue dress fluttered in the wind as she hurried away.

She acted like she couldn't wait to escape him. It had to be his scar. He could come up with a dozen ways to impress her, but he'd never overcome the way his skin puckered around the place on his neck where an enemy saber had sliced down to the muscle.

A wave of fear washed over him. He dropped the basket and whirled, staring at the underbrush growing behind the stable. Sweat prickled his forehead. Where was his rifle? Not again. He'd forgotten the first rule of combat. Don't leave your tent without your rifle.

Ducking, he ran into an empty stall for cover and threw himself flat on the straw. If he didn't move, they'd pass by without seeing him. As soon as darkness fell, he'd find his unit.

"Saxon!"

Curt shuddered. How could the Rebs know his name?

The door of the stall swung open and Curt sprang into a crouch, ready to fight with his bare hands.

A short man with a full beard squatted in front of him. "Take it easy, son. It's Rip." He placed his hand on Curt's shoulder, near the scar. "War's over. You made it back safe."

The darkness inside Curt's head vanished. Rip. The livery. Noble Springs. He took a deep breath, head falling forward as he exhaled. "Happened again, didn't it? Sorry, Rip. I keep hoping each time will be the last."

Rip grabbed Curt under the arms and helped him to his feet. "Been a long while since the last one. Takes time. I wasn't worth much for a couple years after Mexico." He slapped him on the back. "Want to quit early? Go get some supper?"

"Are you buying?" Curt managed a shaky grin.

"Why not? Jake West owes me for a horse rental. We'll see what he's got at the restaurant today."

Curt's sweat-soaked shirt clung to his body. He took a bandana from his pocket and mopped his forehead. It was too soon to think about courting a girl.

On Sunday morning, Faith spent extra time trying to decide what to wear to church. If indeed she'd seen Royal Baxter on Tuesday, he might be among the worshipers today. She wanted to look her best.

She slipped a flower-sprigged purple chintz garment over her head and fastened the cloth-covered buttons. Given her unfashionably stocky frame, the trim lines of the bodice made it the most flattering of her dresses. Gathering her shawl and bonnet, she descended the stairs. Mr. Saxon would arrive any moment to take them to church, and she didn't want to keep him waiting.

Grandpa bent over a table in the parlor, writing. Sheets of paper were strewn across the green and blue patterned upholstery on the sofa. He looked up when she entered. "That your new dress?"

"Not completely new. I finished it a month ago. I haven't worn it yet."

"I see." His eyes crinkled with amusement. "Well, I won't tell Saxon it's new, then."

"Grandpa! You don't have to tell him anything at all. What does he care about girls' dresses?"

43

He wiped the nib clean and set his pen aside. "If he doesn't arrive soon, I'll be telling him he's late."

Faith glanced at the mantel clock. They should have been on their way by now if they were walking. She bit her lip. Morning clouds promised a shower or two—not the best day to wear her prettiest dress.

She pushed the parlor curtains aside at the moment a covered buggy came to a stop in front of the house. To her surprise, Rosemary Saxon, rather than her brother, descended. She wrapped the horse's reins around a hitching rail and walked up the path.

Before she could knock, Faith swung the door open. "Good morning." She peeked around Rosemary's shoulder and didn't see Mr. Saxon on the buggy seat. How curious. "When your brother offered to take us to church, I assumed he'd be driving. I hope we haven't inconvenienced you."

"Not at all. Curt had a restless night and awakened with an acute headache. He asks your pardon."

Grandpa stepped next to Faith's elbow. "It's not every day I attend church with two pretty girls. What is your name, young lady?"

Faith flushed at her lack of manners and made introductions while they walked to the buggy.

"Rosemary Saxon. Hmm." Grandpa rubbed his moustache. "Heard that name somewhere before."

Rosemary's mouth tightened. "I'm the nurse everyone's talking about."

"That's it. I remember now. Good for you, miss. If you ask me, this town needs more helpers and fewer talkers."

Proud of him, Faith took Grandpa's free hand and squeezed it.

Bells pealed from the white steeple on the square brick church as the three of them entered the vestibule. Reverend

French greeted them inside the door. "Judge Lindberg, Miss Faith. I see you're acquainted with Miss Rosemary. Excellent." He beamed at them.

Turning penetrating gray eyes on Rosemary, he asked, "Where's your brother this morning? I'll miss his fine bass voice during the hymn singing."

"He didn't rest well last night."

A meaningful look passed between them. "Ah. Please let him know I'll call on him this afternoon."

"I will. Thank you."

Sunshine flooded through the row of rectangular windows on Faith's right, bathing the oak pews with buttery light and spreading to a vase of dogwood blossoms in front of the pulpit. At the piano, Reverend French's wife, Clarissa, moved her fingers over the keys in a gentle medley of hymns.

Faith followed Grandpa up the center aisle, smiling as he responded to greetings from townsfolk. She didn't see Royal Baxter anywhere in the congregation. When she thought about it, she'd never seen him in church before the war. Feeling foolish, she ran her hands over the crisp fabric of the dress she'd spent so much time selecting. Next Sunday she'd know better.

Questions about Mr. Saxon drove Royal Baxter from her mind. Whatever kept him at home today apparently was well known to Reverend French. She wished she could ask Rosemary for details, but they didn't know each other well enough for personal questions.

When Clarissa struck the first notes of "And Can It Be," Faith rose with the congregation. All other thoughts fled as she poured her heart into her favorite hymn.

That evening after supper, Faith pushed the soiled dishes aside and faced Grandpa across their polished mahogany dining table. "I need to talk to you."

"Last time someone said that, he wanted me to run for county judge."

"Which you did, and served with honor." She lifted her water glass with a trembling hand and moistened dry lips. She couldn't wait any longer. "I think we should join the pioneers going to Oregon."

Grandpa's astonished expression told her all she needed to know. She hurried on with her proposal. "Noble Springs is full of reminders of the past. Papa's gone, Maxwell's gone, Grandma Clara and my mama—all gone. Your plans for Lindberg's Mercantile to be handed from father to son will never happen now. Companies are forming to go west over the next month or two. Why should we stay? We can make a start in a new territory."

He held up a finger to stop her. "I'm not a youngster any-more, and you're a female. A rugged journey like that is best done by men in their prime."

"We can do it. I know how to handle a team."

"A team of horses. Those heavy wagons require oxen—there's no comparison."

"We could hire a teamster."

He reached across the table and took her hands. "You need to stop reading those pioneer guides. They make it sound easy."

"Hundred of families go every year. Mr. Hastings' book says the Willamette Valley in Oregon is beautiful, well watered, productive—"

"Southern Missouri is beautiful and well watered. We don't need to leave. Besides, you know we'd have to sell the mercantile, and who'd want a struggling business?"

Faith sensed she was losing the debate. "What if it weren't struggling? I have lots of ideas to increase trade."

Grandpa set his jaw. "You're just like your mother. Once she got an idea in her head, she wouldn't give up." He lifted his cane and leaned on it when he stood. "First we'll see what you can do with the mercantile, then I'll think about it."

"Thank you!"

"Don't thank me. I said I'd think about it."

During their walk to town the following morning, Faith's mind raced with plans to attract customers to the mercantile.

"I'd like to add more kitchen items to interest the ladies." She slowed her pace to stay in step with Grandpa.

"You're in charge now. Use what's in the till when salesmen call."

When they passed the livery, she glanced over to see if Mr. Saxon had recovered. She thought she saw him at the far end of the adjoining corral, but couldn't be sure. This evening she'd stop and inquire about his welfare.

Once past the courthouse, Grandpa proceeded beyond the drugstore and turned left into the alley that bisected the block. He opened the shed door. "I'll be inside, working on my notes," he said, placing his manuscript sheets on the sawhorse table. "Come and get me if you need help."

"Don't worry about me. I'm perfectly capable."

"Faith—"

She jingled the keys. "I'll see you at supper."

The mercantile smelled stale after being locked for a week. She left the door propped open, pulse hammering with excitement at the opportunity to see her dream come closer to reality.

So much to do. First, she'd need to find someone who could build racks on the wall at the rear of the store. She'd move the hoes, pitchforks, and shovels there, then add shelves near the front to hold bolts of fabric. For now, she could take the bin Grandpa had piled with buttons of all sizes and shapes and sort them by color into individual trays. The ribbons and laces needed to be removed from drawers where they were hidden and displayed with the fabrics.

Faith gazed around the interior. Grandpa had stocked the building with everything a farmer might need, but hadn't given much thought to farmers' wives or daughters. It was a testimony to how well he was liked that any women shopped here at all.

She rolled up her sleeves and tied the clean apron she'd brought from home over her blue calico skirt. Today she'd start by moving the chairs that were next to the stove into the storeroom. The checker players would have to find someplace else to spend their days.

"Where was you all last week, Miss Faith? Heard your grandpap was poorly."

She plunked a chair on the floor and turned to see Mr. Grisbee, one of the woodstove regulars, come through the open door. He shuffled toward her, carrying a tin container. Several days' growth of gray whiskers sprouted from his cheeks.

"Grandpa took a little tumble last Monday. Dr. Greeley thought it best if he stayed home to recover."

"So, where is he now? I need some coal oil."

"I can get that for you. How much do you need?"

He looked her up and down. "Wouldn't want you to dirty your hands, miss. I got enough to get by a few more days. I'll wait for your grandpap."

Faith drew herself up to her full five feet. "Grandpa turned the mercantile over to me while he works on . . . . another project."

"No offense, but it ain't proper for a young lady to be runnin' a store. Tell Nate I'll be back when he's behind the counter."

"I'm afraid you'll be sitting in the dark for a long time if you wait for Grandpa." She held out her hand for the container. "Please, allow me."

He studied her for a long moment. "Nope. Ain't proper. I'll git my boy to take me to Hartfield."

Dejected, Faith followed his progress as he shuffled from the store. Maybe there'd be no need to put the chairs away.

She dragged the heavy oak chair back to its original position beside the stove. No sense alienating possible customers. She brushed dust from the surface of the wooden checkerboard and then arranged the checkers for a game.

Absorbed in her task, she started when something pressed against the back of her leg. Game pieces clattered to the floor as she whirled to face her attacker.

A sable and white collie stood panting in front of her, its feathery tail swishing back and forth.

Faith stroked the top of its head, rubbing the warm silky fur. "You frightened me, puppy. Where's your owner?"

"Bodie! Come here!" Rosemary dashed into the store. "I'm so sorry. He's supposed to stay with me when we walk, but today he had his own agenda. Did he hurt you?"

Faith dropped into one of the chairs and pointed to the one next to her for Rosemary. "No, of course not. Scared me out of my wits, though. I thought I was being attacked." She chuckled. "If I'd been paying attention, I'd have heard his nails clicking across the floor."

Bodie made a circle of the room, then settled at Rosemary's feet. She looked down at the scattered checkers and grinned. "You were playing a game by yourself?"

"I might as well be. Grandpa believes I can manage the

store, but I'm afraid his customers don't take me seriously. The gentleman who was just here refused to let me sell him coal oil." She slid down in her chair and folded her arms across her chest. "He said he'd rather go someplace else."

"Why?"

"'It ain't proper for a lady to be running a store.'" Faith mimicked Mr. Grisbee's growl.

"Don't let him discourage you. You were doing just fine last time I was here. Carry on and don't pay attention to anyone who says you can't do it." Rosemary's warm gaze touched Faith's heart. "You should have heard all of the 'it ain't propers' from our neighbors when I volunteered as a nurse." She rose. "I'll help you gather the checkers, then you can show me some buttons to match the dress goods I bought last week."

Faith smiled. "Funny you should ask about buttons. Want to do some sorting?"

Faith stepped into the quiet house. She hadn't seen Grandpa since they shared the contents of their dinner pails at noon. She prayed he'd gone home and hadn't wandered off. "Grandpa?"

"In here," he called from the dining room.

Mr. Saxon stood when she entered. "Miss Faith."

Astonished, she gazed at the chess game arranged between him and her grandfather. "Mr. Saxon. I trust you're fully recovered from the ailment that kept you home on Sunday."

"I am. Thank you. My sister brewed one of her healing teas."

"Sit," Grandpa told him. To Faith, he said, "I asked our guest to stay to supper. We won't be much longer here. He doesn't know it, but he's about to be checkmated."

A broad grin spread over Mr. Saxon's face. "Don't be so sure."

Faith slipped an arm around Grandpa's shoulders, tears stinging her eyes. "I'm happy to see you playing chess. It's been a long time."

"Curt here mentioned it this afternoon. You know I can't resist a challenge."

Mr. Saxon must have been divinely inspired to mention chess to her grandfather. Nothing she'd been able to do since her father died had tempted Grandpa to set out the carved pieces that had been so much a part of their lives.

In the kitchen, Faith tossed chunks of wood onto the coals in the stove and considered her original plan for supper. Sausage stew wasn't very fancy for a guest, but the simple meal would have to do. She peeled several potatoes and added them to a pot along with sliced sausage and onions. When the mixture came to a boil, she removed a jar of pickles and one of catsup from the pantry shelf and placed them on a tray with plates and utensils. Last night's leftover Dolly Varden cake would be a fine dessert.

When she carried the tray to the dining room, the two men were engrossed in their game. While Mr. Saxon's attention focused on the board, she studied him without his knowledge. Dark brown hair curled at the back of his neck, falling forward over his scar. The ropy muscles along his forearms rippled when he reached forward to move a chessman. Looking at him, she had the impression of power held under tight control. An involuntary quiver crossed her body. She believed Grandpa to be a good judge of character, but still . . .

"Supper's ready." She kept her voice bright. "If you'll move the board to the end of the table, I'll serve the meal."

Mr. Saxon jumped to his feet. "I hope you didn't trouble yourself." He reached for the tray. "Let me help."

She smiled to herself at the sight of the lanky stableman laying out their place settings. Maybe there was more to him than she thought.

*F*aith closed the cash drawer. "Thank you, Mrs. Holmes. I trust you'll be happy with your new baking tins."

"No doubt about it, my dear. My husband will pick them up at the end of the day." She dropped her coin purse into her carryall. "It's good to have a larger selection of kitchen goods here in Noble Springs. I've been needing a fluted pudding pan."

Smiling, Faith watched her leave. New merchandise lined the shelves at the front of the room, where shoppers would be drawn to the displays. Hanging the farm implements on a wall hadn't slowed sales over the past month. At least, not much. She knew a number of Grandpa's former customers no longer patronized the store.

A rotund gentleman stepped toward her after Mrs. Holmes left. "Excuse me, little lady. I'm here to see Mr. Lindberg. He promised to place an order with me the next time I came through." He removed his bowler hat and placed a scuffed leather case on the counter. A label pasted to the surface read "Henry Reed, Boston. World's Finest Cookware."

"I'm his granddaughter, Miss Lindberg. Are you Mr. Reed?"

He rocked back on his heels, a genial expression on his

face. "My name is Roland Dunwoody. I'm Henry Reed's representative in southern Missouri." His vivid blue eyes scanned the room. "Where's your grandfather?"

"He's turned the store over to me. I'm authorized to order merchandise."

"Well, bless me! Dress goods and laces, I suppose."

"Everything, Mr. Dunwoody. I've been thinking of adding more cookware." She pointed at the leather case. "Do you have illustrations of your products?"

"Everything," he repeated in a wondering tone. "This is a first." He unbuckled the case and passed her a booklet, open to a page covered with pictures of frying pans, sauce pans, and kettles, arranged in sets. "You won't find better quality anywhere."

"Please excuse the question, but if they're so good, why hasn't my grandfather ordered from you before? The cast iron we have in stock is from another source."

He leaned forward, and for a moment she thought he was going to give her a fatherly pat on the shoulder. "I'm glad you asked. Until recently, travel within Missouri has been uncertain, as you can no doubt appreciate. Now that the war has ended, Mr. Reed has expanded his territory."

Faith studied the illustrations again. Encouraged by the sale of tinware to Mrs. Holmes, she rested her index finger on the largest display. "We'll take two of these sets."

The salesman's smile grew broader. "Excellent. You won't be disappointed." He flipped open an order book and scribbled the information on a blank page, then wrote a copy for her. "Our supply center is in Rolla. You should have your goods within two weeks, cash on delivery."

She placed her copy of the order in the till as a reminder to have the money on hand when the new cookware arrived. "Good. I'll look forward to adding these to our stock."

He plopped his hat back on his egg-shaped head. "A pleasure meeting you. You're much prettier than your grandfather."

"You're very kind."

He bowed with a flourish and strode toward the door.

A woman approached the counter as he left. "I'd like ten yards of that green flowered calico you have on the shelf."

"Splendid. And do you need buttons and ribbon for trim?" Faith took a pair of shears from under the counter and led her customer to the measuring table.

The bell over the door pealed. "Faith, I want you to read this." Grandpa's cane thudded across the floor. He held a sheet of paper in his free hand.

She took a deep breath and exhaled slowly. "I'm busy right now, but I'll be happy to look at it after supper."

"It'll only take you a minute."

The woman took a step away from the table. "I don't really have much time . . ." Her voice trailed off.

Faith brandished the shears. "Show me which of the flowered designs you want." She shot an apologetic glance at Grandpa in time to catch an expression of hurt cross his face.

"When you have a moment to spare, I'll be out back." He turned toward the door, shoulders slumped.

"Excuse me a moment." She placed a bolt of green fabric on the table, then hurried to her grandfather. Hand held out, she said, "What did you write?"

His eyes lit. "I remembered a story from when I was a boy. Thought you'd be interested."

The page he gave her contained one long paragraph that filled the sheet from top to bottom.

I was sent to a poor mountain school kept by one Bobby Dolliehyde. Why he was named so, I cannot tell unless it was his penchant for hiding the boys and making dolls of the girls. I must have been a rather forward boy for my age, for I recollect . . .

Faith lowered the paper. "Grandpa, I love how you've started this story. May I please finish it at home this evening?" Out of the corner of her eye, she noticed her customer sidling toward the door.

"Ma'am? I'll be right with you," Faith called.

"Some other day. It was impulsive of me anyway. My husband wouldn't have been happy to have me come home with more dress goods."

Grandpa snatched the page from Faith's hand. "You don't know how long I worked on this, and you can't take two minutes to read it. I don't know why I bother."

"I'll take all the time in the world this evening. Just not while I'm busy."

"We won't be home until late, remember? Miss Saxon invited us to supper." He banged his cane against the floor with more force than necessary on his way out.

Faith jammed her hands into her apron pockets and scuffed to one of the empty chairs next to the stove. Balancing her time in the store with Grandpa's needs grew more difficult each week.

Dinner at the Saxons' would be a welcome treat. Maybe she could coax a few words out of Curt. She knew he could talk a blue streak. She'd overheard him sharing stories with Grandpa about his experiences with horses prior to the war. But when she was around, he seldom spoke more than a sentence or two. He was friendly enough when they first became acquainted. She couldn't imagine what she'd done to offend him.

Over the next hour, several patrons came and went. As she dropped coins in the cash drawer, she hoped today might turn out to be their best yet, in spite of losing the dress goods sale. So far, her new ideas hadn't done much to lessen the mercantile's struggles.

She was occupied with showing buttons to Reverend French's wife when three men entered. They headed for the boot display, the scent of tobacco trailing behind them. Faith's fingertips tingled. They looked like the same three men who had ridden past her on that rainy day several weeks ago. The tallest of them had his back to her as he examined a pair of black cavalry-style boots.

Faith dumped several buttons in a paper twist and thrust them at Clarissa French. "Thank you. I trust these will match your mother's dress nicely."

Clarissa stared at her, a startled expression on her face. "These are for my daughter. I told you that when I came in, and I'm not finished with my selection."

"Forgive me." She forced her attention back to the trays of buttons. "Now which color were you interested in?"

"It's so hard to decide. You know how girls are. You must have spent time with your mother choosing dress goods for your graduation."

Faith swallowed. "My mother passed when I was ten. Papa didn't have much patience with fripperies."

Clarissa looked stricken. "I had no idea. Of course, we know there's just you and your grandfather now, but . . ." She dabbed at her eyes. "I'm sorry to bring up painful memories."

The three men moved from the rack of boots toward the ready-made shirts. Faith squirmed inside, anxious to intercept them before they left. She gave the pastor's wife what she hoped was a convincing smile.

"Let's talk about your daughter. Did you say the dress would be white with lavender flowers? Here are some that would be perfect." She showed her a tray filled with glossy white buttons painted with tiny purple dots.

"The very thing. I will need a dozen."

Faith completed the sale, then stepped from behind the counter. "Thank you. See you Sunday." She patted Clarissa on one plump arm, then turned toward the three men.

Her heart beat faster as she approached them. "I noticed you're interested in new boots. Ours are especially fine leather, direct from St. Louis."

One of them frowned. "Ain't there a man here to help us? What would you know about riding boots?"

The tall man turned slowly in her direction. "Give her a chance, Tolly."

Faith took a step backward. "Royal Baxter?" Blood rushed to her head at the sight of his exotic olive skin and full lips. He was more striking than she remembered.

He removed his hat and studied her, a question in his dark eyes. "Do I know you, miss?"

"It's been quite awhile. I'm Faith Lindberg. We met at a going-away rally when you left to enlist." She gave him a wide smile. "You took my hair ribbon as a memento."

Tolly snorted. "That where you got all them ribbons, Baxter? From little girls?"

The third man laughed. "He's got a heap of 'em, for sure."

Royal turned to Faith and shook his head. "I'm afraid you have the advantage over me. I don't doubt you were present when I left, but there was a great crowd at the station. Forgive me."

She wished she could disappear beneath the floorboards. He'd assured her he'd carry her ribbon next to his heart to keep him safe. He must have made the same promise to every girl he met.

Faith dug her nails into her palms and took a deep breath.

"My apologies," she said in her chilliest voice. "How could you be expected to remember something that happened so long ago?"

She turned to Tolly. "Now, what size do you wear?"

"Never mind. The ones I already got will do me just fine."

Faith followed Rosemary into the kitchen. She glanced around the tidy room, with the sink under a window that looked out at her friend's flourishing garden. The cookstove anchored the opposite wall. Drying herbs hung from hooks fastened to a rafter above the stove. "Your kitchen reminds me of ours when my mother was alive. It feels like a refuge." She placed the soiled plates on the counter next to the washbasin. "I'll wash the dishes, since you cooked. It's only fair."

"I cooked it, but you scarcely ate a bite." A worried expression crossed Rosemary's face. "I should have asked what you liked. I could have prepared something else."

"Oh, my word! Please don't think it was your cooking. The chicken was delectable. I'd never have thought to tuck thyme sprigs and cracked pepper under the skin." She sighed. "I'm just preoccupied, I guess."

"Problems at the store?"

"In a manner of speaking." Faith filled the basin and swished the soap holder through hot water until a layer of suds appeared. Utensils rattled when she dropped them into the mixture and settled the plates on top. She bent to her task, scrubbing each plate and stacking them on the drain board.

"If you're not careful, you'll rub the pattern right off my dishes." Rosemary laid her towel aside and touched Faith's arm. "Sometimes it helps to talk things over with someone." She drew a chair away from the worktable and turned another toward Faith. "Let's sit a moment. Your grandfather is busy trying to win a game of chess. He won't mind if you spend a little extra time with me."

Faith smiled. "It's good to see him so occupied. He's been melancholy since my father and brother were killed."

"He's helping Curt too. The war changed him. I try to understand, but I miss his lively nature. Reverend French—" She shook her head. "Enough about us. Please, tell me what's worrying you."

"I'm not worried as much as humiliated." Faith shared her feelings for Royal Baxter and the afternoon's experience. "He had no idea who I was, and here I believed the memory of our meeting would bring him back to me after the war. I feel like such a fool."

"How old were you when he left?"

"Sixteen."

Rosemary took Faith's hand. "And how old was he, do you think?"

"Twenty-three, twenty-four. Somewhere in there."

"I saw many troops leave when the war began. They were always surrounded by young women waving handkerchiefs and weeping." She increased her pressure on Faith's hand. "Call your experience a girlish fancy and let it go. You have more important things to think about."

Faith forced a smile. "Like these dirty dishes."

She wished it were as easy to scrub Royal from her mind as it was to clean the dinner plates.

When the Lindbergs were ready to leave, Curt stood next to the front door, arms folded across his chest. "Please allow me to drive you home."

Faith's grandfather frowned at him. "I've traveled these streets for many a year. I'm perfectly capable." He removed his hat from a peg.

"Yes, sir, but it's going on full dark. You and Miss Faith would be safer in the buggy."

Faith put a hand on her grandfather's arm. "You've been quite content to accept rides to church. The distance is almost the same."

"It won't take long to hitch the horse," Curt said. He took a few steps toward the rear of the house, then paused, waiting for the judge's response.

"Well, Faith is probably tired. Might be good for her to ride." Judge Lindberg dropped his hat over his bald spot and leaned on his cane.

Faith's blue eyes met Curt's. "Thank you. I appreciate your kind offer."

He dared a smile in her direction. "No trouble."

Once they settled in the buggy and started across town,

Judge Lindberg's head drooped forward. A sideways glance told Curt that he'd fallen asleep.

Faith's soft voice reached him through the darkness. "Grandpa rises at daylight. It's a struggle for him to stay awake much past seven."

"I noticed he looked worn out." He kept his attention on the reins. For some reason, the surrounding darkness untied his tongue. "Has he had more trouble with his memory since his fall?"

"Little things. Now that he's not busy with the mercantile, the changes aren't so apparent." She sighed.

Curt guided his horse around the courthouse square and angled left on High Street. Lightning bugs flashed under the spreading limbs of a cherry tree in front of the Bennetts' house.

"Your granddad told me he's writing a memoir. Is that a fact?"

Her skirt rustled as she turned toward him. "Indeed he is." Her voice carried an edge of impatience. "It's good that he's keeping busy, but I wish—"

"Wish what?" Faith's grandfather sat up straight.

"That you had someone else to read your pages. I can't pay proper attention when I'm busy in the store."

"Why didn't you say so? I won't bother you anymore."

Curt heard the anger in the judge's response. "Well, here we are," he said with false cheer. He reined the horse to a stop in front of the Lindbergs' home, then hurried to assist his passengers from the buggy.

When Faith took his hand, a surge of warmth traveled up his arm. She was so small and helpless-looking. He wished he could stand between her and all danger, but how could he? He couldn't control his own memories.

Curt carried a lantern to light his way from the stable to the back porch. Through the kitchen window he saw Rosemary seated at the table with a covered teapot in front of her. She smiled when he entered.

"I brewed some chamomile tea. Thought you might like something to help you sleep." Two teacups rested in matching saucers next to the pot.

"Sounds good. Thanks." Curt sank into a chair, heat from Faith's hand fresh in his senses.

Rosemary filled their cups. "It was kind of you to take them home. I could see Judge Lindberg sinking by the end of the evening." She grinned at him. "It saved the old gentleman's pride to pretend it was Faith who was tired."

"He wasn't pretending. Didn't you notice her yawning?" Curt stirred honey into his cup, watching the sweet threads dissolve in the hot brew. "Wish I could spend more time with him. Miss Faith said something tonight that made me think she needs more help with her granddad than she lets on."

"Why don't we have a picnic on Sunday and invite the two of them?" Rosemary regarded him with a knowing look in her eyes. "You can't go on claiming the judge is the only reason you spend time at their house."

He tapped her shoulder. "Don't start matchmaking. I'm better off single. Miss Faith wouldn't want me if she knew about my . . . spells."

Rosemary stood, hands on hips. "You're certainly not the only man suffering from soldier's heart. Others are struggling too, and many of them have wives. Faith is the dearest person I've ever met. She'd not be one to turn away from difficulties."

"She's your friend. If you want to ask them on a picnic, go ahead. Just don't expect me to start wooing her." He rose and drained his cup. "It's late. Good night."

On tiptoes, Rosemary kissed his cheek. "Sleep well. I'll go to the mercantile tomorrow and extend our invitation."

Shaking his head, Curt left the warm kitchen and climbed the stairs. Once Rosemary settled on an idea, there was no stopping her.

Using a broom, Faith pushed oiled sawdust toward the rear of the store, rolling yesterday's dust away. As she passed the boot display, she stopped to straighten the disorder left by Royal Baxter's cronies.

Given enough time, maybe she'd stop cringing at the memory of the blank look on Royal's face when she introduced herself.

She brushed sweepings into a dustpan and dumped them in a bin in the alley. While standing in the shade of the mercantile, she peeked at the small building where Grandpa worked on his memoirs. The wounded look on his face when she'd blurted her frustration haunted her.

Squaring her shoulders, she marched across the path separating them and tapped on the door.

"Who is it?"

"Faith."

"Thought you were too busy."

She turned the handle and slipped into the room. Clasping her hands together, she said, "I'm sorry, Grandpa. I shouldn't have said what I did. Anytime you want me to read your writing, don't hesitate."

He placed his pen next to the inkwell. "You mean it?"

Faith stepped beside his chair. "Yes." She kissed his cheek. "Get back to your memoir. I'll be inside if you want me."

With light steps, she hurried into the mercantile and hung

the broom on a hook. She heard footsteps through the wall separating the storeroom from the front of the building. A deep voice called, "Is anyone here?"

She brushed through the dividing curtain and stopped short, her heart drumming in her throat. Royal Baxter stood inside the open front door. He removed his hat and pressed it against his trouser leg. "Miss Lindberg, I've thought of your pretty face ever since yesterday. I don't know how I could have forgotten our meeting. Will you forgive me?"

Faith stared at him, speechless. Did he mean he remembered her? Or was he merely apologizing for his comments?

He shook his head. "I knew it. My behavior was unpardonable." He turned toward the entrance. "I won't bother you again."

"Wait." She closed the distance between them. "There's nothing to forgive. I shouldn't have assumed you'd remember me after nearly five years."

"Would you consider getting reacquainted? There's a dance planned at the hotel for a week from Friday to raise money for war widows. I'd like to ask you to accompany me if you're agreeable."

Agreeable? She'd dreamed of such an invitation. But now that he stood in front of her, she hesitated. If all went as she hoped, she and Grandpa would leave in another month or so.

Royal cleared his throat. "You're a quiet one. Shall I ask again some other time?"

"Yes. I mean, no need. I'd be pleased to go to the dance with you."

"Good." He replaced his hat and crossed the threshold.

Faith hurried after him. "Don't you want to know where I live?"

"I already asked someone." He strode to a horse tied out

front and swung into the saddle. "I'll call for you at seven next Friday."

"Yes," she said to his departing back, then flopped onto a bench next to the entrance. Whatever his motivation, this was an invitation she'd waited years to receive. She had no intention of refusing.

Faith reached far into a barrel and dug through the excelsior for a last plate. A full set of tea leaf–patterned lusterware spread over a shelf to her right. The dishes had come at a high price, nearly a week's worth of receipts, but she believed they wouldn't sit long before enticing a buyer.

Rosemary leaned over the counter. "My, those are beautiful."

Rubbing her back, Faith straightened and smiled. "Aren't they? I'm hoping they sell quickly." She wiped perspiration from her forehead with a corner of her apron, then grabbed the empty barrel and rolled it toward the storeroom.

"Let me help you." Rosemary pushed while Faith steered the bulky wooden container across the floor. Bodie followed them, his tail beating the air.

Faith laughed. "He thinks we're playing a game."

"Everything's a game to Bodie."

"My father had a hunting dog named Flint. Grandpa gave him away after we got word of Papa's death." Faith placed the barrel with other empty ones and faced Rosemary. "I used to hug Flint and pretend he was Papa. I cried when he left with his new owner." She shrugged. "Silly of me."

Rosemary's eyes welled with sympathetic tears. "Not silly. Small losses are nearly as painful as big ones."

"Yes." Faith dusted her hands together, dismissing the

moment. "I know you didn't come in today to roll a barrel into the storeroom. What can I get for you?"

"I'm on a mission this morning. Curt and I are going to Pioneer Lake for a picnic Sunday afternoon. We'd like you and your grandfather to join us."

Two invitations in one day. After the somber war years, she relished the prospect of social activities. "Sounds delightful. We'd be happy to come. I haven't been to Pioneer Lake for a long time."

"I have a second reason for being here today." Rosemary whipped a long apron from her carryall and tied it around her waist. "You need an assistant. The mercantile is too big for one person to handle alone."

Faith pushed the burlap curtain aside and attempted to visualize her grandfather's store as it might appear to Rosemary's eyes. The long rectangular room was filled with merchandise on floor-to-ceiling shelves. Cookstoves, crocks and kettles, and a barrel filled with ax handles formed a row down the center. The fabric display occupied a prominent space near the door. A few bright calico work dresses, purchased from a local seamstress, hung from a rack near the notions.

She clasped Rosemary's hands in hers. "I'd love to have your company, but are you sure you want to spend time here? Some of our town gossips can be cruel."

"I can't hide at home forever. If I'm to make a new start, it might as well be here." She raised a questioning eyebrow. "Don't you want me?"

"Oh, you know I do. We don't earn enough to pay wages, though. I hope to change that, but for now my presence in the store has driven away the older customers. They don't think it's fitting for a woman to engage in commerce."

Rosemary hugged her. "I don't want wages. Curt takes

good care of us. I just want to help you. I'll come each morning and stay through the noon hour, starting today."

"Done. Let's see what people think of two women engaged in commerce." Faith chuckled. "We'll create a stir."

Bodie pattered across the floor and sprawled outside on the boardwalk.

"See?" Rosemary said. "He's already comfortable in his new position as doorkeeper."

On Sunday afternoon, Faith filled a basket with cold roast chicken, buttered biscuits, and spice cookies. After a survey of the pantry, she added a jar of apple butter and one of peach jam. She needed to use last summer's preserves. The glass jars were too fragile for travel over the Oregon trail.

Grandpa rapped his cane on the kitchen floor. "Are you ready? They're waiting."

"Coming." She paused at the hall mirror to adjust her bonnet.

He fidgeted at the window. "Look at that sunshine. What a fine day for a picnic."

She smiled to see him so eager. Linking her arm with his, she stepped out the door.

Once she and Grandpa were settled in the Saxons' covered buggy, Curt shook the reins and they rolled west toward Pioneer Lake. Beyond the edge of town the road narrowed, winding between groves of oaks and chokecherry. Sunlight sifted through the branches, gilding water pooled in low spots.

Rosemary poked her brother. "Can't we travel any faster? The day will be over before we ever arrive."

"Moses only has one speed. Maybe you can make him hurry." He handed her the reins.

She flicked them over the horse's back. He jolted forward for several paces, then settled into his former walk.

Curt snickered. "What did I tell you?"

Faith's throat tightened at the sight of brother and sister enjoying each other's company. A shiver rolled over her. She missed Maxwell. Even after two years, memories of her brother never failed to bring tears to her eyes. The sooner they left Missouri, the better.

9

urt stood on the shore of Pioneer Lake, shading his eyes against the sun that ricocheted off the glittering water. An image of himself hiding submerged in a creek jumped unbidden into his mind, obscuring the peaceful scene. He felt the water moving over his skin, and the choking sensation of trying to suck sufficient air through a hollow reed.

He balled his hands into fists. Not now. Not in front of Faith and her granddad. Cold sweat prickled his body. He took a deep breath and held it until he heard his pulse thud. The image faded. Curt raised his head, gasping. The lake sparkled in front of him.

The group sitting on blankets under a shade tree looked up from their conversation when he stumbled toward them.

Faith smiled in his direction. "There's enough here for another meal. I was about to put the leftovers away."

He collapsed next to Rosemary, relieved no one had noticed his weak-kneed gait. "I'll help you eat them." Holding his hand steady, he reached for the jar of peach jam and spooned a portion onto a biscuit. "I can taste summer in this fruit. Warm July evenings. Heat lightning." He forced a smile. "I volunteer to pick peaches for you when they come ripe."

"I hope you'll pick some for us too." Rosemary glanced at him with affection in her eyes.

Faith leaned forward, hands clasped in her lap. "We'll be leaving before July."

Curt dropped the uneaten portion of his biscuit to his plate. Faith would be gone in a few months? A sense of loss rocked through him. Then he forced himself to consider the bright side. He could relax. He'd no longer have to fight his attraction to the petite girl with the ready smile and bottomless blue eyes.

"Where are you going?"

"Grandpa and I are headed for Oregon as soon as we can sell the mercantile."

"Don't put words in my mouth. I haven't agreed yet." Judge Lindberg struggled to his feet.

Faith rose. "Grandpa—"

"This is a family matter. We'll discuss our plans later." He limped toward the buggy.

Rosemary stepped next to Faith. "Why didn't you tell me?" Tears glittered on her cheeks. "I don't want you to go."

Faith looked like she was struggling not to cry. "I didn't mean to blurt things out like that. I wanted to talk to you first. Sometimes my mouth runs off with me." She slipped an arm around Rosemary's waist. "I'm sorry."

"Don't apologize. I shouldn't have assumed you'd always be here." Rosemary swiped at her tears. "You won't be leaving for a month or more, will you?"

"Everything depends on whether we can sell the mercantile. And you heard Grandpa. Sounds like you and I have lots of time."

Curt watched them, wishing he could comfort his sister. Faith's friendship had made a difference in Rosemary's life. She'd overcome her reluctance to face the stares of the proper ladies in town. He'd even caught her humming while she worked in her garden. Without Faith to draw her out, would she isolate herself again?

Grandpa sat at the kitchen table munching a cookie while Faith unpacked the picnic leftovers. She allowed his unspoken criticism to follow her around the room until she could no longer bear the silence. "Aren't you going to light into me?"

He brushed crumbs from his moustache. "I don't need to. You know you spoke out of turn."

"But we're going. You agreed." She flung herself into a chair on the opposite side of the table.

"No, I said I'd think about it. If memory serves, you had plans to turn a profit at the mercantile. How are sales?"

Faith bit her lip. He stopped in at least once a day with his manuscript. He had to notice the lack of customers. "The yard goods are very popular with the ladies. I've sold fabric and notions for graduation and weddings."

"How about plows and cookstoves? It takes a heap of fabric to equal the cost of one stove." Grandpa bit into another cookie, watching her over the frames of his glasses.

"Times are hard. No one has cash money for something as costly as a stove." She shrank under his steady gaze.

"It's plowing season. Anyone come in for a new plow?"

She shook her head.

"I don't mean to hector you, but you've got to look at facts. If we can't sell the store, we can't make the trip." He pushed himself to his feet and walked around the table, resting his hand on her shoulder. "I told you I'd think about this journey. Why don't you do the same? We'll never travel far enough to flee from our sorrows." He drew her against his chest and kissed the top of her head.

Faith leaned against him, blinking back tears. "Perhaps not, but maybe we could forget," she whispered.

That night, she lay in bed staring at the ceiling. Pale moonlight whitewashed the curtains at the window. No matter how she fluffed her pillow or smoothed the sheets, the memory of Rosemary's teary eyes wouldn't let her rest. When would she learn to think before she spoke?

Rolling onto her side, she tugged the blanket higher to block the light. First thing tomorrow she'd go to the Saxons' house and explain her decision. When Rosemary knew why Faith wanted to leave, she'd understand.

A tap at the door awakened her the next morning. "It's after eight. Time to stir."

After eight? Faith swung her feet to the floor and thrust her arms into the sleeves of her wrapper. "I'm up." She filled her washbasin from the pitcher atop her bureau and splashed her face with cold water. Of all the days to oversleep. Now she'd have no time to speak privately with Rosemary before opening the mercantile.

As soon as she and Grandpa finished breakfast, they left for town. Faith matched her stride to his slower one, chafing at the delay. She tossed a wave in Curt's direction when they passed the livery stable. No time to stop and explain herself to him, either.

Once inside the store, Faith hurried to open the shades, noticing the display in the front window needed to be dusted. She drew a breath and released it with a huff. She'd ordered the two new sets of iron cookware, spending almost a week's receipts, certain that ladies would find the burnished gray finish irresistible. Now here the pieces sat gathering dust. There had to be a way to entice patrons through the door. Maybe Rosemary would have a suggestion. Faith would ask her as soon as she arrived.

The morning ticked past, the minutes marked by the eight-day clock behind the cash drawer. Every time the bell over the door tinkled, Faith turned, expecting to see Rosemary. By twelve, she'd lost hope.

She locked the back door and carried her dinner pail to the building where Grandpa worked on his memoirs.

"Noon already?" he asked, placing his pen next to the inkwell. Beads of sweat dotted his forehead.

"Yes." Faith waved her hand in front of her face. "It's like an oven in here. Why don't you leave the door open?" She lifted two tin plates from the top of the pail and placed a wedge of cold cheese pie on each of them.

"Never thought of it. I've been too busy working." He pushed filled pages in her direction. "Take a look. I'm up to the point where my uncle goes off to be a preacher." Grandpa lifted his fork. "Where's Miss Rosemary?"

"I don't know. She didn't arrive this morning. I'm afraid she's upset with me." She poked at her food.

He gave her his Judge Lindberg look and cleared his throat. "What do you plan to do about it?"

How like Grandpa to present her with a Solomon-like question. She'd had all morning to consider the importance of Rosemary's friendship, so her answer came without further thought. "I'll call on her as soon as I close the store this evening. Would you mind if supper is late?"

"Not a bit." His eyes twinkled. "I hoped that's what you'd decide."

When Faith climbed the porch steps, Bodie roused from his nap on the doormat and nosed her outstretched hand. "Good boy." She rubbed his velvety ears.

The door swung open and Curt looked at her, a surprised expression on his face. "Come in, Faith." He turned to Bodie, patting the top of his head. "Some watchdog you are. You're supposed to bark at strangers."

Rosemary peered around his shoulder. "Faith isn't a stranger." In the shadows her skin appeared pale, with dark circles under her eyes.

Alarmed, Faith stepped past Curt to place a hand on Rosemary's cheek. "Are you ill?"

"Nothing serious." She cupped her hands across her abdomen. "I'll be better tomorrow."

Faith nodded understanding.

Curt gestured toward the sitting room. "Sit a spell," he said to Faith. "I'll bring you both some tea—raspberry leaf."

"Thank you." She smiled at Rosemary and lowered her voice. "How did you ever teach him to help in the kitchen? My father and brother . . ." She swallowed. "They never did."

"He was forced to learn when he enlisted. That's the only good thing I can say about that dreadful war." Rosemary led the way toward two chairs accented with needlepoint cushions. "I'm glad you stopped by. I felt guilty about not coming to help today, but I just couldn't."

"I'm the one who feels guilty. You of all people deserve to know why I want so much to leave Missouri."

"Tell me."

Faith settled onto a chair and leaned toward her friend. "When I was ten, my grandmother died, then Mama passed shortly after that. My father and Maxwell, my brother, were all I had left—and Grandpa, of course. Then the war came. Maxwell and Papa enlisted in the Union army right away, even though Maxwell was only sixteen." She closed her eyes for a moment, remembering. "Grandpa and I lived every day in fear they'd be killed, but three years went by and they were spared. Then . . ." She took a deep breath. "Then we got word they'd perished at the Battle of Westport. On Missouri soil—barely two hundred miles from home." She held Rosemary in her gaze. "Don't you see? I want to go somewhere and make a new start, like so many folks have done. The hard part will be leaving you."

"It will be hard on me, also. I wish—"

Curt entered, placing two cups of tea on a tripod table between their chairs. He sprawled on the settee across the room and stretched out his long legs. "If you ask me, running away is a poor reason to pull up roots. Your granddad was born here. He wants to die here."

"How do you know what my grandfather wants?"

"He told me."

Shocked, Faith raised her teacup and then returned it to the saucer, untasted.

"Perhaps you misunderstood him. He's never said that to me."

"In case you haven't noticed, he has trouble denying you anything. Going to Oregon is your idea, isn't it?"

"What if it is?" She glared at him. "Going west will get us away from old memories."

"Your memories will follow you." The scar on his neck reddened. "I know."

Rosemary crossed to her brother. "Curt. This is none of our concern."

"You're right. Forgive me, Miss Lindberg." He shrugged Rosemary's hand off his shoulder and stalked from the room.

Faith stared. She'd gone from being Faith to Miss Lindberg in the space of a few minutes. The man was as changeable as a Missouri spring—warm one minute and biting the next.

By Friday morning, Faith had dismissed Curt's moodiness from her mind. That evening, she'd be attending a dance with Royal Baxter. For once the lack of customers seemed a blessing rather than a curse. She could close the mercantile promptly at five, cook Grandpa's supper, and still have time to bathe and dress for the festivities.

At half past four, Faith hurried to the storeroom, tucked a feather duster under her apron strings, and grabbed a clean rag. Starting in the farthest corner, she flicked dust from shelves and countertops, working her way toward the front door. Halfway there, she surveyed the unsold lusterware dinner set while she polished a matching soup tureen. Maybe if she moved the dishes to a glass case they'd be more likely to catch a customer's eye. With a little rearranging—

The bell over the door chimed. Startled, Faith whirled to see who'd entered, then heard a clink. The handle of the duster connected with one of the stacked teacups and knocked the delicate china piece into its mates. Like dominoes, cups tipped and crashed to the floor.

"No-o-o!" Faith lunged forward to protect the bowls, at the same time losing her grip on the tureen, which shattered on top of several dinner plates. She sagged against a counter, aghast. She didn't know which was worse—destroying a set of expensive dishes, or staying to clean the mess, knowing she wouldn't be ready when Royal arrived at seven.

"Miss Faith?"

She looked up to see Mr. Grisbee holding a tin container. "I need me some coal oil. Decided not to go to Hartfield."

10

Faith caught a section of her hair between heated tongs and rolled a curl. Her stomach flipped with anxiety as she listened to Royal and her grandfather's voices coming from the parlor. Of all the days to be late.

She held the tongs over an oil lamp and waited while they reheated. Precious minutes slipped by while she arranged her thick hair into a fashionable cascade of curls at the back of her head. Dipping her fingers into a bowl of sugar water, she smoothed the sides of her coiffure to control any stray locks, then stepped into her purple chintz dress.

The clock chimed half past the hour as she skimmed down the stairs and arrived, breathless, at the parlor door. "I'm so sorry to keep you waiting. Did Grandpa explain that I was detained at the mercantile late this afternoon?"

"Indeed he did." Royal's face creased in a broad smile. "And I must say, you're worth waiting for." His dark brown eyes glinted approval.

Using his cane, Grandpa levered himself to his feet. "We've been having an interesting discussion. Seems Major Baxter thinks he might have met Sebastian and Maxwell during his time with the Federal militia."

Faith's heart contracted at the mention of her father and brother's names. "You saw them? Where?"

"I can't be sure." He pointed at the oil painting hanging over the fireplace. "But I know I've seen their faces."

She looked at the portrait of her parents with herself and Maxwell. "That was painted years ago. Maxwell looked quite different as a boy."

"The resemblance remains." Royal nodded at her grandfather. "I'll search my memory. We'll talk again next time I call on Miss Faith."

Next time. Faith couldn't keep a pleased smile from her lips.

Buggies lined the front of the Lafayette Hotel when Royal turned the carriage onto Spring Street. He rubbed his chin. "We'll have to tie up in front of the depot. Would you like me to help you down here first?"

Although the entrance to the hotel was well-lit, the remainder of the area lay hidden in dusky shadows. Faith had heard enough rumors about vagrants loitering near the railroad depot to be uncomfortable near the tracks after sundown. "It's not far. I don't mind a short walk."

The horse ambled along the street as though making its own search for a stopping place. Suddenly it whinnied and sidestepped. A dark shape stood in the center of the road, swinging its head back and forth.

"Whoa!" Royal fought the reins to control the horse.

Faith clutched his arm, feeling the strength of taut muscles through his coat. "What on earth is that?"

He stood and peered into the dusk beyond the reach of the buggy lamp. "Looks like a cow. Good thing the horse saw her. She's black as midnight."

"A cow." Faith chuckled over the thrum of her slowing heartbeat. "I thought it was a bear."

"You'd have been safe." He patted her hand, then reached under the seat and brought out a rifle. "This here Spencer repeater saved my skin more than once during the war."

She stared at the polished stock gleaming in the lamplight. "Is it loaded?"

"Always. If it's not, I might as well carry a stick." He shoved the weapon out of sight and handed her the reins. "Hold the horse. I'll run old Bessie back across the tracks." Royal vaulted to the ground and sprinted toward the cow, waving his arms.

The animal bellowed and backed away.

"Keep going! Hoo yah!" He chased her until they were both out of sight.

Faith clutched the reins, thankful he hadn't fired at the animal before identifying it.

Royal huffed back to the carriage and climbed in. "She's on her way home. Hope she stays there." Taking the reins from Faith's hands, he directed the horse to a hitching rail in front of the depot.

She put the incident out of her mind when they entered the hotel ballroom, determined to enjoy the evening. Swags of white muslin, anchored with crossed dogwood boughs, festooned the walls. The fresh-cut branches gave the square room the look and fragrance of a forest glade. For a moment, Faith's mind slipped to the previous Sunday's picnic with Curt and Rosemary. As quickly, she returned to the present with Royal. Lean and handsome in his black frock coat, he drew admiring stares from girls clustered at the edges of the dance floor.

Couples circled to a lively polka, scraped from the bows of two fiddlers. As was the case with every social event since the war, women outnumbered the men. Those not dancing rested on chairs grouped along the sides of the room.

Royal guided her to a seat and whispered in her ear. "You won't mind if I leave you with the other ladies for a moment, will you? I'd like to make a donation to the cause."

"Go right ahead. I'll be fine."

He gave a half bow and skirted the room, heading for a decorated booth near the musicians' platform.

"Faith?"

Faith suppressed a groan when she saw Nelda Raines mincing toward her with exaggerated daintiness. Trapped. During her years at Noble Springs Academy, Nelda was one girl she'd learned to avoid. No one took more pleasure in spreading bad news, whether or not it was true.

Nelda sank into an empty chair. "Did I see you come in with that Royal Baxter? Calls himself a major?" She fanned herself. "My dear, haven't you heard about him?"

"What is it you think I should know?" She glanced across the room, hoping for rescue, but Royal stood at the donation booth, chatting with a gray-haired lady wearing mourning clothes.

"Well," Nelda leaned closer and lowered her voice. "He's fickle. One lady friend after another. Leads them on, then drops them. You'd best be careful." She batted her blonde lashes, looking like a nearsighted mouse. "I thought you should hear the news from a friend—for your own good, of course."

"How on earth would you know that? Unless you . . ."

Nelda's cheeks turned a mottled red. "Me? Of course not! But a man like that—dashing, handsome—what do you think he's been doing during the years he's been away?"

"Since he was in the militia, I assumed he was fighting a war." Blood pounded in Faith's ears. "When did he become your business, Nelda?"

The music stopped, and the other woman's response sounded loud over the shuffle of dancers moving toward their seats. "He's not. I just felt—as your friend—"

Curious glances came their way.

Faith stood. "I'm sure I've taken enough of your time. Your companions must be wondering where you've gone." She turned and walked away, not caring where she went. What difference did it make what Royal had done before they met? She bit her lip.

All the difference in the world.

At the entrance, she paused, inhaling the sweet aroma of forsythia from sprays arched around the doorway. As her pulse slowed, Faith acknowledged her foolishness. Twelve days ago Royal hadn't known who she was. She had no claim on him other than as a dance partner for one evening. Raising her chin, she searched the room and smiled when he strode her way.

"Are you ready for a waltz?" He placed his hand over hers. "I've been looking forward to this all week."

Her heart skittered when he drew her to him. "So have I."

For a few moments, she lost herself in the intoxicating pleasure of gliding over the floor following Royal's lead. When she glanced up, his eyes met hers.

"You're a quiet one."

She chuckled. "Not always. In fact, I was about to ask you what brought you back to Noble Springs. I can't remember whether you have family here."

"My family is in Jefferson City. We're estranged."

The tone of his voice told her not to ask why.

He pivoted, swinging her around before gliding forward. "As

to what I'm doing here, I took my former job at Allen's Cooperage—not that barrel-making is going to be my life's work."

"What do you see as your life's work?"

Instead of answering, he led her through a complicated series of steps that ended with him closing the space between them. His fingers pressed into the small of her back. When the music ended, he held her hand as he escorted her from the dance floor. Out of the corner of her eye, she noticed Nelda looking in their direction and whispering to her companion. Faith wondered how much she embellished her story about Royal each time she repeated the tale.

"I haven't forgotten my question," she said as he drew a chair out for her and turned his own so that they faced each other. "What do you see as your life's work?"

He threw his shoulders back. "I plan to enlist in the regular Army, at my battlefield rank. A man of my experience will be an asset with the Indian troubles out west."

"I'd think you would have had enough of fighting." She shuddered. "You were blessed to survive."

"Enough fighting? Perhaps. But not enough of commanding troops. Beats arching staves for a living. As for survival, it's a matter of skill and luck. I don't know about blessed."

Faith thought of her father and brother. Was he implying they lacked skill? Or were simply unlucky?

"You were blessed. In God's providence, there's no such thing as luck."

"If you say so." His mouth quirked in a smile. "Let's dance instead of debating."

Faith awoke the following morning with waltz music echoing through her thoughts. Her feet ached from dancing all evening. After their disagreement about survival, Royal had kept the conversation light, entertaining her with jokes and stories about his coworkers at the cooperage. Closing her eyes, she pictured him in officer's dress. If he were successful with his goal, he could leave Noble Springs at any time. But while he was here, she'd enjoy his company.

"How was your evening with Major Baxter?" Grandpa asked when she put breakfast on the table.

"Very nice. He's a splendid dancer." She decided not to mention Nelda's gossip.

"I hope he comes to call again. I want to hear about his time with Sebastian and Maxwell." He cut his fried eggs into square bits and pushed the pieces around his plate.

"He wasn't sure, Grandpa. Don't expect too much."

He gripped the edge of the table. "He's got to remember. I want to know."

Faith rested a calming hand on his shoulder. "Now, now. Don't get upset."

"I'm not upset." His fork clanked against the plate. "Please, bring me my hat. It's time to go. Saturdays are busy at the store."

Sensing his agitation, she decided not to remind him that he hadn't helped in the mercantile for weeks. Instead, she went to the entryway and fetched his hat and her shawl. "As soon as I wash these plates, we'll leave."

He paced between the kitchen and the front door while she hurried through her task. Maybe seeing Royal again would be a mistake. It might be better if Grandpa forgot about the man's promise to tell him about his son and grandson.

She threw the damp dishtowel over a drying rack and joined her grandfather.

"About time." He opened the door and was ready to leave when she noticed a ribbon-tied spray of forsythia branches on the top step.

"How sweet of Royal to leave flowers." Faith gathered the aromatic bundle in her arms.

Grandpa tapped a white envelope with his cane. "There's a note."

"I'll just take a moment to put these in water, then I'll read what he said." While she arranged the bright yellow sprigs in a tall opal ware vase, her mind buzzed with what Royal may have written in his message. What a gentleman. Perhaps seeing more of him wouldn't be a mistake after all.

She slit the envelope open as they walked toward town.

Miss Faith,

Please forgive my outburst last Monday. I wouldn't want to jeopardize your friendship with my sister. Perhaps you'd also allow me to be numbered among those you count as friends.

Yours in sincerity,
Curt

*F*aith read the note again before tucking it into her carryall. How unusual to have a man ask to be her friend. She thought of Curt as Rosemary's unpredictable brother. No doubt Grandpa was fond of him, and for his sake she could overlook Curt's flashes of irritability and long silences.

When they reached the livery, Curt leaned over the corral fence. "Morning, Faith. Judge." Uncertainty filled his eyes as they sought Faith's. "Hope the flowers weren't wilted."

"They're lovely. Thank you. Apology accepted." She sent him her brightest smile.

"Good." Flushing, he kicked at a post. "Well . . . better get to work." He loped toward the gate at the rear of the corral.

"He reminds me of your father," Grandpa said as they walked on.

Surprised, Faith glanced at him. "How? They don't look a thing alike. Papa's hair was the same color as mine, and he was short and stocky. Curt's tall and kind of thin."

"Not his looks. His behavior. I watched Sebastian when he courted your mother. It's a wonder she ever said yes, he was so tongue-tied."

"Grandpa! Curt's not courting me. You read the note. He's asking to be friends."

"That's what he said. I wonder what he meant."

She shook her head at Grandpa's fancy. If Curt were interested in courting her, why hadn't he asked her to the dance?

Inside the mercantile, Faith studied what was left of the lusterware. Dessert plates, butter plates, soup bowls, demitasse cups. A few of each. Not enough of any one item to sell as a set. She picked a shard she'd missed off the floor and turned to open the doors.

"Right on time," Rosemary said, entering with Bodie at her heels. She stopped when she saw the meager stack of dishes on a countertop. "Oh, gracious! What happened?"

Faith pressed her lips together. "I had a little . . . mishap Friday afternoon. This is what's left of my expensive folly." She described how she'd bumped one thing and dropped another. "It seemed like they just kept falling and falling." A giggle bubbled up. "You should have seen the mess. Looked like a tornado went through."

Faith snorted, then leaned against the counter, laughing. "It's not a bit funny," she said, gasping for breath, "but have you ever been angry enough to throw a plate against a wall? Don't. You'll just have to clean it up."

Rosemary tipped her head back and joined in the laughter. "I'll keep that in mind."

After a few moments they sobered, patting tears from the corners of their eyes. "The question is, what are you going to do with what's left?" Rosemary asked.

"I have an idea."

The bell over the door jingled.

"I'll tell you later." Faith said, then turned to greet an older couple who entered. "Can I help you find something?"

"Guess you'll have to," the man said. "I'm lookin' for a new ax handle. You've moved things around so much I cain't find my way." He pointed to the woman with him. "The wife here wants some thread, ain't that right?"

She nodded.

Faith gestured in Rosemary's direction. "Miss Saxon will get the thread, while I show you our fine hickory handles."

The woman sidled next to her husband and whispered in his ear. His eyes widened as he scrutinized Rosemary. "It's askin' enough for me to do business with you 'stead of your grandpap, miss, but I ain't going to have my wife talkin' to such as that woman yonder."

Rosemary's eyes snapped fire. "I'll be in the storeroom unpacking the . . ." She waved a hand. "Unpacking something." She stalked past the couple, her chin in the air.

Faith put out a hand to stop her. "Wait." She faced their customers. "Miss Saxon will be helping me as long as we own Lindberg's Mercantile. Her past is to be admired, not condemned. If you don't wish to trade here, I'm told Hartfield has a fine mercantile. It's only a couple of hours away."

The man looked like he'd swallowed mustard paste. Red-faced, he mumbled, "I don't have a couple extry hours. Guess you could show me them handles. Becca, you let that gal git your thread. We got work waitin' to home."

After they left, Rosemary turned to Faith. "Thank you. You'd think I'd be used to reactions like that, but they still make me angry."

"Want to throw something?" Faith offered her a dessert plate.

Rosemary chuckled. "Later, perhaps."

On Sunday morning, Faith settled next to Rosemary in a pew near the center of the church, with Grandpa and Curt on Rosemary's left. Within moments the two men were involved in a whispered discussion of classic chess moves.

Faith rejoiced that Curt's comments drew Grandpa out of the melancholy he'd displayed since meeting Royal. She didn't know whether to hope Royal remembered where he'd seen her father and brother, or to pray he had nothing to tell them. Either way, his words would leave her grandfather disturbed.

As the congregation rose for the opening hymn, Royal ducked into the pew next to her.

"I thought I'd find you here." His voice was meant for her ears alone.

She stared at him, surprised to see him in church. "You were looking for me?"

Instead of answering, Royal clasped his side of her open hymnal and drew it toward him. His deep bass voice boomed out the words to "On Christ the Solid Rock I Stand," while he nodded and winked at her.

Curt leaned forward with a questioning expression on his face. When he noticed Royal, his eyes narrowed.

Faith turned her head toward the front and tried to ignore both of them. It wasn't easy, with Royal's warmth on her right and Curt's scowl scorching her from the left. During Reverend French's sermon, she dared a glance at Grandpa and saw him staring at Royal. She balled her hands into fists until her nails bit into the palms, wishing Royal had waited a few more days.

They left the church as a group, Curt in the lead. At the entrance, the pastor drew him aside. "Would tomorrow evening be satisfactory?" Faith heard him ask as she passed by and descended the stone steps.

Royal took her arm. "May I escort you and your grandfather home?"

"Thank you, but no. We're with—" Before she could introduce Rosemary and her brother, Grandpa interrupted.

"Course you can. I want to hear what you remember about my son and grandson."

Curt joined them in time to hear Grandpa's response. Faith looked at him, hoping he could see the apology in her eyes. "It appears we will travel home with Mr. Baxter."

"You should be comfortable. He rented our finest carriage." He tipped his hat and strode away.

"That fellow needs to learn his place," Royal said. "Rude for a stableman, wouldn't you say?"

"Curt and his sister are family friends." Faith raised an eyebrow. "We don't speak ill of our friends."

Royal's jaw tightened. She watched a brief fight for control cross his face before anger gave way to a thin smile. "In that case, my apologies. Now, shall we leave?"

"Tell me what you've remembered about my son," Grandpa said as soon as they were seated in the carriage.

Faith closed her eyes. *Please, Lord, protect Grandpa from pain.*

"To my best recollection, we crossed paths in Jeff City. General Price was trying to break our defenses. I was there with the militia. Your son and grandson were part of the Federal Army, isn't that right?"

"Yes." Grandpa's knuckles whitened around his cane. "How did they seem?"

"Like the rest of us. Tired. Looking for the war to end. Your son had his left arm bandaged below the shoulder."

Grandpa sat straighter. "No one told me that. He was hurt? He should've been in a hospital. Maybe then he wouldn't . . ." He shuffled his feet. Swallowed.

Faith tucked her arm around his. "It doesn't do any good to think about what might have been. We have each other."

Tears streaked his cheeks. "I had so much more."

"They were both courageous men," Royal said. "You can be proud."

"Proud." Grandpa spat the word. "Pride's not much company on lonely evenings." He pressed Faith's hand. "Glad we have Curt."

Royal slapped the reins over the horse's back, his lips drawn into a thin line.

On Monday evening, Curt perched on the edge of a hard wooden chair in Reverend French's book-lined study. Every inch of the small room was in perfect order. The older man's polished desktop contained one sheet of paper and a Bible sprouting numerous bookmarks. He sat behind the desk, hands clasped across his midriff.

"Tell me how you've been handling your episodes, as you call them, since we talked."

"Only had one last week. I forced myself away." Sweat stung his forehead.

"Good."

Curt sprang to his feet and paced. "I'm tired of fighting. Thought I'd be done with it when I came home. Now I battle memories. When will I be able to sleep through the night? Go somewhere and not look over my shoulder? Court a woman?"

Reverend French cocked an eyebrow. "Court a woman? You haven't mentioned that before. Who's the girl?"

"Blast my mouth. I didn't mean anything. Just thinking out loud."

"Maybe it's time. Nothing like a good woman to settle a man."

Curt thought of Faith leaving the church with Royal Baxter.

Women were attracted to unscarred men—men who had good-paying jobs. She'd accepted his friendship. That would have to be enough.

He placed his hand on the latch. "Thank you for your time."

"Don't be in such a hurry. Last time you were here we talked about turning to prayer when you're tormented by the past. Did you try that last week?"

Curt resumed his seat, remembering the feeling of peace that had accompanied the vanquishing of his ghosts. He felt himself relaxing. "Yes. It felt good. Like handing off a heavy load."

"That's exactly what happened. I believe if you continue, you'll find that your episodes will gradually cease."

"How long is 'gradual'?"

"Only God knows." Reverend French ran his fingers through his graying hair and cleared his throat. "Have you given any more thought to your former profession? We could use a man with your abilities here in Noble Springs."

"Same thoughts as courting a woman. I don't dare."

Faith stepped into the parlor where Grandpa sat in his green-upholstered wing chair staring out the front window. Leaves on the maple tree spun in the morning breeze. "Are you ready? It's half past eight."

"You go ahead. I'm staying home today."

Disquiet buzzed through her. "It's Tuesday. We have to open the store."

He frowned. "I know it's Tuesday. Do you think I'm a simpleton?"

Faith blinked at his sharp words. "Then why aren't you coming with me?"

"Don't feel like it." He rested his head against the antimacassar draped over the chair back. His age-spotted hands lay quiet in his lap.

She placed her fingers against his stubbled cheek. Grandpa always shaved. The buzzing inside grew louder. "Are you ill?"

"Sick at heart. Just let me be for a while."

"Shall I bring your manuscript home at dinnertime?" She kept her voice bright.

"No. I sat down there all day yesterday with nothing to say. Makes no sense to pretend to be busy." He pointed at the clock. "Run along. I'll be fine."

Faith kissed the top of his head. Controlling her trembling lips, she said, "See you at noon."

"Fine."

Once out the door, she fought tears, wondering how she'd keep an eye on Grandpa if he wasn't working in the shed. Drat Royal and his recollections. At the moment she wished she'd never laid eyes on him.

"Faith, would you come out here, please?" Rosemary called.

She brushed dust and cobwebs from her apron. Casting a last look at her project, she hurried through the burlap curtain dividing the storeroom from the front of the mercantile. A young couple stood holding hands under the "Necessities for the Trip to Oregon" poster. He sported a trim beard and moustache and she wore a sunny yellow calico dress. From the glow on their faces, Faith guessed they were newlyweds.

Rosemary stepped forward. "Mr. and Mrs. Potter are outfitting a wagon for the Oregon trail. I thought you could best assist them, since you're planning the trip yourself."

Mrs. Potter turned to her, eyes alight. "Are you and your husband joining our company?"

"I'm not married. My grandfather and I are going together." She bit her lip against the tiny lie. After today, he'd have to admit a fresh start was what they both needed.

"You'd best sign on with a good wagon master," Mr. Potter said. "That trail shows no mercy to stragglers."

"I do know that, Mr. Potter. May I have the name of the captain of your party?"

"Alonzo McGuire. He's made the journey several times."

Faith scribbled the name on a scrap of paper on top of a display case. "Does he live in Noble Springs?"

"He's currently residing at the hotel by the train depot. He'll be there until we're ready to leave—probably by the end of May."

The hotel. Friday night's dance seemed long ago, rather than only four days. From what her customer said, she had less than a month to sell the business and prepare a wagon for the journey if she planned to leave with McGuire's outfit. And she did plan to leave.

Mrs. Potter dropped her husband's hand. "We've read over your list." She pointed at the wall. "Do we have to have everything? After paying what Mr. McGuire charges, we must guard our cash."

Faith scanned the placard. She'd read Randolph Marcy's book so often she had most of the contents memorized. "The journey will take at least a hundred and ten days. You'll need a minimum of what I have listed. For instance, twenty-five pounds of bacon is a ration for one person. Same thing with the flour, coffee, sugar, and salt. Be sure to take a great plenty. West & Riley's has the groceries. We have all the clothing and camp equipment."

Mr. Potter rubbed his fist across his beard. "Let's get started then." He looked at his wife. "You select our clothes and medicines while Miss Lindberg shows me the supplies I need for the oxen."

They left an hour later, their spring wagon loaded up the sides with necessities. Faith grinned at Rosemary. "Finally. I was afraid I'd never have a big sale."

"If this wagon train is just forming, you'll soon have many more customers." Rosemary's eyes moistened. "I'm happy for you, but I must admit to hoping you'll never leave."

"If you'd seen Grandpa this morning, you'd change your mind. He's gone into his shell, just like after we got word about my papa and Maxwell. If I could, I'd take him away from here today."

Rosemary tilted her head, an expression of pity on her face. "What if he doesn't want to go?"

"Of course Grandpa will go. He keeps saying we have to sell the mercantile first. Now that business is on the increase, I'm sure we'll find a buyer."

But when Faith returned to the storeroom, Rosemary's question echoed in her thoughts. The wooden crate she'd dragged to the far corner beckoned. She hefted a cast iron kettle over the edge, settling it on top of four blankets and a painted canvas cloth. Their supplies would be ready the moment they sold the mercantile.

Before going home at noon, Faith stopped at the newspaper office. "I have two advertisements for next week's paper," she said to Mr. Simpkins. She gave him the pages.

He fished his glasses from his coat pocket and read aloud, "Free piece of tea-leaf china with each purchase totaling fifty cents. Your choice. First come, first served." He grinned. "So, if I spend two dollars, do I get four pieces?"

Faith nodded. "Spend ten dollars and I'll give you the entire lot."

Mr. Simpkins impaled the sheet on a spindle and read the second one. His eyes grew round. "You're selling the mercantile? 'Interested buyers call between the hours of nine to five.' Does your grandpappy know about this?"

"We've discussed selling, yes." Her heart fluttered at the half-truth.

"Well, I'll be. Can't imagine the town without Lindberg's Mercantile. You folks made it through the war. Why sell now when things are looking up?"

"We're going to Oregon."

With exaggerated movements, he took several steps backward and flopped on his chair. "Judge Lindberg leaving. This is a front-page story."

Faith gasped. "No. Not yet." Grandpa had stopped reading the *Observer* after Papa and Maxwell were killed. Heaven help her if someone mentioned the advertisement before he'd given his approval. She forced a bland smile. "Wait until we have a buyer for the mercantile. Then you'll have a bigger story for your paper."

"I'm surprised you'd want to leave. I hear Royal Baxter finally made it back. You were right, no news was good news as far as those casualty lists were concerned."

"We can't make our plans around Major Baxter, or anyone else for that matter."

He peered at her over the top of his glasses, chuckling. "You wouldn't be the first gal to adjust her sights to suit a fellow."

"I need to be on my way, Mr. Simpkins. Please let me know the cost of our advertisements at your first convenience."

"Yes, ma'am." He snapped a mock salute.

During the walk home, the truth of what he'd said broke through. Grandpa leaving Noble Springs *was* front-page news. She quailed at the idea that she might be wrong, then shook her head. She had to do something to help him. Oregon was the best idea.

Faith stepped into the entry hall. "Grandpa?"

"In here." His voice came from the parlor.

She hurried to his side. "I brought your manuscript home. Thought you might change your mind about writing."

He took the papers and dropped them on the floor beside his chair. "Thank you. I'll put it away later."

"Well, then, dinner will be on soon." She swallowed a lump in her throat. "Potato omelet. You like that, don't you? And jam tarts for dessert. I stayed up last night to bake them."

"Anything you cook is fine. I'm not too hungry." He stood, straightening his waistcoat over his collarless shirt. "I'll be upstairs. Call me when the food's ready."

While the stove heated, Faith left the kitchen and walked to the stone springhouse to retrieve the ingredients for their meal. Inside, icy water bubbling from the ground poured over rocks before flowing out into the woods behind their home. She paused for a moment and pressed her forehead against one of the cool stone walls.

"Show me what to do," she whispered. "I'm frightened."

She stopped at Ripley's Livery before she returned to the store. Curt had his back to her, currying a horse in the first stall. Faith lifted her skirt and crossed the straw-littered floor.

"Curt?"

He started, then dropped the currycomb into an empty feed bin. A pleased grin spread over his face. "Afternoon. Where's your granddad?"

"Grandpa's the reason I stopped by. He stayed home today." She pressed her hands together. "I'm concerned about him. He spent all morning just sitting in the parlor, and hardly ate a bite of dinner."

Curt stepped out of the stall. "Want me to stop by this afternoon?"

"Would you? I'd be so grateful." Up close, he smelled like horses and fresh hay. She warmed at the pleasant reminder of her childhood with Maxwell. Their horses were another thing Grandpa sold when he learned of his son's death.

"Be happy to. I like your granddad."

"Thank you. You're a blessing."

He took a step away, tugging at his shirt collar. "Best get back to work. See you this evening."

Curt certainly wasn't one for long good-byes. She turned her steps toward town.

Faith closed the double doors of the mercantile and pulled the shades down. As soon as she tallied the day's receipts and swept the floor, she'd be ready to leave. She ran her finger down the ledger entries, adding as she went. The sale to the Potters raised the total higher than it had been since she began operating the business for Grandpa.

She emptied the cash drawer and counted the coins. Potters had paid with bank notes. She'd have to take the paper currency to Noble Springs National Bank first thing tomorrow for deposit. One never knew these days. After dropping the money into a canvas bag, she closed the empty drawer and tucked the bag into her carryall. Grandpa would be pleased to know they'd had such a profitable day.

When she left the mercantile, she noticed two men sitting on one of the benches along the covered boardwalk.

Faith strode past the courthouse, walking faster than normal. A buggy rattled by and she jumped, then laughed at herself. People sat on those benches all the time. She didn't need to be afraid.

When she turned onto High Street and saw Curt walking toward her, she relaxed. She'd be safe in his company. "How is Grandpa?" she called as he drew near.

"He didn't answer the door. I thought he'd gone to be with you."

12

*F*aith's breath caught in her throat. "I haven't seen Grandpa all afternoon." She lifted her skirt above her shoe tops and broke into a run toward their house.

Curt pounded past her. "I'll let myself in," he called over his shoulder.

"Thank you," she said, knowing he was already too far ahead to hear.

The front door stood open when she panted up the steps. She heard Curt's voice upstairs, calling Grandpa's name. She dashed toward the rear of the house and peered into the kitchen, then into the small bedroom at the end of the hallway.

Curt clattered down and met her in the entryway. He shook his head.

Faith dropped her carryall and slumped against the wall. "We have to find him."

"We will." He placed his hand on her shoulder and guided her toward the parlor. "Sit for a moment and tell me what brought this change in your granddad. He seemed in good spirits at church."

She dropped onto the sofa and covered her face with her hands. When she looked up, Curt's image blurred through her tears. "After church . . ." She swallowed. "You know we rode home with the man who sat with us. Royal Baxter."

Curt's mouth tightened, but he said nothing.

She explained Royal's connection to her father and brother, without mentioning the dance. "When he told us my father had a bandaged arm at the time he saw him, Grandpa got upset. He thinks Papa wouldn't have been killed if he'd been in an infirmary having his arm tended to."

Curt's hand strayed to his neck. His eyes hardened. "Unlikely a sore arm would have made any difference. Men went into battle with worse wounds."

"When we find Grandpa, you can tell him that."

"I'm going by myself. You need to stay here in case he just went walking and comes back. He'd be worried if you weren't home. It's past suppertime."

"He's my grandfather. I'm going."

He put both hands on her upper arms, holding her in place. "No. I'll take a horse from the stable and ride out a ways. I have an idea where he might be. You want something to do, pray."

Faith bit her lip. How many times over these past years had she waited and prayed, often to no avail? She followed Curt to the door and stood gazing after his retreating figure.

"Help him," she whispered. "Help me."

Curt saddled his favorite of Ripley's horses, a roan mare. Rip wouldn't mind him taking the animal when he explained why. It would be dark within an hour. There wasn't time for him to go home and saddle Moses.

He rode north on Spring Street and soon left the outskirts of town. The rolling terrain was lush with spring growth on oaks, chokecherries, and hickory trees. Swampy lowland reflected the coral color of sunset from the black water. He swerved right and followed a broad track to the top of a cleared knob.

Inside an iron fence, headstones and crosses dotted the daisy-strewn knoll. Beyond the crest, a bent figure moved among the markers. Curt slipped from the saddle, tied the horse to one of the fence posts, and opened the gate. Not wishing to intrude on someone's private grief, he moved quietly to the top of the rise.

Judge Lindberg sat atop a low brick wall enclosing a section that appeared to be ten feet square. Honeysuckle tumbled over the sides. When Curt drew near, he read the name "Clara Lindberg" carved into one limestone obelisk and "Helena Lindberg" on its twin.

The older man stood and faced him. Defiance showed in the set of his mouth. "I know Sebastian and Maxwell aren't here. They're in the ground in Westport." He gestured toward the markers. "I had this wall built after my Clara died. Then Helena . . ." Tears shone on his cheeks. "She was Sebastian's wife, Faith and Maxwell's mother. She passed when Faith was a girl. I intended this ground for all of us when our time came. I wanted to keep my family together."

He swayed and Curt strode to his side, clasping him under one arm. "It's getting late. Faith has supper waiting. Can you ride?"

"Course I can. Just give me a few minutes. I'll meet you at the gate."

Trudging back to his horse, Curt mentally prepared for a long walk to town. He turned, surveying again the markers spread over the knoll. His vision changed to the sight of battlefield graves—rows of crude wooden crosses jammed in ravaged ground to mark the final rest of so many brave men.

Yet he'd been spared. Reverend French assured him God had a plan for his life. He wished he knew what it was.

Faith paced the hallway from kitchen to front entrance. The sun had set long ago. The roads weren't safe after dark. Too many stragglers. Some were in search of a new place to settle, others looked for an opportunity to rob a lone traveler. She twisted her hands in her apron, maintaining a silent prayer as she walked. Why hadn't she insisted on taking Grandpa with her this afternoon? She'd never leave him alone again.

She opened the door for the dozenth time, peering out into the starlit night. The slow plop of a horse's hooves on the dusty street sounded from somewhere along the road. She leaned outside, straining to see through the darkness. Two shapes appeared, one on horseback, one on foot. Grabbing a lamp from the entry table, she dashed out to the boardwalk.

Yellow light illuminated Curt's features as he tied the reins to the hitching rail and helped her grandfather dismount. *Thank you, Lord!* Faith sagged against the rail, knees weak with relief.

Curt took the lamp from her hand. "The way you're shaking, you're going to drop this."

"Thank you." Her voice wavered. She reached for him, then let her hand fall. "I was so frightened."

Grandpa stepped next to her. "I knew where I was. No need to be upset." He marched into the house.

"But I didn't know," she said to his back.

"He was up at the cemetery." Curt's hand rested on her shoulder.

She shuddered. "That place terrifies me. Grandpa tries to make me visit our family plot, but I refuse." Forgetting propriety, she leaned against him, drawing comfort from his solid presence. "How did you know to search in that direction?"

"I didn't *know*. Just had a feeling."

Warmth from his arm flowed through her. "I'm thankful you're my friend. I don't know what I'd have done without you tonight."

"You'd have found someone else." His voice sounded gruff. He stepped to one side and handed her the lamp.

She glanced up, surprised at his change in attitude. If a more inconsistent man existed, she had yet to meet him. Matching his impersonal tone, she said, "Please join us for some hot soup. I know you must be hungry."

"I'd best get on home. Rosemary will be worried."

"She worries about you? Why?" The moment she asked the question, Faith wished she could retract her words. Her question was far too personal.

Curt's face turned stony. "Guess because I'm her brother."

"Well, I know that, but—"

"Stop by the livery in the morning and tell me how your granddad's feeling, would you?" He walked to the hitching rail. While he untied the roan, a rider on a tall black stallion approached.

Faith's palms moistened. She didn't need to hold up the lamp to know it was Royal. His timing couldn't have been worse. She shot a glance at Curt, hoping Royal wouldn't assume he too had come to call.

Swallowing flutters, she approached the two men. Courtesy dictated that she introduce them. "This is a surprise, Royal. Have you met Curt Saxon?"

"Only at the stable," he said, dismounting. "How d'you do, Saxon?" He stuck out his hand. "Royal Baxter."

Curt gave Royal's hand a brief shake. "Pleasure."

From what Faith could see of Curt's expression, the meeting was anything but a pleasure. He swung into the saddle and kicked his horse into a trot.

Royal joined her on the boardwalk. "I apologize for the lateness of the hour. I'd hoped to have time to talk more with you and your grandfather."

Flattered at his continued interest, Faith glanced between Royal and the open door. Grandpa waited inside, no doubt hungry and most likely exhausted. She shook her head. "I'm sorry. We've had an unsettling evening. Perhaps another time?"

"I hope that Saxon fellow wasn't the cause of your distress. I can discourage his visits if you say the word."

"Oh, my heavens, no! Quite the contrary. He's . . . a good friend." She took a step toward the house.

Royal moved closer. "Truth be told, I wanted to see you again." His warm gaze caressed her face. "Would you accompany me on a buggy ride Sunday afternoon?"

"That sounds splendid." A pulse ticked in her throat.

When he left, she floated into the house. As long as she could prevent him from upsetting her grandfather, everything would be fine.

When Faith answered the door the following morning, Rosemary stood on the porch. "Curt told me about your grandfather's . . . troubles. How can I help?"

Tears blurred Faith's vision. "You're an answer to prayer," she said, seizing her friend in a hug. "I didn't know how I could leave him here and operate the store. I can't expect your brother to run up here all the time to check on him." Faith knew she was talking too fast. Taking a deep breath, she led the way across the parlor rug, patting a space beside her on the sofa. "Could you please open for me today? I'll be there as soon as I can convince Grandpa to come with me to town."

Rosemary's eyes shone above her gentle smile. "I have a better idea. Why don't I stay here with him?"

"But you said you don't want to be a nurse."

"You don't need a nurse, just a companion. D'you think he'd mind having me here?"

"If you're talking about me, the answer is no, I wouldn't mind." Grandpa stood in the doorway. "Can you play chess?"

"Curt's been teaching me, but I have a ways to go before I can beat him."

Grandpa rubbed his hands together. "Perfect. I'll go get the board."

Chuckling, Rosemary stood. "One other thing."

"What?"

"Would you let my dog come in with us?" She glanced between Faith and her grandfather. "He's no trouble."

"Don't see why not." His cane tapped on the wooden stair treads as he climbed to his room.

Weak with relief, Faith leaned back on the sofa and blew out a deep breath. When Curt left last evening, she hadn't known whether he'd want to continue their relationship. She'd thanked him for his help and he'd withdrawn. Then to have Royal arrive—but why should Curt care? All he wanted was friendship, on his terms.

She walked to the door and whistled for Bodie. Rosemary's collie pattered into the house, sniffing around the table in the entry before trotting into the parlor and flopping down on the rug at his owner's feet.

Rosemary reached down and stroked the dog's head. "I plan to have your grandfather help me plant flowers this afternoon. We can't play chess all day. It will do him good to have work for his hands."

"You're heaven-sent. Does Curt know you're here?"

"Absolutely. We discuss all our decisions."

Faith studied her hands, trying to imagine her life had Maxwell lived. What a comfort it would be to have a brother to share her plans. Until Grandpa agreed, she'd have to proceed alone and hope for the best.

Knowing Grandpa was safe with Rosemary, Faith gathered her courage after closing the mercantile and walked the two blocks from the store to the Lafayette Hotel. She carried the scrap of paper with Alonzo McGuire's name in her carry-all. She needed to add their names to a member list for the departing wagon train the Potters had mentioned. End of May was shaving the time a little close, since the *Noble Springs Observer* wouldn't publish her advertisement until Saturday. Surely a buyer would come forward right away. Who wouldn't want to operate a well-established business in a growing town?

As she reached the entrance to the hotel, a train rolled into the station, bell clanging. Smoke poured from the stack and trailed along the top of the cars. Faith paused a moment to watch, wishing the rails stretched all the way to Oregon. Judging from the number of workers reported to live at the rooming house behind West & Riley's, construction was progressing. But she couldn't wait the years it would take for completion.

Faith pushed open the door of the hotel. Plush red lounge chairs in the lobby looked dusty in the late afternoon light. A couple of travelers sat in a corner hunched over a card game, smoke from their cigars smelling like burning hair. She waved her hand under her nose to dispel the rank odor.

The clerk leaned over the registration counter and eyed her carryall. "Is that all the luggage you have, ma'am?"

Heat rose up her cheeks at his suspicious tone. "I'm not a guest. Please, may I ask you to tell Mr. McGuire that Miss Lindberg would like to speak with him for a moment?"

Smirking, the clerk tugged at his chin whiskers. "You can ask, miss, but he's not here. You'll likely find him at West & Riley's Restaurant. It's near onto suppertime." He raised an eyebrow. "I'll give him a message if you want."

Faith's grumbling stomach told her it was beyond suppertime. "No, thank you." She walked to the door, sensing his gaze following her.

Setting sun lit the western clouds with crimson fire. Faith squared her shoulders and trudged six blocks east to the restaurant. She glanced at the horizon from time to time, hoping she could accomplish her goal and arrive home before full dark.

Aromas of fried beefsteak and burned biscuits enveloped her when she entered the crowded eatery. She halted inside the door, quailing at the sight of a roomful of men sitting shoulder-to-shoulder at long tables piled with heaping platters of food. How could she find Mr. McGuire without making a complete fool of herself?

Jacob West made his way toward her, weaving between the tables. His white apron was splotched with dark stains that Faith hoped were from today's meal. "Miss Lindberg, isn't it? Are you here for supper?" He sounded incredulous. Using the back of his hand, he wiped sweat from his swarthy skin, dislodging dark curls at his hairline.

"No." Certainly not, she wanted to add, but refrained. "I was told I might find a Mr. McGuire here."

"That's him over there." The restaurant owner pointed at a narrow-shouldered man wearing a black slouch hat.

"Thank you." Faith drew a deep breath. Any man who would leave his hat on while eating was no gentleman. Her courage wavered.

"McGuire. Lady to see you."

Stopped in the act of turning toward the door, Faith pasted a confident expression on her face and moved in the wagon master's direction. He scraped his chair away from the table and unfolded to a height of well over six feet.

"I'm Alonzo McGuire. What is it you want?"

Some of the diners paused to watch the encounter.

Faith swallowed. Well, in for a penny, in for a pound. She dipped a slight curtsy. "I'm Miss Lindberg. My grandfather and I wish to be part of your company when you leave for Oregon."

"You're funnin' me. Did one of you put her up to this?" He raised an eyebrow and glared at the men around him.

"I'm quite serious." Faith took a step closer. "I know you're leading a company at the end of this month. We want to be included." Her neck felt the strain of looking up into his stern face.

"Go ahead, take 'em," one of the men called. "Least she'd add somethin' good lookin' to your journey."

"Sorry, miss."

"You don't look sorry." As soon as the words passed her lips, she wished she could retract them. "Excuse me, I didn't mean to—"

"I ain't taking no purty little girl and an old man. Last time I did, the old boy died and the rest of us ended up looking after a hothouse flower all the way to Oregon. Then she wanted to turn around and have me take her back to Missouri." He snorted. "No, miss, you and your grandpap ain't going with me."

Faith's cheeks burned at the general guffaws around the

room. She lifted her chin. "You're not the only person who knows the trail. I'll find someone else." She spun on her heel and stalked from the restaurant, catching a sympathetic light in Jacob West's eyes as she left.

The sun dangled low on the horizon, sending fingers of gloom past closed businesses. Faith marched toward home, fuming. She'd pay a teamster to take them across—all she had to do was find the right one.

Out of the corner of her eye she caught movement in the narrow space between buildings. She slowed and peered into the shadows. Outlines of two men, hats pulled low, showed in the dimness. Blood pounded in her ears. She should never have paused to look. Now they knew she'd seen them.

Conscious of the day's receipts in her carryall, she whipped around the corner onto Second Street. One block and she'd be at the Saxons' house. *Lord, please let Curt be home.* Footsteps echoed behind her. She smelled the odor of tobacco smoke mixed with unwashed bodies. Lifting her skirt to her boot tops, she raced along the deserted walk. When she reached the corner, she flew from the boardwalk and dashed toward safety without pausing.

"Faith!" Curt rose from the top step of the porch and ran to meet her. "What's the matter? What are you doing here?" He wrapped an arm across her shoulders. "Come. Sit." He guided her to the porch.

She placed her hand over his and rested her cheek against his chest. He felt warm and strong and safe. "I prayed you'd be here," she said between gasps for air. "Two men followed me."

"I don't see anyone now."

"They must have ducked into the alley." Her voice rose. "They were right behind me."

He took her hand, stroking her fingers with his thumb. "What'd they look like?"

"I don't know. Shadows. That's all I saw."

Curt studied her for a moment. "Why are you in this part of town? I was just going to fetch Rosemary. Thought you'd be home by now."

"I should've been. I've been busy making a fool of myself at West & Riley's." Blinking at the tears that stung her eyelids, Faith told him of her stop at the hotel and subsequent meeting with Alonzo McGuire. "Then I saw those men and couldn't think of anything but finding you."

His face softened. He wiped tears from her cheek with one finger. "I'm here."

13

The following morning Faith stepped out the door with Grandpa at her side. "Are you sure you want to come with me today?"

"First you fuss when I stay home, now you fuss when I leave. Can't ever make a woman happy."

"I'm happy. Just surprised."

"That little Rosemary like to wore me out digging holes for her flowers." He waved rolled manuscript pages in the direction of freshly turned soil. "Thought I'd rest up and work on my book."

It had been too dark the previous evening when Curt brought Faith home for her to appreciate the work Rosemary and Grandpa had done. Columbines nodded in beds freshly spaded on both sides of the steps. Their scalloped leaves swayed the morning breeze. Geranium starts were scattered in a pleasing pattern among plantings of daisies. On one side of the porch, Rosemary had transplanted a climbing rose.

Faith smiled at her grandfather. "It looks like she brought half her flower garden over here."

"She claims she overplanted and had to get rid of these." He flexed his shoulders. "Been a long time since I was acquainted with the working end of a shovel. Felt kind of good. Don't tell Rosemary, though. She'll put me to digging again."

"It'll be our secret."

Curt walked out to greet them when they reached the livery. "Morning, Judge, Faith." His eyes lingered on her carryall. "You going straight to the bank?"

"As soon as Rosemary comes in." She wished she hadn't told him about bringing the cash home with her in the evenings. She didn't need him directing her day.

"No one's going to bother Faith with me around," Grandpa said, brandishing his cane.

Curt's eyes crinkled at the corners. Faith could see he was trying not to grin. Why hadn't she ever noticed how appealing he was when he smiled? Maybe because she'd so seldom seen him wearing a happy expression.

"Thank you again for . . . everything."

"Glad to help." This time his smile broke free, wrapping her in warmth. For a moment she was tempted to reach for his hand, then chastised herself for being silly. He was only being a good friend.

When Faith returned from the bank, Rosemary had one customer waiting while she helped a woman with a fabric selection. "Glad you're back." She pointed to a man standing next to the plows. "This gentleman wants your grandfather to assist him."

Faith tied her apron around her waist and tucked her carry-all behind a counter. "Grandpa is busy with other matters," she said, walking toward the customer. Something about him seemed familiar. She shook her head. The memory would come to her. "Are you interested in buying a plow?"

"Naw." His gaze darted over the goods on display. "I need me one of them shotguns. Figger a man can tell me more about it than you can."

Faith chose the most expensive shotgun from the rack and swung it up to her right shoulder. Sighting along the barrel, she aimed at the remaining pieces of tea leaf china arranged atop a counter, then opened the breech. "This model has served well for birds and deer. Take a look."

He stared at the weapon in her hands. "How would a little thing like you know about a big ol' gun?"

She met his gaze without flinching. "Hunting with my brother. Do you want—"

A deafening crash shook the building, followed by a series of equally loud reverberations. Faith left the shotgun on a counter and dashed to the front window.

Concussions pounded through the livery. Curt ran outside and saw an ominous pillar of umber-tinged smoke rising from the south. Within moments, both church and fire bells began clanging.

"Gotta go," Rip called from the doorway. "That's the call for volunteers."

Curt nodded. "Be right behind you, soon's I settle the horses." He sprinted to the inside of the stable, where the animals whinnied and kicked at the doors of their stalls. The roan mare was first in the row, so he paused and stroked her neck. "Quiet now. Nothing to worry about." She calmed under his fingers. Moving through the building, he gentled each horse in turn.

After closing the rear doors, he stepped out front and secured the building. The cloud of smoke had doubled and now covered the downtown area. Traffic along the street increased to a steady flow of volunteers and gawkers.

Curt's memory transported him to the remains of a burned settlement. His assignment had been to search through the rubble to be sure no enemy soldiers were waiting in ambush. Sour odors gagged him as he made his way through the ruins.

He slumped against the stable doors, rough-sawn wood clutching at his hair. *Lord, deliver me.* He forced himself to open his eyes. The odors changed to coal and wood smoke drifting from the scene of the fire.

Judge Lindberg had gone to the mercantile that morning, along with Faith and Rosemary. What had happened to them? How much time had he wasted reliving the past? He broke into a run, heading south toward the source of the alarm.

Within a block of the stable he saw flames leaping behind the hotel and railroad depot. Bells continued to clang discordantly. Panting, he paused at the edge of a crowd gathered near the tracks, then pushed his way closer. A locomotive, coal car, tender, and baggage car lay on their sides to the south of the rails. Fire roared from the engine compartment, lapping at the wreckage, while the ruptured tender spewed water uselessly onto the ground. The remaining cars had piled into each other and now tilted at crazy angles. The carcass of a black cow sprawled a dozen feet from the front of the train.

A fire brigade was in high gear, ferrying water to the flames. "You, there. If you're able-bodied, get yourself a bucket." Royal Baxter wiped his forehead, leaving a black smear behind. Without waiting for Curt's response, he swung around, jogging toward the cars that remained upright on the track.

Curt clenched his teeth at the man's imperious command. The sheriff should be the one giving orders, not some jumped-up veteran claiming to have been a major in an anonymous regiment. Men carrying water jostled past him.

Travelers stood on the platform holding baggage and gaping at the flames. Shock wrote itself across their faces.

"Get back," Royal yelled. He pointed to a group of townspeople gathered across the street. "You'll be safer over thataway."

Curt looked in the direction Royal pointed and saw Judge Lindberg and Rosemary. Where was Faith? Alarmed, he surveyed the area. He took a few steps toward town, thinking she'd stayed at the mercantile, then spotted her among the passengers. She had her arm linked through that of a woman with a gashed forehead. A man carrying a wailing infant limped beside them as they made their way toward Rosemary.

Relieved, he ran to the pump next to the hotel and filled an empty bucket. Water slopped over the rim as he crowded into the line.

"Let the cars go," Royal ordered the volunteers when they reached the derailment. "Save the engine."

Steam hissed when Curt flung liquid into the firebox. Black appeared where coals had been subdued. Returning to the pump, he noticed other townspeople had followed Faith's example and were tending to the injured. Blankets had been spread in an empty field directly across from the depot. Children sobbed, clinging to their parents. Dr. Greeley's distinctive maroon buggy was tied to a hitching rail, but Curt couldn't pick him out of the crowd.

By mid-afternoon, the remains of the baggage car smoldered next to twisted rails. Broken bones and lacerations were the worst of the passengers' injuries. However, lodging had to be found for the forty or so travelers and crew who were stranded in Noble Springs.

Sweating and filthy, Curt made his way to the makeshift hospital area. He found Judge Lindberg seated on a packing container under a maple tree. He flopped down on the ground and rested his back against the wooden crate. "I don't see Faith or my sister. You here by yourself?"

"Faith went to West & Riley's. You watch. She'll be back with enough food for everyone."

Curt surveyed the size of the crowd. "I'd better go help. She can't carry all that alone."

"She's not alone. That Baxter fellow borrowed a wagon and took her over there."

"Did the cooperage close for the day?" As soon as Curt voiced the question, he realized how churlish he sounded.

Judge Lindberg gave him a knowing grin. "There's nothing stopping you from lending a hand. Don't want Baxter to think he's got a claim on her."

"Good idea." Curt brushed dried grass and ashes from his trousers. "I'll find Rosemary first and tell her where you are." He hoped the judge wouldn't realize why he wanted his sister nearby. With this many people around, he didn't want to risk having the older man wander off.

"She's over there somewhere. Went to help Doc Greeley."

Curt strode in the direction indicated until he spotted the doctor facing Rosemary. A man with a bandaged head lay on a blanket at her feet. Next to him a second man sat hunched over, clutching his arm close to his body.

"Leave them be," Dr. Greeley said to Rosemary. His white goatee bounced with rage. "I won't have a female touching men's bodies. It's indecent."

She glared at him, her face crimson. "You'd rather let them suffer until you have time to tend to their injuries? What's decent about that?"

"Don't sass me, young lady."

"I've had enough of you and your archaic opinions. I'll go where I'm needed." She stalked toward a man bleeding from a gash on his shoulder.

Curt caught up with her. "Thought you were through nursing the sick."

She waved her hand at the injured passengers. "I can't just stand by."

He surveyed the wreckage, the crowd, the wounded. For the first time since returning from the war, he allowed himself to hope he'd left his demons behind. "Neither can I."

Faith stood at a worktable in West & Riley's kitchen slicing bread while Curt and Royal loaded baskets of food into the wagon. Both men were sweat-stained and sooty. Was it her imagination, or did Curt do twice the work while Royal lingered, instructing the harassed cook?

Jacob West entered from the storeroom and stopped at Royal's side. "It'll probably be a couple weeks before the track's repaired. If the hotel fills up, I've got two empty beds over at the rooming house."

"Good. I'll spread the word." Royal straightened his shoulders, looking important.

Faith stacked the bread on a tray and covered it with a towel. "This is all we need for now," she said, smiling over at Jacob. "It's so kind of you to provide this meal."

"No trouble, miss. Nobody was here for dinner anyway. They were all down at the fire. Couldn't let the food go to waste."

Curt took the tray from her hands. The smell of smoke clung to his clothing. Tiny burn holes pocked the fabric of his shirt. "Thanks, Jacob," he said. "We'd better get back. I told people food was coming."

When they reached the accident scene, Royal stopped the wagon at the edge of the grass and strode to the rear to open the endgate. Faith scrambled down after him and ran toward the crowd.

"We brought food," she called, waving her arms to attract attention. "Come line up behind the wagon."

The couple she'd helped earlier walked toward her. The woman didn't look to be more than sixteen or seventeen. Her skirt was torn and dirty, as was her husband's jacket.

"Thank you, miss." She touched a hand to the bandage on her forehead. "I couldn't think of where we'd get a meal. Our dinner basket is somewhere in all that wreckage."

Faith patted her shoulder. "The thanks go to Mr. West. He kindly provided food from his restaurant."

"But you brought it to all of us. You're a blessing." She shifted her baby to one shoulder and offered a slim hand. "I'm Amaryllis Dunsmuir—Amy for short. This is my husband, Joel, and our baby, Sophia."

"How do," Joel said. His straight black hair flopped forward when he nodded at her. He backhanded it off his forehead.

Faith shook hands with the two of them and led the way to the wagon at a brisk trot, talking as she went. "I'm Faith Lindberg." She surveyed Amy's attire. "Were you able to rescue your valise when you escaped?"

"No. The conductor was hollering, 'Get out, get out! She's gonna burn.' We all just got out best we could. Kept my reticule, though." She patted a needlepoint bag draped over her wrist, then turned to look at the smoldering cars. "Guess when they cool off Joel can pick through and see what he can find."

Her husband grunted acknowledgment.

They reached the food-laden wagon, followed by much of the crowd. Curt stood at the left side of the endgate, folding chunks of meat between slices of bread. A stack of sandwiches waited on a tray to his right, next to a roasting pan filled with ginger cookies.

Faith sent him a grateful smile. "You always know just what to do. Thank you."

"Glad to help. Working together, we'll get everyone fed in short order."

"That we will." She handed the food to each of the Dunsmuirs. "Come see me after we finish here," she whispered to Amy.

As soon as the couple stepped aside, another passenger crowded in. Over her shoulder, she noticed Royal lounging against the depot wall, talking to two men. She suppressed a huff of annoyance. He should be helping instead of relaxing with his cronies.

For the next half hour, Faith distributed sandwiches and ginger cookies until it appeared everyone had been served. Wiping perspiration from her forehead, she sagged against the back of the wagon.

Curt put a slice of buttered bread in her hand. "Better eat something. You look tuckered."

"So do you."

He hitched himself up so he sat on the wagon gate next to an empty tray. "Haven't done anything like this since—" His hand moved to cover his scar. "Been awhile."

She studied his face, noting the smile lines in his tanned skin. How could she ever have been afraid of him because he was scarred? Faith wanted to take his wrist, move it away from the red slash, and tell him he looked just fine. Handsome, in fact.

He flushed under her scrutiny. Hunching his left shoulder, he slid to the ground and busied himself stacking empty trays. "Best get these back to Jacob. He'll be needing them tonight."

She pursed her lips, feeling dismissed. Curt and his moods.

Out of the corner of her eye, Faith saw Amy and Joel moving in her direction.

"You said you wanted to see us after we ate?" Amy asked. A drop of red stained her bandage.

Faith's gaze took in both the woman and her husband. "Do you need a place to sleep? We have a spare bedroom."

"This town is plum full of kind folks," Joel said. "Your Reverend French done asked us already. He's bringing his buggy directly to take us there."

"Splendid." She gestured at the pair's torn clothing. "If you come by Lindberg's Mercantile tomorrow—Reverend French can tell you where it is—I'll get you outfitted with some clothes to replace the ones that were ruined."

"We can pay."

"No need."

Tears slid over Amy's piquant face. "God bless you. We'll be there."

Faith waited with them until Reverend French arrived, then crossed to the maple tree and settled on the grass next to Grandpa. Her bones ached with weariness. She leaned against her grandfather's leg and he patted her shoulder.

"I was mighty proud of you today." He squeezed her close. "Bet you're ready to go home."

"Curt said he'd hitch his buggy and take us, but I need to stop by the mercantile first." She looked across the field, spotting Curt and his sister talking to two women dressed in widow's weeds.

She heaved herself to her feet. "I'll let him know we're ready."

As she approached, she noticed the younger of the two had raw scrapes across one side of her face. The braids in her auburn hair had come unpinned and trailed down her back. The older woman standing next to her clutched at one shoulder, where her sleeve had torn from her black silk garment. Sunlight glinted off her unnaturally red-gold hair.

Rosemary turned in her direction. "Faith, this is Miss Cassie Haddon and her mother, Eliza Haddon."

Cassie smoothed her hair with a self-conscious motion. "I'm afraid I look a fright. My bonnet is completely ruined, and my dress"—she gestured toward the torn black lace trim across the bodice—"is in sad need of attention." Her voice carried the softness of southern speech.

"They'll be staying with us until the rails are repaired," Rosemary told Faith.

Curious, she eyed the younger woman. She was introduced as *Miss* Haddon, yet she wore full mourning? Faith shook her head. This was not the time to pry.

"You'll be in good hands," Faith said to them, offering a smile.

Mrs. Haddon pursed her lips and sent her daughter a dark look. "I was in good hands before I left St. Louis. I should never have come on this fool's errand."

"Mother, please." Cassie dipped her head and blotted the corners of her eyes with a handkerchief she removed from her sleeve. "We're grateful to you," she said to Rosemary. Her voice trembled. "First my fiancé, now this." She gestured toward the wreckage, where smoke and ash twisted into the sky.

Rosemary patted her shoulder. "After a bath and a night's rest, things will look better."

"Maybe." Cassie sounded doubtful.

Her mother sniffed. "I've lost my parasol and this sun is ruining my skin." She turned to Curt. "I'll wait under those trees while you fetch a carriage."

He laid a hand on Faith's arm. "I'll come for you and your granddad as soon as we get these ladies settled. D'you mind waiting a few more minutes?"

"Not at all."

After he left, Faith glanced around the area. "What happened to the injured men?" she asked Rosemary.

"Dr. Greeley found beds for them." She made an expression of disgust. "Heaven forbid I should have anything to do with caring for anyone of the opposite gender."

Faith held out her hand and allowed Curt to help her from the buggy, anxiety prickling when she observed that she hadn't padlocked the doors. Flakes of ash swirled over the boardwalk as she walked.

"I'll just empty the cash drawer and be right back," she said to Grandpa, hoping he hadn't noticed the unlocked store.

Curt took her arm. "Could be someone hiding inside. After something like this, you never know." He pushed open one of the doors and preceded her.

She peered around him. Everything looked as she'd left it—Wait a moment.

Where was the shotgun she'd laid on a counter? She whirled to check the rack.

Grooved oak shelves stared back at her, shining and vacant.

"Nooo!" She clapped a hand over her mouth and dashed along the rows of glass-topped display cases. A shelf that had held watches was bare.

Several pairs of boots were missing, as were all of the ready-made shirts.

"We've been robbed." Faith spun and stared at Curt. "And it's my fault."

aith swayed with shock. "If only I'd locked the door. Two more minutes. That's all it would have taken." She bit down on her lower lip to keep from weeping.

Curt put his arm around her shoulder and guided her to one of the chairs next to the stove. "Sit a moment." He pointed to the burlap curtain at the rear of the building. "That's the storeroom?"

She nodded.

"I'll check in the back to be sure they're gone."

"You think—?"

"No, but better be sure." Shirtsleeves rolled to the elbows, he strode toward the curtain.

Faith rocked forward and wrapped her arms around her middle. Her throat prickled when a new thought struck. The cash drawer. Had she locked it?

She jerked upright, dashed to the front counter, and tugged at the drawer. It didn't budge. To be certain, she took the key from her pocket and fitted it in the lock. The tray of coins inside hadn't been disturbed. *Thank you for small mercies, Lord.*

"Got tired of waiting for you," Grandpa called as he walked through the open door. "Where's Curt?"

She drew in a breath and held it until blood pounded in her temples. "We . . . I . . . someone robbed the store while I was at the fire."

He glanced around the display area. "Looks the same to me."

How she wished she could pretend he was right, and just lock up and leave. Instead, she moved to his side and grasped his free hand. "All the firearms and watches are gone. They picked the most expensive things we had."

"Didn't steal the cookstoves, did they?"

She recognized Grandpa's attempt to tease her and ignored him.

"Those new boots from St. Louis are missing. All the men's shirts. I haven't walked around to see what else." Her voice caught. "Oh, Grandpa, I was so sure I could manage the business, and it's been a disaster from the start."

He hooked his cane on the edge of a counter and pulled her to his chest. "Don't cry." His moustache tickled her ear. "It could've happened to anyone. Maybe it did. Most every merchant was down at the tracks today."

"They probably locked their stores," she said between sobs.

"Locked or not, the thief had a choice. He chose to steal. If he wanted in here bad enough, he'd have broken our sad excuse for a lock."

Faith took a step backward, sniffling. "You think so?" She noticed Curt walking toward them past the stoves lined down the center of the store. She swiped at her tears.

He stopped next to her. "Alley door was wide open. Whoever did this must've left that way." His expression softened as he studied her. "Good thing you weren't here. I've seen what men are like when they're bent on thieving. You could've been hurt."

Thankful for his caring tone, she gazed up at him. Depending on Curt in a crisis was becoming a habit.

Sheriff Cooper was waiting outside the store when she arrived the next morning. His leather vest sagged over his rangy form, mimicking the downward droop of his moustache. "Morning, Judge, Miss Faith. Got your message. Sorry I wasn't at the jailhouse yesterday afternoon when you came by." He removed his hat and combed his fingers through his sandy hair. "Had a disturbance at one of the saloons."

"Today's probably better." She unlocked the door and preceded him inside.

Grandpa followed the sheriff and settled in one of the chairs near the woodstove. "Faith can help you more than I can." He looked at her. "I'll wait here in case you need me."

She fought an impulse to kiss the top of his head in gratitude for his continued trust.

Sheriff Cooper turned in her direction. His weary expression made him look older than his years. "You're in charge, eh? Well, let's get on with it then. Did you write down everything that was taken?"

"I think so." She took a folded sheet of paper from her carryall and gave it to him.

"You think? Or you know?"

"It's hard to see something that isn't there, Sheriff. I did my best."

He glanced down the list and whistled. "Looks like they was smart. Nothing here would stand out in town—'cept maybe the new boots." He fixed her with a questioning gaze. "So, how'd they get in? From the alley?"

"Probably by the front door." Embarrassed, she ducked her head. "It wasn't locked. When the train derailed, I just closed the door and ran to the depot. We think they left through the alley, though."

126

He sighed. "Show me the back entrance." As they walked through the room, he asked, "Anyone been hanging around lately? Looking, not buying?"

"Well, just before the crash—"

Aaron Simpkins barreled through the entrance, notebook in hand. "Miss Faith! I saw the sheriff waiting for you. What's happened?"

She bit her lip. With the sheriff standing beside her, she couldn't very well tell Mr. Simpkins nothing was wrong and send him on his way. Her carelessness would be public news by tomorrow.

"Some items were stolen yesterday during the commotion following the train wreck. Sheriff Cooper is looking into the matter." She hoped that would be enough information.

"How about you, Sheriff? Any idea who did it?"

"Simpkins. I just got here."

"But there was a burglary?"

"Yes."

"That's all I need." He scribbled in his notebook. "Between the crash and this, I'll need to print extra copies." Addressing Faith, he asked, "Care to tell me what's missing?"

Sheriff Cooper placed himself between Faith and the newspaperman. "Write 'Several items of value.' Don't want to say more'n that."

He scribbled again and then pivoted toward the door. "Thanks. I'll put in a good word for you, Sheriff. Election's coming up, you know," he called over his shoulder.

The lawman mumbled something under his breath.

Trying not to speculate on what Mr. Simpkins would have to say about her, Faith showed the sheriff around the storeroom and told him about the man who'd been looking at shotguns before the crash. He listened to her sketchy description, shaking his head.

"I'll ask around, but don't get your hopes up. Too many vagrants passing through these days. Meantime, best lock the doors when you leave."

Indignant, she drew herself up to her full height. "I always—" She swallowed the rest of the sentence. "I will."

The bell over the door jingled when he left.

Faith leaned against the cold iron surface of a stove and closed her eyes. Images of the missing merchandise slid through her mind. A representative from Marblehead Gun Works should be here in a few days for his monthly sales call. She could replace the firearms quickly. Then she'd telegraph suppliers in St. Louis for boots and watches. As soon as the rails were repaired, they'd have everything back in stock. The losses were a temporary setback, nothing more. They'd still be able to sell the store when a buyer appeared.

She smiled at her grandfather. "Everything's going to be fine. Don't worry."

At the sound of the bell, she turned to see the Dunsmuirs enter. Amy wore a brown paisley dress that obviously belonged to the much stouter Clarissa French. The bodice drooped on Amy's slight form and the waist was wrapped with a long scarf. She carried Sophia over one shoulder. Joel limped beside them, wearing the coat he'd had on the previous day.

Faith drew in a breath. She'd momentarily forgotten her promise to provide replacement clothing for them. And now the men's shirts were gone. What did she have for Mr. Dunsmuir?

It wouldn't do to seem reluctant to help, so she pasted a pleasant expression on her face and met them at the door. "Good morning." She glanced at the fresh strips covering Amy's forehead. "Is your wound better today?"

"The bleeding stopped. Miss Saxon came by last night with yarrow. She said to leave the bandage on until Saturday."

"We'll never forget the way folks in this town took to us," Joel said. "Couldn't have been kinder if we was to home."

Faith looked at him. Better get the bad news out of the way first. "I'm sorry to say we were robbed yesterday. All the men's shirts are gone. Fortunately for Amy, the thief or thieves weren't interested in women's clothing."

His eyes widened. "If that don't beat all. You're down at the tracks helping, and some no-account robs your store."

She decided not to tell him she'd left the door unlocked. "We do have men's . . . necessities." Faith led the way to a shelf filled with masculine undergarments. "Please select whatever you need."

"Thank you, miss. Don't you worry none about those shirts. Reverend French gave me one of his." He opened his jacket so she could see blue chambray tucked beneath his suspenders. "I come here today for Amy. Miz French said you have a few dresses already made up."

She gestured toward a rack holding calico work dresses. "A local seamstress supplies them. The quality is excellent."

"Are you sure you want to give one away?" Amy fingered a flower-printed indigo garment. "The sign says they cost—"

Faith flipped the placard facedown. "Not this morning." She held out her arms. "I'll hold Sophia while you see if that one would fit you."

After the Dunsmuirs left, Faith sank into a chair next to Grandpa, trying not to think of the cost of her generosity atop the losses they'd suffered from the thieves. "I probably shouldn't have done that," she muttered. "Not right now. Should've just told them our circumstances changed."

Grandpa patted her hand. " 'Withhold not good from them to whom it is due, when it is in the power of thine hand to do it.' Lindberg's Mercantile has prospered all these years following that principle. We're not going to stop now."

Faith nodded, her thoughts on the future. Before long the mercantile would have new owners. She wondered whether they would embrace her grandfather's philosophy.

On Sunday afternoon, Faith rested against the soft leather upholstery while Royal guided the carriage through town. A gentle breeze ruffled the ribbons on her bonnet. After the week's events, their planned ride came as a welcome change of pace.

As they passed a group of girls strolling on the courthouse lawn, she caught a few envious glances. She sat straighter, smiling. Royal cut a handsome figure in his white shirt, open at the collar, and black coat.

He turned toward her, eyes bright. "If you're agreeable, I thought we'd ride out to see how many dogwoods we can find in bloom. Be a nice change from soot and ashes."

"Splendid. As long as we're not away for too long. A friend is staying with my grandfather and I don't want to impose."

"We'll circle around to Pioneer Lake and come back. As I recall, that's where courting couples like to go."

"Are we a courting couple?"

"Aren't we?" He rested his hand over hers. "You're not like other girls, simpery and silly. I like that."

Faith gazed ahead without responding. Other girls. That's what Nelda Raines had said. Now he was interested in her. She didn't want to be another conquest on his list.

He touched her hand. "Did I shock you? I apologize."

"Not shocked. Surprised. We hardly know each other."

"I plan to change that—beginning today. For a start, you can tell me why a pretty girl like you is working in a store. It's not—" He cleared his throat. "Many people would say such a thing isn't done. In fact, maybe that's what prompted someone to rob you."

How did he know? Then she remembered. Saturday's edition of the *Noble Springs Observer* aroused widespread interest. News of the burglary had shared front page space with the train derailment. Faith blew out a breath. "Can we please discuss something else? Anyway, why does it matter to you what I do?"

She turned her head to one side, pretending to study the scenery, while she pondered how he'd answer. The carriage rolled past wooded knolls with dogwood blooms peeking from thick greenery. Redbud trees added their color to the mixture. A stony creek lined with moss gurgled at the side of the road.

"You matter to me. I'm interested. Your grandfather didn't give you full control of the business, did he?"

"Yes, he did." If Royal had objections, she might as well find out now. "He hasn't been himself lately, so I've been able to relieve him of the burden."

A smile flitted across his face. "You must be a comfort to him."

"I'm all he has."

"No more brothers, uncles?"

"Since the war, just the two of us."

"Hmm." He flicked the reins. "Now it's your turn. Ask me something."

"Tell me about your parents."

"Ask me something else." His tone sounded light, teasing.

She smiled. Apparently he wasn't one who relished serious conversation. Remembering the envious glances of the other girls, she decided if she wanted to keep him interested in her, she'd need to think of amusing topics.

"Did you know the thieves even took the jar of peppermints I kept by the door?" She chuckled. "Can you imagine?"

He grinned at her. "You'll have to tell the sheriff to look for someone with a sweet tooth."

"I'll be sure to do that." His laughter joined hers.

When they reached Pioneer Lake, he jumped from the carriage and helped her down, keeping her hand in his after she reached the ground. "Let's take a stroll along the water's edge before I take you home."

"I'd like that." Part of her couldn't believe that she was here with the man she'd dreamed about for so long. His grip on her hand felt strong . . . and thrilling. Faith fought down an impulse to skip for joy. She'd wait until later to share her Oregon plans with him. At the dance, he'd told her of his desire to join the Army and serve out west. For all she knew, perhaps . . . No. She mustn't get ahead of herself.

Still water mirrored trees at the far edge of the lake. A pair of geese, their family of fluffy goslings following in their wake, created ripples near the shore.

"What a fine afternoon. Wish we could linger." Royal's voice echoed her thoughts.

"Next time, I'll bring a picnic." The words were out before she could stop them. A flush heated her face. How presumptuous. He hadn't mentioned a next time.

Smiling, he bent to look in her eyes. "Would next Sunday suit you?"

She slipped into the house, warm with pleasure from her afternoon with Royal.

"We're in here," Grandpa called to her from the parlor, where he sat facing the chessboard. "This young rascal thinks he has me in a corner, but I have a trick or two up my sleeve."

Curt stood. "Faith. Did you have a pleasant afternoon?"

She found it hard to meet his eyes. For some reason she felt she was betraying him by seeing Royal. Yet Curt was the one who'd suggested friendship. "Yes. Thank you for keeping Grandpa company." She untied her bonnet. "I'll have supper ready in a bit. You're welcome to stay."

"No thanks. I promised Joel we'd go fishing before it gets dark."

She had to think a moment before remembering Joel Dunsmuir was the man staying with the pastor's family until repairs could be made to the rails. "Ah. Another time, then."

He gave her a long look. "Another time."

On Monday, Faith studied the gun rack and then checked her list. She wanted to be ready with her order when the salesman from Marblehead arrived. The bell over the door sounded and Mr. Grisbee and Mr. Slocum strolled in, heading for chairs next to the stove.

Faith stared. They'd been absent ever since Grandpa had given her the management of the store.

"Morning, Miss Faith," Mr. Slocum said. "Interesting story in this week's paper." He pointed at the vacant rack. "Looks like they done cleaned you out. No wonder you're wanting to sell. How's Nate feel about it?"

She bit her lip, deciding how to respond. As far as she knew, Grandpa hadn't seen the advertisement and, blessedly, no one had mentioned it at church on Sunday. She cleared her throat, knowing she should have talked it over with him before she placed the notice. "We'll wait and see what happens."

"He out back working on that book of his?" Mr. Grisbee rose from his chair. "Believe I'll go ask him."

"He doesn't like to be interrupted when he's writing. It

makes him forget what he was going to say." Her stomach fluttered.

"Won't be a minute. You coming, Jesse?"

With a sense of doom, she watched them depart and walk down the gravel path leading to her grandfather's work space. She missed Rosemary. If she were here, Grandpa might be less likely to light into her. But as long as the Haddons remained, Rosemary wouldn't be coming to help.

Faith took the feather duster from the storeroom to keep busy while she waited for the explosion. It wasn't long in coming.

Her grandfather stormed in the door, eyes snapping. "The store is not yours to sell. You know that. How could you?"

"We've talked about it more than once. Have you forgotten?" She bit her lip, not intending to refer to his memory troubles.

His face reddened. "I well recall our conversations. I've allowed you to order necessary merchandise. What I can't remember is giving you permission to sell the business out from under me."

"If we're to go west, we need the money. You've said so yourself."

Faith cringed when she noticed Grandpa's cronies standing at the doorway. The entire discussion would be all over town within the hour. She laid her hand on her grandfather's arm. "Can we please wait to discuss this at dinner?"

He shook her hand free. "There's nothing to discuss. I'm going next door and telling Simpkins to print a retraction. Lindberg's Mercantile is not for sale."

15

*H*er grandfather's words reverberated in Faith's mind. *Lindberg's Mercantile is not for sale.* She should never have assumed he'd agree. Selling the business was far different from expecting him to indulge her childish whims for a kitten or a trip to a circus.

The front door clicked shut. Grandpa's cronies walked across the street toward the courthouse lawn, no doubt to spread the news of Judge Lindberg's presumptuous grand-daughter going behind his back to sell the family business. "It wasn't like that," she said to the empty room. "Grandpa told me we'd leave when the store turned a profit. I didn't place the advertisement until we had customers buying equipment for the trail."

Her big mistake had been going ahead without consulting him.

Faith stepped out onto the covered boardwalk and paused to lock the door. Grandpa was probably still in the newspaper office. She needed to pacify him in order to ward off his tendency to wander away when upset.

Mr. Simpkins dropped his head and shuffled some papers on his desk when she entered.

Grandpa raised his eyebrows, wrinkling his forehead up to his bald scalp. "The retraction will be in next Saturday's paper. I told Aaron you made a mistake."

She nodded, relieved that he hadn't shared the details of their personal disagreement. "I did indeed. I'm so sorry."

When they turned to leave, Mr. Simpkins asked, "Did you lock the doors before coming here? I can always use another front-page story." A smile twitched at one corner of his mouth.

Enough was enough. "Why yes, I did," Faith said in her sweetest voice. "Thank you for your concern."

By the end of the week, Faith had grown accustomed to the renewed presence of the woodstove regulars, as she thought of Mr. Grisbee and Mr. Slocum. They'd resumed their daily checker games as though there'd been no interruption.

Repairs to the rail bed gave them plenty to gossip about with customers. Rumor had it, a few more days and horse teams would arrive to help stand the locomotive upright on the tracks.

When a man wearing a frock coat over a plaid waistcoat entered, carrying a leather case, she assumed he was one of the railroad officials visiting Noble Springs to supervise the project.

"May I help you? We have most everything a traveler might need."

"I'm here to talk to the owner." He opened the case and handed her a business card.

"Jerome Jenner. Marblehead Gun Works," she read aloud. "Splendid. I've been expecting someone from your company."

"Good. That makes my job easier. Now, where's the owner?"

From his post at the checkerboard, Mr. Slocum snorted. "You're talkin' to her. Judge Lindberg give her free rein here." He winked at Faith. "Almost."

She ignored him. "I'm Miss Lindberg, and we need to renew our stock of firearms. I've made a list. If you'll come with me, please."

He studied her for a moment before joining her beneath the gun rack. Up close, he matched her in height and probably weighed no more than she did. His white shirt gapped at the collar. Somehow she'd expected someone from a firearms company to have a more commanding presence.

"Looks like you sold all your stock." Admiration colored his words. "That's not easy to do in these hard times."

Her face warmed. "They were stolen. Last week, after the derailment."

"Ah." He removed an order book from the leather case. "What can Marblehead provide you with?"

"A Sharps rifle. Three Henrys. Two of your most reliable shotguns—perhaps the Perkins."

Behind her, one of the woodstove regulars whistled.

Mr. Jenner beamed. "Excellent, Miss Lindberg." His pencil moved rapidly down the page, as though he feared she'd change her mind if he didn't get each item listed. He circled the total at the end of the column. "Since this is such a substantial amount, Marblehead will require payment of half now, and half upon satisfactory delivery."

Previous orders she placed with salesmen hadn't required sizable deposits. She swallowed, trying to seem matter-of-fact. "I'll give you a note to take to Noble Springs National Bank. They'll issue payment."

She removed a receipt book from the cash drawer and drew a line through "Received From," replacing it with "Pay To." After writing the amount, she added her signature and handed him the document. "You'll find the bank at the end of the next block, across the street. Ask for Mr. Paulson. He's the president."

"Pleasure doing business with you." Mr. Jenner bowed, tucked the note inside his coat, and bolted through the door.

Faith rubbed sweaty palms on her apron. She'd never spent so much money in her life.

Mr. Slocum pushed himself to his feet. "Best be heading home. Near time for dinner." He paused next to her. "You surely brightened that young feller's day. Bet he ain't never got an order that big."

"And from a girl, to boot." Mr. Grisbee shuffled past, snickering.

Rolling her eyes, she dropped the receipt book in the drawer. When she glanced up, she saw Rosemary and Bodie entering the building. The dog bounded toward her, wagging his tail.

Faith patted his head and then hurried to her friend. "I've missed you." She pointed to the recently vacated chairs. "Come sit with me a moment. Where are your guests today?"

"Watching the repair work on the railroad tracks."

"How's Cassie?"

Rosemary settled into her chair. "Quiet, as always. She helps with washing up but otherwise doesn't seem to know how to do much in the kitchen. I rarely see her except at mealtimes. She's like the rest of the stranded souls—anxious to return home." She sighed. "Her mother's another story. Bless her, she can't seem to find a single good word to say about anything."

"Send her over here. Maybe she could meet a kindred spirit. Some of the other women come in to the mercantile during the day, just to pass the time. They walk around and look at things, but they're not buying." Faith shook her head. "I can't imagine what I'd do if I were adrift in a strange town.

I walked by the depot yesterday to watch the activity. The place is a beehive. Won't be long now and trains will be—"

Mr. Jenner strode through the door, brandishing a slip of paper. "I wouldn't have thought a woman would pull such a low-down trick. This note is worthless." He marched over to Faith, his coat flapping, and ripped the paper in half.

The pounding of her heart threatened to choke her. "What . . . what do you mean?"

"Paulson was very polite, but he said the mercantile's accounts weren't in a position to cover such an amount." He sneered while he mimicked the banker's words. "Put another way, you tried to cheat me."

Faith felt a flush spread over her body. "I assure you, I had no such intention."

"Then you'll pay me for this order?"

She stood, chin raised, and he took a step away. "Come back in an hour. I'll call on Mr. Paulson myself. There must be a mistake."

"One hour. I'll be here." He stalked out.

"What an unpleasant little man," Rosemary said. "If I may ask, what was he talking about?"

Faith told her about the order to replace the firearms that had been stolen and the note she'd given Mr. Jenner to cover the deposit. "I've drawn on our account a time or two since March. Nothing like this has ever happened. I think Mr. Paulson has us confused with another merchant." As her embarrassment faded, she felt coals of anger glow inside.

"Would you like me to stay?"

"Please. I won't be gone long." Faith leaned forward and squeezed Rosemary's hands. "You're a wonderful friend. Thank you."

On the walk to the bank, she tried to imagine how such an error could have taken place. Each day's receipts were noted in the ledger. After expenses, the balance was deposited in the bank, the way Grandpa taught her. Mr. Paulson had better be ready to apologize for her humiliation.

The imposing two-story brick façade of Noble Springs National Bank dominated the corner of First Street and King's Highway. Faith pushed open the heavy wooden door and entered the quiet lobby. The space had a metallic smell, almost as though coins themselves perfumed the interior. She passed the teller cage, wondering, as she often did, what it would be like to spend one's day working behind narrow brass bars.

Before she reached Mr. Paulson's desk, he noticed her and stood, his rounded stomach straining at the buttons on his gray waistcoat. "Miss Lindberg. I must apologize."

She drew a deep breath and released it with a whoosh, relieved she'd worried for nothing.

"It's quite all right. Mistakes happen. Shall I send Mr. Jenner back to redeem the note?"

He fingered the bow on his maroon cravat. "I'm apologizing for not informing you sooner of the state of your finances. Please sit."

Suddenly weak, she took the chair he indicated. "State of our finances? But I'm here almost every Friday with a deposit."

"Simply put, for the past year or so Judge Lindberg has been spending more than the mercantile takes in. When he bought those four cookstoves last fall, he nearly depleted your funds. Sooner or later things were bound to reach this point." He fiddled with a pen holder on his desk, not quite meeting her eyes. "I saw in last week's paper that the business is for sale. Unfortunately, right now I doubt if anyone would want to invest in such a losing proposition."

"Grandpa cancelled the advertisement," she said, almost in a whisper.

"Very wise." He leaned back in his chair and laced his

hands over his stomach. "You're to be congratulated for doing a fine job of helping your grandfather. If you need any advice, feel free to come to me. In the meantime, however, you must concentrate on building up your account with us."

"But we need those firearms to replace the ones that were stolen. They're always in demand. I know they'd sell."

"Perhaps in another month or so . . ." He rose. "Again, I apologize for not contacting you sooner."

She stepped into the sunlight, barely aware of leaving the bank. She couldn't replace the stolen merchandise. Grandpa had never talked to her about finances. She'd always assumed the mercantile to be profitable, or at least holding its own. She bit her lip to keep from bursting into tears. Her dream of traveling to Oregon had no more substance than the ash that covered the town in the aftermath of the derailment.

Upon her return to the mercantile, Faith noticed Rosemary assisting a woman with washtubs and laundry implements. Grateful for a moment to herself, she headed for the shelf where ledgers were kept and opened the current book to the first entry of the year. "January second. Cold and snow. When I was a boy, snow became covered with a crust hard enough to bear the weight of a man, but would not—"

She skimmed to the bottom of the page. Either Grandpa had no customers that day, or he'd neglected to enter the sales.

She flipped to the next sheet. After a paragraph about his father's musical skills, Grandpa noted, "Arthur Bennett. One lamp. Can of oil. Will pay next week."

Day after day, the entries were similar. Random stories about her grandfather's boyhood, with careless notes about who'd made a purchase and whether or not the item had been paid for. She drew a shuddering breath. He'd instructed her to enter names and purchases for each date, then tally at closing time. How long had it been since he'd followed his own advice? Overwhelmed, she moaned, massaging her forehead with her fingertips.

"Are you ill?" Rosemary crossed the room. Her customer followed, holding a wood-framed tin washboard.

"No." Faith glanced at the shopper and sent her what she hoped was a friendly smile. "Please don't let me interrupt you." She moved aside so Rosemary could open the cash drawer.

When the customer left, Rosemary crossed her arms over her middle and turned to Faith. "What happened at the bank? Obviously it wasn't good news."

She rested a hand on the closed book. "Grandpa's been neglecting the bookkeeping for some time, apparently. There's little money left in our account at the bank. I can't make heads nor tails of these entries." She chewed her lower lip for a moment. "I don't know what to do. It appears people owe us money, and heaven knows, we can use it. Should I ask Grandpa?"

"You can ask, but you don't want to upset him."

"I know."

The two women were silent for a moment, then Rosemary said, "Would you mind if I told Curt? He's a—he's very good with numbers."

A stableman, good with numbers? Faith shrugged. "If you think he can help, please do."

On Sunday afternoon, Faith cast a glance out the kitchen window at rainclouds clustered overhead. She hoped she and

Royal would still go on their picnic. She hadn't seen him since last Sunday's ride to Pioneer Lake. But he'd said two o'clock, so she'd be ready. The promise of an afternoon with him made the week's events fade for the moment.

She tucked a napkin-wrapped plate filled with slices of yesterday's Dolly Varden cake next to a flask of ginger water in the picnic basket, then dashed to the springhouse for the ham salad she'd prepared early that morning. A drop of moisture splashed on her arm. "Oh, go away!" she said. "Come back tonight."

The cool interior smelled of moist earth. Before removing the cloth-covered bowl from a shelf, Faith paused to listen to the friendly murmur of water bubbling from a gap in the ground. After a moment she realized that some of the watery music was coming from the roof of the springhouse. She tried to swallow her disappointment.

Hugging the crockery bowl close to her middle, she dashed into the kitchen and tucked the salad into the basket. She'd waited all week for this day. Maybe the clouds would blow over.

By two o'clock Faith had changed into a sprigged muslin dress with blue forget-me-nots printed on the fabric and settled in the parlor to wait for Royal. At five minutes past, a covered buggy stopped beside the hitching rail. She jumped to her feet and opened the door before he knocked. "I wasn't sure you were coming."

His gaze took in her clothing and the blue shawl draped over her arm. "Do you always dress to go out just in case someone drops by?" His grin teased. "In any case, I keep my promises. The rain's a nuisance, but we're going to have a picnic."

"I hoped you'd feel that way." She settled her loosely woven wool shawl over her shoulders, then lifted the basket from the entry table.

He took it from her, hefting it as though weighing the contents. "Feels like quite a feast. Would your grandfather like to join us?"

"How kind of you to ask. He's spending the afternoon with friends." Mentally, she thanked Rosemary for her offer, and wondered whether she'd told her brother about their financial dilemma. If she had, Faith hoped Curt wouldn't question Grandpa during the visit. She cringed at the idea of what might happen if her grandfather became agitated again.

Royal tucked his free hand under her elbow. "Then we'd better leave right away. Wouldn't want your neighbors to gossip about you entertaining a male caller without your grandfather present."

The columbines next to the steps resembled fairy flowers in the misty rain. Faith held her skirt above the toes of her boots as they walked to the buggy, conscious of Royal's firm grip with every step. He certainly knew how to make a girl feel protected.

At Pioneer Lake, Royal stopped in a sheltered spot under the sprawling branches of a white oak. Rain dripped on the canvas buggy cover, a sound almost as musical as the spring bubbling behind her house. A few towhees splashed in a puddle nearby, the white in their tail feathers flashing in the gray light.

Faith arranged the basket on the floor of the buggy between them and filled a plate for Royal, then served herself.

He took a bite of the salad. "Delicious, as I'm sure everything is."

"Thank you. These are my mother's recipes." She picked at her meal, taking tiny bites of the cake between a couple of forkfuls of ham. Hard as she tried to prevent the intrusion, she couldn't help but worry about finances at the mercantile. They ate in silence for several minutes.

"You're quiet. Is it too cold out here for you? We can always leave." Royal rested his empty plate on top of the basket. "I want you to be comfortable."

She reminded herself that he didn't like to talk about unpleasant subjects. If she wanted to keep him interested, she needed to be bright and amusing. "I'm fine. Just a bit preoccupied."

"Can I help?"

If she'd been at all cold, his gaze would have warmed her. His interest seemed genuine.

"I talked to Mr. Paulson at the bank yesterday. It seems the store's finances are in sad condition—temporarily." She tried to sound positive. "We've been quite busy lately. Customers are outfitting for the wagon train that's leaving in a couple of weeks, so we'll soon be fine." A lump formed in her throat at the idea of the company heading west without her.

Royal shook his head, a sympathetic expression in his eyes. "You're a woman. You shouldn't be working in a store anyway. It would be best if you sold the mercantile. That way you and the old man would be set."

"But Mr. Paulson said this would be a bad time to sell."

"Bosh. A business in distress is bound to look like a bargain." He arched an eyebrow. "Anyway, a pretty gal like you is sure to get married. Maybe sooner than you think."

She flushed at the implication in his words. Was he suggesting—? Disquieted, she placed her dish next to Royal's on top of the basket. She didn't know if she could be happy with giving up her dream and staying in Noble Springs as his wife. Something she thought she'd wanted for so long now seemed less desirable than going to Oregon.

He lifted her hand and stroked each finger, then kissed her palm.

Fire raced up her arm. He cupped her head and drew her

toward him. His lips touched hers, as gentle as a wisp of smoke.

For a moment she lost herself in the fulfillment of the fantasy she'd carried since she was sixteen. Then she jerked away. "We'd best leave," she said in a firm voice.

"I apologize. It won't happen again—unless you want it to." He winked at her and jumped out of the buggy, untying the reins from a branch while she returned their plates to the picnic basket.

The clouds separated for a few seconds, and sunlight poured over Royal. Was the Lord sending her a message? She hugged her shawl closer, wishing she knew.

On the way back to town, they approached a buggy filled with girls she'd known in her class at the academy. Royal's head tilted in their direction as he tipped his hat.

Nelda Raines leaned forward and stared.

Curt stood to one side while Faith's grandfather opened the door and entered his house. Faith met them in the entry hall, her cheeks pink. He suspected she'd spent time with Royal Baxter. Working at the livery gave him the opportunity to see who rented carriages, and Rip had assigned the covered buggy to Baxter for the weekend.

Jealousy seared across his chest. From all he'd heard, Baxter was a ladies' man. Faith deserved someone better. Looking at her flushed face and sparkling eyes, he groaned inwardly. If only he could trust himself to be rid of the visions that blasted to the front of his brain when he least expected them, he'd ask for her hand tomorrow. In the meantime, he was welcome in her home. That would have to be enough for now.

Judge Lindberg crossed to Faith and kissed her cheek. "Too bad it rained. Did you cancel your picnic?"

Curt's ears perked up. Maybe she'd been alone after all.

"No, Royal said we'd go anyway, so we did." Her flush deepened when she glanced at Curt.

He willed himself not to frown. What Faith did was no concern of his. Not at all. None.

She turned to him. "I baked a Dolly Varden cake yesterday.

147

I'd be pleased if you'd join us for an evening treat." An expectant expression filled her face.

When she looked at him like that, he couldn't refuse. "Sounds good. Thank you."

"Glad you and Baxter didn't eat it all," her grandfather said, moving toward the dining table. "Cut me a big slice."

Curt fell in beside Faith as she entered the kitchen. "Can I help?"

She blinked as though his question surprised her. "Yes, if you want to." She lifted a cover from the cake and removed three small plates from a cupboard.

His mouth watered at the sight of the four-layer dessert, light and dark layers alternated with garnet red jelly spread between them. "I remember you served this the first time I visited your grandfather." He shook his head. "Never tasted anything better. Wish you'd give Rosemary the recipe."

She tipped slices onto plates. "I'd be happy to. If you don't mind waiting, I'll write it up tonight. You can take it home with you."

"Be glad to wait," he said, pleased to have a reason to linger.

Once Faith's grandfather finished his cake, he went to the parlor and settled in his wing chair by the fire. Curt cleared the table, then sat while Faith copied the recipe from a stained brown cookbook.

After a few moments, she laid the pencil aside. "Did Rosemary tell you about our . . . financial problems?" Worry lines etched her forehead.

Surprised at the switch in topics from cake to finances, he nodded.

"Did you say anything to Grandpa?"

"No. Rosemary cautioned me that you don't want him upset."

A relieved sigh escaped her lips, but the worry lines

remained. "I don't know what to do. I stayed awake half the night pondering the situation. There's a demand for supplies from people outfitting for the trail, yet we can't order new stock." Her eyes shone with tears. "Do you think I should try to sell the store, no matter what Grandpa and Mr. Paulson say?"

He wished he could kiss the tears from the corners of her eyes and promise everything would be all right. Instead, he reached across the table and covered her hand with his. "Why don't you let me look over the ledgers before you decide? Perhaps things aren't as bad as they seem."

"Would you?"

"I'll be there tomorrow right after you close."

She swallowed. "Not tomorrow. Mr. Baxter has asked to see me home."

Curt stamped up the steps and slammed into the living room of the house he shared with Rosemary.

She looked up from the open book on her lap. "Hush. You'll wake the Haddons."

He thrust a folded piece of paper at her. "This is from Faith. It's a recipe."

"Oh, good." She unfolded the sheet and glanced at the heading. "Dolly Varden cake. I'll thank her tomorrow." She placed the note between pages and closed her book. "Now, tell me why you're in such a black mood."

"That Baxter fellow. Faith seems smitten with him."

"Aren't you jumping to conclusions?"

"Hardly. I offered to help her with the ledgers tomorrow evening, but she can't spare the time. Baxter's coming to see her home."

Rosemary stood and placed a hand on his arm. "Did you offer to go on Tuesday?"

"No."

She released his arm and put her hands on her hips. "You may be my older brother, but sometimes I could shake you. She's not promised to Royal Baxter. If you're interested, why don't you ask her to go for a buggy ride? Or a walk on one of these spring evenings?"

"You know I can't risk it."

"Can't, or won't?"

He turned toward the door. "I'm going out for a while. Don't wait up."

"I'll tell her you'll be there Tuesday evening."

Faith perched on a stool next to Curt, who stood behind a counter flipping through last year's ledger. After several moments, during which the only sound was the whisper of pages turning, he snapped the book closed. "Challenging, to say the least."

"Can you make sense of any of it?" Her voice squeaked with apprehension.

He slid the current ledger in front of him, opened to Saturday's page. "Is this the way he taught you to make entries?"

"Yes. Write the name and the amount sold, or what I paid out for supplies." What had she been doing wrong?

"Where are the weekly totals? The monthly accounting? How do you know whether you're losing money or making a profit?"

She twisted her hands together. "Grandpa said he'd take care of that part."

"Faith." He rubbed his end-of-the-day whiskers while

drawing a deep breath. "Even though you know he's . . . confused sometimes, you still thought he was keeping track? Why?"

She slid off the stool and faced him, hands thrust against her hips. "You make it sound like I'm brainless. If you can't help me, just go away." At the stunned expression on his face, her anger deflated. "Forgive me." She ducked her head and spoke in a strangled voice. "I never had to pay attention to money. It was always there when we needed anything. I honestly didn't know there was more to do than take deposits to the bank." Her face burned. She *was* brainless.

Curt took her hands in his. "Let me take last year's ledger home with me. I'll make a list of names and amounts owed by the people he gave credit to. We'll start there." He released her hands and tucked the book under one arm.

"You said 'we.' You mean you'll teach me?" Her pulse quickened at the thought of his steady presence helping her make sense of their finances. If he told her what to do, she knew she could learn.

He nodded. "We'll have to find a way to work together without your grandfather knowing what we're doing. He may take it as criticism."

Grandpa's voice sounded from the entrance to the storeroom. "Take what as criticism?"

Faith jumped. She'd hoped he'd stay busy in his makeshift office until time to go home.

He marched across the room, his cane thudding. "You're not going behind my back to sell the store again, are you?"

"No. Curt is helping me understand . . . bookkeeping." She flinched inwardly at the half-truth. Once the accounts were corrected, she did hope to sell the mercantile before it was too late in the season to make the journey west. Then there was the matter of finding a driver . . .

151

"I've seen that look on your mother's face." Grandpa chucked her under the chin. "There's more to the story." He turned to Curt. "I'd rather have you hanging about than Baxter, but I don't see what business you have poking into my ledgers."

Curt's face reddened. "I need them to show her how to balance the accounts." He stammered out his reply.

"Find a textbook. Leave my ledgers alone."

Faith stood at her bedroom window in her nightdress, watching ragged clouds scatter the stars. She knew she should have been asleep hours ago. Curt promised to teach her how to total the ledgers, but how could he when Grandpa insisted the books remain in the store?

Maybe Curt could stop in during the noon hour. She shook her head. No. She and her grandfather ate dinner together every noon.

She could copy pages and send them home with Rosemary. No again. It would take forever to duplicate every entry made for the past year and a half.

Her eyelids drooped. Maybe tomorrow, after she'd had some sleep, her thoughts might be clearer. She stumbled to bed and pulled the covers up to her neck. There had to be a way.

When she unlocked the store the following morning, she still had no ideas. As she rolled up the shades, the woodstove regulars marched through the doorway and took their places on both sides of the checkerboard.

"Big doings today, Miss Faith," Mr. Slocum said, sounding like an announcer at an auction.

"What would that be?" She paused on her way to collect a feather duster from the storeroom.

"Going to get that engine back on the tracks. Horse teams will be here this morning. Railroad company sent a locomotive yesterday. It's sittin' next to the station, pretty as you please. Once the engine's upright, they'll tow it back to St. Louis."

Mr. Grisbee inclined his head in her direction. "You going to watch? Everybody will be there."

She remembered the last time most of the town gathered at the depot. Someone had stayed behind to rob the store. "Probably not. Grandpa would enjoy the excitement, though."

"We was planning to fetch him out of his hidey-hole." Mr. Grisbee arranged the game pieces on the board. "Got time for me to whup you before we go?" he asked Mr. Slocum.

"We'll see about that." He pushed a black checker forward.

Chuckling, Faith continued to the storeroom. Once the damaged engine had been moved, stranded passengers would be able to continue their journeys. She'd miss the extra activity in the mercantile, even though most of the visitors made no purchases.

She brushed the duster along shelves and countertops, half-listening to the regulars' good-natured bickering, when the sound of jangling harnesses and pounding hooves carried through the open door.

"Here they are!" Mr. Slocum hopped to his feet. "I'll go for Nate. Be right back." He zipped out the door, followed by Mr. Grisbee doing his fastest shuffle.

"Sure you don't want to come?" he asked.

"You can tell me about everything later." She waved the duster at him. "Enjoy yourselves." Outside, small groups of people hurried by, headed in the direction of the depot.

After the men left, she went to the storeroom and locked the entrance to the alley. Then she closed the front doors and laid an iron poker on the counter above the cash drawer. Just let someone try to rob them again.

She slid into one of the chairs and fixed her eyes on the door, but after several minutes her curiosity overcame her. She stepped onto the boardwalk and darted to the corner of Court Street, where she stood on tiptoe to try to see the tracks. No use. The crowd gathered at the station blocked her view. Disappointed, she turned around and collided with Curt.

"Oh!" She stumbled backward. "You startled me."

He put his hands on her shoulders to steady her. "Rip closed the stable so we could see the engine righted. Thought I'd keep an eye on the mercantile instead."

"I thought the same thing. That's why I stayed behind."

They exchanged a smile. Curt paused at the entrance and brushed straw from his trousers. "As long as I'm here, why don't you go watch the activity? I doubt any customers will come by."

"I'd rather stay here. I spent last night wondering how we could discuss the ledgers out of Grandpa's hearing. Seems like the Lord has provided the opportunity."

Curt sent her a conspiratorial grin. "That he has. Shall we get started?"

She placed last year's book on top of a counter and stood next to him while he opened it to the first page.

"Do you have a blank notebook I can use?"

Faith lifted one from a display on the shelf behind them and handed the lined sheets to him, along with a pencil. "You'll never get all that copied before everyone returns."

"Got to start somewhere. Here's my plan." He sketched columns on a sheet of paper. "We'll write the name here. What they bought here. What they owe here. Leave spaces between names so we can list additional amounts in case the same people have more than one outstanding debt." He tore the page out and handed it to Faith. "You start on the current ledger while I do this one."

She shook her head. "I still don't see how we can finish—"

"We don't have to. Not today." The creases at the corners of his mouth had an appealing way of curving upward when he smiled. "You weren't the only one who spent last night wondering how we'd accomplish our task."

Grateful for his use of the word "our," she clasped her hands atop the lined paper and raised her eyebrows in a question. "And?"

"I'll tell him I'm courting you. That way we can spend time together without your grandfather suspecting anything."

"Courting me?" The pulse in her throat throbbed. What would Royal think about having a rival? She blew out a breath. She'd cross that creek when she came to it.

"Not really courting," Curt added before she could say anything more. "Don't you see? I can call for you evenings, and we'll come here and copy accounts into this notebook. Then I can work on them at home and tell you who owes how much to your grandfather."

"Oh." She stifled an unreasonable wave of disappointment. "But what about Grandpa? I can't leave him alone."

"Has he ever wandered off at night?"

"No, because I'm always at home with him."

Curt shot her an annoyed glance. "You're not awake all night. If he wanted to slip out, you'd never know it until morning."

"Let's get busy, then." With a huff, she tugged the current ledger toward her and turned to a page that began with a paragraph about her great-grandfather's musical skills. She copied a customer's name and his purchase, then noted the cost in the third column.

"I thought you'd be pleased. You seem cross."

"I am pleased. Thank you for your help."

Curt studied her for a moment, then reached for the other ledger. The coarse fabric of his work shirt brushed her wrist.

He smelled clean, like rain and fresh-cut hay. Faith moved a few inches away, wishing she weren't so sensitive to his presence. She should be thinking about Royal—not someone who was merely pretending courtship.

Early Friday morning, Faith and her grandfather walked to the depot under dark skies to join the rest of the townspeople gathered to bid farewell to the stranded passengers. Clouds massed in the distance, promising a thunderstorm before nightfall.

Smoke poured from the stack of the eastbound train. As they arrived, the conductor stepped down from a passenger car. "Boarding! All aboard."

The Dunsmuirs separated from the group and made their way to Faith's side. "Thank you again," Amy said. "You were a blessing."

Joel tipped his hat. "Proud to know you, miss." They hurried toward the train.

Several of the women who'd spent time in the mercantile paused to repeat thanks and good-byes before boarding. Faith dabbed at her eyes with a handkerchief. "It's silly to miss people I've only known for a short time."

Grandpa patted her shoulder. "You have a soft heart, just like your mama's." A grin lifted his moustache. "It makes up for your iron will."

She snickered through her tears. Rosemary joined them, her arm linked through Cassie Haddon's. The bruises had disappeared from Cassie's face, but her woebegone expression remained. Mrs. Haddon walked behind them, her nose wrinkled as though she were entering a stockyard.

The conductor repeated the boarding call. Cassie turned

and clasped Rosemary in a fierce hug, then turned on her heel and followed her mother toward the train, boarding without a backward glance.

"Takes all kinds," Grandpa said. "Good thing they had you folks to stay with."

Rosemary looked around at the gathered townspeople. "Most everyone rallied to help." Her gaze landed on Dr. Greeley. "Some were more openhearted than others."

Faith glanced past her. "Did Curt come with you?"

"He and Mr. Ripley are around here somewhere. I expect most all the businesses are opening late today."

"There you are." A masculine voice boomed behind them.

Faith whirled, expecting to see Curt. Instead, Royal beamed at her. "I've been hoping for a glimpse of the prettiest girl in town before I had to return to work." He stood close enough for her to notice the raw oak aroma clinging to his sawdust-covered clothing. His dark eyes slid over her face. "Will I see you Sunday afternoon?"

She hesitated. If Curt were going to pretend to court her, they should spend Sunday together. But he hadn't said anything. Surely he didn't expect her to wait on his whims.

Royal watched her, a grin on his face. "That wasn't supposed to be a hard question. Yes or no?"

"Yes. Two o'clock."

"Good. I'll be there." He sprinted west toward the cooperage.

Grandpa harrumphed. "I don't trust that fellow. There's something about him—"

The train's bell clanged and with a clashing of cars it rolled from the station. Faith waved at the faces in the windows, one arm tucked through her grandfather's. In his eyes she was still a little girl. He probably wouldn't like anyone who came courting.

The afternoon dragged. Flies bumping against the windows and the scratching of her pencil were the only sounds in the mercantile. The best thing Faith could say about a lack of customers was it gave her the opportunity to copy ledger entries. At this rate, she'd have this year's book completed before Curt ever began on his share of the work. *If* he began. Since they'd made their plan, he hadn't contacted her.

She flipped to a fresh page and saw *20327* written across the bottom. She stared at the numbers, puzzled. They couldn't be a date—Grandpa had entered that at the top of the sheet. Faith rubbed the back of her neck. *20327* had nothing to do with the total for the goods. In fact, there was no total. He'd evidently sold several pieces of cookware, a set of crockery plates, and table utensils without entering the cost. Now she'd have to check the shelves for prices before she could continue her task.

Exasperated, she smacked her pencil down next to the ledger. "Oh, Grandpa," she muttered under her breath. "Why didn't you ask for help long ago?" After brushing past the cookstoves, she stopped in front of shelves holding kitchen goods and climbed a ladder to the one holding copper coffeepots. Once she found the cost, she reached in her apron pocket for a pencil and paper and remembered she'd left them behind. Gritting her teeth, she backed down the ladder and marched to the counter. She should have known she wouldn't get through the ledger entries easily. Where *was* Curt?

"Miss Lindberg?"

She spun around. A tall man leaned against a display case, holding a brown slouch hat in one hand. "I'm Alonzo McGuire. You come to see me at West & Riley's a couple weeks ago."

Heat crept up her neck at the memory of his mocking dismissal. "I know who you are, Mr. McGuire. Do you need something from the mercantile?" She kept her voice one degree above icy.

He fingered the brim of his hat. "Thing is, I want to apologize. I was at the hotel when that train plowed off the tracks. Saw how you took charge of them folks, tending to the hurt ones, feedin' 'em and all."

At the sound of Grandpa's cane, Faith turned to see him coming from the storeroom. He advanced on Mr. McGuire with his hand extended. "You're the wagon master. We talked for a spell down at the tracks the day of the fire."

"Yes, sir. I remember. So you're Miss Lindberg's grandpap?"

"Nate Lindberg in the flesh. You here for supplies?"

"He was just leaving." Faith held her breath, hoping he wouldn't mention her visit to West & Riley's.

"Well, no, I wasn't, miss. I come to say that you and your grandpap are welcome to travel with our company. After watching you, I believe you're up to it." He smiled at both of them. "We'll be leaving a week from Monday. Reckon you're set to go?"

Faith stammered a reply. "Not yet. I mean . . . we won't be joining you. Circumstances have changed." She knitted her fingers together, nails pressing into her palms. Would they ever be ready? Tears stung her eyes at the thought of the wagons leaving—without them—in ten days.

Grandpa turned to her, his face thunderous. "You already talked to this man about joining his company? Without telling me?" His voice rose. "What's gotten into you?"

Mr. McGuire backed toward the door. "Sorry to disturb you folks." He clapped his hat over his grizzled hair. "You change your mind, let me know." He directed the last comment at Faith before fleeing.

Faith stared after his retreating form. He would have taken them west. *Why, Lord? Why did things turn out this way?* Shoulders sagging, she walked to one of the chairs and sank onto the smooth wooden seat.

A moment of silence passed before Grandpa moved next to her and lowered himself into another chair. He drew several deep breaths before speaking. "I had no idea the thought of going to Oregon was this important to you. First you try to sell my store and now I find you've gone behind my back to arrange for wagon passage." He bit off the words.

"I didn't think of it as going behind your back. We talked about the trip. I was just getting everything ready for the day the store changed hands." She pointed at the empty gun rack. "Now it appears the day is a long ways off."

"Is that so bad?"

"Not if I wanted to stay in Noble Springs, but I don't." She leaned over and laid her hand over his wrinkled one. "Everywhere I look there's a memory of someone I loved who's gone. I want to live somewhere with grass and flowers and trees and a future. All we have here is the past."

He rested a sorrowful gaze on her. "The past is your future,

Faith. You're a child of these hills, whether you realize it or not. Our people have always lived here."

"Not always. Once upon a time they came from Virginia. You say so in your memoir. Why can't it be our turn to move west?"

He closed his eyes for a moment, then pushed himself to his feet. "All right. I'll think on it some more."

"Really?" She jumped up and kissed his cheek. "Thank you."

"What is it you're thinking on, Judge?" Curt ambled over the threshold.

"Faith here is wearing me down on the subject of Oregon." Grandpa shot her a glance that was more irritated than loving. "Only way I can get any peace is to promise to consider what she says." He headed for the rear entrance, mumbling as he went. "This whole thing reminds me of when I enlisted to go fight in Mexico. I'm going to write everything down. You want me, I'll be out in my workroom." The burlap curtain swayed as he passed through.

Curt grinned at her. "So talking to you reminds him of going to war."

"I'm sure that's not what he meant—and it's about time you got here. We can work on the ledgers while Grandpa's busy writing."

"Can't stay right now. Came by to ask if you wanted to take a stroll with me Sunday afternoon." He winked. "Might as well start this courtship."

Why did she tell Royal she'd see him Sunday? If Grandpa were willing to consider leaving, working with Curt on the ledgers was more important than showing her former schoolmates that she could interest a dashing bachelor. "I already have an engagement for Sunday." She bit her lower lip. "I'm sorry." As she said the words, she realized she meant them, and not only because she needed help with finances.

Disappointment flickered across his face before his eyes narrowed. "I'm helping you because Rosemary asked me to. When you think you can make time for me, let her know. She'll give me the message."

Faith leaned forward when Royal directed the buggy north instead of continuing west. "I thought we were going to the lake."

He shook the reins and urged the horse up Spring Street's steep incline. "Not today. I feel like doing something different."

Uneasy, she shifted on the seat.

The road leveled off, winding past dense groves of oak. Black willows outlined a clear stream that gurgled past limestone outcroppings. Somewhere out of sight a whip-poor-will called.

Be cheerful, Faith reminded herself, trying to shake off her growing dread as they traveled farther north. She gave Royal a bright smile. "What makes today special?"

"Hoped you'd ask." He slipped an arm around her shoulder and squeezed, then dropped his hand back to the reins before she had time to object. "I been thinking on how to get my battlefield rank when I enlist, and came up with an idea. Some of the men I met during the war were sent from a fort in Oregon." He stopped, as if that comment explained everything.

Faith waited a moment for more, then asked, "How is that a plan?"

"I'll go to Oregon and enlist there. I heard the fort was being run by civilians after the war started. The soldiers were sent east to join regiments."

"You never mentioned Oregon before. Going there has been my dream since the war ended, but Grandpa won't leave until we sell the store." She felt a thrill of interest. "Where is this fort?"

"Slap in the middle of the Willamette valley. Army put it there to keep Indians and settlers apart. Heard it's real pretty—meadows, good soil. A man could have himself a right nice home once he quit soldiering." He sent her a side-long glance. "Lots of wildflowers for his wife to pick."

She sucked in a breath when he mentioned marriage. "When . . . when are you going?"

"I have to get the money together so I can sign on with a wagon company. I've got some side jobs in mind." Leaning close, he touched her with his shoulder. With one eyebrow raised, he said, "Then I'll be asking someone to be my wife."

He pulled back on the reins and guided the horse through a wrought iron fence. "Thought you'd like the view from the top of this hill."

Faith froze. "This is the cemetery." Her heart thudded in her chest, making it difficult to breathe. "Get me out of here. Now."

"You're white as that dress you're wearing." He put an arm around her and drew her close, patting her shoulder. "No one's going to hurt you here. They're all dead." She heard suppressed laughter in his voice.

Perspiration popped out on her forehead. "Please. I . . ." Gray mist swirled around Royal's face. His image receded. As though coming from a great distance, she heard him slap the reins over the horse's back.

"Giddup." The buggy jolted forward.

When she opened her eyes, they'd left the cemetery fence behind and were rolling toward town. She took several deep breaths to clear her head.

Royal slowed the horse to a walk. "You all right? What happened to you?"

"I've had nightmares about that place ever since I was a child. I know it's silly, but I can't seem to forget."

He looked at her with a confused expression. "You going to tell me, or do I have to guess?"

"A bit after Mama died, my brother took me with him to put flowers on her grave. It was dusk and I guess he thought it was funny to sneak off and leave me there. But then it got pitch dark." She wiped sweating palms on her skirt. "I called and called, and he didn't answer. I ran, looking for him, then something reached out and grabbed my ankle. I fell flat on top of a grave." Faith held her hand against her chest, feeling the thump of her heart. "Anyway, when Maxwell came for me, I was hysterical. He pointed out that I'd only tripped over a honeysuckle vine, but it made no difference." She shuddered. "When we got home, my father fixed me warm milk and put me to bed, then marched Maxwell to the woodshed and gave him a good hiding."

Royal gestured up the road in the direction of the cemetery. "So all that carrying-on was about something that happened years ago? Time you got over it, Faith." He shook the reins and the horse resumed a trot.

She shouldn't have said anything. Royal liked to keep the conversation light. For a moment she thought of Curt. Something about his nature told her he would have understood. But Curt wasn't courting her. Royal was, and Royal intended to go to Oregon.

A week later, Faith stood with Rosemary on the lawn at the foot of the church steps. "It was good of Reverend French

to pray for the wagon company," Rosemary said. "I imagine
more than a few of the women are nervous about leaving
tomorrow." She squeezed Faith's arm. "I'm glad you aren't
going with them."

"I can't pretend I'm not disappointed."

"The Lord has other plans. If he means for you to go, there
will be plenty of other opportunities."

Faith thought about Royal. "Perhaps so. We'll see." She
fanned herself. "I wish Grandpa would hurry on out here so
we can go home. It's terribly warm in the sun."

Three young women came down the steps and joined them.
She smiled at Hilda and Marguerite, suppressing a groan
at Nelda's presence. Faith introduced Rosemary, noticing
that her former classmates greeted her friend with the same
warmth they'd have used if she were a leper.

Nelda moved to Faith's side. "I saw you and Mr. Baxter a
couple of weeks ago riding in from the country in a covered
buggy. He's going to ruin your reputation if you're not careful." Her pale lashes blinked rapidly. "As your friend, I feel
it's my duty to warn you, since you have no mother."

"Nelda. Come over here." A buxom woman wearing an
overabundance of ruffles waved from across the lawn.

Faith watched as Nelda scuttled toward Mrs. Raines.
Perhaps there were worse things than not having a mother—
having one like Mrs. Raines, for instance.

Marguerite winked at her. "Nelda can't get over Royal
Baxter favoring you. She's swooned over him since before
the war. Tell me, what's your secret?"

Pretty and vivacious, Marguerite had always been the girl
most sought after at dances and other social events. Faith
couldn't prevent a smile from crossing her face at the thought
of her former classmate asking *her* for advice. She chuckled.
"It's as much a surprise to me as it is to you."

Rosemary stepped next to her. "Maybe it's Faith's kind nature."

"No doubt." Marguerite's voice turned chilly when she spoke to Rosemary. "She does tend to welcome the oddest people."

Her rudeness gave Faith another reason to wish she could leave Noble Springs. How could she ever have envied girls like Marguerite?

She took Rosemary's arm. "Let's find your brother. It's time we left."

Faith rolled her shoulders to loosen tight muscles. Across the counter, Curt scribbled names and amounts into a notebook. He flipped to a new page and stopped. "What's this?"

She leaned over and followed his pointing finger. *20327.* "I don't know—I've run across those numbers a few times in this ledger too. I hoped you'd have an answer."

"Doesn't mean anything to me." He rubbed his temple. "You know how your grandfather can be forgetful. Maybe these numbers jumped into his mind and he wrote them down, like he does his stories."

Faith doubted the explanation. Grandpa's stories were random. This set of numbers was consistent.

Curt straightened. "Maybe they're a combination for a lock. Does he keep a money box at home?"

"I've never seen one." A draft blew across her feet. The burlap curtain that concealed the entrance to the storeroom slid forward, then dropped back. She glanced at the front door, but it remained closed. A prickle of alarm marched up her spine. "Did you feel that?" she asked Curt in a whisper.

"What?"

"Cool air, like someone opened a door." She kept her voice low. "You don't suppose Grandpa followed us, do you?"

"It's late. He's probably fast asleep."

A floorboard creaked.

Curt's eyes widened. He tugged off his boots and laid them down without making a sound, then slid from his chair and crept toward the storeroom.

Faith gripped the edge of the counter, listening to the thrum of her heart. Her grandfather would never sneak up on them. She wished she'd listened when he suggested she keep a revolver under the cash drawer.

With a swift movement, Curt flung open the curtain. She hoped he had enough light from the lamp overhead to see into the room. Boots thudded. Another burst of outside air lifted the burlap. She heard crates being shoved aside as Curt pushed his way to the alley door. Then the bolt slid into place and he padded back to the circle of light.

"Couldn't see a face. Might've been another one in the alley." He pinned her with a stern glance. "Why wasn't that door bolted?"

"I leave it open during the day so Grandpa can come and go." She fought to control the quiver in her voice. "I just forgot to secure it when we left today."

He gathered her hands in his. "You've got to be more careful. You've been robbed once, and it looks to me like whoever it was came back for more." The expression on his face conveyed a depth to his feelings she hadn't seen before.

She swallowed the flutter in her throat at the sensation of his large hands enclosing hers. *What would it be like—?*

Stop it, she told herself. *He's only worried about a robbery.* Drawing away, she lifted a pencil. "Maybe we should see if we can finish this tonight."

Curt's face flushed. He took his boots from the countertop

and slid his feet into them. "I'd rather look around outside. We'll finish another time." He closed the ledger he'd been using. "Stay here. I'll walk you home in a few minutes."

After he left, she leaned forward and rested her head on her arms. Her whole body trembled. *Thank you, Lord, that Curt was here.*

18

*T*wo evenings later, Faith and Curt stood in the mercantile beaming at each other. "We did it." She held up the list of uncollected debts. Names covered two pages, including those who had the mysterious numbers below their purchases. She turned and paced toward empty shelves. "We'll soon be able to replace our stocks."

She swung around and faced Curt. "I can't thank you enough. I'd never have been able to do this without you."

A pleased smile crossed his face. "Now you need to remember to keep track like I showed you, so you'll always know how much you have in the bank."

"I will." She thought again how handsome he looked when his eyes crinkled at the corners.

"You may not be able to collect from everyone."

Deflated, she eyed him. "Why not?"

"These are hard times. Some folks won't have the money. That's why they ran up a debt in the first place."

She rattled the list in front of him. "There are customers on here who come in every week. They just need a reminder. I'll start first thing tomorrow with Mrs. Wylie. She's had her eye on that glass caster set over there, and she said she'd be in Friday to buy it."

He gave her an indulgent look. "I hope everything goes as smoothly as you think it will."

"Why wouldn't it?" She shook her head. Curt could be so gloomy at times.

Faith turned to Rosemary when she saw Mrs. Wylie approach the front doors. "She's the first person I plan to ask about paying up old accounts. Grandpa said not to give her credit, but he didn't tell me about their back debts. I know they have the money."

Rosemary raised her eyebrows. "Maybe I should talk to her. Let her be angry with me, rather than you."

"My grandfather got us into this. It's up to me to get us out."

"Then I'll be in the back praying." She squeezed Faith's hand. "Call me if I can help."

Faith turned toward the door when the bell chimed, arranging her face in her brightest smile. "Good morning, Mrs. Wylie. Are you here for the caster set?"

"I want to take one more look before I decide." She swept past in a cloud of lavender scent. After fingering one of the pressed glass cruets, she turned. "This set will do nicely. You'll have it delivered?"

"I'm afraid not, ma'am. It's too small an item to warrant hiring a horse." Faith held her breath. They needed this sale.

The yellow flowers on Mrs. Wylie's bonnet quivered. "I wish your grandfather was here. He's a more accommodating person."

Faith lifted the caster set by its silver handle and carried it to a counter where she kept a stack of newsprint. Placing one of the cruets on a sheet, she tucked the edges under and rolled the paper tight. "I wish he were still interested too, but he's placed me in charge." She set the wrapped piece aside and picked up the next one, her hands busy while she talked. "Speaking of my grandfather, he allowed your husband credit for a selection of woodworking tools last fall. When you settle for the caster set, I'd appreciate it if you could clear that debt from our books."

Mrs. Wylie's face turned the color of a boiled crawdad. "Mr. Wylie gives me money for the household. He'll have to settle his own accounts."

Faith felt perspiration tickle under her bodice. She opened the cash drawer. "There's also the matter of a toiletry set, a perfume vial, and a porcelain doll. These would be your purchases, I assume?"

"We made our arrangements with Judge Lindberg. You have no right . . ." She sputtered to a stop.

"Yes I do, Mrs. Wylie. We depend on the mercantile for our livelihood." She held her voice steady, praying that the quaking she felt inside wasn't visible to her customer.

The woman's eyes darted between the wrapped caster set and the open cash drawer. With her mouth set in a grim line, she opened her reticule and handed Faith three five-dollar gold pieces. "This should be sufficient." Her voice could have frozen a July day.

Faith checked her list. "I'm afraid not. If you would ask your husband to drop by, I'll go over the balance with him."

When Mrs. Wylie left with her purchase bulging the sides of her carryall, Faith's knees buckled. She grabbed the edge of the counter to keep from sinking to the floor. This was nowhere as easy as she thought it would be. There were two pages of people who owed money to the mercantile. She couldn't afford to make that many enemies.

Bodie padded over to her and bumped his nose against her leg. Faith reached down and stroked his head. "At least you're not angry with me, are you?"

"That's why I like having a dog. They always love you," Rosemary said, making her way toward the front. She made a "tsk" sound with her tongue. "I could hear Mrs. Wylie clear back in the storeroom."

"At least she paid part of their bill." She subtracted the woman's payment from the amount due. "I don't look forward to speaking with her husband, though, provided she gives him the message."

"Why are you putting yourself through this?"

Faith massaged her temples. "Right now, I'm not sure. I wanted to have the shelves fully stocked before asking Grandpa again if he'd agree to sell the business. Royal thinks we should take what we can get right now."

"Why is this his concern? I know you've been seeing a lot of him, but still . . . Has he spoken of his intentions?"

"Not directly. He's hinted a bit, though."

Rosemary put a hand on her arm. "Congratulations. From what I hear, it's a feather in your cap to have captured his interest." Her smile didn't quite reach her eyes.

"I'm not sure how I feel about him. His attention is flattering, but I disagree with his opinion about selling. Not that I'm attached to the mercantile, but Grandpa has poured his life into this store. To just let it go in this state seems . . . disrespectful."

The bell over the door chimed. "I'm sure you'll do the right thing," Rosemary said, turning to greet their customer.

What was the right thing? Faith wished she knew. Without Grandpa's permission, she couldn't put the mercantile up for sale even if she could collect all the back debts. She slipped down the aisle between the stoves and the wall where the firearms had been displayed. The empty case that had held watches looked sad and dusty. She tightened her jaw. Lindberg's Mercantile had been a leading business in the community for as long as she could remember. She couldn't let it die now.

Thunderclouds bruised the sky to the southwest. Faith kept her arm tucked under her grandfather's as they walked home through the humid June evening. When they approached Ripley's Livery, she craned her neck to see if Curt might be inside. She had something important to ask him, if she could leave Grandpa for a moment.

"You looking for your young man?" he asked.

Faith drew a quick breath. "He's not my young man. We're friends."

"Doesn't seem like it to me, with all the evenings he's called to take you out for a stroll. You could do worse, you know. Like that Baxter fellow. Told you before, I don't think he's been honest with us."

She bit her lower lip. "You're not being fair. Once you get to know Royal, you'll like him."

"Bet he can't play chess."

"Evening, Judge, Faith," Mr. Ripley called from the entrance to the stable. He wiggled his eyebrows at Faith. "Reckon you're looking for Curt. He's already gone home. I'll tell him you was here, though."

"Thank you." She glanced between him and Grandpa. Let them think what they wanted. "Would you ask him to stop by the store tomorrow sometime if it's convenient?"

His eyes twinkled. "Sure thing. I don't mind playing Cupid."

She opened her mouth to object, then closed it. The more she protested, the less convincing she sounded.

An arrow of lightning zigzagged from one of the clouds, followed by a rumble of thunder. Grateful for the distraction, Faith tugged at Grandpa's arm. "We'd better get in before this hits."

When they reached their front walk, a wagon rumbled to a stop next to the hitching rail. A fleshy man wearing canvas pants and a rumpled plaid shirt jumped down and poked a finger in Grandpa's chest. "My poor wife come home sore upset today, thanks to this gal right here."

Faith cringed. This could only be Mr. Wylie. As far as she knew, she hadn't offended anyone else's wife.

Grandpa confirmed her suspicions when he said, "Calm down, Wylie. Come in and tell me what's bothering you." He used his authoritative Judge Lindberg voice.

"Nope. Ain't got time. Just wanted to give you this." He handed Grandpa a bank draft. "You can close your books on us. We'll go to Hartfield from now on." The irate man stomped back to his wagon and rattled away.

Once inside, Grandpa peered at the draft. "Eighteen dollars." His forehead wrinkled. "What in the name of heaven did you do to Mrs. Wylie?"

Faith removed her shawl and hung it on the hall tree, stalling for time while she thought of a way to tell him about collecting their debts. She'd hoped she'd be able to order new stock without Grandpa learning about their lack of finances. A look at his confused expression told her it was too late.

"The Wylies owed us more than thirty dollars. This morning I asked Mrs. Wylie for the money."

"Thirty dollars! How'd you come up with that?"

"Let's sit in the kitchen and I'll tell you."

He stalked ahead of her, his cane rapping on the floor.

"This better be good. I've known Cletus Wylie for a number of years. Never saw him so angry."

As Faith explained her encounter with the banker and her subsequent investigation of the ledgers, Grandpa looked stricken. She was careful not to mention Curt's involvement. The idea had been hers.

She concluded, "So I made a list of debts, and plan to collect them. We can't get new merchandise unless we pay cash."

He leaned toward her, both of his hands clasped over the top of his cane. "You be mighty careful when you talk to folks. I won't have you raising a ruckus all over town."

"Mr. Wylie raised the ruckus. I didn't. Not everyone will be so touchy." She prayed she was right.

Curt grinned at his employer. "She asked for me?"

"Sure did. Looked disappointed you wasn't here too." Rip cut open a bag of oats and scooped some into a bucket. "You want to run down there right now?"

"Might as well." Curt attempted to sound casual. "Shouldn't be gone long."

When he passed the courthouse, Sheriff Cooper hailed him from the jail building across the street. "Got a couple questions for you, Saxon."

Curt sprinted over. "Did you find the thieves who robbed the mercantile?"

"That's what I want to talk to you about. Miss Faith says she had another intruder last week."

"Yup. I ran him off, but never got to see his face. Guess she told you that."

"So you were the only one who saw him." The sheriff

surveyed Curt, his gaze pausing at his neck before traveling to his face. "How'd you get that scar? Not a rope burn, is it?"

A chill doused Curt's insides. "Rebel knife." He took a step backward, narrowing his eyes. "What're you getting at?"

"You and that sister of yours spend a lot of time at Judge Lindberg's store. Then expensive merchandise turns up missing. Makes a man wonder."

"While you're wondering, you might check some of the stragglers camped in the hills. I don't think it's likely a thief will come walking up to you and ask to be arrested." Curt spoke through gritted teeth.

Sheriff Cooper rested his hand on the hitching post in front of the jail. "Mind yourself, Saxon. I've got my eye on you."

Curt raised his hat in a mocking salute and strode toward the mercantile, enraged. The sheriff wouldn't have looked at him twice if not for the scar. Memories of supercilious officers ticked through his mind. He wondered if rank made men bullies, or whether they were bullies to start with. When he entered the store, he was still angry.

Faith hurried over, smiling. "I'm so glad to see you." She took a second glance at him and her smile vanished. She jammed her hands on her hips. "You look like someone marched you here with a rifle to your back. You didn't have to come, you know."

He pulled off his hat and swiped his forehead with his shirtsleeve. "I'm here, aren't I?"

A hurt expression crossed her face. She didn't respond.

Curt felt the pain he was inflicting. "Sorry." He tried to smile. "What did you want?"

She studied him for a moment, then evidently deciding he was sincere, said, "I need help with the lists we made."

"You found more names?"

"No." She walked behind the counter and pushed the pages

in his direction. Spots of color showed in her cheeks. "I spoke to Mrs. Wylie yesterday about what they owed and stirred up a hornet's nest. She'll never shop here again. Then Mr. Wylie came to the house last evening and hollered at Grandpa." She shook her head. "I didn't think of this until after Mr. Wylie left, but I can't go out in the evenings to collect debts from customers—particularly the men. And I don't dare trust Grandpa out alone at night. Could you please talk to some of these people?"

She looked fragile standing at a counter with floor-to-ceiling shelves looming behind her. Much as he admired Judge Lindberg, he questioned the man's decision to turn such a large enterprise over to Faith. Of course, he'd never say as much to her.

A thought came unbidden. *Take her in your arms and kiss the worry lines from her forehead.* He forced the impulse away, angry for allowing his thoughts to take him where he had no right to go.

He compelled himself to focus on the sheet in front of him. "I don't work here. How would your customers feel about me telling them to pay up?"

"I'll give you a letter of introduction." Her teary blue eyes pleaded with him.

Curt knew he'd lost the battle. "Let me see what I can do. There are several names here I recognize."

A smile spread over her face. "Thank you." While he reviewed the lists, she wrote a brief message on a fresh sheet of paper and handed it to him.

Curt folded the letter and the lists of names and tucked the pages in his pocket. "Give me a few days. I'll go evenings after the livery closes. Meantime, if any of these folks come in, you talk to them." He squeezed her hand. "You can do it."

"I don't know how to thank you."

"That's what friends are for."

At the end of the day, Curt stopped at home to change his clothes, then stepped out into the sticky evening to walk to Ivar Harrison's house. By starting with people he knew best, he hoped to shorten the task. Harrisons lived not far from the livery and had rented a buggy from them more than once.

Curt's knock was answered by a pretty blonde woman. A boy of about seven peered around a doorway to the right.

"I wonder if I could have a word with your husband, ma'am."

She nodded and left him standing on the porch while she walked past the boy. He eyed Curt, then scuttled after her. In a moment, Ivar appeared. His spectacles were perched on top of his springy dark hair. "Saxon. What brings you here?"

"A matter of business. You may know Miss Lindberg is now managing her grandfather's mercantile."

"Yes. Heard that."

"Things got a little out of hand there the past year or so. She's asked my help in collecting a few back debts." He handed him the letter of introduction.

"Why are you telling me this? I don't owe the judge any money."

Curt cleared his throat. "Appears you do." He showed Ivar the amount written next to his name.

The man shook his head and continued to shake it while he spoke. "Judge Lindberg said that was between him and me. There'd be no debt." He glanced over his shoulder, then stepped onto the porch and closed the door behind him. "Our house burned down last year. Lost every last thing and had to start over." He lowered his voice. "The judge gave us cookware and blankets and such. *Gave* it to us. Said we could do the same for someone else one day."

Curt rubbed the back of his neck. Why would Harrison's

name be entered if the judge didn't charge him for the merchandise?

Ivar broke the momentary silence. "Couldn't pay you now anyway. Had to quit my job so we could move to St. Louis to take care of the wife's mother. She's poorly." He sighed. "Hated to leave the academy with no mathematics teacher, but couldn't be helped."

"We must've made a mistake. Sorry I bothered you." Curt studied the figures on his list. It was Harrison's word against the ledger, and somehow the man didn't seem like a liar.

He hoped he'd have more success at his next stop, which was—he consulted his list—Jesse Slocum's house on Third Street. Rosemary had mentioned the man often. Faith called him one of the woodstove regulars.

How could Slocum visit the mercantile almost daily and not settle his debt? Curt thought of what Faith said about Mr. Wylie's explosion and crossed his fingers. He'd promised to help, and help he would.

He stepped up to the door of a tidy cottage set back from the street. On one side of the property a vegetable garden flourished. He noticed mustard greens and onion tops in the first rows. Sucking in a breath, he knocked.

After a moment of silence, he knocked again.

"No need to beat the door down. I was coming." Jesse Slocum stood in stocking feet, one suspender hanging loose. "You're Miss Rosemary's brother, ain't you? What brings you over this way?"

"Helping Miss Faith collect some leftover debts." He hoped his smile looked friendly. "Seems the judge has been a little lax the past year or so."

"You'd be lax, too, if'n you lost your son and grandson at the same time." He gave Curt a sharp glance. "Looks like you know a thing or two about battles yourself." Swinging the door wide, he said, "Come on in. Tell me what Nate has me down for and I'll get you the money. Been meaning to take care of this."

After two more successful stops, Curt walked toward home. Maybe Ivar Harrison's response was an anomaly. He hoped so. He enjoyed being able to provide something Faith needed.

He paused at the entrance to West & Riley's, pondering whether to have supper there or go home and see if Rosemary had saved anything for him. A man rode past seated on a tall black stallion, his hat brim shadowing his face. Baxter. Couldn't mistake that horse. Or the arrogant tilt to the man's chin.

He had to be going to call on Faith. Curt clenched his fists. The evenings they'd spent with the ledgers had started to feel like a real courtship. Weeks had passed since he'd had any recurring visions of wartime. It was time to let her know how he felt.

Curt slipped into the shadows and trailed after horse and rider. Once he reached the Lindbergs' home he'd tell her, even if he had to say his piece in front of Baxter.

As he passed Dr. Greeley's office, he heard someone ask, "Going somewhere, Saxon?" Sheriff Cooper stepped out from the shadows. "Been noticing you around town this evening. Let's see what you've got in that bag."

19

*G*randpa glowered at Royal from his wing chair across the parlor. "So you say you knew my son, but you can't tell me what he looked like. Maybe you didn't know him at all."

"Grandpa. Please. Royal came for a pleasant visit, not an interrogation." Faith glanced between the two men from her position at one end of the sofa.

Royal sat at the other end, a cup of tea balanced in one hand. "Our paths crossed, I'm sure. We didn't often have a father and son serving together. But know him?" Royal placed his cup and saucer on a side table. "There wasn't time for that. Wish I could tell you more."

Grandpa made a derisive sound. "You play chess?"

"No, sir, I don't."

Faith saw her grandfather mouth, "Told you so" as he rose to his feet. "It's getting late. Reckon you'll want to be on your way."

She shot an apologetic look at Royal.

He dropped a wink in her direction, his expression unperturbed. "I came by to ask Faith if she'd like to attend a musicale next Friday evening. Now that the trains are moving again, a gentleman's quartet will be here from St. Louis."

"I'd enjoy that. Thank you," Faith said, hoping to head off any more remarks from Grandpa.

"Good." Royal took her hand and kissed her fingertips. "Until next Friday. Now if you'll be kind enough to see me to the door, I'll be on my way."

She lingered on the porch a moment, watching him ride toward town. A tiny thrill passed through her. If Marguerite were to be believed, Faith was the envy of half the girls she knew. What an amazing turn of events.

The next morning, Faith hummed as she prepared for church. Maybe Royal would be there. She wished she'd invited him. Grandpa's rudeness had her so flustered she hadn't been thinking. After checking her reflection in the pier glass on her wall, she sped downstairs. Curt and Rosemary would arrive any moment to take them to services.

Grandpa waited in the parlor, apparently over being crotchety. "Maybe afterwards Curt would like a game of chess. You'd like to spend time with Miss Rosemary, wouldn't you?"

"Sounds lovely. Rosemary and I are often too busy at the store to visit much."

Saxons' buggy stopped out front, Rosemary holding the reins. Faith put a hand to her mouth. A long time had passed since Curt missed church because of headaches. She hurried to the door and opened it just as Rosemary raised her hand to knock.

"You've got to come right away. Curt's in jail."

Faith clutched her grandfather's arm as they pushed through the jailhouse door. The stone building stank of stale food, vomit, and unemptied slop pails. She covered her nose with a handkerchief. An interior door comprised of flat metal bars crisscrossed in narrow rectangles blocked the stairs leading to the basement where prisoners were held. Her stomach clenched at the thought of Curt being locked up because of her.

Sheriff Cooper rose and nodded at them. "Judge Lindberg. I didn't expect you this morning. Or you either, Miss Faith." His gaze slid over to Rosemary. "Figured you was bluffing when you said the judge would vouch for your brother."

Faith pounded her fist on his desk. "This is an outrage, Sheriff. Mr. Saxon has been a blessing to Grandpa and me. I can't tell you how many times he's stepped in to help us. Let him out this minute!"

"Whoa now. He claims you asked him to go knocking on doors to collect money. That's where he got that bag full of coins."

Faith opened her eyes wide. "A bag full? That's splendid." She cupped her hands around her mouth. "Thank you, Curt," she yelled through the barred door.

"Wait a minute," Grandpa said to her. "You sent Curt to collect those debts? Thought you were going to do it. Shouldn't be his job."

"That's my opinion, Judge," the sheriff said. "Thought I'd better lock him up."

"Now unlock him." Faith gripped her fingers together. "Grandpa and I will straighten out our misunderstanding. Regardless of who's right, Mr. Saxon is innocent. Didn't he show you the letter of introduction I gave him?"

"He did. Not that I believed it. Anyone can write a letter."

"Let him out, Thaddeus," Grandpa said.

Grabbing a key ring, Sheriff Cooper flung open the barred door. His boot heels echoed on the wooden steps, then they heard keys jingle and the screech of iron on iron. In a moment he reentered the room with Curt at his heels.

Rosemary rushed to Curt and studied him. "Are you . . . all right?"

"Yes. Fine." He glared at the sheriff. "Like I told you, that bag of coins belongs to Miss Lindberg. I know how much was in there, so don't try to cheat her."

"You're not making a friend of me, Saxon. Lucky for you the judge is here, or you'd be right back in that cell."

Faith held out her hand. "The money, please."

After he handed the bag to her, she turned to Curt. "I am so sorry. We'll make it up to you somehow."

He returned her gaze with an expression that melted her all the way to her toes.

The following Friday evening, Faith couldn't help stealing occasional glances at Royal during the musicale performance. He looked over at her and smiled, then turned his attention back to the stage. Or appeared to. Marguerite had swished up to them when they arrived, batting her vivid green eyes as she demanded an introduction. Once they were seated, she'd placed herself across the center aisle, giving Royal an unobstructed view of her trim figure sheathed in teal green watered silk. Faith felt certain his eyes had drifted from the performers more than once.

On the stage at the front of the hotel ballroom, a pianist accompanied four men dressed in dark trousers and identical scarlet waistcoats. They'd sung several wartime tunes in perfect four-part harmony, and now were tapping their toes and swaying as they sang "Camptown Races."

The song ended and during the applause she smiled at

Royal. "Wonderful music. I'm glad you suggested this evening."

His eyes met hers. "Good. I hoped you'd enjoy the quartet. Perhaps afterwards we can take a short ride in the moonlight before I take you home."

The pianist played the introductory bars to "Jeanie with the Light Brown Hair." Royal squeezed her hand. "This should be called 'Faith with the light brown hair,'" he whispered.

She leaned against his shoulder and sighed as the quartet sang through the verses. "I dream of Jeanie . . . I long for Jeanie . . . I sigh for Jeanie." Maybe she'd imagined his glances at Marguerite.

When Royal drove away from the hotel after the performance, he turned right on King's Highway. "I thought we'd take a turn around the square."

"Sounds lovely," Faith said, relaxing against the cushioned seat. They rolled past the closed mercantile and the newspaper office. Across the street, moonlight transformed the grass behind the courthouse into glittering spears. Over the clop of the horse's hooves, she heard crickets chirping their evening melodies.

"Seeing the mercantile reminds me." Royal's voice cut through the night. "Have you had any luck selling the place?" He guided the buggy left up the next street.

"There are a few things I want to set right beforehand. The business is not for sale at the moment."

"I told you, just go ahead and sell it. Let someone else take over. You shouldn't have to be involved."

She scooted away from his side. "I *am* involved. My grandfather founded Lindberg's Mercantile before I was born. I'd be dishonoring his years of work to walk away now."

"Even for a chance to go to Oregon?" At her surprised expression, he grinned. "I heard about you asking McGuire to take you with his company. What if someone else asked you to go? Would you?" He slowed the horse to a sedate walk, turning onto the street that passed in front of the courthouse.

"Are you asking—?" Out of the corner of her eye, Faith noticed a shadowy figure standing on the courthouse steps. She gasped. "Stop the carriage! There's my grandpa."

As soon as Royal drew up on the reins, she scrambled down and ran to the entrance door. Grandpa turned at the sound of her footsteps. "Clara?"

"It's me. Faith. Your granddaughter. What are you doing here?"

"I have a trial scheduled. You know that." He wore his black frock coat buttoned over his nightshirt. His feet were shoved into his best boots. Moonlight illuminated his bare calves.

Faith struggled to keep from weeping. She'd dared to think he was better since he'd slept through the evenings she spent with Curt. Slipping an arm through his, she kept her voice gentle. "You're a little early. Let's go home now."

"Who's out there in that buggy?"

"Mr. Baxter."

"Do I know him?"

"Yes." She tugged at his arm.

Royal moved toward them through the shadows cast by an oak tree. "C'mon, old fellow, let's get you to your house." He reached toward Grandpa.

"Don't need your help." He sidestepped and marched to the buggy.

Faith followed, Royal's hand on her elbow.

"There's a place in Fulton for folks like that," he whispered.

She stared at him, horrified.

"Never."

Faith watched Grandpa while he ate his breakfast. He'd dressed to accompany her to town as though nothing had happened the night before. After swirling a biscuit through the gravy on his plate, he spoke around a mouthful. "You're staring at me like I was a stranger. What's on your mind?"

She set her fork on the edge of her plate. "Do you remember being at the courthouse last night?"

He gaped at her as though she'd begun speaking Chinese. "I don't know what you're talking about. I was home last night. You went to a musicale with that Baxter fellow." He patted her hand. "Did you have a bad dream?"

It wouldn't do any good to tell him. If she jogged his memory, he'd only be humiliated at being found in public in his nightshirt, especially by Royal Baxter. In fact, was her evening with Royal the reason for one of his spells?

She stood to clear their empty plates. "Yes. It must have been a dream."

As they walked to town, she marveled at how he could be so chipper when she'd barely slept for worry. Royal's suggestion that she put Grandpa in the lunatic asylum in Fulton frightened her. If he slipped into one of his cloudy moments and failed to recover, she didn't know what she'd do. To see him this morning, such a thing didn't seem possible. But the concern failed to leave her thoughts.

Rosemary arrived at the mercantile soon after the doors were unlocked, Bodie at her heels. She took one look at Faith and asked, "You have raccoon eyes this morning. Were you out late with Mr. Baxter?" A teasing smile played over her lips.

"Nothing so romantic." Faith leaned against a counter with her arms folded. "On the way home from the performance we passed the courthouse, and there was Grandpa standing by the door, thinking he had a case to hear. Royal brought him home." She shuddered. "What if I hadn't seen him? Who knows where he'd have gone."

Rosemary hugged her, then stepped back. "I'm so sorry. Where is he now?"

"Working on his memoir, just like always. He's fine. He doesn't remember a thing about last night." She chewed her lower lip. "Royal suggested sending him away to the asylum in Fulton, but I could never do that."

"Of course you couldn't. Don't even consider the idea."

"That's all I did last night. I considered his suggestion and then tried to think of how I could manage alone if Grandpa gets worse."

"You know things always look bleakest after midnight. You're not alone. Remember that. Curt and I are very fond of your grandfather." Rosemary put a finger to her cheek. "I'll brew him a special tea that's said to help memory. Curt can bring a jarful over this evening."

Some of the tension left Faith's shoulder muscles. "The Lord must have sent you into my life. You're a gift."

"Fiddlesticks." Nevertheless, Rosemary looked pleased. She went to the counter where she'd placed her belongings when she entered and drew a canvas bag from her carryall. "If you want a real blessing, Curt has managed to collect from several more names on the list you drew up." A frown crinkled her forehead. "Remember the man you talked to the other day who said your grandfather gave him merchandise free of charge?"

Faith nodded.

"Curt has spoken with three such people. He doesn't understand why their debts were listed."

"I don't either." She smiled to herself. Solving the mystery would give her a legitimate reason to spend more time with Rosemary's brother. She'd raise the subject when he brought the tea.

She took the bag from Rosemary and counted the contents. Curt's tidy handwriting listed each name and amount. After making ledger entries, Faith consulted her totals. "We can order more stock now. Boots, some firearms—not all, but some—and maybe two or three watches. I can't wait to see the shelves fill up again." She clapped her hands in delight.

Bodie jumped to his feet and woofed when she clapped. Faith giggled. "This is a happy day. Seeing the supplies decline has been almost as sad as Grandpa's spells. If the store prospers, maybe he will too."

"That's certainly possible."

Faith grabbed her reticule and dropped the canvas bag inside. "I'll go to the bank with this right now. If Grandpa comes in, please tell him I'll be right back." She hugged Rosemary and dashed out the door.

The porch roof brought welcome shade from a day that promised to be a scorcher. With the weather this hot in mid-June, she dreaded the prospect of August. Faith hooked her reticule over one finger. Using her free hand, she dug in her pocket for a handkerchief to dab her forehead. As she passed the alley between the mercantile and the newspaper office, someone stepped from the shadows and jostled her.

A man's voice said, "'Scuze me."

Faith whirled to see who'd nearly knocked her off her feet, and saw nothing but his back as he ran down the alley toward the railroad tracks. Her breath caught in her throat.

He'd taken her reticule.

20

Faith sat in front of the sheriff's desk, swiping tears from her cheeks. "I told you, all I saw was his back as he ran down the alley. He had a hat on so I couldn't see his hair."

Sheriff Cooper leaned back in his chair, his thin face weary. "Been too much of this lately. Not sure I want to stand for reelection." He tugged at a corner of his drooping moustache. "How d'you suppose the feller knew you carried all that money?"

"Maybe he didn't. Maybe he just thought he was stealing my reticule." She sniffled. "Imagine his surprise."

"Who knew you'd be going to the bank this morning?"

"Just my helper, Miss Saxon."

"Ah, the Saxons." He scribbled something on a scrap of paper. "It's safe to say if she knew, so did her brother."

Anger flared through her. "If you'd stop trying to find Mr. Saxon responsible for our misfortunes, you might have time to catch the real thieves."

"Miss Faith, you forget yourself. I've been sheriff here for a dozen years. I know dishonesty when I see it."

"Apparently you do not. Good day, Sheriff."

Faith marched from the jailhouse, spine rigid, mind whirling. There had to be a way to find whoever had taken her reticule. Could he be the same person who robbed the store? And what about the intruder Curt had surprised last week?

Clouds piled overhead, adding to the stickiness of the morning. One thing she knew, she needed to warn Curt of the sheriff's suspicions.

That evening, she kept watch out the parlor window for Curt's promised arrival with the tea for Grandpa. A light rain fell, glistening on the pink petals of the climbing rose twining through the porch rail.

She stepped out into the warm twilight, settling into a wicker chair on the covered porch to wait. Moisture plinked from the roof with a musical note, joining drops from the roses and the maple tree to fill the air with an orchestral chorus. Faith closed her eyes, allowing the soothing sounds to cleanse her mind of worry.

She stood when she heard footsteps on the walkway, smiling as Curt approached carrying two jars bound at their tops with a wire handle. Strands of his dark brown hair visible beneath his hat looked almost black with dampness. Once he climbed the porch steps, he shrugged off his oiled coat and draped it with his hat over the chair she had just vacated. "What a nice welcome. I expected you'd be inside where it's dry."

"It's not wet here under the roof." She took the jars from him. "I love to listen to the rain. The sound is like tinkling keys on a piano."

An expression of pleasure crossed his face. "We're kindred spirits, then. Rain always acts as a lullaby for me on restless nights."

Faith led the way into the house, appreciating the warmth of his closeness. A dozen thoughts tumbled through her mind. Foremost was the importance of warning him about the sheriff.

Then somehow she needed a private moment to talk to him about the customers who claimed to have received merchandise as a gift.

Grandpa waited for them in the entry hall. "Faith said you were coming. I've got the chessboard ready on the dining table."

"In a moment, sir," Curt said. "Rosemary gave me specific instructions about these teas. As soon as I pass her words on to Faith, I'll come and checkmate you."

Grandpa guffawed. "We'll see about that."

Curt followed Faith into the kitchen. After she placed the jars on the table, he unwound the wire binding them together. Each container had a square of paper tied around the zinc lid. One had the words "Judge Lindberg" written on top, the other said "Faith."

"What did Rosemary send for me?" Faith lowered her voice. "I thought the tea was to help Grandpa's memory."

"This one is." Curt pushed the first glass jar toward her. "Rosemary said to mix it half and half with hot water and give him a cupful with his evening meal."

Faith eyed the greenish-amber liquid. "How long before it works on him?"

"She said to give it time. When you run out, she'll make some more." He lifted the second tea so that the lamplight made the lemon-colored contents appear golden. "This will help you sleep. Warm a cup at bedtime." He took her shoulders and turned her to face him.

"She told me about the money being stolen this morning. I was sorry to hear the news, after all the work we've done."

Tears stung her eyes at his caring tone. "That's not the worst of it," she said in a soft voice. "The sheriff thinks you're responsible."

His fingers tightened. "We'll have to prove him wrong." His voice held an edge of steel.

"But how?"

"Are you two finished whispering in there?" Grandpa called. "Time's a'wastin'."

Curt released her. "May I come 'courting' Monday?" He smiled. "We can go for a walk after supper."

"I'm afraid to leave Grandpa. Did Rosemary tell you about Friday night?"

"She did. Told me the circumstances too. Let's try it anyway. We won't be away for as long as you were." His voice carried a hint of condemnation.

Faith leaned against a counter in the mercantile listening to a train rumble out of the station. A glance at the clock told her it was close to noon. Seven more hours and Curt would come to the house to escort her on a stroll around town. Thinking of his caring ways brought a smile to her lips.

She gave herself a shake. She shouldn't be daydreaming about Curt when Royal was the man courting her. Or so he said. She hadn't seen him since the night of the musicale.

The door to the mercantile opened so slowly that the bell gave a single clink and fell silent. Amy Dunsmuir stood in the entrance, hugging baby Sophia to her chest. Her pale skin looked almost translucent.

Faith hastened to her side. "What a pleasant surprise. Is your husband not with you?"

"Joel's dead." Tears filled the young woman's eyes.

"No! It's not possible. You were here just a few weeks ago. What happened?"

Amy swayed and Faith put an arm around her waist and

guided her to a chair. "Rest a moment. I'll bring you some water."

She moved behind the counter and poured from a covered jar into a waiting glass. "Rosemary Saxon brings ginger water for me each morning. She claims it helps avoid cramping in the summer heat." Faith placed the filled glass on top of the checkerboard, thankful that the woodstove regulars had departed earlier.

The baby whimpered and Amy turned her to face forward.

"Come here, little one." Faith held out her arms and cuddled the infant on her lap. With a pang of sorrow, she noticed Sophia had her father's straight black hair and round nose. "She favors your husband."

Amy nodded. "Everyone says so. Now she's all I have to remind me. We wanted to have a picture made, but it cost too dear. That's why Joel took a job . . ." She sucked in a breath. "Took a job in the quarry. The pay was good. First week, an edge of the pit broke away. He was standing right underneath. They brought him to me in the back of a wagon." She closed her eyes, her head shaking from side to side. "I didn't hardly know him, he was so tore up."

Faith squeezed her hand. "You can tell me later."

"No, I want to say it all now. Get it over with. We had a nice burying. Joel's boss, he gave me the wages Joel had coming. They weren't much. After thinking on things, I didn't know what else to do but come here. We neither of us have any kinfolk left." She met Faith's concerned gaze. "I hoped maybe you could tell me of a place to stay and some kind of a job I can do."

"Didn't you stay with Reverend French before?"

"We did, but it doesn't feel right to go to them. His son's there, and now that I'm a widow . . . It's not seemly." Amy took a sip of ginger water.

Faith recalled the Frenches' son. He'd served in the Army and returned home missing an arm. In his late twenties, he now lived with his parents and taught classic literature at the academy. Although she was sure he was a perfect gentleman, she could understand Amy's reluctance.

She shifted Sophia on her lap and patted Amy's hand. "I'd be pleased if you'd come home with me. My grandfather and I will be going to our house for dinner in a few minutes."

Amy lifted her chin. "I'm not here to make you feel sorry and take us in. I hoped you knew someone who needed a housekeeper or some such."

"If I came to you in need, wouldn't you help me?"

"Well, naturally. That's what folks do where I'm from."

"Folks do that here too." Smiling, Faith passed Sophia to her mother. "I hear Grandpa coming. Are you up to walking several blocks?"

"Been sitting all morning on the train. A walk will be nice." Tears starred her lashes. "I don't know how to thank you."

As soon as they reached the house, Faith took Amy upstairs and showed her to the bedroom across the hall from her own. "This was my brother's room." She waved a hand at the dark mahogany bedstead and heavy chest of drawers.

Amy shrank away from the door. "I don't want to discommode your memories. We can sleep somewheres else."

"Nonsense. As you can see, his things are gone. Packed away." She swallowed the lump that rose in her throat. "We'll be glad to see the space put to use."

"You're certain?"

Faith nodded. "I'll fetch clean bedding from the storeroom

and be right back. We still have the family cradle Grandpa made when my father was born. I'll bring that too."

Amy placed Sophia in the center of the bare mattress. "Let me help."

A few minutes later, Faith dashed down the stairs. "Dinner will be on the table in a few minutes, Grandpa."

He leaned back in his chair. "I couldn't say this before, with Mrs. Dunsmuir around, but I'm proud of you for bringing them here. 'Withhold not good from them to whom it is due, when it is in the power of thine hand to do it.'"

She dropped a hug around his shoulders. "I hoped you'd feel that way. There was no opportunity to ask you ahead of time."

"You never have to ask my permission to do good to another person. You should know that by now. Besides, it will be nice to have a young'un around."

"We'll enjoy them while we can. Amy said she's hoping to find work as a housekeeper." Faith walked into the kitchen and slid a crock of baked beans from the warming oven. As she put the meal on the table, she noticed Amy coming down the stairs.

"Sophia went to sleep soon as I put her in the cradle. I'm sorry I didn't help with setting out the food."

Faith smiled at her earnest expression. "I didn't expect you to. Sit and eat with us, then why don't you rest this afternoon? We're usually home by half past five."

Amy caught her trembling lower lip between her teeth. "I can't thank you enough for your kindness. I'll pay you back somehow, I swear."

"There's no need," Grandpa said. "One day you can pass a blessing on to someone else."

Faith's heartbeat increased when she heard the knock at the door. Curt was early. In spite of the events of the day, she'd been counting the hours until he arrived. Now she'd have even more to tell him.

She swung the door wide—and stared into Royal's face. "What . . . what are you doing here?"

"That's a nice greeting."

"I apologize, but I expected we'd go for a buggy ride Sunday like we always do, and—"

He touched the tip of her nose with his index finger. "If I promise to see you, I'll keep that promise. But you can't assume. As it happens, I had to be in Hartfield Sunday afternoon." He grinned at her. "Come for a stroll with me. I'll tell you all about my visit there."

She glanced over his shoulder and saw Curt crossing the road, Bodie at his heels. Her face warmed. "I have something else to do this evening. I wish you'd asked sooner."

He turned his head, following the direction of her gaze. "The stableman? You can do better."

"We're just friends. He's been helping me with matters at the store."

Royal rested his fingers against her forearm. "I'll see you Sunday afternoon. That's a promise." He stepped off the porch, nearly colliding with Curt. "Evening, Saxon."

Curt touched his hat brim. "Baxter."

Faith moved to one side to allow Curt to enter. Bodie flopped down on the porch to wait. When she closed the door, she had the uncomfortable feeling she might be turning into one of those girls who kept men on a string like so many fish. "I had no idea he would be stopping by," she said, her voice apologetic.

"Not your fault. We're just pretending to court, remember?" His tone put distance between them. "I'll greet your granddad, then we'll go for our walk."

He crossed to the parlor entrance and stopped. "Mrs. Dunsmuir. Good evening. I hadn't heard of your return." He glanced around. "Where's Joel?"

"He's—"

"Killed in an accident." Grandpa spoke from his wing chair. "Amy's staying with us for a bit. I'm sure Faith can tell you the rest."

"Yes. I can. As soon as I get my bonnet we'll be on our way."

Curt walked to the sofa and made a half-bow in Amy's direction. "My sincere condolences. Joel was a fine man. I admired his spirit."

Her hazel eyes brimmed with tears. "Thank you. Your words are a comfort."

As they walked toward town, Bodie ran ahead and then circled back, busy sniffing at shadows. Faith told Curt what she knew of Joel's death and Amy's decision to return to Noble Springs. "When she recovers, she plans to look for work here."

"I'll keep my ears open and let you know if I hear of anything." He smiled at her, his earlier chilliness apparently forgotten. "Maybe Mrs. Wylie needs someone."

She loved the way his whole face lifted when he smiled.

"She wouldn't hire Queen Victoria on my recommendation." Faith chuckled. "I'm afraid we've lost a customer. You seem to have been more successful with collections."

"Except for those few who claim your granddad gave them the merchandise."

"Yes, there's that. How many people have told you they didn't have to pay?"

"Five so far. What about you?"

"Three. That's quite a bit of uncollected debt. I don't understand."

"I have several more calls to make. Once I've talked with everyone, we'll try to make some sense of this."

She sighed. "I was so thrilled when Rosemary brought me the money you collected. The first thing I planned to do was order supplies to replace what was stolen. And now we're back to zero."

He took her arm when they reached the front of the livery stable. "Careful. The ground's still slippery from Saturday's rain." His hand remained around her elbow after the board-walk resumed. "You won't stay at zero for long. Rosemary tells me you have customers supplying for a wagon train that may leave by late summer. They'll travel partway, then winter over somewhere, I hear."

Disappointment flickered inside at the mention of late summer. The date might as well be never as far as she was concerned. The mercantile was months away from rebuild-ing a strong financial foundation. "Rosemary's right. The thieves didn't take basics like cookware and buckets, ropes and shovels. But those items don't bring a profit like rifles do."

" 'For who hath despised the day of small things?' "

"This must be my day for Bible quotations. You sound like Grandpa."

He squeezed her arm. "Just trying to bring a smile to your pretty face."

Her eyebrows shot up. Curt had never said anything like that before. Did he really think she was pretty?

As they neared the courthouse, Faith glanced across the street, noticing a light burning in the window of the jail. "Has the sheriff bothered you again?"

"Not yet. He's probably biding his time."

"I'll be glad when the thieves are caught and we can prove you had nothing to do with the robberies."

"That's what I want to talk over with you. I had—"

Bodie came to an abrupt stop in front of them, his fur raised. A low growl rumbled from his chest. Faith felt Curt's body tense. He dropped her arm and stepped in front of her, shielding her with his body. His hand went to his side, as though he were reaching for a pistol.

He wore no holster.

Curt stared at the low shrubbery beside the courthouse. "Identify yourself." His voice sounded menacing.

Faith peeked around him. Fading daylight showed no one next to the building. Who did Curt see?

Bodie crept forward, continuing to growl. After a moment, he pounced. A black cat burst from hiding and tore across the street, the dog in full pursuit.

At the sight of the chase, Curt's body relaxed. He turned toward her, his face a picture of shame. Faith put her hand to her throat. "Curt? What happened?"

"I'll take you home." He set off ahead of her. Bodie abandoned the cat and ran after him.

She stood motionless, hands on hips, and hollered at his retreating form, "If you're going to take me home, hadn't you better get back here where I am?"

21

Curt stopped at the sound of Faith's teasing voice. Heat suffused his body. He'd done the unthinkable by losing control in front of her. He marveled that she could still want his company. She should have turned and run the other way.

With dragging steps, he returned to her side. "I'm sorry you had to see that," he mumbled.

She slipped her small palm into his hand. "We're not far from the mercantile. Let's sit a moment on the bench out front." They walked the length of the courthouse square in silence and then crossed the street.

Once they were seated, Curt stared at his shoes, uncertain how to proceed.

Faith cleared her throat and spoke in gentle tones. "Please tell me. What is it you're afraid of?"

"*You* should be afraid of me."

"Hardly. I've felt something was wrong for quite a while. You've shared in all my troubles for months now, let me share yours." She held him with her eyes.

Perspiration prickled his forehead. Would she think he was deranged? In spite of Rosemary's assurances, he half-believed it himself. He leaned forward, digging his fingers into the flesh of his thighs. "Ever since the war—" He cleared his throat. "I have visions. I see battlefields, burned-out towns, soldiers dying. I never know what will touch them off."

Faith squeezed his hand. "Go on."

His breath shredded. "I thought I had them licked. It's been a long time. Reverend French suggested I pray when I feel one coming on, and it's helped some. Tonight . . ." He slumped forward. "I'd give anything if you hadn't seen that."

"After all you've been through, I don't wonder you have horrible memories. I wasn't anywhere near a battle, but I still have nightmares about what must have happened to my brother and father." Her hand felt soft and cool on his. "You don't need to be ashamed."

"That's what Rosemary says."

"She's right."

He dared a glance at her face. A soft smile lifted her lips. "You're not afraid of me?"

"Why would I be?" She squeezed his hand again. "We're friends, aren't we?"

Curt felt like jumping to his feet and dancing a jig, but the thought of Royal Baxter gave him pause. Faith was right—they were friends. It was Baxter who held her heart.

After seeing Faith home, Curt detoured past his house to leave Bodie with Rosemary, then crossed the street to the parsonage. Reverend French opened the door at his knock.

"You look mighty happy. Come in and tell me about it."

Curt recounted the events of earlier that evening, leaving out nothing. "She wasn't afraid of me. Said she understood."

"Praise God."

"I did."

"So what are you going to do now?" The reverend laced his fingers together, steepling his thumbs.

"Same as always—work at the stable, help Rosemary at home."

"And what about this young lady? Faith Lindberg, if I'm not mistaken."

Curt's heart stirred at the sound of her name. "Yes. Faith. She's interested in someone else."

Mrs. French stepped into the room carrying a tray containing a plate of cookies and two steaming cups of coffee. The aroma of molasses drifted past Curt's nose. His stomach growled and he remembered he'd skipped supper to call on Faith.

"Thought you men might like a bite of something sweet." She placed the tray on a corner of the desk. "There's plenty of coffee if you need more."

"Thank you, my dear." Reverend French helped himself to a cookie and pushed the plate toward Curt. "You sure she's really interested in him, and not just infatuated with his looks? All the girls think Baxter's quite the charmer. You should hear my daughter."

"How'd you know who I meant?"

"I've got eyes. Thing is, until he declares himself she's not committed. You've got as much chance as he has." He rose and leaned against one of the bookcases. "Have you given any more thought to finding a job that suits your talents? All your schooling is wasted at Ripley's Livery."

The abrupt change of subject caught Curt off guard. He had been considering going back to his former profession, but how could he leave Rip without a helper? Especially after all the man had done for him.

Faith propped open the front door of the mercantile to try to corral any breeze that might ruffle the day's promised heat. Rosemary bustled in, fanning herself. She dropped her carryall on a counter and turned to Faith, her expression curious. "Curt told me Joel Dunsmuir was killed in a quarry accident and Amy and her baby are staying with you."

"She's hoping to find a job as a housekeeper, but the poor thing is too distraught right now. I thought it best that she wait awhile."

"Would she welcome a caller? I'd like to offer condolences."

Faith nodded. "I'm sure she'd love to see you again. She showed me that gash you treated on her forehead. It healed beautifully, thanks to you. She's very grateful."

"She's alone at your house today?"

"Grandpa stayed home with her. He's quite taken with little Sophia." Faith smiled at the image of her grandfather bouncing Amy's four-month-old baby on his knee. She knew he had hopes of seeing her babies one day. God willing, he would.

Rosemary tilted her head, her index finger resting on her cheek. "Maybe Amy's the Lord's provision for you. She can keep an eye on your grandfather. I know you worry about him."

Faith considered her words for a moment before responding. "I don't know. I'd feel I was taking advantage of her. How could she refuse?"

Mr. Slocum and Mr. Grisbee drifted through the open door, tipped their hats to Faith and Rosemary, then settled next to the checkerboard and commenced disputing whose turn it was to go first.

"They're as reliable as roosters," Rosemary said with a grin. "Time to start our day." She reached into her carryall. "I brought you something."

Faith hefted the bag of coins Rosemary handed her. "Feels like Curt was successful. He must've gone out last night after taking me home." She kept her voice low so the woodstove regulars wouldn't overhear. She didn't want her troubles spread all over town.

"He only has a few more names he hasn't crossed off the list." Rosemary tied her apron around her waist. "Has the sheriff discovered anything new about the person who stole your money?"

"I haven't heard a word. I doubt he's trying very hard. He seems fixed on the idea that Curt's the thief." She dropped the bag in the cash drawer and turned the key. She'd count the money later.

Mr. Slocum raised his head. "Someone stole your money? When was that?"

Faith grimaced. Rosemary might as well have told the editor of the *Noble Springs Observer*. "Awhile ago."

Rosemary mouthed a regretful "I'm sorry," and busied herself rearranging bolts of fabric.

Mr. Grisbee shuffled to her side. "Me and Jesse can take turns watching the place, Miss Faith. Bad enough your guns was stole. Now they're takin' your cash money." He shook his head, his wrinkled features sorrowful. "Don't know what this town's comin' to."

"You're very kind, but I wouldn't dream of asking you to spend your days here." Images of the woodstove regulars patrolling the mercantile made her cringe. Then she grinned to herself. They already watched the door like hungry puppies waiting for feeding time.

"We'd be glad to help out," Mr. Slocum said. "Give us something to do."

Rosemary and Faith exchanged a glance. Rosemary shrugged.

"Then I accept," Faith said. "You can start today. I'm going to the bank later. Who wants to come with me?"

While they argued among themselves, she returned to the cash drawer and counted the money Curt had collected. The salesman from Marblehead Gun Works was due soon. Maybe she had enough to order one shotgun.

When she left for the bank, Mr. Slocum stuck close to her side. "Me and Harold decided to trade off. Next time he'll go with you, and I'll guard the store."

His neatly trimmed gray beard matched his keen gray eyes. In spite of her initial reluctance, Faith felt safer in his company. She hadn't wanted to admit it, but the theft on Saturday had shaken her, both mentally and physically. For the time being, she'd welcome an escort.

Faith turned toward the teller cage on her left when she entered the hushed interior of the Noble Springs National Bank. "Miss Faith," Mr. Slocum whispered, "Paulson's trying to get your attention." He pointed to the president's desk at the far end of the lobby.

She glanced at Mr. Paulson, wondering what he wanted. She'd been meticulous with the store's records since Curt taught her how to make entries. While the teller entered the amount of her deposit in her passbook, Faith noticed Mr. Paulson hurrying toward them.

"I have some good news for you." He smiled broadly at her. "Would you have a moment to discuss an important matter?"

"I'll wait over there." Mr. Slocum pointed to a bench inside the door.

The banker took her elbow and guided her to a chair in front of his desk. "I had a visitor yesterday. This person is very interested in purchasing the mercantile—lock, stock, and barrel." He rubbed his hands together. "I knew you'd be happy. We just have to set a fair price."

Faith sucked in a breath and held it for a moment. Sell the store, just when she was beginning to see results from her efforts?

He studied her face. "You don't look pleased. My understanding was you wanted to unload the business. You did place an advertisement in the *Observer.*"

"That was over a month ago. I told you my grandfather cancelled the item." She paused a moment, pondering. "Who would come out of nowhere and offer to buy the mercantile now?"

"A local businessman."

"Who?"

"Gilbert Allen. He owns the cooperage."

Faith planted her elbow on the arm of the chair and rested her face on her hand. A jumble of thoughts spun through her mind. This was their chance to be part of the next wagon train to leave. But now she had Amy to consider. They couldn't go off and abandon her and Sophia.

"How much did he offer?" she asked in a small voice, half afraid he'd name an amount so high she couldn't refuse.

"Not as much as the mercantile's worth, unfortunately, but if you're interested I'll tell him your price and see if he'll match it."

Relieved, she pushed herself to her feet. "Right now there is no price. I want to see the business attain its former luster first."

"You're making a mistake. It could be months before you see much profit."

"So be it. Tell Mr. Allen I said no."

22

By the time Faith arrived home that evening, she'd decided not to tell Grandpa about Mr. Allen's desire to purchase the mercantile. She had questions about the cooper's proposition, and they centered on Royal. He had to be the one who prompted the offer. When she saw him Sunday, she'd demand an explanation.

The stench of lye combined with the odor of burned bread overwhelmed her when she entered the house. Grandpa sat at a table in the parlor, writing. He smiled at her when she closed the door.

"It smells terrible in here," she said. "What happened?"

"I think Amy had a mishap in the kitchen. Glad you're home. I'd say she needs your help."

Faith dropped her carryall next to the hall tree and hastened toward the source of the odors. A wash boiler sat on the stove, billowing steam. Amy sat at the kitchen table scraping at the charred surface of a pan of cornbread.

"Amy, what are you doing?"

She turned teary eyes toward Faith. "I thought I'd surprise you and have fresh bread ready for supper. But then I had to wash Sophia's diapers, and I forgot about the oven temperature when I heated the stove. I'm so sorry."

Faith dashed to the back door and flung it open. "Let's get some air in here. I can't breathe."

Amy slumped in her chair. "You probably want me to leave."

"Not at all." Faith hugged her thin shoulders. How had Amy managed her home when Joel was alive? She couldn't imagine deciding to heat a wash boiler on an afternoon when the temperatures hovered in the high nineties. She gave the girl a pat on the arm. "Why don't you go see to Sophia while I prepare supper?"

Amy nodded and scurried from the room.

The surface of Pioneer Lake sparkled like scattered jewels. Faith leaned against the trunk of a white oak and emitted a deep sigh. Light filtered through the canopy of leaves, dappling her muslin skirt.

"That sounded heartfelt," Royal said. "Did you have a trying morning?"

"I've had an unusual week." She rummaged in the picnic basket and drew out a plate of shortbread. The cookies had dark brown edges. "Amy Dunsmuir's been helping me with the cooking as a way to pay for her keep. But she's easily distracted. When I arrive home in the evenings, I never know if we'll have an edible meal, or one that's cooked beyond a fare-thee-well."

He selected a shortbread and took a bite. "A little charred. Not too bad." He reclined on the quilt covering the grass, resting his weight on his elbows. A lock of black hair dropped over his forehead. Her pulse increased at the sight of his muscular body stretched out next to her. If only he weren't so handsome . . .

"So you have both young Mrs. Dunsmuir and your grandfather to look after, not to mention the store. No wonder you're tired. Have you given any more thought to selling the business?" His voice sounded casual, but his gaze sharpened.

Faith folded her arms across her chest. "I planned to ask you about that. It seems Mr. Allen visited the banker and told him he wanted to buy us out." She raised an eyebrow. "Did you tell him we were ready to sell?"

Royal studied the cookie in his hand as though the answer to her question was written on its surface. After several moments he sat upright. "He knows we're courting, and asked me what my intentions were."

"You talk about me?" She felt herself flush. "How dare you!"

He dropped the shortbread onto the plate. "I'd never say anything improper, but I have mentioned how taken I am with you, and that your struggles worry me."

Speechless, Faith tried to comprehend what he'd just said. She remembered her brother talking about his sweetheart before he left to join the Army. He'd left no doubt that he wanted to marry the girl when he came home. Was this the sort of conversation Royal had with his employer?

He slid closer, so that their shoulders touched. He slipped an arm around her waist. "I told Gil Allen that my intentions toward you were honorable. I said if you'd have me, I wanted you to be my wife."

Her breath whooshed from her lungs. She met his intent gaze. "Are you asking me?"

"I'm asking you." He cupped a hand around the back of her head and leaned forward, placing a gentle kiss on her lips.

She leaned against him. The elusive Royal Baxter had just proposed marriage—to her.

The throbbing of her pulse filled her throat. Her head screamed at her to say yes, but her heart hesitated. "You've taken me by surprise. I don't know what to say."

"Say yes." He lifted one of her hands and kissed each fingertip. "We'll have the wedding just before we leave for Oregon."

"There's no time."

"What?"

"June's half over. By the time we're wed, it will be too late to start west. According to the guidebooks—"

He nuzzled the palm of her hand with his lips. "We can winter over somewhere on the way and wait for spring."

In spite of the logic of his statement, Faith felt like she was in a runaway carriage, headed downhill. She slipped from his embrace and gave him a shaky smile. "It's too hard to think when you're this close."

"What's there to think about? You know I'm drawn to you, and I believe you feel the same toward me. You're a perfect partner for a new life in Oregon. Of course, in the meantime the mercantile will have to be sold. You realize that, don't you?"

With a sense of unreality, she felt she was observing a stranger from a distance. He had no right to make decisions for her.

Apparently interpreting her silence for acquiescence, Royal leaned close. "Just imagine our home on Officer's Row. You'd be an ideal major's wife."

But you're not a major yet, she wanted to say. You're a cooper with big ideas.

She reached for his hand. "Will you give me a little time? I have more to consider than my personal desires."

A hurt expression crossed his features. "Take all the time you need." He squeezed her hand. "I'll be waiting."

Faith sat close to his side on the ride home. His proposal spun through her mind until her thoughts bumped against a wall.

Royal hadn't said he loved her.

When Faith entered the mercantile on Monday morning, she surveyed the large room with fresh vision. She tried to imagine how she would feel when she handed the keys to a new owner and left Noble Springs forever.

Rosemary's arrival interrupted her musings. Faith rested her eyes on her friend's bright face. Rosemary had blossomed since she'd begun helping at the store. A few of the women in town sought her out for advice, both regarding merchandise and her herbal remedies. And Curt—Faith took a deep breath. She'd fought down images of Curt ever since Royal left her at her door the previous afternoon. An almost-betrothed woman shouldn't be thinking of anyone but her fiancé.

"Your head's in the clouds today," Rosemary said. "I've said good morning twice and you haven't answered."

"I'm sorry. My mind is elsewhere." She stepped close to her friend and glanced around to be sure no customers approached. Thankfully the woodstove regulars hadn't yet arrived. "Royal proposed marriage yesterday. He plans to go to Oregon and take me with him as his wife."

Rosemary's jaw dropped. "What did you say to him?"

"I asked for time to think about it." She gestured at the room. "There's Grandpa to consider, and Amy, and the store . . . and you."

"You have to follow your heart. I have a feeling if you truly wanted to marry Royal, you'd have said yes in spite of the difficulties."

"He took me so by surprise. I just wasn't ready." She walked to one of the chairs and sank down. "Royal said he'd wait."

"But for how long?"

By the end of the week, Faith was no closer to a decision about Royal than she'd been on Sunday. She knew he worked long hours at the cooperage. Somehow not seeing him on a daily basis made it easier to ponder the issues raised by his proposal. Until she was sure of her choice, she wouldn't mention marriage to Grandpa. He made no secret of his distrust of Royal. Faith trembled at the thought of broaching the subject.

As she rolled down the shades preparatory to closing the mercantile for the day, Mr. Slocum walked out of the storeroom. "Door's bolted. Never saw nothing suspicious this afternoon."

"It's good of you and Mr. Grisbee to take turns staying every day, but it's been two weeks since the money was taken. I'm sure the thief is long gone."

"Doesn't matter. Girl like you, alone here. Might give someone else ideas. Me and Harold will watch out for you." He held the door open after she gathered her bonnet and carryall.

"You're a blessing. Thank you." She snapped the lock securing the door. "Until Monday, then."

He tipped his battered felt hat and strode away.

She couldn't imagine why she'd ever thought the two old men were nuisances. She'd come to appreciate them in spite of their gruff natures.

When she turned the corner and headed west toward home,

she faced a molten ball of heat shimmering above the hills. Mentally, Faith crossed her fingers, hoping Amy hadn't decided to cook anything that required a hot oven. A light supper of eggs and salad greens sounded perfect.

She sighed with relief as she left the boardwalk and hurried up the stone path to their door. Summer was a season to be endured with as much grace as possible. Once inside she could take off her boots, no matter what Grandpa said about the impropriety of going barefoot.

"Evening, Faith." Curt's voice called when she entered the house.

"I didn't expect—" Faith stopped at the doorway to the parlor, shocked by the jealousy that sliced through her. Curt sat on the sofa near Amy, while Grandpa jiggled Sophia on his lap. Curt and Amy? She forced a pleasant smile.

He stood. "I wanted to talk to you this evening, so came on by after Rip closed the livery."

"If you wanted to talk to me, why didn't you go to the mercantile?" Her voice sounded sharper than she intended.

He raised an eyebrow. "Your house is closer. I didn't think you'd mind."

"Well, please talk then. I'm listening."

"I meant later. We'll go for a walk."

She almost groaned at the thought of going back into the heat. "Let's at least stay inside until sundown. It's suffocating out there."

Grandpa cleared his throat. "We've been waiting for you. Amy has supper ready."

As if sensing the tension in the air, the girl sent Faith a hopeful look. "I made something from your mother's recipe book—egg salad and greens."

Amy's earnest expression melted Faith's ill humor. She shouldn't take her anxieties out on the poor girl. If Curt were interested in Amy, it would probably be a good thing for both of them. She ignored a tiny stab of pain at the idea.

"That's exactly what I had in mind. I'll set out the plates."

Faith and Curt walked toward town in silence for the first few moments. Lightning bugs blinked in the shadows.

He slowed his steps to keep pace with her shorter stride. "We saw those lights over silent battlefields at night. You wouldn't think they'd exist in such a place. They reminded me of home during times I sorely needed the reminder." Curt's voice sounded wistful at the remembrance.

Faith stifled an impulse to take his hand. Since he'd shared with her the visions that tormented him, he'd been far more open about his past life. His words created a bond between them that she didn't feel with her almost-fiancé. It wasn't right that she felt closer to a family friend. She promised herself that next time she saw Royal, she'd ask him to talk to her about some of his experiences.

Her thoughts returned to Curt. "I like lightning bugs too," she said. "Maxwell and I used to capture them."

He grinned at her. "Who caught the most?"

"Me. I was quicker."

He tucked a hand under her elbow. "Now that I've finished collecting your debts, I'd like to take another look at your grandfather's ledgers. I think I may have discovered a connection between those customers who say they don't owe you anything."

"Tell me."

"I want to be sure first." They turned at Courthouse Square.

Faith shuddered when they passed the jail. She wished she knew whether the sheriff had found any trace of the thieves.

Almost as a reflex, she tightened her elbow against her side, pressing Curt's hand close. In response, he squeezed her arm.

Once inside the mercantile, he lowered the lamp above the cash drawer and touched a match to the wick. An island of light spread over one side of the darkened room.

Faith placed the ledgers within the borders of the island, pushing the books in Curt's direction. "If you can explain this, maybe we can press our claim with them. No one's offered anything in writing to prove that their merchandise was a gift."

"It's possible you don't have a claim."

Her jaw dropped. "Why not?"

He took a sheet of paper from his shirt pocket and opened last year's ledger. "It will take me a few minutes to find pages with these names. Be patient."

She blew out an exaggerated breath. Placing her elbows on the counter, she rested her face on her palms. "I'm waiting, but I'm not patient." Her toe tapped against the floor.

"You of all people know how hard it was to make sense of these pages." His eyes crinkled with amusement. "Unless you've organized everything since I last looked through these books."

She laughed. "I'm afraid not. Tell me what you're looking for. Maybe I can help."

"We had to fill in prices for some of the goods, remember? Do you remember which people you talked to who told you their merchandise was given to them?"

She thought for a moment. "Mr. Bingham—he has that run-down farm a couple miles south of town—was one. The milliner, Miss Lytle, was another."

He shoved a ledger in her direction. "Please look for their names, and mark the pages if you find them."

Faith crossed the room and retrieved the shears from the

216

table she used when cutting fabric. While Curt turned pages, she clipped a piece of newsprint into strips.

"Here are bookmarks." She placed them on the counter between the two ledgers.

Nodding acknowledgment, he continued his perusal.

Twenty minutes or so passed while they searched for names and marked entries. Finally, Curt closed the book he'd been reviewing. Its edges bristled with limp strips of white paper. He looked at Faith. "Have you finished?"

"Yes. Now tell me—"

"Did you notice anything in particular about those accounts?"

She grinned at him. "I did. These were the ones we had to write in the amount owed. All Grandpa did was enter what they bought."

"Notice anything else?"

Flipping back through the pages she'd marked, Faith took a second look, then sent Curt a questioning glance. "In this book, they all have *20327* written at the bottom. Do yours?"

A triumphant expression crossed his face. "Yes. That's what I thought we'd find. When your granddad didn't enter an amount due, I think it meant he didn't intend those customers to pay."

Faith's hopes for recovering the remaining debt sank to her shoes. If her grandfather gave the listed items away, she had no right to press anyone for payment. Silently berating herself for counting on profits she'd never receive, she asked, "So, what do the numbers mean? Added together, they don't equal the price of the merchandise. None of the customers bought—were given—identical goods."

Curt rubbed his forehead. "Beats me. You'll have to ask your granddad."

"Then he'll know we've been pestering people. He warned

me to be careful who I approached. At the time, I didn't realize what he meant."

"I'm sorry." He took her hand in his callused one. "I know you were hoping for more. Between the theft of what I collected earlier and now this . . ."

She closed her fingers around his, wishing she could lean against his broad shoulder for comfort. Instead, she took a step backward. Curt was a friend, but he was also a man. A very attractive one.

Faith released his hand. "Thank you for all you've done to help me." She straightened her shoulders. "Without you, I'd still be floundering. At least now I know how to keep track of the money when it comes in. It may take a long time, but I'm determined—"

The bell over the door jangled. Faith jumped at the sound and spun toward the doorway. "Sheriff Cooper. What on earth?"

"I might ask your friend there the same thing." The lawman eased his lanky frame into the room. "Saw a light shining around the shades. Wondered who was here so late." He pointed at the open ledgers. "You sure it's a good idea to let a stranger know your business?"

Anger burned Faith's cheeks. "I told you before, Curt is a family friend." She spoke through clenched teeth. "I do appreciate your checking when you saw our light, but now I suggest you turn your attention to finding the man who robbed me."

He tipped his hat. "That's what I'm doing, Miss Faith."

23

Faith surveyed the flowers planted next to the porch. Morning glory weeds and wild clover threatened to choke the blooms Rosemary had planted. She looked down at her sprigged muslin skirt. If she had the time, she'd change into a work dress and tackle the intruders, but Royal would be arriving any minute.

It had been two weeks since he proposed and she'd promised an answer today. Her stomach fluttered. He'd been part of her daydreams for years, and out of all the girls in Noble Springs, he had chosen her. She ought to be ecstatic.

His buggy rumbled into view. Faith slipped inside the front door and said to Grandpa, "I'm leaving now."

He turned in his chair. "Amy and I will be fine. You watch yourself with that fellow."

She bent to kiss his cheek, wondering how he'd respond if she told him "that fellow" wanted to marry her. "I'll be back in time for supper."

He grunted and resumed his writing.

Faith closed the door behind her as Royal approached on the stone walkway. He carried his hat in his hand, his dark hair shining with Macassar oil. Her heart lifted at the sight of his confident stride. When they were together, he charmed her doubts into submission.

He slid an arm around her waist. "You're prettier than those flowers."

Conscious of Grandpa at his post in front of the parlor window, she stepped to one side, but her smile didn't leave her lips. "Thank you."

"I've been counting the hours until this afternoon," he said as he helped her into the buggy.

"Today has been on my mind, as well."

Royal shook the reins and guided the horse along the road toward town. "Have you seen the bandstand that's being built in the new park across from the tracks?"

"Not yet. Everyone who comes into the store is talking about it."

"The mayor's committee has a bang-up Independence Day celebration planned for Wednesday." He squeezed her hand. "Won't be anything compared to how I'll celebrate when you say yes."

Faith swallowed hard when Royal drew the buggy to a stop in front of the bandstand. He jumped down, then reached up and circled her waist with his hands, swinging her to the ground. They walked toward the new structure, Royal holding her arm. "See the fine latticework?" he asked. "We cut those pieces at the cooperage."

"Beautiful."

Afternoon sun slanted across the roof and spread gold over the freshly mowed field. Mourning doves scooted about, foraging for seeds among the cuttings. When Faith and Royal drew close, the birds flared up and disappeared.

Royal dusted off the top step before patting the empty space at his side. Faith spread her skirt and settled next to him. The fragrance of his hair oil mingled with the sweet smell of cut grass.

He reached over, cupping her cheek with work-roughened

fingers. "What have you decided?" His breath felt warm on her skin.

A tingle tripped down her throat. When he was this near, she couldn't think straight. It would be so easy to say yes, to sell the mercantile, and leave for Oregon. She thought of lush meadows, high mountains, broad, flowing rivers.

Trembling, she straightened. "I cannot let the business go while it's so depleted. I must ask you for more time." She fought to ban the quiver from her voice.

Royal stared at her, a stunned expression on his face. "You don't have to sell that blasted store before you say yes. I'm asking you to marry me. We can work out the details together." He clasped her hands, beseeching her with his eyes.

"It would be unfair to you if I agreed. The mercantile's fate is ultimately up to my grandfather."

"You said he turned it over to you." His eyes narrowed.

"I'm to run the business. He's made it very clear that I can't make the decision to sell."

He'd turned his proposal into an argument. If he loved her, he would respect her wishes. She slid a few inches away. "Please give me a couple of months. We're at a turning point. I'm sure profits will increase."

Royal gathered her into his arms. He slipped one hand around the back of her neck and kissed the lobe of her ear, then moved his lips to her mouth. The heat from his kiss sent sparks flying through her.

"Are you sure you want to wait?" he whispered against her cheek.

Breathless, she put a hand to her throat, feeling her heart pound through the thin fabric of her bodice. "No, Royal, at this moment I don't want to wait." She stood on shaky legs and descended the steps. "But I must. I pray you'll agree."

A puff of wind whirled grass cuttings through the air. With

an annoyed frown, he brushed chaff from his black trousers. "I've been planning to visit Jefferson City. I'll leave tomorrow to give you time to decide. When I return, I expect you to set a date."

Still reeling from the effects of his kiss, she stammered, "How long will you be away?"

"How long will it take you to make up your mind?"

It appeared Royal could turn his charm on and off at will, and during the ride home it had been off. He walked her to the door without a word, then spun on his heel and strode away.

Faith entered the house and ran upstairs without greeting her grandfather or Amy. She couldn't let them see her so upset.

She flopped on her bed and stared at the ceiling. If only she had someone to help her make sense of her conflicting desires. Royal's magnetism drew her toward him, the way a cyclone sucked up everything in its path. But once she was alone, she could see past her whirling emotions enough to wonder why he pressed so hard for a commitment, yet never said the word "love."

Sighing, she stood and paced, his passionate kiss burning in her memory. *Lord, please show me what to do.*

Talk to Rosemary. Faith sensed, rather than heard, the words. The mantel clock downstairs chimed four. She had time to walk to her friend's house and return before supper.

Standing in front of the pier glass, she settled her bonnet back over her braided chignon and smoothed loose tendrils of hair behind her ears.

"You're a Jack-in-the-box today," Grandpa said when she descended the stairs. "Up, down, up, down." He chuckled at his own humor.

"I'm going to visit Rosemary, but I shan't be long."

She smiled at Amy, who sat sewing a garment for Sophia. Amy returned the smile. "Have a nice visit."

Faith wished she could invite her along, but five blocks would be too great a distance to walk carrying a five-month-old baby, and the idea of leaving Sophia in Grandpa's care gave her pause.

Over the three weeks Amy had been with them, she'd become a part of their household. Faith knew they'd miss her when she found a position as housekeeper. So far, neither she nor Curt had come up with any prospects.

She huffed with mild frustration as she set off toward town. Life grew more complicated every day.

Curt answered the door when Faith knocked. His shirt was rolled up to the elbows and sawdust clung to his trouser legs. A broad grin lit his features. "This is a nice surprise. Guess you're here to see my sister."

She nodded and stepped around a dozing Bodie to enter the room. "It appears I've interrupted you in the middle of a project. I apologize."

Rosemary walked up behind him. "Curt's making a carriage for Amy Dunsmuir's baby. Wait until you see it. He's done such a clever job."

Faith felt the same stab of jealousy she'd experienced when she saw Curt and Amy together in her parlor. What was the matter with her? She'd come to talk to Rosemary about marrying Royal, and here she was jealous over Curt's attraction to their young guest.

She forced a smile. "How thoughtful of you. The poor girl can't get out for any exercise unless I'm home to watch Sophia. This way she'll be able to take the baby with her."

Curt's warm brown eyes lit with pleasure. "Thank you. I hoped you'd be pleased."

He must have meant he hoped Amy would be pleased. Sure he'd misspoken, she turned to Rosemary. "If you have a few minutes, could we talk?"

Rosemary slipped an arm around Faith's shoulders. "Come in the kitchen. I made some chamomile tea this afternoon. It's cooling in the springhouse."

Curt stepped around them, headed in the direction of the back porch. "I'll take a glass of that tea if you're willing to share."

His sister shook her head and gave him a playful push. "Go on with your task. I'll bring your tea." She bustled past him and soon carried a jar filled with pale green liquid toward the house. After taking a glass of the cooled beverage to her brother, she placed two more on the kitchen table and sat facing Faith.

"Wasn't this the day you were to give Royal your answer? You look too disquieted to be announcing an engagement."

Faith's composure crumpled. "I told him I needed to wait longer." She blinked back tears. "I just can't abandon the mercantile the way it is. Once upon a time our store was the finest establishment in town. One day, it will be again."

"What did Royal say?"

"He's angry." She twisted her hands in her lap. "He's leaving for Jefferson City tomorrow, and demanded an answer when he returns."

Rosemary studied her in silence for a moment. "Is this the kind of man you want to marry?" she asked in a gentle voice. "A bully?"

"He's not like that, not normally. I don't blame him for being frustrated. I promised him an answer, now I tell him to wait." Faith leaned back and folded her arms across her chest. "There's so much about him that draws me. But at other times . . . I don't know what to do. When he comes back, what will I say?"

"You'll know when the time comes. The Lord will give you the words."

Faith lifted her glass of tea. "Thank you. I needed the reminder." She sipped the lemony-tasting beverage. "I'm so glad I have you to talk to."

Through an open window, she heard sounds of a saw ripping wood. A bittersweet smile crossed her face. Amy was a fortunate girl to have captured Curt's interest.

As Curt's hands fashioned a hood for the baby's carriage, his mind stayed with the conversation he'd overheard. Baxter was a fool if he didn't know what a treasure he had in Faith. She worked in her granddad's store without complaint, took care of their meals and their home, and still managed to look fresh and desirable every time he saw her. If she were his, he'd wait as long as necessary to claim her as his bride.

He jerked the saw through a thin board, then groaned when he saw the wood split along the grain. *Slow down, Saxon*, he admonished himself. He wanted this carriage to be perfect enough to elicit Faith's admiration. Now that they'd completed their work on the ledgers, he needed another reason to see her. Crafting a carriage for Amy's baby was a stroke of genius. They could visit while Amy took Sophia for walks.

The back door creaked. Rosemary walked onto the porch carrying a tiny flowered quilt. "We can line the bottom and sides with this to make it soft." She ran her fingers along the side walls. "This wood is as smooth as satin. You must've spent hours sanding."

He shrugged, trying to seem offhand. "Gives me something to do. D'you think Faith will like the carriage?"

"I thought you were building it for Amy." Her voice teased.

"I am." Grabbing a piece of sandpaper, he rubbed at a support bar for the hood. "But only because I can't think of anything to build for Faith." As soon as the words were out, he wished he hadn't said them. No sense admitting he cared about a woman he couldn't have.

Rosemary tucked the quilt under one arm and reached up to put her free hand on his shoulder. "Why don't we ask Faith, Amy, and Judge Lindberg to join us for the Independence Day celebration? We can take a picnic and watch the parade and speeches." Her eyes sparkled. "The carriage will be finished. What a perfect opportunity to show it off—and spend time with Faith."

"She's as good as promised to that Baxter fellow."

"I don't believe so. I think she's hoping for a reason to turn him down. She just hasn't realized it yet."

Curt stared at his sister. How did women know these things? Judging from the amount of time Faith spent with Baxter, it looked to him like she was practically engaged. He placed the support bar and sandpaper on the porch railing, allowing enthusiasm for Rosemary's suggestion to build in his heart.

"You think she'd agree to come with us?"

Rosemary jammed her hands on her hips and sent him a mock frown. "After all the time we've spent together, why wouldn't she? You're making this too difficult. 'Faint heart never won fair lady.'" She poked his upper arm. "Ask her when you deliver the buggy."

During her walk home, Faith thought about the baby carriage Curt was crafting for Amy—and Sophia. She pictured his intent gaze concentrating on the small pieces of wood necessary to build something for a baby. Amy would be thrilled.

She picked up her pace, walking faster to outdistance unworthy jabs of envy that pricked at her heart. If anyone deserved kindness, it was their young guest. As intense as Faith's feelings of loss were for her brother and father, she didn't believe they could compare with losing a husband.

As she drew close to home, Faith realized she hadn't worried once all afternoon about leaving her grandfather alone. In fact, ever since Amy arrived, she'd had no need to worry about Grandpa. He seemed content to work on his memoirs at the house, with occasional evenings out spent with his friend, Dr. Greeley.

An idea buzzed through her mind. After supper, she'd see if Grandpa agreed.

*F*aith dried the final plate and stacked it with its mates in a cupboard next to the stove. Grandpa's cane bumped against the floor as he crossed the entryway. She assumed he was heading for the stairs.

She poked her head out of the kitchen, wiping her hands on a towel. "Have you got a moment? I want to ask you something while Amy's busy with the baby."

"I always have time for you." He tugged a chair away from the table and sat. "Any of that cake left? Amy's almost as good with pastry as you are."

"It's Amy I want to talk to you about." She cut a slice of Dolly Varden cake and placed it in front of him.

Grandpa separated the layers and forked up a bite of the filling. Faith grinned at the sight. She'd instructed Amy to spread extra berry jam on the cake, knowing her grandfather's fondness for eating the filling first. Taking a chair across from him, she watched for a moment, then asked, "What would you say to inviting Amy to stay on permanently as our housekeeper?"

"Excellent idea. She's a great help, and surely needs a home." He poked at his cake, cutting one of the layers into squares. " 'Withhold not good from them to whom it is due, when it is in the power of thine hand to do it.' "

His words jolted something loose in her memory. "Where is that in the Bible?"

"Proverbs." He pointed his fork at her. "You need to spend more time memorizing Scripture. God's Word never fails."

"You're right." As soon as he finished eating, she'd run upstairs and ask Amy if she'd be willing to stay on—officially. Then she'd take her Bible and search for the verse Grandpa so often quoted.

Faith walked through the store late Monday afternoon, flicking a duster over countertops and merchandise. Today was Mr. Grisbee's turn to act as watchman. She imagined he was somewhere out back, patrolling the alley, but she didn't need protection any longer. Several weeks had passed since the theft of her reticule.

She strode toward the storeroom. She'd tell Mr. Grisbee that he and Mr. Slocum could relax their efforts. The thief was probably long gone.

A rattling sound came from the storage area, followed by a crash and muffled curses. She pushed the curtain aside. "Mr. Grisbee! Are you all right?"

Light from the open door illuminated buckshot pellets strewn over the floor inside the back entrance. Faith lifted her skirt and stepped with care around the scattered lead balls. Mr. Grisbee must be in the alley. *Lord, I pray he's not hurt.*

Outside, a heated breeze blew a puff of dust down the pathway between buildings. Mr. Grisbee came toward her in a fast shuffle from behind the newspaper office. "Blast it. He got away."

"Who?"

"Your thief." He put his hands on his knees and drew several deep breaths. Sweat trickled through his gray whiskers.

Faith's hand flew to her throat. "He was here?" A shudder ran through her. She tucked her hand under the older man's elbow. "Come inside and sit. I'll get you a glass of ginger water and you can tell me what happened."

When they stepped into the storeroom, she pointed at the floor. "Careful. A box of buckshot got spilled."

"Hah! Me and Jesse come up with that. Worked too, 'cept I was too slow." With the toe of his boot, he rolled the pellets aside.

She stared at him. "Buckshot?"

"Yep. Dumped it on the floor. Figured anyone who tried to sneak in would slip and fall, then we'd grab 'em. Only trouble was, he was too fast."

He shuffled to a chair and mopped his forehead with a bandana while Faith poured a glass of ginger water. Her hand trembled when she handed him the beverage. "We need to tell the sheriff." She sank into the chair next to him.

He patted her shoulder. "I'll talk to him directly." He chortled. "Meantime, we did a pretty good job of scaring that fellow off. Bet he's got a bruise or two."

After Mr. Grisbee left, Faith swept up the shot pellets, dumping them into a bucket in case the regulars wanted to use their trap again. Her head spun with worry. As far as she knew, none of the other merchants had been robbed. She was being targeted.

She hung the broom on a hook, then cocked her head and listened. A squeaking sound came from the alley. Her nerves tingled. Tiptoeing, she crept to the tool display and wrapped her fingers around a crowbar.

Someone knocked at the bolted door.

Clutching the iron bar in her right hand, she shot open the bolt and peered into the alley.

Curt stood outside, a sheepish expression on his face. He gripped the handle of what looked like a cradle on wheels.

"Finished the carriage." He took a second look at her. "Who are you planning to attack with that weapon?"

"Mr. Grisbee scared off an intruder awhile ago. I thought the man had come back."

"Thieves don't knock."

"I know." She took a deep breath. "I wasn't thinking." She sagged with relief at the sight of his friendly face. "Come on in."

Curt bolted the door behind him. "You weren't harmed, were you?" His jaw tightened.

She shook her head.

"Did you tell the sheriff?"

"Mr. Grisbee did." She paused a moment while her heartbeat slowed to normal. "I'd hoped to see you today."

He shot her a smile and rolled the white-painted buggy into the mercantile, parking it near the front windows. "Thought you'd be the best one to take this to Amy."

"It's beautiful. But why did you come the back way?"

"Can you picture me pushing this down the street? I took the alley all the way from our house."

Faith bent over to examine the workmanship. She patted the quilted lining, admired the curved hood, and exclaimed over the perfectly matched wheels. "You even made a tiny pillow."

"Rosemary did that. I draw the line at sewing."

They exchanged a smile. "I'm glad you're here," Faith said, remembering the news she wanted to share. "I have something to tell you."

Did she imagine it, or did his face pale for a moment?

Curt swallowed. "First, I've got a message for you from Rosemary. She . . . we want you to go to the Independence Day celebration with us. The parade starts at ten. We can pick you up a few minutes earlier." A proud expression crossed his face. "Amy will have the carriage for Sophia."

"I know she'll be pleased." She tried not to let a disappointed edge creep into her voice, but from his expression, she'd failed.

He eyed her for a moment, then moved toward the front. "Wednesday, then." He turned the knob, jingling the bell.

"Wait."

The bell chimed again when he closed the door. Faith scooted around to the cash drawer and slapped two ledgers on the counter. "Come see what I discovered." She flipped a book open to one of the marked pages, then took her Bible from her carryall.

"You've got my curiosity up. Did your granddad explain his system to you?"

"In a way." She opened her Bible to the third chapter of Proverbs and pointed at the twenty-seventh verse. 'Withhold not good from them to whom it is due, when it is in the power of thine hand to do it.'" She smiled at Curt, triumphant. "Grandpa says that all the time. Last night I counted the books from Genesis on, and Proverbs is the twentieth one in the Old Testament."

She moved her hand to the open ledger and ran her finger under the numbers *20327* at the bottom of the page. "Twenty. Three. Twenty-seven. The numbers written below each name when he gave merchandise away. Do you see?"

"Well, I'll be." His eyes shone. He took her face in his hands and planted a kiss on her forehead. "You're a smart one."

Faith stepped backward, the imprint of his lips warm on her skin. She stared at him with widened eyes.

He stared back, a flush climbing his cheeks. The scar on his neck pulsed red. "Forgive me. I had no right."

She lifted a hand toward him and then let it drop. Her heart thrummed. "Of course I forgive you. We had something to celebrate, after all."

"No. I was wrong," he mumbled, striding toward the entrance.

The bell jangled. The door slammed.

Faith watched him lope down the boardwalk, wishing there'd been more she could say. Words that would keep him by her side.

Independence Day arrived. Faith and Amy waited on the front porch with Grandpa for Curt's arrival, filled picnic baskets at the ready.

"Here comes a wagon. Must be him," Grandpa said, pointing with his cane.

"How can you tell at this distance?" Faith asked.

"Slowest horse in town—bound to be young Saxon."

Once Moses plodded to a stop at the hitching rail, Curt jumped down and sprinted toward the house.

Faith took a deep breath, ready for his greeting, but instead his gaze fell on Amy. "Does the carriage roll smoothly? I put bricks in it to test weight load, but bricks aren't a baby."

Amy lifted Sophia into her arms. "It's perfect, Mr. Saxon. I've enjoyed taking her for walks. Thank you."

He winked at Faith. "'Withhold not good from them to whom it is due . . .'"

A flutter tickled her throat at the reminder of their shared discovery—and his kiss. Her lips curved upward. "It seems you're accomplished at any task you undertake. Is there anything you can't do?"

A shadow displaced his cheerful expression. "Hide from memories," he said in a voice meant for her ears alone. "As you well know."

The pain in his eyes penetrated her heart. She wished she could promise him that in time the memories would fade, but how could she? She was planning to run to Oregon to hide from her own memories.

When they reached the site of the celebration, Curt tied the horse and wagon in front of the depot and helped his passengers to the ground. He paused before carrying the picnic baskets to a grassy area under a maple tree. "Rosemary's waiting for us. Earlier this morning we staked a spot with a quilt."

The number of quilts spread over the grass formed a solid pattern of their own. Faith's eyes lingered on the red, white, and blue bunting draped over the latticework on the bandstand, remembering her visit there with Royal a few days before. She hoped he wouldn't appear today and disrupt her time with Curt and Rosemary, then felt a nudge of guilt at the thought.

At the far end of the parklike area, she noticed a string of booths labeled "Cold Lemonade," "Soda Water," and "Beer and Libations." The beer concession seemed to be doing a brisk trade. Men's raucous voices carried over the murmur of families gathered for the parade. Faith frowned, thankful the revelers were far enough away not to disturb their picnic.

In the distance, a band struck up "Columbia, Gem of the Ocean." Flag bearers marched down Court Street, preceding the musicians. Faith tucked her hand under Curt's arm. "Let's hurry. I want to get close enough to see the parade."

They gathered with the rest of the spectators lining the street facing the railroad platform. Faith stood between Curt and Grandpa, while Amy pushed the carriage over the grass to join Rosemary.

"I've never seen so many people turn out for the Independence Day celebration before," Faith said.

Grandpa responded in a low voice. "We're a Union again. That's something to celebrate."

The band marched into view, followed by a farm wagon filled with children dressed in costumes featuring stars and stripes. A brightly polished buggy was next. A portly red-faced gentleman in a frock coat and top hat sat behind the driver.

"One thing we can count on," Faith whispered to Curt. "Mayor Hayes will treat us to a long speech."

Several more entries passed by, including a small boy driving a dog cart and waving a flag. The Saint Bernard that pulled him had a red bow around his neck and flags flying from makeshift saddlebags slung over his back.

The home militia unit concluded the parade. As the crowd began to disperse, the soldiers halted, pointed their rifles into the air, and fired three volleys.

Curt froze.

Reacting without thinking, Faith clasped one of his fisted hands between hers. "You're here with me. You're home. You're safe."

Slowly his hand relaxed. His fingers wrapped around hers. He closed his eyes, breathing in short gasps.

In front of them, the leader of the militia led his men in a brief close order drill, then formed them up to march forward. As they moved down the street, the smell of gunpowder lingered in the air. Curt removed his hat and wiped sweat from his forehead. "I didn't expect that, or I wouldn't have come."

Rosemary hurried over to them. A worried frown creased her forehead. "Are you all right?" she asked Curt.

"Yes. Faith here kept me from embarrassing myself."

"The Lord helped you. I was just in the neighborhood." Faith disengaged her hand from his.

"Why don't we get comfortable? We can listen to the mayor speak and enjoy our picnic at the same time." Rosemary pointed to their quilt in the shade of a maple tree. Amy sat next to the baby carriage, her dress a pool of black engulfing her slight figure.

"I'm ready to get out of the sun." Faith exchanged a smile with Rosemary, then turned—and stopped short.

Sheriff Cooper stood near the tree watching them, arms folded over his chest. He tipped his hat. "Morning, folks. Fine parade, wasn't it?"

"Indeed it was, Sheriff." Faith's mind went to the day their store had been robbed. Most of the townsfolk had been gathered near the railroad tracks then too. "But shouldn't you be uptown keeping an eye on things?"

"Can't be everywhere at once. Heard there might be a disturbance down here between Rebs and Union men. War's not over for some, seems like." His gaze flicked in Curt's direction and then returned to Faith.

Feeling a surge of protectiveness, she stepped between the sheriff and Curt. "Any progress on finding the thieves who stole our merchandise?" She hoped he noticed the sharpness in her voice.

"I've got a pretty good idea who it was." He tipped his hat again and ambled past them.

"He probably never gives it a thought unless I prod him," Faith muttered under her breath.

Mayor Hayes concluded his lengthy speech at the same moment Faith rose to gather the picnic leftovers and stow them in baskets. Once the man's strident oration ceased, sounds of voices raised in argument drifted from beyond the bandstand. Undisturbed, Grandpa dozed, slouched forward on the camp stool Curt had provided for his comfort.

She turned, noticing Curt and Rosemary strolling under the trees with Amy, who pushed Sophia's carriage over the uneven ground. Faith stared after them. Judging from Curt's attentiveness, it wouldn't be long before he courted Amy in earnest. Why else would he continue to call at the house now that they'd concluded their work on the mercantile's ledgers? A shadow of jealousy stole some of the luster from the afternoon.

Faith picked her way across the grass toward their wagon with a filled basket in each hand. As soon as her friends returned, she'd suggest that Curt take them home. Her grandfather looked ready to tip over in the afternoon heat.

"Look out! They've got knives."

Startled, she pivoted to locate the source of the alarm. A woman pointed in Grandpa's direction. Behind his slumped figure, a blade flashed in the sunlight.

Two men circled one another, coming closer to Rosemary's quilt and paying no attention to anything but their dispute. One of the men staggered, his weapon coming within inches of the stool on which her grandfather napped. Didn't they see him?

Fear coursed over her body. How could he sleep through their grunts and muttered curses? She tore past picnickers, running straight at the two men. Part of her mind recognized that she still carried the baskets. She flung them aside without pausing.

"Stop! Don't hurt him!" She waved her arms to attract their attention. A few more yards and she'd be able to thrust herself between the brawlers and her grandfather.

Her right foot sank into a soft mound of earth, twisting her ankle with an explosion of pain. Momentum carried her forward and she sprawled on the ground.

25

$\mathcal{F}$aith struggled to her knees, gasping for breath, pain a blazing pitchfork in her ankle. Her bonnet had come loose and dangled in front of her eyes. She flung it aside. Where was Grandpa? Had he been hurt?

Through a haze of tears she saw Curt sprinting toward her. He dropped to one knee at her side. "What happened?"

"I . . . I stepped in a gopher hole. My ankle. I think it's broken." Speech left her breathless. "Grandpa . . ."

"He's coming." Curt slipped his arms around her waist and with a gentle motion turned her to a sitting position.

She leaned against him, fighting nausea. "It hurts so much."

Several people gathered around. Her grandfather pushed his way past them. "I woke up just as you fell. Why in heaven's name were you running in this heat? Was someone chasing you?" He brandished his cane. "You should have called me."

Faith covered her mouth, unsure whether to laugh or cry. "There were two men fighting. Behind you. They had knives."

"She's right," someone said, pointing toward Court Street. "Sheriff's got 'em now."

The two men, hands in the air, were being prodded by Sheriff Cooper in a quick step toward the jailhouse. From the set of his right shoulder, Faith assumed the sheriff had his revolver pointed at their backs. She breathed a silent apology to him for doubting his reason for attending the festivities. Thank goodness he'd been there to stop the fight before anyone, particularly her grandfather, had been injured.

Curt's voice rumbled in her ear. "What did you think you could do against men with knives?" He drew her closer. "You could've been hurt."

"She is hurt." Rosemary appeared at her brother's side. "Please carry her to our quilt so I can see what's wrong. Be careful."

Faith drew a sharp breath when Curt lifted her in his arms. The agony in her leg intensified as he stepped across the ground and settled her in the shade of the maple tree. She gritted her teeth to keep from moaning.

Rosemary knelt beside her. Her soft palm stroked Faith's forehead. "Tell me where the pain is the worst."

"My right leg."

Mortified, Faith closed her eyes when Rosemary drew her skirt up. She hoped Curt couldn't see her exposed limb. Her friend slowly unwound the laces on Faith's boots, each motion a fresh burst of agony.

Faith caught her lip between her teeth while Rosemary's fingers probed the ankle area.

"Is it broken?"

"Just sprained. We'll get you home and soak it in a basin of cold water."

"So I can go to the mercantile tomorrow?"

"Not so soon—"

"What's happening here? I heard someone was injured." Dr. Greeley stepped next to Grandpa and peered down at Faith.

Rosemary sat back on her heels. "Faith caught her foot in a gopher hole and turned her ankle. It's just a sprain."

His white goatee seemed to bristle. "I'll thank you to allow a professional to make the diagnosis." He turned to Grandpa. "Can you transport her to my office for a proper examination?"

Grandpa looked at Curt, a question in his eyes.

Curt nodded. "I'll bring the wagon over here. We can meet you at your office, but I don't think it's necessary. My sister is perfectly qualified to care for an ankle sprain."

Rosemary stood, her cheeks redder than the bunting draped over the bandstand. "Let it go," she said to her brother. "I'll see you at home." She stalked away.

"Rosemary." Faith tried to stand, only to crumple to the ground. Anger at the doctor burned in her throat. "Dr. Greeley, Miss Saxon was a nurse during the conflict. She's no doubt treated worse injuries than my ankle."

"She treated them, perhaps, but not before they were diagnosed."

In the uncomfortable silence that followed, Faith avoided the doctor's eyes by tracking Curt's path to the wagon. He paused to speak to Amy for a moment, then crossed the street and unhitched Moses.

Amy gathered the discarded picnic baskets and held them in one hand while pushing Sophia's carriage toward the edge of the grass. When Curt brought the wagon around, she lifted the baby into her arms. He placed the carriage in the wagon bed, then swung Amy up to the front seat.

Faith stifled a jolt of jealousy. Whatever Curt decided to do with his life was his own concern.

"Please stretch out flat." The doctor lifted one corner of Rosemary's quilt. "We'll wrap this around you before placing you in the wagon."

Her eyes widened at the thought of being transported through town like a stack of lumber. "Why can't I sit next to Grandpa?"

"We need to keep your leg elevated. From what I could see, it's quite swollen." He tucked the corner of the quilt under her hip.

Faith winced at the motion. Perhaps Dr. Greeley was right. She tried to ignore the stares of several small boys who'd gathered nearby while he bundled the quilt from her waist to beyond her toes.

One of the lads stepped forward. "Excuse me, miss, did you drop this?" He held a shiny object toward her. "After that man covered you up, it was sitting in the grass right there." He pointed to a crushed area where the quilt had rested. "I never stole it, honest."

With a thrill of recognition, she clasped her fingers around the smooth silver case. "Thank you. I know you didn't steal it."

But someone had. It was one of the pocket watches that had been on display in the mercantile.

An hour later, Faith trundled home in the rear of the mercantile's delivery wagon. An unbidden thought crossed her mind. If she'd said yes to Royal when he first asked, she and Grandpa might already be on their way west and away from the ongoing turmoil stirred up in the wake of the war. Mr. Allen would own the mercantile and its problems.

How foolish she'd been to postpone her decision. She thought of Mr. Allen's offer. As soon as she could, she'd inform the banker that she was interested. After today's events, her grandfather was bound to see things her way.

"Are you comfortable?" Curt asked, pushing the curtain aside with one hand while keeping the other on the reins.

She shaped the pillow behind her head into a mound so she could see his face. "This is better than being out in the open with people staring." Her mouth quirked in a half-smile. "But comfortable? No."

"After a couple weeks' rest, your sprained ankle will be as good as new." He chuckled. "I can't wait to tell Rosemary her diagnosis was correct. Dr. Greeley merely reinforced everything she said."

Faith had no intention of resting for two weeks, but she didn't say so. As soon as she could hobble well enough on the crutches the doctor provided, she'd go straight to the sheriff with her find. One of the men he arrested must have been carrying the watch.

She smiled at Curt's back. Before she and Royal left, she'd have the satisfaction of knowing Curt was no longer suspected of robbing the store. Her smile faded when she imagined herself leaving Noble Springs as Royal's wife. No more Curt and Rosemary. No more mercantile.

A lump rose in her throat. She forced it down. Grandpa would be happier away from reminders of the war, and so would she. While she waited for Royal's return from Jefferson City, she'd do all she could to get their affairs in order. He would be pleased.

Curt carried Faith into her house. Her hair tumbled loose, surrounding him with the fragrance of rose oil. He savored the softness of her body against his chest. For a moment, he pretended he was carrying her across a threshold as his wife. Baxter could go hang. Until there was an official engagement, he had an equal chance with Faith.

One day soon, he'd be ready to ask her. All he had to do was give Reverend French the word and the last barrier would be removed.

Amy led the way past the kitchen to the same small bedroom where Faith's granddad had recuperated from his fall earlier in the year. Curt maneuvered through the hallway with care to avoid striking Faith's injured foot against the wall.

"While you were with the doctor, I freshened the bedding and moved things so you can see out the window," Amy said to Faith.

"Thank you." Her voice wavered.

Curt felt her tremble as he placed her atop a quilt spread over the cot. He folded her hand in his. "Rest now. Amy can help you change your . . . garments. Rosemary said she'd look in on you later."

Faith nodded, shivering.

Past scenes of men in tent hospitals painted themselves behind his eyelids. He drew a long breath and held it for a moment, then moved to the doorway and motioned Amy to follow him. Once in the hall, he spoke in a low tone. "She's experiencing delayed shock from the fall. Keep her warm and see if she'll sleep."

"I'll be happy to tend to her. It's the least I can do after all she's done for me."

A pang squeezed his chest at the sight of her earnest young face, so pale above her severe black dress. He hoped the day would come when she'd meet someone who'd be as good to her as Joel had been.

Curt placed a hand on her shoulder. "Faith is blessed to have you here. You've been a godsend with her grandfather."

Amy blushed.

He heard a rustling sound from the bedroom. Glancing back, he saw Faith propped on one elbow watching them, sorrow in her eyes.

The popping of firecrackers greeted Curt when he left the Lindbergs' house. Flinching at the sound, he supposed he'd have to endure the crackling until long past dark. Little boys hadn't changed since he was a youth.

He untied his horse from the hitching rail and drove the delivery vehicle toward the alley behind the mercantile, where his own open wagon waited. Moses plodded along at his usual snail's pace. As they approached the jailhouse, the door opened and two sullen-looking men stumbled onto the boardwalk.

Sheriff Cooper leaned against the door frame with his arms folded. "You two git now. Any more trouble out of either of you boys and you'll spend a few weeks enjoying my hospitality."

One of the men turned his skinny neck toward the sheriff as though he planned a retort, then looked away. The other clapped a slouch hat over greasy-looking curls and stomped off toward the train station.

The sheriff angled his head at Curt. "Hope you didn't steal that wagon. Belongs behind the mercantile."

Seething, Curt pulled up on the reins. "Were those the brawlers you arrested at the festivities?"

"What business is it of yours?"

"They're the reason I'm driving the Judge's wagon. Miss Faith hurt her ankle when she saw them carry their fight too close to her granddad. I just got done taking her home from Doc Greeley's."

Sheriff Cooper's expression softened. "I grabbed 'em right after she fell. Sorry to hear she's hurt."

"So, why'd you let them go? You know they'll have a couple more mugs of beer and start all over again."

"Now you're a lawman? Let me handle miscreants. You stick to currying horses." He stepped inside and banged the door behind him.

Curt clenched his jaw, wishing he knew a way to shake Sheriff Cooper out of his shortsighted complacency.

Early Thursday morning, Curt sat across from Reverend French's desk sipping stout black coffee. No wonder the man was such a passel of energy behind the pulpit. If he started his Sundays with this brew, it was a wonder he didn't bound up and down the walls of the sanctuary.

"You came for a letter of introduction?" the reverend asked. "You really don't need one."

"Then call it a referral. I want something besides my word to prove I'm who I say I am."

"Your reputation will speak for itself."

"It's been more than four years. Reputations are like bread—they're only good when they're fresh."

Reverend French rubbed his upper lip. "Malcolm Robbinette's the man you want to see. I'll write the letter now if you want to wait."

"Thanks, Reverend. I appreciate the boost."

He opened a drawer and placed a single sheet of paper on top of his spotless desk. After fitting a nib to his penholder, he favored Curt with a warm gaze. "I'll write this on one condition."

"Anything."

"Stop calling me Reverend. My name's Ethan."

With Ethan's letter folded in his shirt pocket, Curt strode at top speed across town to the livery stable. Rip had given him permission to arrive after nine, but he didn't want to abuse the man's good nature, especially since Rip didn't yet know he planned to seek another job.

When he reached the livery, his employer burst out of the open double doors. "Of all the days for you to be late. Thought you'd never get here."

"I'm not late. I asked yesterday—"

"That's right. You did. Sorry." Rip tugged at his beard. "I got some bad news this morning. I need you to run things here for a few weeks."

Curt struggled to frame a response. The letter in his pocket whispered its promises to him. Now that he was ready, he didn't want to postpone his decision for several weeks.

As the silence between them lengthened, the other man's eyes grew moist. "It's my brother in Arkansas," he said in a choked voice. "His wife telegraphed. He's dying."

Ashamed of his selfish reaction, Curt rested a hand on his boss's shoulder. "Go. Don't worry about the livery. I'll take care of everything."

26

_F_aith's ankle throbbed as she swung her legs over the side of the cot. She shouldn't be lying about in bed. She needed to tell Sheriff Cooper about the watch while the two men were still in jail. Then she had to see the banker about selling the mercantile.

Propelled by a sense of urgency, Faith pushed herself to a standing position, teetering on one foot. Her crutches were propped against the wall just out of reach. Flapping her elbows for balance, she hopped to the wall and grabbed at a crutch, gripping the hand piece while she tried to fit the second one under her left arm. After two wobbly tries, she gave up and hopped back to the cot.

Amy poked her head around the open door. "Did I hear you up and around?"

"Trying to be. I can't seem to manage those sticks." She swallowed, hating to ask for more assistance from the already overworked girl.

Amy's eyes flicked from Faith to the crutches. "Are you sure you're ready to walk?"

"You heard what Rosemary said. Twenty-four hours."

"She meant the hot and cold soaks."

247

"I'm better now. I know I can walk if you'll help me get started."

"We'll see." Amy handed Faith her wrapper and waited while she slipped her arms into the soft flannel garment. "Now, hang onto me and stand on your good leg. I'll give you the crutches one at a time."

Chafing at Amy's slow pace, Faith fitted the wooden devices under each arm.

As soon as she rested her weight on her left leg, Amy stepped away. "Now, move both crutches ahead a little bit, then put your weight on them and swing your good leg forward."

Faith took a tiny step and stopped. "What now?"

"Do it again."

Another tiny step. Pain pounded through her ankle. Dismayed, she saw she'd moved only a dozen inches closer to the bedroom door. How would she get to town at this rate?

A slight smile tugged at Amy's mouth while she watched her. "D'you think you can make it to the table? Dinner will be ready soon."

"Of course I can." She sucked in a breath. "How do you know so much about crutches?"

Amy lifted her skirt, revealing shiny scars covering her left leg. She touched a finger to her disfigured skin and said in a soft voice, "When I was twelve, sparks set my dress afire. Mama threw water on me, but this leg was burned bad. My papa made me some sticks and taught me to use them."

"Oh, Amy. I'm sorry." Faith berated herself for her impatience with Amy's slowness. If only she'd known. She lurched another step forward. "At this rate, it looks like I'll be at home for another day or two. Why don't you spend some extra time with Sophia? Grandpa and I will be fine."

"Thank you. I'd love that. I'll take her for a long ride in her carriage after we eat."

Faith smiled after her when Amy returned to the kitchen. If Curt's attraction blossomed into love, Amy's life would take a glorious turn. A man with his qualities would make any woman a perfect husband.

That evening, Faith showed the silver watch to Rosemary while the two of them sat on the sofa in the parlor. Grandpa had retired early, and Amy was up in her room with a book from their shelves, so Faith could enjoy Rosemary's company uninterrupted. A breeze from the open window bore the fragrance of the climbing roses her friend had planted that spring.

Faith's right leg rested on the green brocade ottoman that matched her grandfather's wing chair. She wiggled her toes inside her white silk stocking. "See why I can't take the watch to the sheriff? It'll be days before I can walk all the way to town."

"More like weeks."

"Worse yet. There's no time to lose. What if he lets those men go?"

"Let me show it to him. I'll explain how it came to light."

"I can't ask that of you. You're already spending your days at the mercantile. Besides, Sheriff Cooper doesn't seem too friendly to the Saxon family. If you have the watch, he'll say Curt stole it."

Rosemary bit her lower lip. "That didn't occur to me, but you're probably right." She stared at the ceiling.

Faith waited, knowing from her friend's expression that she was formulating a solution.

After several silent moments, Rosemary walked to the window and gazed into the dusk, hands clasped behind her.

"Would you have any objection to Sheriff Cooper coming here to talk to you?" She spoke with her back to Faith.

"Do you think he would?"

Rosemary turned to face her. "I don't see why not. He respects you and your grandfather. I'll tell him something turned up at the Independence Day celebration, and you want to talk to him about it."

"You're a wonderful friend. Tell him we'll expect him tomorrow evening, if that's convenient. I'll see to it Grandpa stays awake." Excitement bubbled through her. Perhaps more of their missing merchandise could be recovered. She pictured the stolen firearms back on the shelves and drew a satisfied breath. If their stock were restored, they could get a better price for the mercantile. Royal would be pleased indeed.

"Are you sure you want me to stay downstairs with you when the sheriff comes?" Amy asked Faith the next evening.

Faith patted the sofa cushion next to her. "You're part of this household. You should share in our celebration at catching the man who robbed our store."

"We didn't catch him. Sheriff Cooper did." Grandpa winked at her. "He just doesn't know it yet."

The clock struck seven at the same moment they heard the knock. Amy jumped to her feet and dashed to the door. Faith noticed the look of wide-eyed wonder that passed over the sheriff's face when he stood on the threshold and looked down at her.

He whipped his hat from his head. "Good evening. I was told Miss Faith had something she needed to discuss with me."

"Indeed she does." Amy reached for his hat and hung it

on the hall tree. "She'd greet you herself, but guess you know she sprained her ankle pretty bad."

"I heard." He remained at her side, unmoving.

Faith cleared her throat. "We're in here, Sheriff," she said.

He bowed in Amy's direction and gestured at the parlor entrance. "After you."

Grandpa gestured with his cane. "Great snakes, Thaddeus. Stop the bowing and scraping and come on in. Faith told me to stay awake until you arrived, but I'm not going to wait all night while you fuss around our Amy."

"Amy, is it?"

"Amy Dunsmuir," she murmured, settling beside Faith on the sofa.

The sheriff tucked his thumbs in the pockets of his leather vest, assuming an official pose. He tore his gaze from Amy and focused on Faith. "You have something to show me?"

She opened her hand and held the watch up for his inspection. "This was stolen from the mercantile along with several other watches and firearms. I believe you have the report."

He took the silver timepiece from her hand, turning it over. "How do you know it was yours?"

"We had half a dozen Walthams. If you'll look on the back, you'll see the number 405315 stamped into the silver. Miss Saxon brought me my record book this morning. That's one of our watches, without a doubt." She took a small leather-bound volume from the sofa cushion and opened it to a marked page. "Here's the proof."

"Supposing you're right, what do you want me to do about it?"

Did she have to tell him how to do his job? "I'm sure one of the brawlers you arrested on Independence Day lost this. It got kicked under our quilt during the fight. You've got them

251

both in jail. All you have to do is determine which one is the thief." She leaned back, unable to keep a smile of satisfaction from her lips. "I told you Mr. Saxon was innocent."

The sheriff's face flushed. He held up two fingers. "One. The men are no longer in custody." A finger went down. "Two. This doesn't prove Saxon's innocence, or the other man's guilt, for that matter." He closed his fist.

Faith felt the air whoosh from her lungs. "Did you record the names of the men when you arrested them?"

"Of course. It's the law."

"Then can you go after them? At least ask questions?"

Grandpa stirred in his chair. "Speaking of the law, judges don't look too kindly on incompetence. Maybe you need to put some effort into this."

Amy looked from Grandpa to the sheriff, her face a picture of confusion. "The store was robbed clear back in May. I remember how kind Miss Faith was to me at the time, in spite of her losses." She inclined her head in Sheriff Cooper's direction. "I hope you solve this soon. I'm afraid to step outdoors alone with such men running loose."

Lowering her eyes, Faith hid her amusement. Amy wasn't a bit afraid.

The sheriff drew himself up to his full height and smoothed his moustache. "Don't fret, ma'am. I have a good idea where to find these fellows." Turning to Faith, he added, "I'll be back soon with a report."

After he left, she squeezed Amy's hand. "I think he's smitten."

"I don't care about that." She frowned. "Maybe now he'll stop acting like a lazy hound and get after those varmints. I think it's terrible he blames Curt."

"Yes. So do I." Her voice sounded flat. She'd been thrilled when the watch turned up, but they were no closer to catching the thief. She doubted the sheriff planned to arrest anyone. His focus seemed to be on impressing Amy.

Faith surveyed the exterior of Lindberg's Mercantile from her seat in Curt's buggy. She sighed with pleasure. "It's good to be back. Everything looks the same."

Curt grinned at her. "You were only at home for two weeks."

"I missed being here—the customers, the activity, mornings with Rosemary."

"She missed you too." He propped her crutches against the hitching rail and clasped her around the waist, swinging her to the boardwalk.

"Well, this is a pretty picture," said a familiar voice.

She swiveled in the direction of the sound. Her face flushed. "Royal. When did you return?"

He strode toward them. "Not a moment too soon, it seems." His gaze swept over the crutches and back to Faith. "You're hurt."

She leaned on the rail while she fitted the crutch pads under her arms. "I sprained my ankle. This is my first day back at the store. I can't walk far, so Curt offered to bring me in his buggy. He had to close the livery in order to help me." Faith knew she was babbling. Stepping forward, she crutched toward the entrance, hoping to end the awkward moment.

"Very good of you, Saxon." Royal sprang ahead and opened the door for her with a flourish.

Faith turned, hoping the apology in her eyes would be apparent to Curt. "Thank you."

"No trouble." Curt climbed into the buggy. "Got to be getting back. I'll be here at five to take you home."

"Faith will travel home with me." Royal growled the words.

Curt glanced between them. "As you wish." He flicked the reins over the horse's back. Dust sprayed from the wheels as the buggy sped down the road.

Tears stung Faith's eyes. Of all the times for Royal to appear. Five more minutes and she'd have been in the store and Curt would have been on his way to the livery. He didn't deserve the other man's jealousy, yet she recognized how the scene must have looked to Royal when he first saw them.

Rosemary sent Faith a welcoming smile when she crossed the threshold, then her eyes widened when Royal entered behind her. "Mr. Baxter. What a surprise. We thought you to be in Jefferson City."

"I returned this morning and came directly here." He placed a possessive hand on Faith's shoulder. "She's promised me an answer to a very important question."

Faith felt her pulse throb in her throat. The memory of the knife brawl returned. She thought of Grandpa, visiting the cemetery to grieve the loss of most of his family. She was all he had left. It was her responsibility to take him somewhere where peace would overcome his pain.

Royal bent his head close to her ear. "What have you decided?" His warm breath slid over her neck.

She gripped the hand pieces on her crutches. "Yes," she whispered, "I'll marry you."

oyal whooped and swung Faith into the air. Her crutches bounced against a counter and clattered onto the wood floor. With his hands tight around her waist he kissed her, then set her back on her feet, supporting her with one arm.

Dazed, she glanced at Rosemary in time to see her shocked expression replaced with a polite smile.

"How wonderful for both of you." Her friend advanced, hands extended, smile fixed in place. "I wish you every happiness. I'll help all I can with your wedding plans."

The suddenness of the decision left Faith with nothing to say. She hadn't thought ahead to wedding plans. Most girls dreamed about the day they'd say "I do." And here she was, speechless.

Royal came to her rescue. "We haven't discussed exact plans. I can promise you we won't have a lengthy engagement. Summer's winding down and we need to start west as soon as possible."

At the promise of the trip west, Faith relaxed against his side. She'd done the right thing.

"I must leave you for now. When I fetch you this evening,

we'll talk to your grandpappy." He gave her waist a squeeze. "Tomorrow we'll go to the bank and—"

The bell over the door jingled. Marguerite sashayed in, followed by Nelda. "I thought I saw your beautiful stallion tied to the rail outside," Marguerite said to Royal in a syrupy voice. She paused when she noticed his arm around Faith. She batted her eyelashes. "Excuse me. It appears I've interrupted something."

Faith lifted her chin. "May I help you with a purchase? My fiancé was just leaving."

"Your . . . fiancé?" Nelda blinked at them, mouth agape.

Marguerite tried for a smile. "My goodness, you're full of surprises, Major Baxter."

Royal swept Faith's crutches from the floor and handed them to her. "I'll come for you at five." He dropped a light peck on her cheek before bowing in Marguerite's direction and striding through the door.

Nelda wandered across the room to the fabric counter and fingered a bolt of peacock blue velvet.

Her companion broke the silence. "I hadn't heard of your engagement. When did all this take place?" Spots of pink tinged her cheeks.

"This morning, just before you came in."

"Well, that explains how he could be in Hartfield last week with another girl. Nelda saw them when she was visiting her aunt."

"I'm afraid she was mistaken." Faith moved toward Marguerite, her crutches thumping in time with the pounding of her heart. "Royal's been in Jefferson City."

Nelda turned, raising a pale eyebrow. "If you say so."

"I do. Now, how much of this velvet would you like?"

She backed away from the counter. "None. I was just looking."

"And you, Marguerite? Some lace, perhaps?"

She shook her head. "I only stopped in to say hello to your . . . fiancé."

After they left, Faith's shoulders drooped. If anyone else but Nelda had spread the gossip, she might have believed the story. Still, the thought wouldn't quite leave her mind. He said he was going to Jefferson City, but she had no way of knowing that's where he went.

Rosemary patted Faith's arm. "Don't let them upset this happy day. You know they're jealous."

"If I weren't trying to keep from falling over these sticks, I'd hug you."

"We'll need to get in all the hugs we can." Tears brimmed in Rosemary's eyes. "You'll be gone before summer's out."

Faith's smile disappeared. "I know," she murmured. "I'm trying not to think about leaving you behind."

Curt paused inside one of the stalls, a scoop of oats in one hand. A shadowy figure stood in the entrance to the stable. "Anyone here? I'm in need of a carriage."

The voice couldn't belong to anyone other than Baxter. Curt dumped the oats into a trough. "Be right with you," he called. He trudged the length of the stable at a dilatory pace.

Baxter drummed his fingers against the door of the little room Rip used for an office. "I don't have all day. It's almost five, and I promised to fetch my fiancée home." He smirked. "I'll be renting a carriage from you for a few weeks, until after the wedding."

Ice raced through Curt's veins. "Fiancée? Wedding?" He cursed himself for sounding like a parrot.

"Your friend Faith Lindberg has accepted my proposal. Once we're wed, we plan to take her old grandpappy and head for Oregon."

The words struck Curt with the force of a blow. "Congratulations. She's a fine girl. You're blessed." His voice sounded as tight as a wagon spring.

"Blessed, or lucky. Whatever you want to call it."

"I'll bring the phaeton up for you. Likely you want the best."

"I'm a little stretched right now, what with supplying for the journey and all. A plain buggy's fine. Do you have weekly rates?"

Curt ground his teeth. "We do. Paid in advance."

Baxter counted out several coins, dropping them in Curt's palm. "Things'll be better once she sells that store. I'll get the phaeton from you then."

"Fine." Curt placed the grain scoop at the edge of Rip's desk and scribbled out a receipt. "The buggy you want is out back. Just give me a moment to get it ready."

Baxter lifted a silver watch from his waistcoat pocket and clicked open the lid. "Make it quick. It's almost five."

"Nice watch." Curt angled to get a closer look while keeping his tone noncommittal.

"Friend gave it to me." He snapped the timepiece shut, tucking it out of sight. "You getting that buggy or not?"

After Baxter left, Curt grabbed the scoop and flung it against a wall. "Idiot! Why didn't you tell her how you felt about her?"

Out of habit, he ran his fingers over the scar on his neck. When he lowered his arm, he brushed against the paper he'd carried in his pocket since Ethan gave it to him. He jerked it out. "Won't need this now." Crumpling the folded sheet into a ball, Curt sent it flying onto a pile of manure.

Faith perched at one end of the sofa. Royal fidgeted next to her while Grandpa sat with his hands on his knees, staring at both of them. The pain of betrayal shone in his eyes.

"What does it matter now?" he asked. "You want my blessing on something you've already decided. I'm disappointed in you, Faith."

Pain coursed through her at his words. She bit her lip and said nothing.

Royal stood. "Please don't blame your granddaughter. I took her by surprise this morning. I know I should have called on you first." He fumbled in his coat pocket and removed a small cloth-covered bundle. "This belonged to my grandmother." Unfolding the cloth, he showed a ring to Grandpa. "She told me to give it to someone special. With your permission, it will belong to Faith when we're married."

"I can hardly refuse now, can I? Faith always gets what she wants. She wants to marry you, fine. I won't stand in your way."

A jubilant expression crossed Royal's face. "Thank you, sir."

Faith rose, limped over to her grandfather, and kissed his cheek. "It's for the best," she whispered. "You'll see."

He blew out a weary sigh. "Time will tell."

Royal took Faith's left hand in his. "I want to see how the ring looks on you." He slipped the gold band onto the fourth finger. The garnet and opal setting glowed in the light from the window.

She turned her hand from side to side, noticing colors flickering within the opal. The stone mirrored her heart. To one not wearing the ring, the colors looked like heat, but to her it was a cold fire.

As promised, Royal knocked on the Lindbergs' door shortly before nine the next morning. When Faith answered, he looked at her in surprise. "No crutches?"

"I want to practice walking. My ankle needs to be stronger before we leave."

"Good idea, but be careful." He took her arm. "You could have a setback. We wouldn't want that to happen."

"Certainly not."

When she was settled in the buggy, he flicked the reins over the horse's back and they rolled into town. Royal cleared his throat. "So, did you tell your grandpappy *all* our plans? Selling the mercantile, outfitting a wagon?"

Faith hunched her shoulders. "Not just yet. He's a little upset right now."

Royal slapped his hand on his leg. "Hang it! He'll be upset if you don't tell him. You heard him last night."

She shrank from the anger in his voice. "He's my grandfather. I'll tell him when I'm ready."

The muscles in his jaw twitched, but he didn't respond. They rode in silence until reaching the mercantile. With exaggerated courtesy, he helped her from the buggy and held her arm while she limped to the entrance. "Be ready at noon. I think we should speak to the banker today about the sale of the business."

"Today?"

"Yes. The sooner the better. Don't you want to get as far west as possible before winter sets in?"

She nodded.

He lifted her hand and kissed her palm. "See you at noon."

Faith pushed open the door, surprised to see Rosemary talking to the salesman from Marblehead Gun Works. Bodie stood sniffing the man's trouser leg.

Faith dismissed Royal from her mind and moved as quickly as she could toward the empty gun racks. "Mr. Jenner. I'm so glad to see you." She gave him her biggest smile, thankful he'd returned after the debacle of his last visit.

Rosemary snapped her fingers at Bodie. The two of them moved toward the woodstove, where Mr. Grisbee sat whittling. Faith shook her head, amused. She'd had an audience the last time the salesman called. The only person missing was Mr. Slocum, who was probably patrolling the alleyway.

Mr. Jenner gestured at the wall. "I see no competitors have been here."

"After your unfortunate visit in May, I felt it only right to place our order with you. We do have the funds to acquire a good shotgun and a Henry rifle."

"Only one of each?" His voice squeaked.

"For now. Maybe two more next month." After the work she and Curt had put into collecting bad debts, the thought of the firearms being replaced filled her with satisfaction. She'd tell Curt as soon as she saw him.

The salesman whipped out a notebook and scribbled the order. "Half up front," he said. "No bank draft." He showed her the total.

She breathed a silent prayer of thanks for the money she knew was in the cash drawer. Rosemary had kept careful accounts while Faith was forced to stay at home. Every afternoon she took extra cash to the bank and every morning brought a sum to keep in the till. Faith unlocked the drawer and removed two gold eagles.

Mr. Jenner beamed. "You'll have your merchandise within the next two weeks. As soon as I return to Jefferson City, I'll see to the loading personally."

A smile twitched her lips as she watched him stride out the door, shoulders back, head high.

261

"Guess a small order's better'n none," Mr. Grisbee said. His knife flicked wood shavings over Bodie's coat. "Be good to see this place packed with goods again."

"I agree." Faith leaned against a counter to take weight off her ankle. Her eyes roamed over the store, making note of the changes she'd wrought since Grandpa put her in charge. Placing new cookware on top of one of the stoves had helped sell both cookware and a stove. Hoes, shovels, and rakes sold well in spite of being relegated to a back wall.

She was most proud of the ladies' area she'd established near the front door. Fabric, laces, buttons, and thread were all arranged by color, making it easy for women to find what they needed. What had started as a burden had become a joy.

"You look pleased with yourself," Rosemary said, joining Faith at the counter.

"It felt wonderful to order those firearms. Curt spent hours and hours helping me with the finances. I can't wait to thank him."

"You may have to do it soon. Last night he mentioned that he was considering a return to St. Louis."

Faith stared at Rosemary. "Then you'd be alone here."

"Without you or Curt, I'd have no reason to stay either."

"I'm so sorry. I wish it could be otherwise, but ever since witnessing that fight all I've been able to think about is getting Grandpa away."

"Not marriage to Royal?"

She flushed. "Well, that too."

"Faith, you can't marry him for someone else's sake. You have to listen to your heart."

"I can't hear my heart anymore. I've tried."

Rosemary hugged her shoulders. "I'll help you listen."

Shortly after noon, Royal entered the mercantile and strode directly to Faith. "The buggy's outside. Are you ready?"

She noticed sawdust particles clinging to his shirt. The fragrance of fresh-cut oak hovered in the air. "The bank's at the next corner. We don't need the buggy."

"I don't want you to tax your ankle, sweetling."

She smiled at the pet name. Meeting with the banker would be one more step toward Oregon.

"I got a long dinner break," he said as they walked to the hitching rail. "Hated to ask after being gone for over two weeks, but Mr. Allen seemed glad to cooperate." He tucked his hand under her elbow. "He wished us well."

"Tell him thank you."

"I did." With his hands at her waist, Royal lifted her into the buggy.

Faith knew they could have walked during the same amount of time it took to ride to the corner, cross the intersection, and tie the horse to the rail outside the bank, but she appreciated his concern.

The bank president stood when Royal escorted Faith past the teller cages and stopped in front of his desk.

"Miss Lindberg." Mr. Paulson looked at Royal, his eyebrows raised.

"This is my fiancé, Royal Baxter," she said in response to his implied question.

The banker's eyebrows lifted higher as he surveyed Royal's work-stained clothing. He sat, resting his hands on his round belly. "This is quite a surprise. So tell me, what can I do for you today?"

Faith took a chair in front of his desk, extending her right leg to relieve a jab of pain in her ankle. "I've reconsidered Mr. Allen's offer. Could you talk to him and draw up sale documents for the mercantile?" Her stomach did a little flip.

"Once we're married, Royal and I plan to leave Noble Springs and emigrate to Oregon." The flutter in her stomach rose to her throat. She coughed.

Standing behind her, Royal rested his hands on Faith's shoulders. "We'd like to proceed without delay. When do you think you'll have an answer for us?"

Mr. Paulson's eyes narrowed. "Until Miss Lindberg is your legal wife, any matters regarding the mercantile are none of your concern." He turned to Faith. "If Gilbert Allen agrees, I'll have papers drawn up for your grandfather's signature."

Royal's grip on her shoulders tightened. "Faith is managing the store. Shouldn't she sign?"

"Young man, ownership of the business is in Judge Lindberg's name. There can be no sale without his signature."

Faith quailed at the thought of presenting her grandfather with sale documents on the heels of announcing her engagement. Perhaps having to wait for Mr. Allen's reply was for the best. She gathered her composure and stood. "Thank you, Mr. Paulson. I appreciate your assistance."

"I'll contact you soon." He eyed Royal. "Mr. Baxter. Congratulations on your engagement to this fine girl." His emphasis on the final two words carried more warning than blessing.

*U*nable to sleep, Faith went to the open window in her bedroom and stared out into the humid darkness. Lightning bugs blinked under the chokecherries that grew wild behind the springhouse.

She'd have to talk to Grandpa about Mr. Allen's offer tomorrow. Heaven help her if one of his friends heard the news and told him first.

Heaven help her. Rosemary had told her to listen to her heart.

Never mind her heart. How long had it been since she'd listened to the Lord?

Faith dropped to her knees beside her bed, something she hadn't done since she was a small girl. "Father, I've been busy chasing my own ideas of what's best. If Royal is part of your plan for me, please show me. Open or close the door on our marriage." She covered her face with her hands and heard nothing but crickets chirping in the silence. With a ragged sigh, she added, "Please."

The following morning, she awoke with one thought in mind—persuade Grandpa to agree to her plans. Faith slipped into her light blue calico gown and combed her thick hair, pinning it back into a coil. Before she rolled her stockings on, she studied her ankle. No swelling. Maybe today she'd go for a walk with Rosemary during the noon hour.

Across the hall, she heard Sophia whimper and Amy's soothing voice in response. After a moment, Sophia quieted. Faith knew Amy was nursing her before going downstairs to cook breakfast.

If she hurried, she could brew Grandpa's coffee and talk to him before Amy finished with Sophia. She dashed into the kitchen, poked up the fire, and poured beans into the coffee mill. Water heated while she turned the handle of the mill, grinding the beans into fine fragments. As she poured the boiling water over the coffee, the fragrance drifted over her head and filled the room.

Grandpa's cane thumped in the doorway. "You're up early." His moustache prickled when he kissed her cheek.

"I wanted to talk to you."

He drew a chair away from the worktable. "I'm listening."

Faith gulped. She sat facing him, her hands clasped in her lap. "Royal has arranged for a team and wagon to take us to Oregon as soon as we're married."

An alarmed look crossed Grandpa's face. "And when will that be again?"

"We've decided on August 21, here in our parlor." She didn't mention she'd already told him the date several times.

"That's just a month from today." His knuckles whitened as he gripped the top of his cane. "What about the mercantile?"

She leaned forward and placed a hand over his. The pounding of her heart threatened to choke her. "Mr. Allen, the cooper, has offered to buy the business. I hope to bring the sale documents home Monday."

Grandpa's head dropped forward until it rested on his clenched hands. "I never thought it would come to this. I hoped you and young Saxon . . ."

266

"He's not interested in me. I think he fancies Amy."

"You've got your life all planned, and mine as well."

"This is our only way out of Noble Springs. We need to go somewhere where we can begin anew."

"I want to see you happy. If Baxter is the means, so be it. We'll go to Oregon—but don't expect me to sell this house too. It can sit here and rot away before I turn it over to another owner."

The sadness in his eyes tore at her. Mute, she watched him through a shimmer of tears.

He rose to his feet as though every joint in his body ached. "You can't run away, Faith. I hope you find that out before it's too late." He leaned heavily on his cane as he left the kitchen.

Faith threw her hands over her face and wept. What had she done?

"You've been quiet all morning," Rosemary said. "Do you want to tell me what's wrong?"

Faith took a deep breath. "Today I told Grandpa about going to Oregon and Mr. Allen wanting to buy the store." She shot an agonized look at her friend. "I thought if I took care of all the details, he'd see the wisdom of the move. Instead, he was heartbroken. Oh, he didn't say so, but I could see it in his eyes." Tears trickled down her cheeks. "He said he wants me to be happy." She choked. "That's what I want for him! I'd never have—"

Rosemary gathered her into a hug and waited until she stopped sobbing. "Give him time. Older folks can be set in their ways."

"D'you really think he'll change his mind?" Faith sniffled.

"Once he sees how happy you and Royal are together, he'll come around."

Faith nodded. She would be happy with Royal. Of course she would.

Rosemary glanced at the clock. "It's almost noon. Shall we walk to the park by the depot? We can sit in the bandstand and eat our dinner."

"I'd like that. My ankle should be good for two blocks."

Carrying their dinner pails, they covered the distance to the train station, Bodie frisking behind them. Two horses harnessed to buggies were tied to the hitching rail in front of the hotel. Otherwise, the town simmered silently in the midday heat.

When they reached the shade of the bandstand, Faith noticed a woman dressed in black strolling away from the depot. She walked the distance of the train platform, then turned and walked back. After she'd repeated the action several times, Faith looked at Rosemary.

"There's no train scheduled to leave today, is there?"

"No. One stopped around eleven. The next one through won't be until tomorrow."

Faith set her dinner pail down, snapping the lid closed to keep Bodie from stealing her food. "That poor woman's going to perish out in that sun. Perhaps she'd like to sit with us for a bit."

"It won't hurt to ask."

They crossed the street at the same time the woman turned toward them. Rosemary's eyes widened. "Cassie Haddon? What are you doing here?"

Faith stared as she recognized the young woman. Cassie and her mother had stayed with Rosemary during the time the tracks were being repaired after the train derailed.

"Rosemary." Cassie's mouth spread in a tremulous smile. "You were in my thoughts when we got off the train this morning. I didn't dare hope I'd see you."

Rosemary clasped Cassie's hands. "It's providential Faith and I came to the park today." She waved in the direction

268

of the bandstand. "We noticed you walking in the sun, and wondered if you'd like to share our shade."

The woman glanced over her shoulder at the hotel, then nodded. "I'll sit where I can watch the door."

Once they were settled on the benches that circled the interior walls, Cassie untied her bonnet strings and removed her simple black bonnet, trimmed with ivory rosettes. Faith noticed she had touches of lavender lace at her throat and wrists, so apparently her period of full mourning had passed.

Rosemary leaned forward, facing Cassie. "You said 'we' got off the train. You're not here alone, then?"

Cassie's fair skin flushed. "My mother is in the hotel . . . with her new husband. That's his buggy tied out front. I preferred to remain outdoors rather than sit in the reception area with traveling salesmen." She wound her handkerchief around her fingers.

Studying the somewhat dilapidated buggy that Cassie had indicated, Faith couldn't stop the question that rose to her lips. "Is her husband from Noble Springs?"

"Yes. He has a large farm south of town. He's taking us there today."

Faith and Rosemary exchanged glances. This time Rosemary asked the question. "You live in St. Louis. How did your mother meet a man from Noble Springs?"

Cassie's flush deepened. "They were introduced by mutual friends when Mr. Bingham visited the city. Mother wanted to go someplace where we could start over, so she married him."

At the name Bingham, Faith straightened. She'd encountered that name on one of the *20327* pages when she and Curt pored over the ledgers. If he was the same man, his farm was far from large. In fact, it was small and neglected.

Cassie turned to Rosemary, shaking her head. "After the war, we had nothing left. Papa was dead, our farm in ruins.

Papa's brother in St. Louis took us in." Her tone pleaded for understanding. "I should have told you this when we stayed with you in May, but it's important to Mother to keep up appearances—as she often reminds me."

Faith cleared her throat. "You said she married a Mr. Bingham. Do you mean Elmer Bingham?" she asked in a tentative voice, hoping she was wrong.

"Yes, Elmer's his Christian name."

The door of the hotel opened and Cassie's mother stepped into the sunlight, her bright hair unmistakable.

Cassie sprang to her feet. "As soon as I can, I'll come to town for a visit." She kissed Rosemary's cheek and pressed Faith's hand. "Thank you for being here." She dashed toward the hotel, tying her bonnet on as she ran.

A lump the size of a stone lodged in Faith's throat as she watched Elmer Bingham help the two women into his buggy. Poor Cassie. What a shame her mother had chosen a hasty marriage as a means to improve their lives.

At the end of the day, Faith leaned back against the buggy seat, spent, while Royal drove her home.

"You're quiet," he said.

"I was thinking about Grandpa. This morning I told him about Mr. Allen's offer, and our intention to leave for Oregon soon after our wedding."

He slowed the horse. "What did he say?"

"He said he wants me to be happy."

"That's good, isn't it?" He grinned at her. "Opens the door, you might say."

She flinched at his choice of words. Grandpa's demeanor had resembled more a locked gate than an open door. "He's sacrificing his desires for me. I don't know if I can live with that."

Royal stopped the buggy in front of the Lindbergs' house, but turned to face her instead of helping her down. "He's had his turn. It's your life now. If he doesn't want to go, let him stay behind."

"You don't understand. He can't manage on his own anymore."

"We can leave him in Fulton before setting out for Oregon."

Horrified, Faith stared at him. "I'd never do that."

The hardness in his eyes softened. He stroked the side of her face, then leaned forward and pressed a gentle kiss to her lips. "You're exhausted. The store, the wedding, our plans to leave—it's too much for you. I hope you sleep well tonight."

She rested her forehead against his shoulder, grateful for his caring words. He was right about one thing. She *was* exhausted.

When he swung her to the ground, he kissed the tip of her nose and said, "I'll be here before nine to take you to church tomorrow."

"We always ride to church with Rosemary and her brother."

"Not anymore you don't, sweetling. When I talked to the preacher about marrying us, he made it clear he expected to see us together in a pew from now on."

Faith smiled, grateful to Reverend French. Having Royal beside her every Sunday would be a good foundation for beginning their life together. In the meantime, she'd explain to Curt and Rosemary about Royal's invitation when they arrived tomorrow. She prayed they'd understand.

She leaned on his arm as he escorted her to the porch. Would Grandpa still be as upset as he'd been when she left that morning? She hesitated a moment before going inside.

Amy opened the door before Faith put her hand on the latch. At the sight of her tear-streaked face, a wave of alarm rolled through Faith. Panicked, she pushed into the entryway. "Has something happened to Grandpa?"

"No. He's fine. He's been writing all day."

"Then what's wrong? You've been crying." She put a hand on Amy's shoulder, but the girl jerked away.

"Judge Lindberg told me about your plans to leave after you and Royal are married. Why didn't you tell me yourself?"

Faith clapped a hand over her mouth. She'd been so engrossed with the mercantile and wedding arrangements, she'd neglected to share her intentions with Amy. "I just assumed . . . I thought you . . ." Her shoulders drooped. "I've been beyond thoughtless. Forgive me."

Amy dabbed at her eyes. "So I have until late August to find a new position and a place to live?"

"Come with us," Faith blurted, wondering why she hadn't made the offer in the first place. In Faith's heart, Amy had grown from a stranger to a younger sister. She couldn't leave her behind.

"No."

Faith grabbed her hands. "Why not? There's nothing tying you here."

"I've heard stories about how many children die along the trail. Sophia's all I've got left of Joel. I'm not taking her out there."

Faith opened her mouth to protest, then closed it again. She'd heard the stories too.

An idea tickled the back of her mind. She squeezed Amy's hands. "Let's go talk to Grandpa. I think I know exactly where you can live."

Curt and Rosemary. Now Amy. The cords binding her to Noble Springs drew tighter.

On Sunday morning, Curt tied Moses to the rail in front of the Lindbergs' home while Rosemary remained in the buggy. Faith flew out the front door, her eyes darting from his face to the street behind him.

"I wish there'd been some way to tell you sooner," she said, breathless.

"Tell me what?"

His spirits sank when Faith explained the change in their routine—Royal would take her to church from now on. She hoped Curt would understand.

She looked distractingly beautiful in her dress with the blue flowers that matched her eyes. He swallowed a desire to fling her into his buggy and spirit her away.

It's better this way, he told himself. *The less I see of her, the easier it will be to say good-bye.*

While she talked, Judge Lindberg made his way from the porch to the hitching rail. Amy followed, wheeling Sophia in her carriage.

"I'm sorry you came all this way for nothing," Faith said.

"It wasn't for nothing." Her grandfather spoke from behind her. "I'd rather have Curt's company this morning, and yours too, Miss Rosemary." He tossed his cane onto the floor at Rosemary's feet and pulled himself up onto the seat next to her.

Curt arched his eyebrows at Amy. "How about you? There's room."

"Thank you, but I'll walk." She smiled at him. "Sophia's enjoying her carriage rides."

At that moment, Baxter's horse pranced to a stop next to Curt's buggy. "Hope we didn't put you out, Saxon," he said, vaulting from the seat of his vehicle and crossing to Faith's side.

"Not at all." He masked his jealousy with a bland smile. "I was just leaving."

Baxter tipped his hat. "See you in church."

As he drove through town, Curt forced himself not to look back at Faith and Baxter. Once he was inside the sanctuary, he'd wait until they were seated, then find a spot toward the front where he couldn't see them.

"Four weeks," Judge Lindberg said.

Curt knew what the older man meant. "So Rosemary tells me."

The judge leaned forward and nailed Curt with a steely gaze. "You gonna let this happen?"

For a moment, Curt thought of criminals impaled by those eyes before being sentenced to jail. He squirmed. "Not much I can do about it. Can't interfere in matters of love."

"Faith hasn't said she loves him. She's set on going to Oregon, and he's promised to take her. I believe it's the idea she loves, not the man."

"I think he's right," Rosemary said. "She's so wrapped up in making plans, she hasn't thought ahead."

Curt clenched the reins. He felt they were both looking to him for a solution. He didn't have one. Whether Faith loved Baxter or not, she'd agreed to marry him.

On her way to the mercantile on Monday morning, Faith paused at the corral next to the livery. The humid air carried the pungent aroma of dust and dung past her nostrils. Leaning over the fence, she waved to get Curt's attention.

"I didn't get a chance to talk to you after church."

He ambled toward her, not smiling. "Where's your escort?"

"I told him I'd rather walk from now on. My ankle's much better."

"What did you want to talk about?"

"Thanks to you, I was able to order some firearms to replace the ones that were stolen." She sent him her brightest smile. "You have no idea how wonderful it will feel to see the shelves filled again."

"Glad to help. I . . . I liked working with you." He pushed up his hat brim with one finger. "Think you'll be here long enough to see the shelves restocked? Thought you were leaving near the end of next month."

Faith felt a pang of loss at the finality in his words. "Maybe not. A few things have to happen first."

He stepped up to the fence and placed a hand on her arm. "Like your granddad signing the papers to sell the store?"

"How did you know?"

"He told me yesterday. He's not ready, Faith. It's not my place to speak, now that you're engaged, but I think too much of the old gentleman not to say something."

"I care about him too. More than you do." She jerked her arm away. "I can't stand watching him pine for what used to be. Leaving is the best solution."

"He'll pine for Noble Springs if you take him west."

Tears sprang to her eyes. She dashed them away with the

back of her hand. "I'm in too far to back out now." She flung the words at him, then turned and marched toward town.

In the storeroom, Faith rummaged through crates she'd filled with supplies for the journey west. Iron clanged against iron when she stacked kettles to one side. Had she overlooked anything? Extra clothing and boots for Grandpa, tin plates and bottled matches for her traveling kitchen, a medicine chest with quinine, purgatives, and bandage strips. After reviewing her entire list, including spare wagon parts and extra hemp lariats, she folded her arms over her chest, satisfied. Nothing further would be needed until they were ready to stock the wagon with the necessary food.

"Heard someone back here. Thought I'd better take a look."

Hand to her throat, Faith whirled around to see Mr. Slocum standing at the door to the alley.

Her heartbeat slowed at the sight of his genial expression. "Thank you. You and Mr. Grisbee are the reason there hasn't been another robbery."

"Well, Sheriff Cooper sure ain't no help. Long as you're here, we'll be guarding you." He leaned against the door frame. "Heard you was getting married, and you done sold the mercantile. Going to Oregon, so the story goes."

"Yes and no. My wedding is next month, but the sale of the store isn't final as yet. The papers aren't signed. We can't leave until then."

"You waiting on the judge?"

She nodded.

Mr. Slocum's gray eyes brightened. "What if he don't sign? Why cain't you and your new husband stay in Noble Springs? It ain't such a bad place to raise up a family."

She considered his words after he left. Would she have chosen Royal if it weren't for the promise of traveling west?

Faith shook the thought from her head. Enough of listening to naysayers. Lifting her chin, she pushed through the curtain and walked to the fabric display near the front entrance. Today she'd choose a style and start sewing a wedding dress.

Rosemary joined her while she flipped through *Godey's Lady's Book* and *Peterson's Magazine*. "You haven't much time to sew a gown."

She bit her lip. "There's time enough. The wedding will be small, in our parlor. I don't need anything too fancy." Turning to a page showing day dresses, she pointed to one with a fitted bodice and skirt made of joined panels of fabric. "The princess style would be just the thing."

Frowning, Rosemary tilted her head. "It's awfully plain. Maybe if you added some bows."

"We're settling in the west. Anything elaborate wouldn't be practical for later."

In spite of her words, Faith paged back to a gown with cascading ruffles over a wide skirt. "If I weren't leaving, I'd choose this one. It looks like icing on a cake."

"You mean if you weren't marrying Royal."

Faith looked down at the illustrations blurring through sudden tears. "Yes."

Royal and Oregon were linked with an unbreakable chain.

Sweating, Curt wrestled with a heavy coil of chain that Rip used to suspend feed sacks from the rafters of the livery. By hanging the grain in the air, he believed mice couldn't get at the oats. Curt had seen evidence to the contrary, but once Rip's mind was set there was no changing it.

"Got them sacks up there yet?" Rip hollered.

"This is the last one." Curt balanced the fifty-pound burlap bag upright and bound the top to a hook.

His employer joined him and together they hoisted the lumpy bundle. One by one, the links clunked over a wooden rafter until the feed dangled fifteen feet in the air.

"That ought to stop the little beggars," Rip said, dusting his hands on his trousers.

Curt anchored the chain to a stout nail beside one of the stalls. "Should slow them down, anyway."

Rip stomped to his office on his short legs, talking while he went. "Good to be back. You did a fine job taking care of this place whilst I was gone. Knew I could count on you."

"Couldn't do any less, considering all you've done for me."

"You don't have to stay on now, ya' know. I'll not be leaving again."

Despite the heat inside the building, Curt felt a chill. "You just said I did well. Why are you letting me go?"

Rip took a stained sheet of paper from his desktop and handed it to Curt. "Found this tangled up in the sumac out behind the corral. Appears to be a letter to Mr. Robbinette recommending you for a position." He massaged his curly beard. "Told you all along you was free to take something more suitable. Knew I couldn't keep you forever."

Curt took the paper and flopped onto a chair next to the desk. Although crinkled and splotched with uneven tan streaks, the letter from Ethan French was readable. "I threw this away. Thought it was gone for good." He rubbed his neck. "How'd it get stuck in the bushes?"

"Maybe divine providence? You'd best go see the man. Don't want to bring holy wrath on your head." Rip chuckled.

Shaking his head, Curt turned the document over in his hands. "I don't know. When I asked Reverend French for a recommendation, I had a good reason. That reason's gone. Working here's as good as anywhere."

"That don't sound like a compliment."

"Didn't mean it that way. Some of my best days since the war have been here at the livery—thanks to you."

Rip straightened in his chair, jabbing an index finger at Curt. "Hear what I'm saying. You're way beyond a stable-hand. It's time you trusted yourself to move on. Go see Rob-binette."

"But—"

"If he hires you, you can spend all your time off in here if you want. I can always use free labor." He rose and slapped Curt between the shoulder blades. "Come back and tell me what he said."

Curt chose to travel High Street on his route home so he wouldn't have to pass Lindberg's Mercantile. He missed his talks with Faith. Her engagement had moved her out of his world, even though she still stopped at the livery to say hello in the mornings. In a little over two weeks she'd be Mrs. Royal Baxter, and then who knew how much longer she'd remain in Noble Springs.

He half-smiled. At least Judge Lindberg wasn't making it easy. He still hadn't signed the sale papers for the mercantile.

After bathing, Curt dressed in his Sunday trousers and a crisp white shirt with a fold-down collar. Wearing a jacket was out of the question on such a sweltering afternoon. He brushed his hat until it looked new, then settled it on his damp hair.

He covered the blocks between his home and the academy with a brisk stride. A park-like setting at the north edge of town gave the three buildings on campus a dignified appearance. He could almost imagine himself in St. Louis, teaching mathematics in his former classroom at Spencerhill.

Steady, Saxon, he warned himself. *It's been a long time.*

Choosing the largest of the brick structures, he mounted the steps and entered the building. Several open doors lined the hallway. Curt walked through the first one and found himself in a library. He drew a deep breath, savoring the fragrance of dusty volumes.

A rail-thin man rose from behind a table near the door. "Are you looking for someone in particular, or did you drop in to browse our collection? We have some lovely editions of the classics." His hair fuzzed out around his head like sheep's wool.

"I was told to ask for Malcolm Robbinette."

"That would be me."

Curt extended his hand. "My name's Alexander Curtis Saxon. Reverend French encouraged me to see you."

Mr. Robbinette pumped his hand with enthusiasm. "There used to be an excellent instructor at Spencerhill by that name. He was the talk of the academic world in St. Louis before the war." He cocked his head. "You wouldn't be the same man, would you?"

Muscles twitched up and down Curt's spine. He lifted his shirt collar to cover his scar. "I'm . . . I'm what's left of him."

"It's a pleasure to meet you." He looked as though he meant it. "Come back to my office so we can talk."

Their boot heels echoed on the stone floor as Curt followed the taller man to a room at the end of the hall. Afternoon sun slanted through the high windows, brushing the grain of a substantial oaken desk with amber strokes. Framed diplomas lined wall space above shelves filled with books. Rather than seat himself behind his desk, Mr. Robbinette slid two ladder-back chairs away from the wall, arranging them so that they faced each other.

"Tell me what brings you here," he said, settling onto one of the chairs. "I hope you're offering to join our humble faculty. We desperately need a mathematics instructor, but I never dreamed we'd get one of your caliber." He shook his head. "I'm getting ahead of myself. Sorry. Habit of mine."

"Reverend French prepared a letter of recommendation for me." Curt took the folded paper from his pocket and passed it to the other man.

"Looks like it had a rough journey," Mr. Robbinette said, a smile lurking at the corners of his mouth as he scanned the wrinkled missive.

Curt nodded. "I had some hesitation about coming here. I haven't taught students since before the war. I'm not altogether sure I'm up to it." He allowed his collar to drop in order to reveal his scar. "This puts some people off. Figure you should know what you're getting."

"I'm pretty sure of what we'd be getting to have you teach here. It would be a privilege."

"Sometimes I have . . . memories. They sneak up on me."

"Like what happened to your neck?"

He flinched at the man's boldness but felt relief at the same time. Might as well lay everything on the table. "That was my own fault. Heard a noise outside our tent and stepped out with no weapon. Couple inches closer and he'd have slit my throat. Good thing another trooper heard the struggle."

"You're not the only one returning troubled with soldier's heart. My younger brother's never been the same, but he carries on with his family and his job."

At the mention of family, Curt's throat tightened. To have Faith—and regain his former profession—would be all he could ever ask. He'd have to settle for part of his dream. "So, you'll take me on?"

"Without hesitation. Come back at the end of August for orientation. In fact, come anytime so we can get acquainted. School year starts mid-September. That's probably later than you're used to, but many of our students need to help on the family farm through harvest."

Mid-September. He'd be able to work at the livery until Rip found a new stablehand. Curt leaned forward. "Thank you for the opportunity. I'll try not to disappoint you."

After Mr. Robbinette's effusive farewell, Curt stepped out into the oppressive evening heat, stunned. The interview had seemed too easy.

Thunderheads climbed over each other in the southwestern sky. Illuminated by the sun's orange rays, they looked like pillars of fire. Awed at the sight, he paused and stared upward, wondering if they were a sign of divine favor.

When he turned his attention to the road in front of him, he noticed a rider galloping south on a tall black stallion.

Curt tightened his jaw.

What Baxter did was none of his affair.

aith peered out the front window of the mercantile at the sight of Mr. Bingham's shabby buggy stopping in front of the boardwalk. "Here she comes again."

"I hope she brought Cassie with her this time," Rosemary said. She snapped her fingers at Bodie and pointed to the woodstove. "Down."

The dog trotted to a folded blanket and turned around three times, then flopped on his belly. "Good boy." She rubbed his head. "Cassie's mother acts like Bodie's going to tear her throat out every time she shops here. Poor old boy wouldn't hurt anyone, even a sour pickle like her."

Faith snickered. "Miss Saxon. How unkind."

"You'll have to forgive me. After all I did for her—"

"Good morning, ladies. I see you're not particularly busy. Perhaps you can assist me." Mrs. Haddon, now Mrs. Bingham, swished into the building.

"Of course." Faith smiled when she saw Cassie. "How nice to see you. We were hoping you'd join your mother on her trips to town."

Mrs. Bingham sniffed. "I'm the one who needs supplies, not Cassie. It seems Mr. Bingham misrepresented the extent of his holdings. Just getting him to buy a new blanket is an effort. Never mind china, or any fripperies."

That explained her frequent visits to the mercantile for one item at a time. Faith folded her hands. "What can I show you today?"

"The wash basin in our bedroom is in shameful condition. It's a wonder the cracked thing holds water at all. I hope you have something suitable as a replacement."

Faith led the way to the shelves where she displayed pottery. "I have a blue and white transferware set." She placed a curved bowl and an elegant matching pitcher on the countertop.

The woman's forehead wrinkled as she studied the pieces. "Perhaps this is a little dear. I'm hoping to have enough left to buy a new hat. Is there anything else?"

"This would be serviceable." Faith placed an unadorned brown pitcher and basin next to the transferware.

Mrs. Bingham darted a glance at the price, then smiled. "Perfect." She dug in her bag and handed Faith two silver quarters. "Here you are. Mr. Bingham will come for us in an hour. Please have this wrapped for travel." She turned toward the entrance. "Could you direct me to a milliner?"

Pointing north, Faith said, "Across King's Highway, next to the bank. Miss Lytle does lovely work."

"That remains to be seen. Are you coming, Cassie?"

"I'd rather wait here."

"As you wish. Don't wander off." She swept onto the boardwalk and moved up the street like a ship under full sail.

Cassie untied the lavender ribbons on her bonnet and settled into one of the chairs near Bodie's blanket. "I'm so happy I got to come to town today. It's terribly lonely on the farm."

"I wondered how you were faring," Faith said, her hands busy cushioning the bowl and pitcher in brown paper. She couldn't imagine being in Cassie's position.

Cassie fanned herself. "Mr. Bingham was certainly less than forthcoming when Mother met him in St. Louis. His farm appears to have been neglected for years. He told her he had servants, but there's no one there but an old man who sleeps most of the day. He's a dreadful cook too."

"I imagine you're quite busy cleaning," Rosemary said.

"Heavens, no." Cassie stared at her with wide eyes. "Ladies don't clean. Servants do that."

"Ah. Then how do you pass the time?"

"Needlework. Reading. I've been taking walks around the property. There's a little trail where things aren't too overgrown." She leaned forward. "That reminds me. I saw something curious on one of my walks last week. I must have wandered off the trail. I found a big tent, like soldiers use. No one was around, so I peeked inside."

"That was dangerous," Faith said. "There are lots of squatters living in the woods."

Cassie shuddered. "Believe me, I won't go near there again. The tent was full of guns, boots, shirts. Everything looked new and shiny, like someone was outfitting an army."

Faith's fingertips tingled. "Where was this exactly?" The question came out sharper than she intended.

"Up in the woods near Mr. Bingham's farm."

"Could you find the spot again?"

"I think so. Why?"

Rosemary crossed the room to Faith. "Don't get your hopes up. There could be a logical explanation."

"I can't think of one." She tied the paper-wrapped pottery with string and set the pieces aside, then turned to Cassie.

"Come with me, please. We're going to see the sheriff. I want you to tell him what you saw."

Cassie paled. "Did I do something wrong?"

"Not at all. We were robbed the day the train derailed. I think you've found the thief."

At Cassie's incredulous expression, Faith described what had been stolen and the subsequent theft of her reticule. She added the information about the man Mr. Grisbee had chased away in July.

"I think you're brave to stay here at all," Cassie said. "I wouldn't."

"You don't know what you can do until you try." Faith opened the door. "Let's go. You too, Rosemary. We'll leave Bodie here to guard the store, since my watchmen are late today."

"I'll be glad to see Curt's name cleared."

Faith patted Rosemary's hand. "So will I." She missed Curt. This news would give her a reason to visit with him, even if it was over the fence at the livery.

After fastening the lock on the front doors, Faith led the two women across Court Street to the jailhouse.

Sheriff Cooper looked up when they entered and hastily covered a salmon-colored dime novel with a wanted poster. "Good morning, ladies. Are you taking up a collection for some worthy cause?" He shoved a hand in his pocket.

"Miss Haddon here has something interesting to tell you," Faith said.

He nodded in her direction. "I'm listening."

Cassie's hands trembled. Faith moved behind her and whispered, "Don't be nervous. Just tell him what you saw."

"My mother is married to Mr. Bingham."

"Heard that. You here to complain about the state of his property?"

"No. Last week I saw something in the woods that Faith thinks is important." Her voice gained strength. She explained how she'd happened upon the tent, and what she'd seen inside.

The sheriff placed his palms flat on the desktop. "I'll look into this soon as I can. No law against a man having firearms and extra clothes. If I rousted every squatter around these hills, I'd have no time for anything else."

"Don't you see?" Faith stamped her foot. "If a squatter who's camped south of here is the thief, you'll have to stop blaming Mr. Saxon."

"Not necessarily. They could be in cahoots."

She narrowed her eyes. "I'll be sure to tell Amy how hard you're trying to protect our town."

He flushed. "No need to be hasty." He flipped the wanted poster over and dipped a pen in a bottle of ink. "Now, exactly where was this tent?"

When they left the sheriff's office, Cassie turned worried eyes on Faith. "Do you think we've been gone more than an hour? Mr. Bingham gets very upset if he's kept waiting." She hurried ahead of them, but slowed her steps when she reached the corner. Her mother was pacing back and forth in front of the locked doors, her face set in furious lines. Mr. Bingham sat in the buggy with his arms folded across his chest.

"I'm late. He's already here." Cassie clutched Faith's arm. "Please don't say anything about visiting the sheriff. He hates lawmen."

"Sooner or later he's bound to find out. Sheriff Cooper may need to talk to him."

Cassie's hand flew to her mouth. "Heaven forbid."

"Miss Lindberg." Cassie's mother strode toward her. "What's the meaning of this? I step across the street for a moment, and you lock the store. I demand my parcels."

"I apologize, ma'am. I had urgent business to attend to."

"If you keep your store locked, you won't have any business at all." She huffed out an exasperated breath.

"Yes, ma'am." Faith opened the doors and grabbed the paper-wrapped items from the counter. "Thank you for your trade." Over Mrs. Bingham's shoulder, she met Cassie's eyes.

"I hope you'll both return in spite of this inconvenience."

"I hope so too," Cassie said.

Faith walked home that evening praying Curt would be at the livery, but it was Mr. Ripley who greeted her when she stepped into the pungent-smelling interior.

"Saxon's left already. He don't hang around much in the evenings since—" He cleared his throat. "Guess he's found better things to do."

Now that she thought about it, she hadn't seen him on her walks home for several days. He must be avoiding her.

She forced a smile. "I'll stop by in the morning. I had some good news I wanted to share."

Mr. Ripley pulled a straw from a mound of fresh hay next to a stall and stuck it between his teeth. "Just between you and me, I think the good news he'd like to hear is that you've called off your wedding. 'Course he ain't said nothing to me, but I know him. Wears his heart on his sleeve where you're concerned."

"You must be mistaken." A flush climbed her cheeks. "If you're thinking of his visits to our house, he's shown an interest in Amy Dunsmuir, and my grandfather, of course."

"Don't be so sure." He gave her a sideways glance. "Anyway, I'll tell him you'll be here tomorrow."

"Thank you."

Faith's thoughts whirled as she covered the remaining distance to her home. Surely Mr. Ripley was wrong about Curt's feelings toward her. Curt saw her as his sister's friend, someone who needed his help from time to time. He'd never once asked her . . . well, he did invite her to the Independence

Day celebration. But Amy and Grandpa were included. They'd never spent any time alone . . . wait. Yes, they had. She touched her forehead where he'd kissed her after she explained the *20327* mystery. A friendly kiss, nothing more.

Grandpa sat in his usual place near the window when Faith drifted into the parlor, her mind still on Curt. Amy held Sophia in her lap and smiled at her over the baby's head. "I finished basting your dress. After supper I'll help you with the fitting."

Her words snapped Faith's thoughts from Curt to her wedding. Ten more days and she'd be Mrs. Royal Baxter. Soon after, they'd be off for the west. Perspiration dampened her palms.

Grandpa tucked his pen into a holder on the table in front of him. "I made arrangements for Amy today." He gestured at several papers. "Wrote up a statement giving her possession of the house for as long as she needs it."

Faith bent and kissed the top of his head, then looked at Amy. "I told you not to worry about where you'd live when we leave."

"Judge Lindberg. Faith. I don't know what to say." Tears trembled on Amy's lashes. "You didn't have to do this."

"Did it because I wanted to, not because I had to," Grandpa said in a gruff voice.

Pretending to study the document her grandfather signed, Faith riffled through the other papers on the table. The sale agreement for the mercantile ought to be there too.

"I know what you're looking for, and it's not here. I put it somewhere safe until the time is right."

Her shoulders slumped. Royal had made it clear that they couldn't leave without the proceeds from the sale. "Time's growing short, Grandpa."

"Won't take but a minute—when I'm ready."

She recognized the steely tone. Further persuasion would be wasted.

"I do have something you might like to hear," he said, drawing a page from another stack. "I remembered this today."

After clearing his throat, he read, "When my sister Charlotte Anne was twenty, she worried so much about her spinster status that she accepted a proposal from a prosperous farmer, in spite of her affection for a local blacksmith. Our family opposed the match, knowing she didn't love her intended, but she was determined to see herself married and settled in a fine home. But as fate or providence would have it, several days before the unfortunate event was to take place she—"

A loud hissing sound erupted, followed by a noxious odor. Faith dashed toward the source of the smell, which could only be the kitchen.

Amy followed at her heels. "Oh my word. The soup." She plunked Sophia on the floor next to the pantry door and wrapped her hands in a towel, then lifted a kettle onto the worktable. Black liquid smoked on the stovetop and around the lids.

Amy sent Faith an agonized look. "I thought pea soup would be an easy supper, so we could spend more time on your dress. Now see what happened. I'll be half the night scrubbing."

"We'll work on it together as soon as the stove cools."

"But it wasn't your doing."

"You're helping me with my dress. Why shouldn't I lend a hand out here?" Faith sniffed at what was left of the kettle's contents. "Doesn't smell too scorched. This will be fine for supper." She felt relieved at the interruption of Grandpa's morality tale, wondering whether he really had a sister named Charlotte Anne. He'd never mentioned her before.

Later that evening, Faith stood in her bedroom while Amy

slipped the pale green and gray shot silk dress over her head. In the lamplight, the colors appeared iridescent, shimmering like moonlight on water.

Amy sighed. "What lovely fabric. I've never sewn anything so fine."

"Rosemary convinced me to make this selection. I don't think it's going to be practical for pioneer life." She stroked the skirt, secretly thankful for her friend's persuasion. If Royal succeeded in his plans to command a western fort, perhaps there'd be dances or parties where she could wear the gown.

When Amy had the rear panels arranged, she led Faith to the pier glass and handed her a small mirror. "How do you like the train?"

Faith held the mirror so she could see her back. A long swath of silk swept from the neckline to trail on the floor behind the hem. She sucked in a breath. "I don't recognize myself. You've done splendid work. Have you ever considered becoming a dressmaker?"

"I like to sew. I don't know that anybody'd want me to make their dresses. What do I know about fashion?" She brushed a hand across her plain over-dyed black frock.

"You could learn. I'll bring home some *Godey's* and *Peterson's* magazines tomorrow." She turned around and surveyed the front of her gown, appreciating the simple lines.

"Rosemary said I should make bows for the front, maybe from dark green ribbon. Here, here, and here." Amy tapped places where pins marked future buttons.

"It's fine the way it is." Faith bit her lip. The closer the date loomed, the less she felt like celebrating. Bows would be a festive touch she preferred to avoid.

aith slowed her steps as she neared the livery on Saturday morning. Curt deserved to hear about Cassie's discovery. She hoped for an opportunity to talk to him without Mr. Ripley listening, but when she didn't see him in the corral, she knew her hopes were in vain.

Sighing, she lifted her skirt over her boot tops and walked through the door, her eyes seeking Curt.

"He's up there," Mr. Ripley said, bounding out of his office and pointing at the loft. A forkful of fragrant hay dropped into a bin inside one of the stalls, confirming the man's statement. "Saxon! You got a special visitor."

Faith cringed. He made it sound like the governor's lady had come to call.

Curt's shoulder muscles strained at the fabric of his shirt as he descended the ladder. She averted her eyes, ashamed of the direction her thoughts were taking.

"Rip told me you were here last night. Must be something important." His voice held a note of curiosity.

She noticed Mr. Ripley lingering nearby. "I have news you'll be pleased to hear. Would you be able to step outside for a moment?"

"Go ahead, Saxon. Take all the time you need." Curt's employer sent a broad wink in her direction.

Curt took her arm and guided her to a shaded area on the west side of the building. His eyes studied her face as though he were memorizing her features. "Last night, Rosemary told me about Cassie's discovery. Is that your news?" His tone was guarded.

Faith hoped her disappointment didn't show. "Yes," she said, deflated. "I wanted to tell you myself. I should have realized Rosemary would be even more excited than I am."

"I'm glad you stopped by." His expression warmed. "It's nice to know you're interested in my welfare."

Faith dared to place a hand on his arm. "Of course I am. You said a long time ago that you wanted to be my friend. Nothing has changed."

"Everything has changed. You know that. If Baxter happened by at this moment, do you think he'd be pleased to see us together?"

"No." She let her hand fall to her side.

He took a step toward the front of the livery, then turned to face her. "You'd better go." His jaw was set in a tight line.

Faith fought the impulse to run after him when he entered the building. He didn't look back. The memory of the tale Grandpa read last night entered her mind.

How did Charlotte Anne's life turn out? Did she marry to attain her goal of a fine home, or did she follow her heart?

Torn, she directed her steps toward town. Royal had promised to take her for a buggy ride after church tomorrow. When they were together, his charm had the effect of casting a spell over her. She wasn't plagued by indecision. At least, not much.

As she approached the jailhouse, she saw Sheriff Cooper untie his horse from the hitching rail and swing into the saddle. He tipped his hat to her and rode south on Court Street. Faith hurried toward the mercantile, eager to tell Rosemary what she'd seen.

Mr. Grisbee met her outside the locked doors. "Got bad news, Miss Faith. Someone tried to break in to the store last night."

"How do you know?" Her gaze swept the storefront. "Nothing's disturbed."

"Not here. In the alley."

"Did you tell Sheriff Cooper?"

"Haven't had time. Only been here a couple minutes."

"I just saw him ride away. Maybe we can stop him." Faith whirled and dashed to the corner, but the sheriff had apparently turned on the street fronting the railroad tracks and ridden out of sight.

She stomped back to Mr. Grisbee, anger rising in her throat. "I've had enough of this. If the sheriff won't stop the thieves, I'll do it myself."

"Now, calm down." His faded blue eyes filled with concern. "We got no more idea who to arrest than Cooper does. Anyways, all that happened last night is some ax marks cleaved in the door. I'll show you." He shuffled to the corner of the mercantile and followed the gravel path to the alley. Faith matched her steps to his slow pace.

Morning sun angled between the buildings, lighting the alleyway but leaving the storeroom door shaded. Faith clamped her teeth together at the sight of raw wood chips on the ground. Half a dozen gashes stood in pale contrast to the weathered exterior around the door frame.

"That door would've been chopped open if'n you wasn't using that bolt."

"Why do you suppose he didn't finish?" She studied the damage. "A wooden bar wouldn't stop an ax."

"Likely making too much noise. We're a stone's throw from the jailhouse."

"But Sheriff Cooper doesn't *sleep* there. Who would hear?"

Mr. Grisbee spread his hands. "I'm just an old teamster. Don't expect me to think like a thief."

Faith chuckled and linked her arm through the older man's. She'd come to depend on Mr. Grisbee's watchful care. She'd miss him when she left. "Let's open the store. We'll talk to the sheriff when he returns."

The back door of the adjoining business creaked open. Mr. Simpkins poked his head out of the newspaper office. "Thought I heard voices. Something wrong out here?"

Faith released Mr. Grisbee's arm and planted her hands on her hips. "Just a robbery attempt is all." She didn't care if he printed the story. Maybe it would spur Sheriff Cooper to try harder.

The editor whipped a notebook from his pocket and hustled toward them, whistling when he saw the damage. "Thought I heard something last night." He pointed at the stairs that led to his living quarters above the *Noble Springs Observer*. "My bedroom's behind that corner window up there."

"Did you see anyone?" Faith's voice rose to an excited pitch.

He shook his head. "I opened the window and looked out, but it's black as coal down here once the sun sets. The noise stopped, though."

Faith and Mr. Grisbee exchanged a knowing glance. "You're the reason he didn't break in," Faith said. "Thank you."

Mr. Simpkins slipped a pencil from behind his ear. "This'll be in today's paper. It's early enough to make room on the front page."

"As long as you're writing the story, be sure to tell the whole thing. The mercantile's been plagued with trouble for three months. I can't get the sheriff to take me seriously."

The editor's eyes brightened. "Start at the beginning."

Sheriff Cooper marched into the mercantile late Saturday afternoon. He waved the *Noble Springs Observer* at Faith. "Did you tell Simpkins I'm not helping you solve the robberies?"

"Please wait a moment," Faith said in her sweetest voice. "I'm assisting Mrs. Raines here with her purchase." She unrolled a bolt of red calico, patterned with yellow flowers. Lifting the shears, she asked, "You said six yards, is that correct?"

Mrs. Raines nodded, then glared at the sheriff. "I think it's disgraceful when a defenseless young woman has to turn to the community for help with her dilemma. What did we elect you for?"

His face outshone the red calico. He slapped the paper down next to Mrs. Raines and pointed to the second paragraph of the front-page story. "Citizens are asked to report any suspicious sightings to the editor of this paper," he read in a voice tight with anger. "A vigilante committee will be formed to carry out justice in the absence of proper law enforcement." He paused and drew several breaths. "Vigilante committee? You're suggesting anarchy."

Unperturbed, Faith folded Mrs. Raines's fabric. "That will be thirty cents, please."

She waited while the woman tucked her purchase into a carryall and left the store, then raised her eyes to meet the sheriff's infuriated gaze. "Mr. Simpkins added the part about vigilantes. I pray things won't come to that point." She replaced the bolt of fabric on a shelf, aware of the sheriff steaming behind her like a kettle on the boil. "By the way, I noticed you riding out of town early this morning. Were you by any chance verifying Miss Haddon's discovery?"

He snatched the newspaper from the countertop. "No. But rest assured, I will. Soon."

The bell over the door jangled for several extra seconds when he slammed out of the mercantile.

"Whoo-ee," Mr. Grisbee called from the entrance to the storeroom. "Simpkins sure lit a fire in Cooper's tail feathers."

Faith snickered at the image. "It needed to be done." Then she sobered. "I do think Mr. Simpkins shouldn't have mentioned using vigilantes, though. There's been enough trouble in these hills without starting more."

"Likely you'll be gone before things come to such a pass." Mr. Grisbee dropped the curtain. She heard him throw the bolt locking the rear entrance.

By leaving, she was locking herself away from Noble Springs's future. The thought left her feeling bereft.

On Sunday, Royal guided the buggy under a canopy of white oaks overlooking Pioneer Lake. He jumped out to assist Faith.

"You've haven't said two words since we left your house. I'm glad I'm not marrying a chatterbox." He chuckled and took her hand. "Shall we stroll to the water's edge?"

She gazed up at her fiancé's handsome face. He'd removed his hat, and his black hair shone with spice-scented oil.

When he caught her eye, he smiled and squeezed her hand. "Ten more days. Before you know it, we'll be leaving this stodgy town for Oregon. That is, once your grandpappy gets those papers signed." He cleared his throat. "Gil Allen was asking me about them yesterday. If you wait too long, he may change his mind. There's other properties available, you know."

Faith removed her hand from his. "I've told you before. I have no control over when my grandfather decides to sign. You know how hard this is for him." *And for me.* She blinked with surprise when the unbidden thought crossed her mind.

Royal led her to a fallen log and brushed leaves from the bark, then patted the cleared space. "Let's sit and watch the ducks." Near the edge of the lake, orange-billed waterfowl paddled in small groups. A light breeze blew from the water.

She untied her bonnet to capture the cooler air, fanning herself and sinking gratefully onto the curved surface of the log. "It's pleasant here."

"This is nothing compared to the lakes we'll see in the west. I'm told some of them are miles wide."

"So I understand."

He moved closer to her side, slipping an arm around her waist. "I figure this Tuesday wouldn't be too soon to start moving our supplies to Hartfield. Our wagon's waiting. I'll come for the first load when you close the store."

"Tuesday," she repeated in a faint voice.

"I have other plans for Monday," he said, apparently misinterpreting her hesitation. "The fellow who built the wagon is getting a mite testy at having to wait for his money."

Faith lifted her eyebrows. "You said you'd paid him." Did he expect her grandfather to supply the means for the entire journey?

"He wouldn't start work without cash up front." Royal dropped a kiss on her head. "I told him we'd have the rest sometime in August."

She slid away, leaving a gap between them. "You presumed on my grandfather's funds? Is that why you want to marry me?" Her throat constricted. Did his choice of her over other available girls depend on who had the most money? She blinked back tears at her foolish vanity.

"Not at all." Royal stood and drew her to her feet. Once she was standing, he wrapped his arms around her and buried his face in her neck. His warm breath sent tingles through her body. "I want to marry you for you." She felt his lips shape the words on her skin. "I can't imagine life in Oregon with anyone else." His mouth sought hers.

For a moment, she relaxed in his arms. Royal Baxter wanted her. His lips were proof of his love, even if he didn't say as much. But when his arms tightened, she pushed away, frightened by her body's response. In truth, he *was* a cyclone, overwhelming everyone in his path.

Faith drew a shaky breath. "I'll talk to Grandpa as soon as I return home."

"That's my sweetling." He grabbed her hand. "Let's go."

On the ride back to town, she sat with her hands clasped in her lap while her pulse returned to normal. In the clarity that followed Royal's kisses, she knew she wouldn't say a word to her grandfather about the sale. Then she'd see how much her fiancé's assurances were worth.

Monday morning came with no word from the sheriff. Faith was kept busy talking with curious customers, all of whom wanted to know more details about the thefts than what had appeared in the *Noble Springs Observer*. Rosemary waited on the few people who had come in to make a purchase.

Sometime past noon, Mr. Wylie stomped in and, in a loud voice, volunteered to head up a vigilante committee if Sheriff

Cooper failed to bring in the guilty party. Faith masked her surprise at seeing the man who had vowed never again to do business with Lindberg's Mercantile.

"Please, no vigilantes," she said.

"We'll see about that. Anytime you need help, you holler, little lady. I can get a slew of fellas together in no time." His fleshy jowls quivered. "Long as I'm here, I need a few tools for my wagon shop. Where'd you put them things?"

"I've moved the hardware to a special section in the back. I'll show you where it is."

"No need. I see it now." He clomped past the cookstoves and selected three hammers, a maul, and a splitting wedge, then scooped nails from a barrel into a cloth sack. After he dumped his purchases in front of her, he took a handful of coins from his pocket. "What do I owe you?"

She totaled his purchase and returned his change, feeling triumphant. One more customer had returned.

In the lull after Mr. Wylie left, Faith strolled to the window. Rosemary joined her, Bodie trailing in her steps.

"You should have Mr. Simpkins write an article about you every week. We've never been this busy on a Monday."

"If the story prompts the sheriff to pay attention to what Cassie discovered, that's all I ask. I'm eager to have the mercantile filled with goods and shoppers again."

"Even though you won't be here to see it?"

Faith closed her eyes for a moment. "I keep forgetting."

"I'm praying for you." Rosemary gave her a one-armed hug.

"I'm praying for myself," Faith said. "I'm asking for open or closed—" She leaned forward, staring at the street. "Well, look at that."

Sheriff Cooper rode past, a lead rope fastened to his saddle horn. Two horses were tied behind him. Each animal held a man with his hands bound together. As the procession clopped by, she hurried out the door to get a better view, wondering who'd been arrested, and why.

The bound men both wore dusty slouch hats low on their foreheads. In spite of their shaded faces, Faith felt a stirring of recognition. She'd seen them before, but where?

Once Faith locked the mercantile for the night, she hurried over to the jailhouse to ask about the men Sheriff Cooper had arrested. Were they the thieves? Their faces nagged at her. Somewhere there was a connection, but she couldn't drag it out of her memory.

She clicked the latch on the heavy wooden door and stepped inside Sheriff Cooper's office. His chair was empty. Perhaps he'd gone downstairs, where prisoners were held. She crossed the room to the barred door and called through one of the spaces between bars. "Sheriff? Are you down there?"

"Come and find out," a raucous voice hollered. "Bring the key with you."

Someone snickered. "We'll tell him you was here."

Faith jumped back and bolted from the building, the sound of their laughter following her across the threshold. Whatever they'd done, she was glad they were locked away.

As she neared the livery on her walk home, she kept her eyes forward. If she didn't see Curt, she wouldn't miss talking to him. She longed to tell him about the two men the sheriff arrested, but he'd made it clear their friendship was over.

Tears threatened. Buggies and men on horseback passed

on the dusty street, but she paid little attention until a voice called, "Miss Faith."

She swiveled to see Sheriff Cooper leaning over the saddle on his chestnut gelding. "I was on my way to call on you and the judge." His voice held an edge. "If it's not inconvenient, what with you organizing vigilante committees and all."

"I told you, Mr. Simpkins was responsible for that paragraph." They were steps away from the path to her porch. She gestured at the front door. "By all means, do come in." Faith waited next to the hitching rail until he dismounted, then led the way into the parlor.

Using his cane, Grandpa raised himself to his feet. "What brings you here, Thaddeus?"

"I needed to talk to both of you—Miss Faith in particular." Sheriff Cooper fingered the brim of his hat. He held a small, paper-wrapped parcel in one hand.

Faith felt a bubble of excitement. He *had* arrested the thieves.

"Sit down," Grandpa said to him. He patted a copy of the *Noble Springs Observer* on the table next to his chair. "Been reading Aaron Simpkins's opinions about you."

"Less said about that, the better." The sheriff sat on the edge of a chair facing the sofa, his long legs stretched in front of him. He balanced the parcel on one knee. "Miz Amy's not here?"

"Yes, I am." Amy stepped into the room, wiping her hands on an apron. Flour dusted the sleeves of her black dress. "What is it, Sheriff?"

"Brought you a couple of books. My mother liked to read novels, rest her soul. I was thinking, what with you here all day . . ." He gulped, then blurted, "You might want something to pass the time." His face glowed crimson from his neck to his hairline.

Amy took the bundle and untied the string. "*The Missing Bride* and *The Hills of Home*," she said, reading the titles. "Thank you. I like novels."

"When you finish, I can bring you some more."

Faith felt a pang at the warmth in his eyes when he looked at Amy. She'd never seen such an expression on Royal's face.

Amy's pink cheeks matched the flush on Sheriff Cooper's. "I'll send word when I'm ready." She ducked from the room, clutching the books.

"Thought you wanted to talk to me and Faith," Grandpa said. "If you want to call on Amy, just say so. You don't have to dodge around."

The sheriff rested his hands on his thighs. "Like I said, news for you and Miss Faith is what brought me here. But I figured as long as I was coming this way . . ."

"Please, Sheriff," Faith said. "I've been wanting to talk to you ever since I saw you bring those men into town this afternoon. Who are they?"

"You're not going to like this. They're friends of your intended."

Faith rocked back on the sofa. That's where she'd seen them. They were with Royal the first time he came to the mercantile. "Why did you arrest them?" She forced the words past the constriction building in her throat.

"Went out to that tent Bingham's stepdaughter told me about. Sure enough, there was your firearms, like she said. Saw just about everything you named on your list, 'cept for the watches. Didn't find a one." The badge on his vest flashed in the late afternoon light. "Here's where I got lucky. I'd left my horse hidden in some brush, so when I heard voices I ducked behind the tent. Didn't have to listen long to know they was the ones who stole the goods. Sounds like they was behind everything that happened to you."

Faith's heartbeat threatened to choke her. "Did you . . . arrest Royal too?"

He shook his head. "They swear he had nothing to do with it. Seems they figured they'd be doing him a favor if they could scare you into selling your store. Then they'd follow him to Oregon. Least that's their claim."

"So Royal's innocent."

Grandpa huffed out a breath but didn't say anything.

"Appears so," Sheriff Cooper said. He tugged at a corner of his moustache. "I'll take a wagon out there tomorrow and bring back your goods."

Faith visualized the empty gun rack refilled and shiny boots restored to their places on a shelf. She smiled at him. "Thank you. I'm so grateful."

"Be sure you tell that to Simpkins. I want to see another front-page story next week about how the thieves was brought to justice."

After he left, she leaned against the door frame for a moment. Royal hadn't said a word to her about his friends accompanying them on the journey west. What else was he hiding?

With slow steps, Faith reentered the parlor and sank down on the sofa. The sunshine that illuminated the sheriff's badge now sent shards of light across the rug at her feet. When she raised her eyes, Grandpa was watching her.

Faith swallowed. "Your sister, Charlotte Anne. How did her story end?"

"You'll have to discover that for yourself." He stood, leaning on his cane, and left the room.

When Faith awoke the next morning, the first thing she saw was her wedding dress hanging from one of the open doors of her wardrobe. Brilliant jet buttons marched down the front of the gown from throat to hemline. Amy must have finished the garment last night after Faith fell into an exhausted sleep.

She rolled over in bed and covered her head with the pillow. Humiliation seared through her body. How could she have been naïve enough to believe that Royal wanted her for herself? She'd seen how he looked at Marguerite.

Nelda Raines's gossip returned to her ears. She claimed to have observed Royal in Hartfield with another woman. No doubt she was correct. If Faith married him, she'd be one of those unfortunate wives who looked the other way while their husbands made a mockery of their marriage vows.

I will not cry. She grabbed the pillow and flung it at the silken gown. The garment crumpled in a heap on the floor. Faith sprang from the bed and kicked at the lustrous fabric, stubbing her toe on a triangular-shaped wooden hanger.

Limping to the washbasin, she splashed cold water over her face. She'd asked the Lord to close the door if her plans weren't part of his will. He'd slammed it in her face.

At breakfast, Grandpa looked as tired as she felt. "One more week," he remarked in a dull voice. She studied the weary lines her stubborn determination had etched on his dear face. Tonight she'd have a surprise for him.

Amy placed a platter of scrambled eggs spooned over biscuits in the center of the table, then joined them for the meal, Sophia on her lap. While she fed the baby tiny bits of egg, she chattered about her day. Faith half listened, her mind on her own plans.

" . . . and I'll have time to start reading one of the novels."

Faith cocked her head in Amy's direction. "What did you say?"

"Dr. Greeley invited your grandfather to supper tonight.

If Sophia doesn't fuss, I'll have time to read for a bit, unless you have something you want me to do."

"Not a thing. Enjoy your book. I intend to be busy arranging the merchandise Sheriff Cooper promised to return."

Color rose in Amy's face. "He's nice, isn't he?"

"He likes you too." Faith patted Amy's shoulder, wondering how Curt would feel about having a rival.

She rose and kissed Grandpa's cheek. "Have a pleasant evening. I'll see you when I get home."

As Faith walked to the mercantile, she viewed her surroundings with fresh eyes. The houses she passed on her street looked tidy, with bright flowers blooming inside picket fences. Maple trees extended patches of shade over the boardwalk. Noble Springs's stone courthouse had survived the war when many other counties had theirs destroyed. Now it stood like a proud sentinel in the center of town. She paused and stared up at the three-story edifice, her mind on Royal.

He'd said he'd come at closing time to transport a load of their trail supplies to Hartfield. She couldn't wait. Thankfully, she'd have all day to decide what to say to him.

Soon after she unlocked the mercantile, the woodstove regulars strolled in and settled on their chairs next to the checkerboard. "Didn't see nothing unusual in the alley this morning," Mr. Grisbee said. "After I whup Jesse at checkers, I'll go out and keep an eye on things."

"That won't be necessary." She rested a hand on the back of his chair. "I'm happy to say Sheriff Cooper found most of our stolen merchandise yesterday—and arrested the thieves." She didn't mention the men's motive. Some things were better kept to herself.

"Well, by gum." Mr. Slocum said. "I liked feeling useful." He combed his fingers through his trim gray beard. "How about we go on escorting you to the bank?"

"Thank you. I'd appreciate that." She added a talk with Mr. Paulson to her mental list of things to do.

Rosemary dashed through the door. "I'm sorry I'm late. Curt needed—he had to—" She took a breath. "Something came up."

"Is he hurt?" Faith's heart lurched.

Rosemary shook her head. "Nothing like that. He's well." She scrutinized Faith. "On the other hand, you look dreadful. Wedding nerves?"

"You might say so. The sheriff paid us a call last evening." She repeated what she'd told Mr. Grisbee and Mr. Slocum, again eliminating the information about the connection to Royal. "Please tell Curt as soon as you can. I think Sheriff Cooper owes him an apology."

"Why don't you tell him yourself?"

"He's not at the livery anymore when I walk home, and he never comes to see Amy in the evenings. I think he's avoiding me."

"Oh, that's not the case at all." Rosemary seized Faith's hands and gave them a reassuring squeeze. "Curt's been spending evenings with Mr. Robbinette. They talk for hours."

Surprised, Faith remembered the tall, affable principal of Noble Springs Academy from her days as a student.

"What do they have in common? Does Mr. Robbinette like horses?"

"Curt didn't tell you?" Rosemary dropped her hands. "He was hired to teach mathematics at the academy this fall. I thought you knew. He taught in St. Louis before the war. He's brilliant with numbers, although I admit to being prejudiced."

Stunned, Faith gaped at her friend. No wonder Curt

brought quick order to the mercantile's ledgers. "Why didn't he say anything to me?"

Rosemary's face clouded. "He probably felt it inappropriate since you're engaged to Royal."

Curt stood in the doorway of Rip's office. "You sure you don't mind?"

"We ain't exactly got customers lined up to rent buggies, now, have we? Go on with you." Rip winked. "I won't even dock your pay the extra half hour."

Curt shook his head. "You're a good man. Thank you." He left the livery, energized at the prospect of an invitation to supper with Malcolm Robbinette's family. That morning, Rosemary had completed a new high-necked shirt for him, so he wouldn't have to worry about Mrs. Robbinette being disquieted by the sight of his scar.

If only he were escorting Faith to the Robbinettes', instead of attending as a bachelor. He prayed Malcolm's wife hadn't provided an eligible young woman as his table companion. He had no room in his heart for anyone but Faith.

Before setting off for home, he glanced over his shoulder at the Lindbergs' house. One more week and she would be Mrs. Baxter.

He set his face forward and strode toward town.

Faith put the "Closed" sign in the window of the mercantile, then rolled down the shades. Where was Royal? He should have been here twenty minutes ago.

She paced to the storeroom, a smile crossing her face as

she studied the now-empty crates that had held supplies for the journey west. After replacing the items she'd accumulated onto their proper shelves and adding the merchandise the sheriff had returned, the store looked almost as good as it had before the war. She couldn't wait to share her news with Grandpa.

Her nerves jangled in tune with the bell when the front door opened. As much as she'd rehearsed what to say to Royal, now that he was here the words died in her throat.

"How's my sweetling?" Royal removed his hat and drew her close. His shirt was sprinkled with sawdust and smelled of sweat. "Ready to—"

She placed her hands against his chest and shoved. "Don't touch me."

His dark eyes glinted. "What's come over you? You said tonight we'd start packing our supplies for Oregon."

"No, that's what you said. You also said I should prod my grandfather to sign sale papers. Neither of those things is going to happen. Not tonight, not any night." Faith moved behind one of the counters to put distance between them.

Black anger crossed his face as he stared at her. She watched as he composed himself, his frown reshaping itself into a contrived smile. "I've said this before, working here is too much for you. Women aren't strong enough for daily commerce. Perhaps we could talk tomorrow, after you've rested."

"I understand your friends won't be joining you on your trip west."

"My . . . friends?"

"Tolly Grubbs and Frank Kagan. The sheriff visited us last night. It seems they're the men who robbed me."

He took a step backward. "I had nothing to do with that."

"But you had everything to do with trying to charm me into selling my grandfather's store so we could provide for your journey to Oregon. You knew those men would follow you, just like they did all through the war." She glared at him through a haze of anger. "You never knew my father or brother at all, did you? A few questions around town, and you learned everything you needed to know about the unfortunate Lindberg family."

"Didn't take much to win you over, did it? Plain girl like you, daydreaming about the day you sent a heroic soldier off to war." He sneered at her. "You were ripe for the picking."

Shaking with rage, she stamped to the door and flung it open. "Leave. Now. Maybe you can explain to the man in Hartfield why that poor, silly girl in Noble Springs won't give you the money for that wagon you ordered."

He slapped his hat over his sweaty hair and brushed past her without a word. She banged the door shut behind him, then sagged against the smooth wooden surface.

"Thank you, Lord," she whispered.

Twilight had settled over the streets when Faith left the mercantile. As soon as she got home, she'd tell Grandpa there'd be no wedding, and no departure for Oregon. Then she'd heat water and take a long bath. She wanted to throw the memory of Royal's touch out with the soap scum.

A feeling of freedom lightened her steps. Her obsession had nearly led to disaster for herself and her grandfather.

She dashed into the house, expecting to see Grandpa waiting by the window, but his chair was vacant.

"Grandpa! Where are you?"

Amy came down the stairs, carrying Sophia. "Dr. Greeley is going to bring him home. They must have a drawn-out chess game going. He's never been this late."

"I'll go fetch him. I have news he'll want to hear."

She covered the three blocks between their home and the doctor's house with rapid steps. Shadows lengthened over the streets. If they didn't hurry, it would be full dark before they got home.

Lights from the front windows brightened the doctor's broad porch. Faith paused to dab perspiration from her forehead, then raised the horseshoe-shaped knocker and rapped on the door.

Dr. Greeley peered out at her. He wore house slippers and an open-collared shirt. "Faith. What are you doing here? Is your grandfather ill?"

Her senses prickled. "He's not here?"

"He left an hour ago. It's a warm evening. Said he wanted to walk."

Faith gaped at the doctor, the sound of her heartbeat loud in her ears. "Grandpa didn't come home," she said. Her voice shook. "I need to find him."

"Maybe he stopped on the way to visit a neighbor."

"You don't understand." She half-turned toward the street. "He gets confused sometimes. He comes to his senses in a strange place and doesn't know how he got there."

Dr. Greeley raised a skeptical eyebrow. "Nonsense. Nate checkmated me this afternoon in five moves. There's nothing wrong with his mind."

Faith tightened her jaw. If a more opinionated man than Dr. Greeley existed, she had yet to meet him. "Thank you. I'll not trouble you further." She skimmed down the steps and trotted toward Curt's house. Whether he wanted to talk to her or not, she needed his help.

Rosemary opened the door in response to Faith's frantic knock. "My goodness. It's almost dark. What brings you out so late?"

"Is Curt here?" She wheezed, trying to catch her breath.

"No, he had a supper invitation at Robbinettes' this

evening." She took Faith's hand and led her to the sofa. "Sit down and tell me what's wrong."

"Grandpa's missing. He left Dr. Greeley's some time ago and hasn't come home."

"And I'm sure the good doctor was no help."

Faith puffed out a breath. "No, he wasn't. Claims there's nothing to worry about." She shifted on the cushion. "I need to start looking. Too much time has passed already."

"You won't be safe out after dark. A woman alone—"

"I have to find my grandfather. If it weren't for me, he'd be sitting in our parlor right now."

"You can't blame yourself." Rosemary pulled her into a hug. "Please stop at the jailhouse and get the sheriff. Better if he goes than you."

On the way to see the sheriff, Faith walked past the mercantile and entered the dim alley, in case Grandpa had returned to his old writing room in the shed. She tried to stay in the shadows so she wouldn't attract unwelcome attention. Peering into the shed's dusky interior, she saw nothing but stacked crates.

Her hands clammy with fear, she crossed the street toward the sheriff's office. No light showed through the windows.

"Then it's up to me," she said, squaring her shoulders.

A blinding thought flared in her mind. She knew where Grandpa had gone.

"Please, God, not there," she whispered. "I can't do it."

Fear not, for I am with thee.

She clung to the promise from the book of Isaiah as she dashed through town.

Faith stopped at home to tell Amy what had happened and where she was going. The girl pressed her hand to her lips.

"You can't. It's dangerous. What if something happens to you?"

"I'm going." Faith went to the pantry and lifted a lantern from a shelf, then struck a match against the edge of the stove and lit the wick. "Should Grandpa come home while I'm gone, please make sure he stays here. I'll come straight back if I don't find him."

Amy wrung her hands. "I'm scared."

"I am too." Faith leaned over and kissed Amy's cheek. "Please pray for both of us."

With trembling legs, she pressed into the humid darkness. The lantern threw light three or four feet ahead. She tried not to think of all that lurked beyond the yellow beam.

Retracing her steps toward the livery stable, she turned north on Spring Street and began to climb the hill. Green eyes glowed from under humped shrubbery. Skittering noises behind her caused her to whirl, holding the lantern high. *Keep walking*, she told herself. *One step at a time.*

After what felt like hours, she saw the iron fence. Every nerve in her body vibrated. She knew where Grandpa was, but she lacked the courage to enter the gate and walk past dim crosses and headstones to the Lindberg family plot. Faith shuddered when a faint breeze tickled past her ankles.

Paralyzed, she stood rooted outside the cemetery.

Fear not, for I am with thee.

Her grandfather had to be inside, a hundred yards away, at the top of the rise. Faith took one step, then another. Then another. The lantern light bobbed over carved stones as she moved steadily toward the low brick wall where she expected to find him.

A choked voice spoke through the darkness. "Who's there?"

Her perspiring hands slipped on the handle of the lantern

and it swayed. Grandpa's face shone in the sudden brightness. Faith dropped the light and ran to him.

"Praise God. You're safe."

Grandpa's arms held her close. "You shouldn't be out here. It's risky for a woman after dark." His breath brushed her ear.

"I came to find you."

"I wanted to say good-bye to Clara."

"We're not leaving. That's what I came to tell you." She stepped away and lifted the lantern, thankful it hadn't tipped over, and placed it on the brick wall around their plot. "Sit beside me and I'll explain everything that happened today." While she talked, she marveled that she could remain calm enough in the middle of a cemetery to have a conversation with her grandfather.

Fear not, for I am with thee.

As they walked down the road toward town, they heard hoofbeats. Grandpa seized Faith's arm and pushed her into the shadows, then dropped his hat over the lantern. "Be still," he whispered. "Maybe he won't see us."

She nodded.

The horse's steps slowed as the rider approached. A glowing circle appeared on the crown of Grandpa's hat, followed by a thin column of smoke.

She gasped, then sneezed when the smoke reached her nose.

The hoofbeats stopped. "Faith? Judge?"

"That you, Saxon?" Grandpa jerked his hat off the lantern and stomped on the glowing embers.

Faith raised the light in time to see Curt dismount. His high-necked shirt was unbuttoned at the collar. Caring eyes sought hers. "Rosemary came to the Robbinettes' and told me what happened. She was afraid you'd try to find your granddad on your own, no matter what she said."

"Rosemary warned me about the danger of being out after sunset and then she braved the dark to fetch you." Faith shook her head, humbled at the magnitude of her friend's action. She wondered how she could have believed she needed to leave Noble Springs to be happy.

She studied Curt's shadowed face. "How did you know where to find me? When I left your house, I didn't have any idea where to start looking for Grandpa."

"Amy told me this is where you went."

Amy again. She'd have to get used to them being together.

Curt patted Grandpa's shoulder. "I'm relieved to see you."

"You both act like I was lost. I knew exactly where I was. Glad you're here with your horse, though. It's a long walk to town."

"Seems like we've done this before." Curt laced his hands together so Grandpa could have a boost into the saddle.

"Obliged."

Curt turned to Faith. "I know how you feel about this cemetery. Why didn't you ask Baxter to come with you?" He took the reins and led Moses down the road.

Faith walked next to him, holding the lantern in one hand. "Baxter's out of my life."

"What about Oregon?"

"Noble Springs is my home."

She heard his sharp exhalation over the sound of horse's hooves and singing crickets. After a moment he said, "Good. You've made a lot of people happy."

She waited for him to say he was one of those people, but he said nothing further. They covered the distance to town in silence.

The next morning, Faith gazed into the hall mirror and straightened her bonnet. She wanted to look her best when she called on Mr. Paulson at the bank.

Shuddering, she considered how close she'd come to marrying Royal. Six more days and she'd have been Mrs. Baxter. How could she have been so blind? *Thank you, Lord, for opening my eyes.*

On the way to town, she'd stop at the livery and thank Curt again for coming to her rescue. Even though he was interested in Amy, they could still be friends.

Grandpa walked up next to her and handed her the sale documents. He'd drawn a large "X" across the pages. "Give this to Paulson." His eyes twinkled. "Tell him Lindberg's Mercantile is not for sale. Not now. Not ever." He looked happier than he had in months.

Faith hugged him. "I'll tell him just that."

Was it her imagination, or was the sun shining more brightly than usual? With light steps she strolled toward the livery. A black buggy sat in front of the building. As she drew close, she saw Curt bent over polishing one of the wheels. Her eyes widened. The vehicle looked like the one Royal had been using.

Curt straightened when she approached. "How's your grandfather this morning?"

"Never better. Thank you again for coming to find us." She tilted her head. "Did Rosemary tell you that the sheriff caught the thieves who robbed the mercantile?"

"She did." He dropped the rag he'd been using and leaned against the buggy, his thumbs tucked into his front pockets. "You must be relieved."

"I am relieved, for more than one reason. The thieves were

friends of Royal Baxter's." She shook her head. "I feel like I've awakened from a bad dream."

Curt rested his hand on top of a wheel. "He's gone, you know. Left the buggy here with a note saying he wouldn't need it anymore."

"Good riddance."

He stared at her for a moment, joy dawning on his face. "I thought I'd lost you." He moved forward and laced his fingers through hers.

The look in his eyes shivered through her body, leaving her knees weak. "Lost *me*? Aren't you interested in Amy?" she asked in a faint voice. "You built that carriage for Sophia."

"I did it to impress you."

Out of the corner of her eye she noticed Mr. Ripley watching them from the doorway. When he realized he'd been observed, he sent her a knowing grin and slipped inside the livery.

Faith gripped Curt's hand. "All this time I believed . . ." She held her breath, praying he'd say what she longed to hear.

"I've been blessed with second chances." He cupped her face, sliding his long fingers along the hair at her temples. "I love you, Faith. I want you to marry me, if you'll have me. I'll wait as long as necessary for your decision."

"Are you sure you want me for a wife, after the way I stubbornly pushed my grandfather toward something so wrong for him? I almost ruined both of our lives."

He gathered her in his arms, as he'd done when she injured her ankle. "I'm absolutely certain."

"Then you don't need to wait. The answer's yes." She tipped her face up. "I love you too, Curt."

He bent his head and she tasted his lips for the first time. And the second. And the third.

Faith clung to him when he returned her to the ground.

She lifted one hand and pressed it against his cheek. "I can't wait to tell Grandpa—and Rosemary."

"Let's tell them together this evening. Rosemary and I will pay a call on you after supper."

She smiled all the way to town.

34

osemary arrived at the mercantile soon after Faith unlocked the doors. "My goodness, you're blooming this morning. Knowing those men are behind bars must be a great relief."

"The first of many. They were Royal's friends."

Rosemary's mouth dropped open.

"I didn't tell you yesterday," Faith continued. "I wanted to talk to him first."

"What did he say?"

Faith's cheeks heated, remembering his hurtful words. "It's what I said that matters. I sent him packing, for good."

"My prayers have been answered." Rosemary grabbed her hands. "Curt told me you're staying in Noble Springs, but he didn't explain why." Her gaze probed Faith's. "You'd never have been happy, even if you did get to Oregon."

"Did he—?" She bit down on her lower lip to keep from blurting the rest of her news.

"Did he what?"

Faith swallowed. "Nothing." She took a deep breath. "Everyone I love is here in Noble Springs. Why should I leave?" She grinned to herself, thinking of Curt. "The first thing I'm going to do this morning is call on Mr. Paulson at the bank and tell him we're not selling Lindberg's Mercantile."

Rosemary released her and stepped behind a counter. "I'll take care of customers." She flapped a hand toward the door. "You go on."

Faith strode into the bank's cool lobby with light steps. When Mr. Paulson saw her approach, he rose from behind his desk.

"Miss Lindberg. Please, have a chair." His face wore a worried expression. "I was planning to stop by the mercantile today. Mr. Allen was here on Monday. He's found another property he's interested in. If Judge Lindberg doesn't sign those papers soon, I'm afraid you'll lose the sale."

She passed the cancelled papers across his desk. "There will be no sale. Please let Mr. Allen know he's free to purchase the other property."

The banker rocked back in his chair. "Are you sure? This isn't the first time you've told me the mercantile isn't for sale. If you recall, you changed your mind shortly thereafter. Your indecision puts me in a bad light with Mr. Allen."

"I'm quite sure. My grandfather and I are staying right here in Noble Springs."

He raised an eyebrow. "May I ask how your fiancé feels about this?"

"I assume you're referring to Mr. Baxter. We are no longer engaged."

"A wise decision, if you'll pardon my familiarity." He stood. "I wish you all the best with the business. I've seen much improvement in your accounts over the past couple of months."

"Thank you. I've had excellent help."

Faith ducked inside the doors of the livery on her way home that evening. Curt looked up at her approach and strode to meet her, arms wide.

She hesitated, glancing around the interior of the building. "Where's Mr. Ripley?"

"He left early. I've been waiting for you. Thought the day would never end."

"I felt the same way." She nestled close and raised her face for his kiss. Her heart raced when his lips met hers.

"I waited for *this* all day too," Curt murmured in her ear when their embrace ended.

She twined her fingers through his. "I asked Rosemary if she'd come by this evening and bring some of the special tea she brews for Grandpa. You'll escort her, of course."

"Of course." He grinned his beautiful grin. "Can you keep our secret that much longer?"

"It'll be a struggle. I almost blurted it out more than once today."

"We'll be there in a couple of hours." He put his hands on her waist and lifted her off her feet before planting a kiss on her nose. "Then the whole world can know."

If happiness were wings, I could fly home, Faith thought as she skimmed up the porch steps and entered her house. Grandpa smiled at her from his chair in the parlor. "You must have had a good day. Did your talk with Mr. Paulson go well?"

She planted a kiss on the top of his head. "Yes. He knows we aren't selling the mercantile. In fact, he said our account is looking better and better."

"Amy made a Dolly Varden cake this afternoon to celebrate the fact that we're not leaving." The aroma of cinnamon and cloves drifted from the kitchen, confirming Grandpa's words.

"Now we can be thankful for the mercantile's recovery too." She tamped down the desire to burst out with her news.

"Rosemary and Curt will be here later. They can share our joy—and our cake."

Curt caught Faith's eye across the table. "Now?" He mouthed the question.

She nodded and stood, her pulse drumming in her throat. "Curt and I have something to tell you."

She gazed around the room. Grandpa rested his fork on his empty plate, a questioning expression on his face. Next to him, Amy bounced Sophia on her knee. She put a hand over her mouth, hiding a smile, as she glanced from Faith to Curt.

Rosemary's eyebrows shot up. "You and Curt? What is it?"

Faith walked to his chair and rested her hands on his shoulders. "We plan to be married. He asked me this morning, and I said most definitely yes!"

Grandpa slapped the table, making the plates rattle. "That's the best possible news. You've made me a happy man—two nights in a row." He beamed at her.

"I should have asked your permission first," Curt said to him. "I apologize."

"This has been my hope for months. No apology necessary. Unless you want to apologize for being so slow about it." He chuckled.

Curt rose and held Faith's hand as Rosemary ran toward them, tears slipping down her cheeks.

"I've prayed for this moment." She clasped Faith in a tight embrace. "I've never had a friend like you, and now you'll be a permanent part of my life. I'm overwhelmed."

Faith's tears mingled with Rosemary's. "I'm overwhelmed too. When I think of how close I came . . ."

Rosemary took a step away. "Instead of looking at what's

past, let's get busy planning a wedding. Have you decided on a date?"

"Soon." Curt pulled Faith close to his side.

"Very soon," she said. "But first Amy and I need to sew a certain ruffled dress."

Acknowledgments

*W*riting a novel may be a solitary pursuit, but mine would never see the light of day without assistance from many people.

Thanks to Scott and Kristen Melby, and to Leilani Weatherington for providing the local Ozark information that decorated the pages of this book.

Nancy Shaner contributed more than she realized when she suggested I research the steamboat *Arabia* story. Much of the stock on the shelves of Lindberg's Mercantile was inspired by the contents of the Arabia museum.

Diane Morton was the winner of the "Name That Doggie" contest on my Facebook page. Her entry of "Bodie" as the name for Rosemary's dog was a perfect fit. Thank you, Diane.

Thanks to my wonderful agent, Tamela Hancock Murray, for being my champion and for providing prayers and unfailing guidance.

Special gratitude to my editors at Revell—Vicki Crumpton and Barb Barnes, who made this novel shine; to Michele Misiak, Cheryl Van Andel, and all the members of the Revell team. Your godly attitudes make the process a joy.

I appreciate the insightful comments provided by my critique partners Bonnie Leon, Sarah Sundin, and Sarah Schartz. Extra appreciation goes to Judy Gann, who interrupted her busy schedule to advise me all the way through the end of the story.

My husband, Richard, contributed two weeks of his time to chauffeur me around Missouri while I researched the location of this series. Thank you for your patience, my love, and for putting up with a wife who spends most of her time glued to a computer.

My highest thanks goes to my Savior, Jesus Christ, who guided the words as they went onto the page. He holds me by my right hand.

Ann Shorey has been a full-time writer for over twenty years. She made her fiction debut with the At Home in Beldon Grove series in January 2009.

When she's not writing, she teaches classes on historical research, story arc, and other fiction fundamentals at regional conferences. Ann and her husband live in southern Oregon.

Ann loves to hear from her readers, and may be contacted through her website, www.annshorey.com, or find her on Facebook at http://www.facebook.com/AnnShorey.

Don't miss any of the
AT HOME IN
Beldon Grove series!

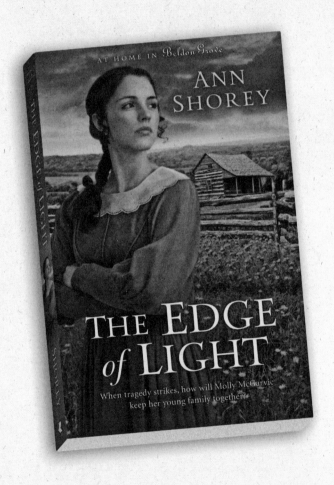

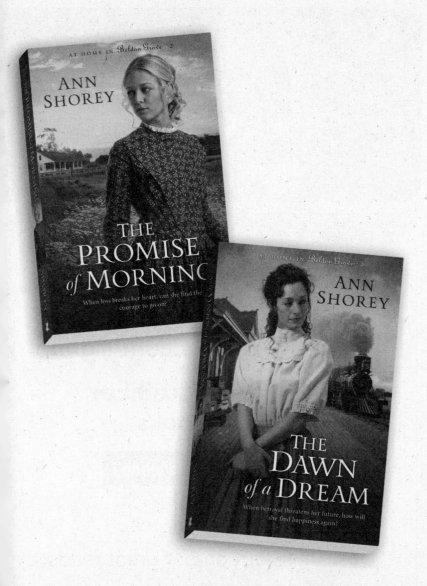

Ann Shorey weaves three emotional love stories of strong women who are determined to make it despite the difficulties of prairie life.